Fla.
F
New

Newell, David
    McCheyne

The trouble of it
is

c. 1

A883   8.95

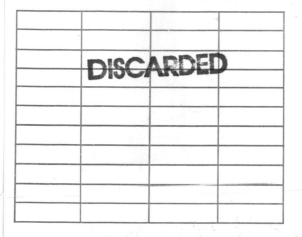

DISCARDED

Also by David M. Newell

IF NOTHIN' DON'T HAPPEN

The Trouble of It Is

Illustrations and calligraphy by Mark Livingston

 ALFRED A. KNOPF   NEW YORK   1978

The Trouble of It Is
by
David M. Newell
SHERIFF OFFICE
M. LIVINGSTON

THIS IS A BORZOI BOOK
PUBLISHED BY ALFRED A. KNOPF, INC.

Copyright © 1976, 1978 by David M. Newell

All rights reserved under International and
Pan-American Copyright Conventions.
Published in the United States by Alfred A. Knopf,
Inc., New York, and simultaneously in Canada
by Random House of Canada Limited, Toronto.
Distributed by Random House, Inc., New York.

Library of Congress Cataloging in Publication Data

Newell, David McCheyne [date]
    The trouble of it is.   I. Title.

PZ4.N543Tr   [PS3527.E83]   813'.5'2   77-74976
ISBN 0-394-40413-0

Manufactured in the United States of America

FIRST EDITION

Contents

Introduction

This is more about the Withlacoochee Driggers family—where they came from, how they fought and drank and made love, how they hunted and fished and "carried on" in general. It is a story of bad bulls and rattlesnakes, of bears and panthers and brave dogs and dogs that were not so brave; the story of folks who did the right thing and some who did not; of brotherly love and brotherly hate; of Cracker humor and Cracker politics, all told by Billy Driggers, a good old Cracker boy himself, who held to the faith his ma had taught him and tried to pass it along to his sons. He goes way back to describe a breed of backwoods people from the Carolina mountains and the Florida swamps who often "just settled their differences theirselves with guns, knives or fists."

This is also the story of Loofy Henry who married Billy and gave him a daughter and six sons: Kelly who ran for Sheriff and David who sneered at the law; poor little old Winton who never had a chance and Burr whose "bread weren't quite done when they taken him out of the oven"; big Jim, the first-born, who "couldn't tell turkey scratchin' from squirrel diggin'" and cared less; Charlie, named after famous Sheriff Charlie Dean; daughter Etta, unlucky in love though beautiful of body and "graceful as a doe deer jumpin' a log."

Here also is the story of Billy Driggers's older brother Tarley, who married the little black-haired Yankee gal and lived nearby on the edge of the Hammock. Billy rambles around some, like a bear trail through Seminole Swamp, but he gets it all told in fairly decent language—from Grandaddy Epps's mules to the shooting at Mink Island and the little dead chameleon and all that it meant. The trouble of it is he must tell of brother against brother, the hunter and the hunted, a terrible thing indeed.

The Trouble of It Is

The Eppses & the Driggerses —Mostly the Eppses

My name is Billy Driggers of the Withlacoochee River Driggerses, nephew to Winton Zebulon Epps who busted the mold when they made him. I reckon that's a good thing for the world because even his own folks couldn't of stood two of him.

He liked his likker and I remember one night when he were over to our house after a big ruckus he'd had with Aunt Effie.

"She says she can't stand me when I'm drinkin' and I say I can't stand her when I ain't. So we're in a deadlock and I don't see no solution unless the whiskey gives out."

"Well," Ma told him, "at least you ain't tom-cattin' around like you done before you married her." She were referrin' to a time when Uncle had been messin' around with a Yankee widow-woman who had three young-uns. The kids wouldn't let him sleep in the daytime and she wouldn't let him sleep at night and it liken to have killed him. Folks said she were an infomaniac and them women are trouble, I mean.

Uncle were a pistol, all right, and his sayin's and doin's is hard to forget. His sister, my ma, were different. She were a real double-dyed, triple-dipped, stomped-down, godly Christian and I'll whip ary man who says different. And I'll never forget her sayin's neither, especially about the Lord. She'd done got her ticket for crossin' the big River when her time come.

"Jesus paid for it," she'd say. "And I believe Him." She weren't specially what you'd call *religious*, but like I said she were a real Christian. And there's a heap of difference.

Some of the Eppses was regular religious fanatics. In fact they had a feud goin' with the Danielses that all started over what they called a question of doctorin'. I'll tell about that directly. Right now I want to get on with the Eppses and the Driggerses and how they got together which, naturally, is how come me to be here.

Most of the Eppses I ever seen was sandy-haired, freckledy-faced folks like Ma—all but Uncle Winton Epps, who were a hairy old bear of a feller with black mustaches and black hair on his head, chest, back and most anywhere you wanted to look. I'll be talkin' a lot more about him because, like I said, there just ain't never been nobody to equal him.

Way back in the days when most people was children Jeremiah Epps come over from England and settled near Front Royal, Virginia. He married a Zachary from over in North Carolina near Raleigh. They had three sons and bein' as Jeremiah were a religious man they give the boys Bible names—Ezekiel, Zachariah and Zebulon—Zeke, Zack and Zeb. Zeb were my ma's and Uncle Winton's daddy. Accordin' to her he were a big, rawboned knocker, about two ax-handles long and with feet so big he got skeered of his own track when he seen it in the snow.

All three of the boys was great hunters and they kept a-pushin' deeper into the mountains as the country got settled up. Zack and Zeb finally wound up near Franklin, North Carolina. Zack built him a sawed-lumber house near town but Zeb moved way up on the mountain near Wayah Bald and built a log house. There was deer, bear and turkeys in the woods, trout in the streams, ducks on the ponds and livin' were easy.

Ezekiel Epps went over into Georgia and married a Bolton—Medora, I believe her name was, but I ain't sure. When I think back and try to keep track of all the Eppses, let alone the Driggerses, I just get more wicks out than I can keep fire on.

Anyhow, Ezekiel and his wife settled near what is now Tiger, Georgia. Like his daddy, he were very religious but he were a Calvinist. Most folks around there was Baptists but there were a family of Methodists named Daniels and old man Aiken Daniels were the he coon of 'em. Him and Great-uncle Zeke and some of the Baptists used to have some hellacious hassles about questions of doctorin'—like head sprinklin' as against dunkin', keepin' the Sabbath Day, what Paul said, what Peter said, what James said and somethin' about lettin' a woman keep silence, accordin' to Pauline teachin'. Whoever Pauline were, she sure didn't know Aunt Effie. But their main difference were over what they called "fordination." Mr. Zeke claimed God knowed and ordained just when a feller's time would come. Mr. Daniels said a feller had to stay right in there pitchin' if he wanted to go to heaven.

The arguments had got so hot that one evenin' them two old fellers tangled in a fist fight and Zeke Epps whipped Aiken Daniels within a inch of his life. Daniels were a big feller, too, but he ought to of knowed better than to pick a fight with a Epps. All of the Eppses would fight and even the kids would just choose up and fight when they come home from school.

Well, not long after the big fight over doctorin', one of the Daniels boys tried to bushwhack Zeke Epps but the old muzzle-loader missed—the bullet goin' through his coat but missin' the meat. It were then that he started carryin' his rifle to church.

My Uncle Wint told me that when he were just a shirttail boy the Zeb Epps family went down to Georgia to visit the Zeke Eppses.

"We was all a-walkin' to their little Presbyterian church that first Sabbath mornin'," he said, "and Uncle Ezekiel were totin' his rifle. 'Why are you carryin' a gun to church, Uncle Zeke?' I asked him. 'Daddy says you believe the Lord has ordained ahead of time when you are goin' to heaven and there ain't nothin' goin' to happen to you till your time comes. Don't you believe that?'

" 'Course I do, sonny,' he told me. 'But the trouble of it is I just might meet a Daniels whose time had done come!' "

That's the way the Epps-Daniels feud started and it sure must of grieved the Lord—fellers a-fightin' over what they should of been rejoicin' over. There was some wild times up in the hills back in them days. Of course all these tales about my ma's folks come down through the family and I ain't got no way of knowin' if ever'thing happened just the way I heered it—like what they said about Great-uncle Zack's boy, Cousin Staunton.

Staunton Epps hadn't never been too bright and when he were near 'bout thirty years old he went crazier than a outhouse rat and had to be sent off. After about five years he got better and they let him come home to see how he would do. Well, back in them days ever'body used a big old straight razor and the very first day he were home Cousin Staunton went in the bathroom to shave. He poured some water in the basin, lathered up his face and started.

About that time one of the dogs went to barkin' and he stepped outside the door to see what the dog had found. But the dog were just barkin' to be barkin' and so Cousin went back in to finish shavin'. While he'd been out lookin' at the dog the mirror had slipped off the wall and slid down behind the washstand. Well, he picked up his razor, taken one look at the blank wall and said, "Just my luck! My very first day out and I've already done cut my damn head off!" I could go on and on about the Carolina and Georgia Eppses but right now I got to get along with how the Eppses come to Florida.

A feller don't suffer too much comfort in the winter back up in them Carolina mountains and along about eighteen and ninety Grandaddy Zeb decided to head south. Maybe he were tired of gettin' skeered of his own track in the snow. Maybe he were just tired of seein' it in snow. Anyhow, he fixed him up a regular old prairie schooner rig like them old-timey settlers used a-headin' west. Eppses always had good mules and his wagon team was extra fine—not too big but lively and strong. He tried to get his brother Zack to go along and look over the country but he wouldn't do it—said a travelin' man had told him that Florida weren't nothin' but alligators, sand flies and fan-bushes.

In tellin' about their trip, Uncle Winton would say, "I were just twelve years old and I couldn't hardly sleep at night for thinkin' about all I would see. I hadn't been nowheres but down to Clayton in my whole life. Now I might see big cities like Atlanta and Macon and no tellin' what."

But Mister Zeb had got him a ruler and laid it down on a map and drawed him a line from Franklin to a little old place called Lisbon. The nearest town of any size were Leesburg and it weren't much. Lisbon were near Fort Mason and Eustis, too, where the army had fought the Seminole Indians.

"Instead of goin' through the cities," Uncle Wint said, "Daddy tried to shun 'em and just follered the line he had drawed and he taken whatever kind of roads he could find."

There had been six in the wagon—Zebulon Epps, his wife Virginia and four kids—Winton, Hubbard, Sophronia and Rosa Belle. Uncle Wint had wrote his first poem on that trip:

> *A feller's a fool*
> *To trust a mule.*
> *They kick over the traces*
> *And poop in our faces.*

Uncle told me that his daddy got onto him about writin' out that word, but inside he must of been tickled because after old Zeb died they found the poem in his papers and he had wrote on it, "My boy Winton's very first poem." There were several others and I remember the first part of one which went:

> *My sister married a feller named Driggers*
> *And moved on down with the skeeters and chiggers.*

Uncle always had a knack for findin' a rhyme even if he had to use a Yankee word—like callin' a redbug a chigger.

Along with all the kids, Zeb Epps taken along a couple of mountain black and tan pups named Bawl and Squawl. They come from a strain of hounds that was bear dogs from their hearts and they had deep bellerin' tongues that would raise a feller's hackles. It were young Winton's job to look after them dogs, feed 'em and clean up after 'em, and he used to say, "I love a good hound but that trip liken to have soured me on all dogs for the rest of my life." It didn't though, because later on he had a slew of dogs and I mean some good ones.

Well, Uncle Winton and his parents and the other kids settled for a while near Lisbon and set 'em out a orange grove near a big lake. They met up with a old settler named Robertson who helped 'em a heap. Just when the grove were gettin' ready to bear, along came the big freeze of eighteen and ninety-five and wiped 'em out. That's when they moved on over to the west coast and got 'em a place on the River. They liked it better there in the Hammock because there were a heap more game and all manner of fresh and salt water fish and oysters.

Back in them days land were cheap—around three dollars a acre—but a heap more when there were river front. An acre that fronted on the water would cost a feller as much as two hundred dollars. Zeb Epps were lucky. A widow-woman wanted to sell a real nice old home place with some orange trees and about four hundred feet on the River. It taken in a point at a bend where the deep water come right up to a good high shell bank and a feller could tie up his boat right in his front yard.

There was some fine old shade trees, too—water oaks, magnolias and a big old hickory that turned yeller in the fall; and there was two or three big slash pines and some cabbages that was sixty feet tall if they was a inch. When us Crackers talk about "cabbages" we mean cabbage palmettos.

The house were built out of heart pine from trees that hadn't never been tapped for turpentine and them boards was hard as iron. They had weathered till they was a soft, pretty, gray color. Like most all houses along the coast it were built up on piers near 'bout three feet above the ground on account of the big storm tides. Some of the piers was red cedar hearts and some was light'd pine. By "light'd" I mean old fat pine full of gum. When lightnin' would kill a pine tree the sap wood rotted off and the hearts was great for fence posts and house piers and also for startin' fires. That's why it were called lighter wood—or just "light'd." Some folks spell it "litard" but that don't rightly explain it. Anyhow, the Eppses had 'em a house that would be there.

The property taken in about three hundred acres back inland toward the Hammock, so the Eppses could have their livestock, specially their goats. Zeb Epps had chronicle belly trouble and he had found that goat milk done him good.

At the north end of the Widow Larrigan's property, there were a little side creek comin' in from up toward Brantley Marsh and along it were some fine muck soil where a feller could grow sugar cane ten feet high.

Grandaddy Zeb hadn't had much money left after the freeze-out over in Lake County but he made a down payment and moved in—wife, kids, dogs and all. It suited him to a fare-thee-well and I reckon he figured there'd be an Epps right there as long as there were a world.

Old man Zeb died in 1900 and his wife, Virginia Tarley Epps, in 1902. After they was gone, Uncle Winton stayed on at the home place. He married a gal named Euphemia Thaxton from across the River and his sister, Froney Epps, my ma, were livin' down South. Uncle Hub had gone up to Georgia to study to be a tooth dentist and Rosa Belle had married a Yankee and moved up to Chicago.

2 The Eppses
& the Driggerses—
Mostly the Driggerses

Now the way the Driggerses joined up with the Eppses were like this. My daddy, Jim Driggers, and his folks had been Florida Crackers since before the gator bellered. They lived out from Fort Myers near a little old place named Bokeelia on Pine Island. Some of 'em guided, some brewed a little corn, some net-fished and some done all three. Mainly they done what they wanted when they wanted. There didn't nobody push a Driggers about nothin', specially my daddy's branch. His grandaddy had been a army scout with the Florida Volunteers at Fort Cooper, over near Inverness, when the government were fightin' the Seminoles. He must of been a regular Indian in the woods hisself to escape gettin' massacreed there or at Wahoo Swamp when they ambushed Major Dade.

Some folks said Great-grandaddy had married a Choctaw woman. I don't know. I do know my daddy, Jim Driggers, had black hair and a black mustache near about like Uncle Winton Epps. Ma used to say they both looked like they had swallered a couple of minks and left their tails hangin' out of their mouths. Anyhow, whether because of Indian blood or Driggers blood, my daddy were knowed as a quick-tempered feller it didn't pay to mess with. But there didn't nobody know then what terrible things was goin' to happen from that headstrong streak. While he were growin' up my daddy lived in the house he were borned in. It had been built by his daddy, Len Driggers, along about eighteen and seventy but it caught afire one night from a woods fire while everybody were off at a frolic and burned to the ground. The old folks moved in with Uncle Joe Driggers and Daddy built his own little house on Pine Island Sound, close to the beach where he could look after his boat. He were guidin' most of the time and doin' right well. A feller didn't have to mortgage his home in them days to hire a guide boat and he only got ten dollars a hide—not as much as Uncle Joe Driggers who run whiskey but better'n Uncle Frank who mullet-fished.

There were a rich old Yankee who come to Fort Myers ever' winter who had him a big home on the Caloosahatchee River. He were a great tarpon fisherman and my daddy guided for him and looked after his boat. All the guides envied this boat. The hull were mahogany and she had teak deckin' and Daddy really babied her. "This boat'll take whatever comes along," he'd say, and I reckon that were so because a feller gets some mighty seas in sixty-foot-deep Boca Grande Pass with a high wind buckin' a big tide. The rich old Yankee wanted to go tarpon fishin' every day, rain or shine. He mortally loved to hook them big silvery scoun'els, see 'em jump and then get shed of 'em. He didn't want to kill 'em nohow and he weren't able to fight one very long.

But the old feller had done got non compass mentis. This meant that his compass weren't workin' right and sometimes he didn't know where he was at or who he was. But he did know Jim Driggers and trusted him so when spring come nothin' would do but that Jim would go up on the train with him to North Carolina to help look after him. He wouldn't leave Florida though till late in June after the tarpon run had peaked.

Like a heap of them effluent folks he had places all over the country. The one in North Carolina were a big log lodge on the Nantahaly where he used to fish for trout when he were young and could get about in that fast water and slippery rocks. He'd only stay there a couple of weeks and then move on up to his place in Maine on a lake with a name about a moose lookin' somewheres. Then he'd go across into New Hampshire to another place he had on a lake with a name I couldn't even write if I were lookin' at the map. Some of them Yankee Indians could turn out some tongue-twisters too!

The time Jim Driggers went up on the train with him were the same summer that Froney Epps, my mother, were stayin' with the Zack Eppses at Franklin, while she were takin' nurses' trainin' at the hospital. She'd got a job helpin' to take care of the rich old Yankee out at the lodge on the Nantahaly and that's how come her to meet Jim Driggers, my daddy, and to marry up with him, like I've been tryin' to tell you all along.

But they couldn't go back to Florida till after the old feller went on up to Maine in July. Froney wouldn't leave her patient and Jim Driggers wouldn't leave her, so he had just hung around and fished for a solid month. My earliest recollections are of my daddy talkin' about that fishin'.

"Billy," he'd say, "them trout was little old speckledy fellers, hardly big enough for tarpon bait but they was some kind of good when you fried 'em in bacon fat. You had to catch 'em with what they called a 'fly rod,' somethin' like a buggy whip and made specially for slingin' a teentsy little old fly no bigger'n a skeeter. It taken me a few days to get onto it before I could flip that fly up under the tree branches and into the deep holes. Mostly the water went a-boilin' along over the rocks not even knee deep and it were so clear it looked like there weren't no water at all. But back of the big rocks and where there were a sharp bend in the river, the current had dug out holes and that's where them fish laid."

Well, the rich old Yankee finally took off for Maine and my parents was married by a Methodist preacher in Franklin. My daddy wanted to wait till they got back to Florida where a Southern Baptist could do it and he'd be sure of the knot but Froney said she weren't goin' nowheres with a man in a railroad car with beds in it unless she were married to him.

If I had time, I'd tell you about what my son David Driggers done with a gal in one of them sleepin' cars, but that'll have to wait till later, too. Right now I got to get my folks settled back on Pine Island.

A feller might of thought they would stop off to see Ma's

folks in Gulf Hammock but they was all mad at each other. The Eppses was mad at their daughter for marryin' a feller they hadn't never even seen and Ma were mad because they were mad and hadn't come to her weddin' and Daddy just said, "To hell with ever'body. We're goin' to Pine Island. If anybody wants to see us they can come there."

The rich old Yankee who Daddy guided for usually showed up back in Florida along about the first part of December. He didn't have no kinfolks that anybody knowed about so he didn't fool around up in that snow waitin' until after Christmas and all. In the meantime my daddy looked after his place and his boat. He let Daddy use the boat for guidin' other folks when he weren't there and business were real good when the snooks and redfish was runnin' in the late summer and fall.

Toward the last of November of the first year my dad and Froney Epps was married, the rich Yankee keeled right over while he were gettin' packed to come back to Florida. The bank sold his big old place on the Caloosahatchee and notified Daddy that he had been left the guide boat and ten thousand dollars. Course me and my brother Tarley hadn't been borned but my ma swore Tarley jumped up and down and clapped his hands in her belly when she heered the news—though it hadn't been hardly five months since the train trip. Anyhow, they was able to fix up the house with screens, run a water pipe from the cistern right into a tank in the kitchen, so they didn't have to tote drinkin' water and cookin' water, buy a few more hogs and chickens and Daddy got him a long-barreled, breech-loadin' shotgun and three new hounds that would ever more drive a old buck out of the worst cypress pond in Lee County.

"On top of everything else," Ma told me years later, "we put half of that money in savin's at the bank for 'mergency." And that time sure did come for us later on.

Ma never were too happy livin' down there amongst all them Driggerses. Like I said, her daddy and grandaddy had been real God-fearin' folks and the Pine Island Driggerses didn't fear nothin'. Of course the Carolina Eppses hadn't been no shrinkin' violets neither. Ma's brother, Uncle Winton, liked his whiskey from the time he were just a young bucko and when he were drinkin' a feller could get a fight out of him without half tryin'.

About a year after my parents was married, Winton Epps got on a excursion train and went down to Fort Myers to visit 'em. They met him and drove him twenty miles in the buggy out to where they lived on Pine Island. He liked it there all right but he said there was just too many Yankees around and about. There weren't hardly no Yankees any closeter than Bokeelia, about four miles away, but Uncle Winton said even that were too close. "Y'all come up and see us," he told Daddy, "and I'll show you some real wild country . . . with nary a Yankee." That were even before old man Knott come down and started Yankeetown.

It were another year before Ma seen her brother again. Folks didn't dash off a couple of hundred miles back in them days without good reason and it meant a long train trip when they did go. But when her father, Grandaddy Zeb, died in 1900, Ma and Daddy took off for the funeral. They left my brother Tarl, who weren't but two years old, with Jeff Driggers's wife, Julie Ann. Jeff were the most peaceablest of all the Pine Island Driggerses and his wife and Ma was always real friendly and she was about the same age as Ma, twenty-one or so.

That were my daddy, Jim Driggers's, first visit to Gulf Hammock and he liked what he seen. They didn't stay but three or four days but he killed a ten-point buck and a gobbler with a beard a foot long just walkin' out from the house one evenin'. Of course, I don't remember nothin' about any of it because I was lackin' about a year and a half of bein' there at all, but I do know that my daddy talked about that country from as far back as I can remember, specially them oysters down at the mouth of the River.

"I must of eat a bushel of them oysters," he'd say, "and them were the biggest, juiciest ones I'd ever seen. They'd hang 'em overnight in a burlap bag and let 'em wash and fatten in that fresh water."

When Grandma Epps died two years later, Ma didn't try to make the trip again. She were carryin' me and feelin' puny a heap of the time. But she'd kept in touch with her brother and Uncle Wint would write to her now and again. Sometimes he'd send a poem he'd wrote. There's one that Ma kept all through the years. It were the whole poem about his sister marryin' a feller named Driggers and it went like this:

My sister married a feller named Driggers
And moved down south with the skeeters and chiggers.
And bein' as how she's a full-blooded Epps,
I doubt if she'll ever take backward steps.

Folks say he's big and rough and tough,
But if my sister gets enough,
She'll tell him off and slap him down
And pack her stuff and walk to town.

But if this couple stay together
Through thick and thin and stormy weather,
I'll tell you now the kids they raise,
Will make a feller's eyeballs glaze.

A blood of Epps and Driggers mix
Will scare off h'ants and keep off ticks.
There ain't no tellin' what could happen
With kids that's borned with such a wrappin'.

The Driggers folks from all I hear
Drink moonshine whiskey and home-brewed beer.
So when I go to visit Sis,
I hope they have enough of this!

I reckon they must of had because they say he taken on a load right soon and got into a big argument with one of the cousins, Virgil Driggers, about what the Bible had to say about drinkin'. Cousin Virgil claimed that Jesus changed water into real 'toxicatin' wine—not grape juice or nothin' like that, but real wine.

"And it says to take a little for your belly's sake," Virgil said. And he claimed that wine were all right because it come from natural fermentin' of the grape. But whiskey and gin and beer and such as that had to be brewed by men and so it were wrong to drink 'em.

"Shucks," Uncle Winton said, "it's alcohol right on, no matter how you make it, and I like it. So you drink your wine and I'll drink my beer. Now, I don't want to hear no more about it."

But Cousin Virgil tried to tell him more, so they tangled. That cousin were the fightin'est of all the Pine Island Driggerses so that even today folks down yonder still talk about "that big feller Epps that come down from Gulf Hammock and whipped Virgil Driggers." Virgil went on to be a professional heavyweight prize fighter and whipped ever'body else he ever fought. But I heered that he died a wino.

I don't remember too much about them early days of my life on Pine Island because I were only nine years old when we left there to move up to the Hammock. But I do remember when Daddy would let me go with him in the boat to catch tarpon bait. Sometimes we'd haul a short seine for silvers or pick up our mullet soon in the mornin' at Uncle Frank's dock—if he'd made a good strike the night before. Sometimes we'd drift and hook-and-line fish for pinfish or rockfish or small catfish. One day them tarpons would prefer a catfish or a pinfish and another day they wouldn't hit nothin' but a little old blue crab about the size of a silver dollar. But whatever we done were all right with me. I purely loved any kind of fishin' . . . and still do.

A few times Tarley, my brother, went along when Daddy guided a sport but I weren't big enough he said. I didn't agree but if Jim Driggers's kids didn't agree with their old man they kept it to theirselves!

Ever since his trip up to Grandaddy Zeb Epps's funeral my dad had talked more and more about movin' up to Gulf Hammock. I remember his tellin' us about the big woods—all kinds of hardwood trees that made cool shade. Down where we lived there weren't nothin' but palmettos and pine trees and white sand and it got some kind of hot in the summertime in spite of coolin' Gulf breezes nearly every evenin'. Course we had fine fishin' of all kinds right where we was—tarpon and snook and trout and redfish and jacks and a world of them fancy-jumpin' ladyfish. And way offshore there was grouper and red snappers that would tear up a feller's tackle. But Daddy loved to hunt and he couldn't get them deer and turkeys and squirrels out of his mind. Of course, Ma were all for the idea because she were real fond of her brother Winton, spite of his drinkin', and she said all the Driggers men was too stubborn and hot-headed.

"Somethin' bad'll happen," she said, "if ary body pushes Jim Driggers a little too much . . . even one of his own brothers. I'd be happy to move away from here. Brother against brother—that would be terrible." I'll always thank the good Lord she didn't live to see that very thing happen with her grandsons.

³The Move to the Hammock

When my folks decided to make their move to the Hammock, the movin' part weren't no real big problem. They hadn't 'cumulated much furniture and such so they just sold out lock, stock and barrel—hogs, chickens and a couple of dogs that weren't fit for nothin' but to feed and turn out. Daddy's only good deer dogs had been killed by a bear when he were huntin' over in Fahkahatchee Swamp. What few things they really wanted to save and couldn't be packed in our two skiffs they crated to be sent up by rail to Dunnellon.

Of course Daddy would need his boat and skiffs wherever he went, either to net-fish or guide, and he figured it would save money for us all to ride the boat instead of the train.

One of the things Ma packed in a box to go in one of the skiffs were a big, black iron cockroach about a foot long—or at least what looked like a roach or a beetle. It really were a bootjack that Great-uncle Zachariah Epps had given to Ma when she got married at his house in Franklin. She called it a heirloom so maybe it come over from England with old Jeremiah. Anyhow, you stepped on the dern thing, put the heel of your other boot between the feelers and pulled. Ma prized it but packed it to go in the skiff because it wouldn't break and water wouldn't hurt it.

Then there were a wood duck deecoy that had been carved out by some famous feller in Maryland. I reckon it were a duck, though it looked like its daddy must of been a sea gull. Ma were right proud of them family heirlooms because they was all she had got when she married Jim Driggers up in Franklin. Her mother and daddy never sent her the first weddin' present, nor went down to Pine Island to see her. Only her brother, my Uncle Winton, ever come to see her or wrote her.

"I don't know who's stubborner, an Epps or a Driggers," she'd say. "I just hope the Lord will forgive us all."

Of course she never had no chance to make up with her daddy but when she went up to the funeral she and Grandma got together and the old lady taken quite a likin' to my daddy after she got to know him a little. It's just too bad that me and Tarl never did even get to see our old folks, specially Tarley who were named after his granny's family.

If it had took us as long to load them skiffs as it has for me to tell about them heirlooms and the family trouble, we'd still be on Pine Island, but maybe the reason will be plain when you know how much them things meant to Ma.

Well, we finally got all loaded and pushed off for the last time from our dock. We had meant to get gone by an hour by sun so as to make it up around Tarpon Springs that first day, but like always a feller don't hardly never get started on time.

As I remember, we didn't hit the open Gulf till after we'd went out big Boca Grande Pass. There were some low-hangin', swirlin' clouds to the southwest and Daddy said he didn't much like the looks of 'em. The wind kept pickin' up and the seas buildin' a little higher. By five o'clock we was really doin' some rollin' and the skiffs started to cut up—runnin' off to one side and tryin' to bury their noses when a wave would break under 'em and the tow lines would come tight. The wind were blowin' spray off them breakin' waves and howlin' so that a feller couldn't hear nothin' but that hissin' and howlin'.

I don't reckon a feller could get any scareder—specially a nine-year-old like me when all this happened. Even a growed-up man don't really know what it is to be scared until he gets caught in a little boat in a big storm. A bad bull or a bad boar hog or even a bad man ain't nothin' compared with that. A feller can kill a bull or a hog or even a man but he sure can't do nothin' about the howlin' wind and rollin' seas. Give me my thirty-thirty and I ain't scared of nothin' that walks or talks, swims or crawls. But nothin' helps when old Mother Nature goes on a tear.

There probably weren't no more dangerous a pass on the whole dern west coast of Florida than Pelican Pass but it were the nearest one and we made for it. My dad could near 'bout always read the water pretty good, even where there weren't no channel markers, by watchin' the swirls and eddies and rips. But it were almost dark and that whole inlet were one solid sweep of white caps. The wind howlin' from the southwest and the tide runnin' out strong agin it so there was seas five feet high, breakin' white wherever they'd hit a sand bar. The one thing in our favor were that Pelican Pass ain't a rocky pass. A feller can go aground on a sand bar and maybe get off on the next wave but if he hits rocks in wild water like that he's done dropped his candy.

Though Pelican Pass ain't rocky, the trouble of it is that it changes with every storm and a feller has to pick his way. Of course, I didn't know nothin' about all that then, but I were a scared little boy I'll have you know.

It's bad enough to have to run ahead of followin' seas without tryin' to tow one skiff and we was towin' two. They was loaded right, weight to the rear, but when we hit that pass and got into them cross currents and followin' seas, them skiffs really went to cuttin' up—runnin' off to one side, duckin' back and near 'bout swampin' when we'd ride the top of a breaker.

Well, directly it happened. A sea broke under us, we went hard aground, and them skiffs come a-chargin' at our stern. Daddy seen what were goin' to happen and turnt the wheel loose and tore out for the stern, just runnin' over whatever got in his way. He were able to check that first skiff a little bit before it come a-drivin' into our stern and then he shoved it to one side and it and the second one slid on past and run together and switched around broadside and both of 'em swamped. About that time my dad whipped out his fish knife and cut the towin' rope and I remember hearin' Ma holler, "Oh no, Jim! There go my precious heirlooms."

And Daddy hollered right back, "If we don't get off this sand bar, there goes your precious ever'thing."

By this time the skiffs was out of sight and Daddy hollered out, "Now listen close, y'all. Billy, you stay in the boat. Just hang on and stay in the boat no matter what happens. Tarl, me'n you will get overboard, one on each side, and we'll try to help back off. Froney, I'm a-goin' to open her up hard astern. You keep the wheel and if and when we come free just back straight off and don't let her swing broadside under no condition. There'll be some more water come in but keep backin'. Now Tarl, don't turn loose of this boat whatever happens. There could be quicksand under your feet."

Then Dad went forward, put her in hard astern, and handed the wheel to Ma. Between that old engine a-throbbin' and the wind a-screechin', I couldn't hardly hear Daddy when he hollered to Tarley to jump in.

Well, I'd just as soon not even tell about the rest of that evenin'. We got off the bar but liken to have lost both Tarl and Daddy when the boat come free and went to backin' off. Their feet had bogged down in that sand halfway to their knees. At last we made it to the beach on the north side of the pass, found some driftwood and built up a fire and tried to dry out. Durin' the night the wind went around into the northwest and it faired off and turnt cold. I never were so glad to see anything as that old red sun raisin' up over them mangroves and hittin' that cold sand beach. I hadn't never seen or felt snow, but I could sure imagine it.

By nine o'clock the wind had laid, the tide were swellin' and Pelican Pass were near about a slick calm, nothin' like the screechin' hell it had been the night before. Ma fried some bacon, made a kettle of grits and a pot of coffee and Daddy said, "All right ever'body. Let's get gone while we got this good high tide." He'd been up near about all night worryin' with the boat—changin' the anchor, keepin' her pushed off and bailin' her out. In between he'd set around that fat pine driftwood fire and were some kind of sooted up. Ma said if the border patrol had ever seen him they'd of sure took him away.

There was a few ground swells rollin' in right at the mouth of the pass but nothin' bad and only a light surf on the beach as we rounded the north point and turned into the open Gulf. You might wonder how a nine-year-old kid would remember all these things but that particular nine-year-old were so skeered you couldn't of drove a needle into his butt with a sledge. Maybe it were because he was so keyed up that he was first to see the skiff. Just around the point were a little old mangrove key and wedged in among them roots were one of our skiffs. The tide had carried it out and bein' built out of cypress it hadn't never plumb sunk. Anyhow, there it were and we was able to get it and bail it out and take it in tow. There wasn't but two things left in it though—a cast net and that dad-burned iron cockroach. We never seen a trace of the other skiff nowhere.

The rest of the trip were pretty smooth sailin' and I don't remember too much about it. Most of it were outside and one chunk of Gulf looks a heap like another. Of course Daddy had charts and we hit the channel markers off the mouth of the Withlacoochee late that evenin'. There were deep water all the way in where sizeable boats come in to load phosphate back in the days when Port Inglis were flourishin' and old Captain Inglis had him a fine home and there was a church and a school and a customs house and no tellin' what all.

Anyhow, we went on up the River and kept inquirin' from fishin' boats till we learnt where the Zeb Epps place were and found it and tied up alongside their dock. Uncle Winton himself were out to meet us and Ma were so happy she went to cryin'.

"Is it all right to leave her tied up right where she is?" Daddy asked.

"Who?" Uncle Winton said.

"My boat," Daddy said. "Will she be in the way there?"

"That'll be fine," Uncle said. "All you salt water fellers call a boat *she* but I sure don't. I'd be afraid a she would turn bottom-side up when I were least expectin' it. And I know dern well a she'd be hard to steer!"

We didn't understand all that right at the time but then we hadn't met Aunt Effie neither.

4 Aunt Effie & Uncle Wint

We learnt a few things about Aunt Effie right soon after we got there. She didn't waste nothin' and you eat what she dished up—every bit of it, I mean. The rations was good but sort of on the few side. And nobody didn't say nothin' to stir her up. I remember Uncle Wint sayin' to Ma, "She's the most even-tempered woman I ever seen in my life. She's always mad. And she's always tryin' to tell me what to do. I hear fellers say, 'Ain't no woman goin' to tell *me* what to do,' and it tickles me because there ain't no way to stop her. Oh, there *is* but it's agin the law. So I let Effie go ahead and tell me what to do and I don't *say* nothin'! I just don't *do* it; not every time, anyhow."

A feller could tell a heap about how Aunt Effie felt by the way she said, "I declare." She said this a lot—when somethin' surprised her, when she were put out at somethin' or somebody, and just to be usin' up the air when there come a break in somebody else's talkin'—lettin' folks know she was there, you might say, though she probably couldn't even tell you what they had been talkin' about. She done this a lot when she'd be on the telephone with old lady Burchell. Mrs. Burchell would talk a blue streak for a half an hour and about every five minutes Aunt Effie would say, "Well. I declare." She were readin' a book all the time but she had to let Mrs. Burchell know she were still there.

But if Aunt Effie said, "I declare . . ." and stopped as if there was a lot still to be said, you could bet she were put out and you could be glad she didn't say the rest. So when she said, "I declare," everything depended on the reflection she put on it. One time Uncle Winton told me that the reason she never would have any kids were that he had threatened to name any gal child Ida Claire.

About the third week we was there me'n Tarl was out in the yard gettin' acquainted with some of Uncle Winton's hounds. Daddy and Ma had gone up the River to hunt a place where we could build our own house. I had just got a tick off the neck of a big old blue-speckled pup when there come a feller to buy some cane syrup. Like I said a while back when I were describin' the Larrigan place where the Eppses lived, there was some mighty fine muck down along a little old creek where they growed sugar cane and made the very best syrup to be had—thick and sweet and clear as honey. Aunt Effie were in the kitchen puttin' up a gallon in a lard can and Uncle Wint had come out and were settin' on the porch steps talkin' to this feller.

Now this feller were deef and like a lot of them hard-of-hearin' folks he talked kind of loud hisself.

"How's Effie?" he said.

"About the same," Uncle said.

But Aunt Effie had heered the feller all the way to the kitchen and she hollered out, "I'm fine. Tell him I'm fine, Winton."

So Uncle said, "She says she's fine but she seems about the same to me."

So after the feller had left they had a big hassle and she said, "I reckon you just hate my guts, don't you?"

And Uncle just said, "Well, no. I wouldn't hardly go so far as to say that. But I sure don't love 'em as much as I used to."

A few mornin's later somethin' happened down at the cane grindin' mill that liken to have been right pitiful. Uncle had cooked down a big kettle-full of juice and were sittin' on a orange crate waitin' for it to cool enough so that Ma could put it up in the lard cans. A hog went to squealin' over in the saw grass across the creek and Uncle got up to see what were makin' the hog squeal. He had told us that sometimes a bear or a big gator would catch a hog right out in the big broad open daytime.

Anyhow, whilst Uncle were gone, I'll be derned if a big, gawky hound pup named Ranger didn't jump up onto that crate, rare up and try to get a piece of venison Uncle had hung on a nail in a shed post. Uncle got back just in time to see the crate tip and flip the dog over into the syrup kettle. Me'n Aunt Effie had just come out of the house to go to the shed and feed the chickens when we seen him grab that dog and throw him twenty feet. It were a good thing the syrup had cooled enough so that it didn't scald nobody.

"We'll just dump that batch out," Uncle Winton said. "We ain't sellin' folks no syrup that a hound dog has been into."

"Oh yes we are," Aunt Effie said. "Every drop of syrup that touched that dog is still on him. That syrup ain't hurt. We'll sell it right on." And they did and three other dogs helped Ranger clean hisself. I couldn't help wonderin' though, if the syrup had been hot enough to kill the fleas.

Aunt Effie usually had her way. "I let her have her way about little things," Uncle would say, "but when it comes to the big decisions, I make 'em." There didn't no real big decisions come up, I reckon, whilst we was livin' with the Eppses.

Another thing about my Aunt Effie were that she weren't to be outdone by nobody about nothin'. Whatever it were a body had, she'd had it worser. If they'd had double pneumonia, she'd had triple. If they'd growed a big melon, she'd growed a bigger. If somebody was to claim he'd gone around the world in three days, she'd probably claim she could take a short cut down through the middle and do it in two.

Somebody told a yarn one evenin' about a old couple who lived way back in the woods toward Bayport. They had a cravin' for a strikin' clock and saved up their money and bought one. Well, the first night they laid there listenin' to that clock strike nine and ten and eleven and each time it were music to their ears. Somewheres between eleven and midnight the old lady dozed off but the old man were bound and determined to go all the way and hear all there was to hear. So after while there were a little click and the old clock went to strikin': . . . one . . . two . . . three . . . four . . . five . . . six . . .

seven . . . eight . . . nine . . . ten . . . eleven . . . twelve
. . . thirteen . . . fourteen . . . fifteen . . .

"Hattie, honey, wake up," the old man hollered, shakin' her by the shoulder. "It's later than I have ever knowed it to be!"

Aunt Effie didn't even laugh—just said, "Huh! Winton Epps has stayed out later'n that a heap of times."

That certainly were the truth and the other day when I heered a baby with the hiccups I thought of one time when Uncle really come home late. When I remember somethin' about Uncle Wint I got to tell it before I forget it—whether it happened in nineteen and ten or nineteen and forty. Anyhow, I were over spendin' the night at the Eppses one time and Uncle had gone to Ocala to carry one of his yearlin's over to the stock show. He come in about half past two in the mornin' and the sound of the car woke me up and set all the dogs to barkin' at the strange car. One of the Haddonses had drove him home. He could walk, but just barely, and you could have lit his breath with a match. Aunt Effie jumped him time he stepped in the door.

"Winton Epps, you're drunk," she hollered. "Get into bed before you fall down and break your butt." So Uncle pulled off his shoes and pants and got into bed but right away he taken the hiccups. She tried to give him a drink of water but he wouldn't have it.

"Try holdin' your breath," she said.

"You try holdin' your tongue," he said.

Well, them hiccups kept on and on. You could hear him all over the house and that were the last thing I remember before goin' back to sleep.

Next mornin' at breakfast Uncle were real grumpy. Aunt Effie were fryin' bacon and directly she hollered, "Ouch!"

"Burn yourself?" Uncle asked her.

"Well, no . . . not really," she said.

"Then try again," Uncle told her. He could be rough as a cob all right and she could most always hand it right back. But this time she didn't say nothin' at all. She were so meek she were near about meechin'.

While we was walkin' down to the shed to feed the stock Uncle told me what all had happened durin' the night. The hiccups had just kept on until Aunt Effie had got desperate. She had been over to a neighbor lady's and their baby had taken the hiccups and they couldn't get 'em stopped. So they had tried a remedy the lady's grandma used to use. They tied a string around the baby's little spigot and the hiccups stopped. Maybe it hurt the little feller so much he forgot about the hiccups. Anyhow they stopped.

Well, Aunt Effie knowed somethin' had to be done for Uncle so she decided to try the turnaket treatment. She couldn't find no cord but she had some ribbon scraps in her sewin' basket and she tied one on him. That didn't stop 'em so she tied another one on, even tighter.

"Boy, them things was hurtin' me," Uncle said, "and I got up and lit a lamp and went in the bathroom and seen them ribbons and I said, 'Well, I don't know where I've been or what I've done but I've sure placed first and second!' "

I didn't even dare laugh, but I said, "I seen you was walkin' sort of spraddle-legged and I wondered if you was crippled or somethin'. But you didn't have no hiccups at breakfast and you ain't got 'em now, so it must of worked."

"Somethin' did," Uncle said. "But boy, let me tell you one thing. Some women are great on tryin' new-fangled ideas but don't never let one try a *old-fangled* one on you."

"I'll remember that," I told him. "And I'm sure glad you have overed them hiccups."

"You ain't jokin'," Uncle said. "And if I ever get 'em again I hope it ain't nowhere in hearin' of Effie Epps!"

From all I've been tellin' about my Aunt Effie and her ways, I reckon folks will think I'm agin all women, but I ain't. I grew up and married one of the finest ones God ever made and I've already done told about my fine Christian mother. But I don't mind sayin' that there's some that I call contentious wenches. I got that name from one of Uncle Winton's poems—the part that went:

> *I've knowed a heap of pretty wenches*
> *And they was nearly all contentious.*
> *The only gentle ones I've seen*
> *Was very few and far between.*

If Uncle was here today no tellin' what he'd write. Just a month or two ago there come a woman to Gator Crawl who said she were a activist, whatever that meant, and she were campaignin' for more rights for women folks. I don't know how come she picked on me but we got in a discussion up at the post office and after while she said, "Mr. Driggers, you are a perfect example of the shovin'est male."

"I don't know why you say that, Ma'am," I told her. "But I will have to say you sure are the shovin'est female I ever seen." That lady and Aunt Effie would of got along fine, I'll bet a pretty.

The sewin' circle from the Second Baptist Church—there weren't but two churches in Gator Crawl then, the First Baptist and the Second Baptist—used to meet at Aunt Effie's every Wednesday and have some coffee and homemade cake before goin' on to prayer meetin'. Us boys always looked forward to Wednesdays and we would hang around to get some cake and sometime listen in when we wasn't supposed to. I remember one meetin' when them women really got down to some serious gossipin'. Aunt Effie said she were thinkin' about divorcin' Uncle on account of his drinkin'.

"Well," said Mrs. Ertle, "I'm thinkin' about a divorce myself."

"Why, I declare," Aunt Effie said, "I didn't know Roger drank."

"He don't," Mrs. Ertle said. "The trouble of it is he don't do nothin' else either."

That set 'em all to talkin' about men folks in general and how they was all just a bunch of infidelities and impotentates.

"Take that new feller workin' in the Commissary," Mrs. Hawkins said. "They say he's really hired by the company as a undercover man."

"I wouldn't be surprised," Mrs. Johnson said. "And they sure picked the right one. From all I hear he's already been under more covers than ary body ever come here."

Nobody didn't say nothin' and directly they changed the subject and begun talkin' about their sewin' and cookin' and such.

That night after I'd gone to bed I heered Aunt Effie talkin' to Uncle Winton out in the kitchen. She were tellin' him about the undercover man.

"It's plumb disgustin' to me the way some of them younger

women take on about that feller," she said. "Why, them two Yarnigan gals go moonin' around like a couple of heifers comin' in season."

"Ain't nothin' the matter with them gals that a good cold enema wouldn't cure," Uncle said. "And I notice them kids' bedroom door is cracked open." So I didn't hear no more that night.

I remember another night when Aunt Effie had took Ma to prayer meetin' and Uncle Wint and my dad were talkin' in the kitchen—and they weren't drinkin' tea, neither. Somehow or 'nother our door weren't tight-closed again. Mostly the talk were about huntin' and fishin' but just before I went to sleep I remember Uncle Wint sayin', "I don't know about you and my sister, Jim, but I can always tell when somethin' don't please Effie. Her upper lip will draw down till it looks four inches long."

"Froney just sets her mouth like a catfish on a trot line," Daddy said. "It ain't no touble to tell when she's mad neither."

"Well, at least we know the storm signals," Uncle said, "and can trim our sails and head for shelter. And we'd better put the jug away . . . I think I hear the buggy."

5 School Days & Tarley's Buck

School had already took up when we moved up to Gator Crawl and Daddy started us right off. They put me in second grade and Tarl in fifth. He were worried about makin' it but not as much as a big old boy from down River who said he had trouble passin' fifth grade and told us, "I was so nervous the day them exams come that I couldn't shave."

There was some rough boys but there weren't no worser young-un in the school than Hull Jordan's boy Spencer. Spence weren't only mischeevious he were mean and talked dirty and cussed right out in school. His teacher told him that she had a good will to write a letter to his daddy but she knowed it wouldn't get delivered.

"The hell it wouldn't," Spence said. "I ain't skeered of you nor my old man neither." This were a dern lie itself because ever'body were skeered of Hull Jordan when he got mad.

"All right," the teacher said. "Here's a letter—let's see you take it to your daddy. Will you?"

"You're damn right," Spence said. "You're damn right I will."

Well, in a couple of days here come old Hull Jordan to the school, madder'n a wet owl.

"What's all this?" he wanted to know. "What's my boy done now?"

"He's been naughty," the teacher said. "He curses and talks dirty and won't study his lessons. I'll show you what I mean. I'll ask him a question right out of today's lesson."

"All right," Mr. Jordan said. "Ask him."

So the teacher asked, "Spencer, who wrote the Declaration of Independence?"

"I don't know and I don't give a damn," Spence said.

"You see?" the teacher said. "That's the kind of impudence I get from him all the time."

Well, Hull Jordan really got mad then. He grabbed Spence by the collar and shook him and said, "All right, you dirty-mouthed little bastard, if you writ that thing you tell this lady!" So Spence admitted it. I sure felt sorry for him, mean as he were.

Just how much good schoolin' does for a feller depends on his payin' attention to what they're tryin' to learn him. Most kids ain't really payin' attention. Like me when Aunt Effie's cousin come to visit. He had went in the army when he were a young feller and had worked up to be some kind of a general . . . a "Bring a deer General," were what I understood her to say. She were some proud of him and said that he'd be a full general before he got through. Well, I sure did look forward to seein' him and his deer and were some kind of disappointed when he showed up without one. But she were right about his soon gettin' to be a full general. Uncle Winton brought out his jug and they taken care of that the first evenin'.

Durin' most of the time we was gettin' our own house built, me and Tarl come straight home from school and went to helpin' any way that we could. Daddy had found a hundred and sixty acres up River about a mile and a half from the Eppses. It had a good long front on the water and the house were goin' up on high ground about thirty steps from the River bank. There were a sort of sandy, shallow beach directly in front, before it dropped off deep, so we could have a dock for our boat as well as a place where us kids could go a-swimmin'. The front porch would look south right out across the water at some big old mossy cypresses on the other side and miles of hammock and marsh that stretched plumb down to Crystal River. There just couldn't hardly be no prettier place.

"—if you writ that thing you tell this lady!"

Saturday mornin's Daddy let us off to go fishin' or huntin'. Before we started off the first time Uncle Winton said, "That Hammock out yonder is a mighty big chunk of country and it's easy to get lost in it, so tell your boys to be careful."

"I reckon they'll be all right," Daddy told him. "I've had Tarl out with me a few times down in the Big Cypress and he's just like a Indian in the woods."

So one Saturday mornin' me and Tarl got a early start and sort of went explorin'. If a feller headed straight north from the Eppses' place, he passed through some pretty open glades of cabbage trees and big pines before he come to the heavy palmettos along the outer edge of the main Hammock. There was always a heap of birds in them glades and plenty of fox squirrels in the big pines. When a Florida Cracker hunter says "birds" he means partridges, quail, or what Yankees call "bob-whites." When he says "fox squirrels" he's talkin' about Florida fox squirrels, which are near about as big as rabbits and got tails long as a fox almost.

To the west the Hammock went to breakin' up into islands scattered along the big marsh. Some of 'em was big islands with pines and oaks and bay trees and such, along with the cabbages, which was everywhere. All them islands was pretty rocky, specially along the creek banks. We'd been down the River a few times with Daddy in our boat, lookin' over the country and runnin' through some of the creeks, but we hadn't yet gone ashore huntin'.

Out toward the open Gulf the islands got smaller and they weren't hardly nothin' but oyster shell with just a few little old twisted cedars and mangroves on 'em. At low tide, the marsh would go near 'bout dry and a feller could walk it if he'd watch where he put his feet and not step in the same places comin' back. It would get boggy real quick if any kind of trail got beat out in that black mud.

On this mornin' we started workin' toward the westward till we hit the marsh. We seen a big old island that looked to be about a quarter over in the marsh and headed for it. The goin' were just a little boggy, I remember, and there was some real heavy saw grass and high palmettos along the edge of the island. What were about to happen on that island I can't never forget.

When we busted through them high palmettos on the edge, we come out into a great big old open island—big pine trees, a few cedars and some of the tallest cabbage palms I ever seen. There was a thicket of oaks ahead of us and they was loaded with acorns. We didn't know too much about turkeys back then but it sure looked like the sort of a place a feller would find 'em. We was tippin' along, me with my .22 and Tarl with Daddy's old .44–40, when all of a sudden we heered somethin' comin' through the leaves behind us. There was a big clump of myrtles back of us so we couldn't see for a second just what was comin' but I mean we was ready! I eased the bolt back to cock and I heered the hammer click back on Tarl's .44.

Then we seen it—a dog! That old blue tick pup had done follered us off. He'd took a likin' to me ever since I got the ticks off'n him and he'd sneaked off after me. Of course Uncle Wint wouldn't never of let any of his hounds go off with a couple of greenhorn kids, if he'd knowed about it, but here we was.

"Come here, Blue," I said and that pup come a-waggin' his whole body sideways. He sure were proud to see us. If there'd been any turkeys around they'd done left, so we figured we had just as well go home. With this big old gawky scoun'el bouncin' around, a feller wouldn't even get to see a squirrel.

About that time Blue stopped and raised his head and sniffed and tore out into that oak thicket. Over on the far side he let out a squall that made my hair stand up. I mean that old pup had a mouth—a deep, bellerin' mouth—and he went to usin' it.

There weren't hardly time to realize what were happenin' until it happened. Here come a buck, a great big old gray feller and he were stretched out and jumpin' high. I seen his big, shiny horns and the wild look in his eye as he come sailin' over a palmetto and I'll never forget that picture so long as I live. And I'll never forget the roar of that old .44 and the sight of that deer just sort of stoppin' and plungin' down. Tarl had broke his neck and he never kicked. My brother Tarl is a cool customer all right but this were his first deer and he just couldn't say nothin' or do nothin' but shake. And I reckon that pup, Blue, were the most excited one there. I thought he'd knock a hole in his own ribs with his tail.

The buck were a ten-pointer and fat as butter. I ain't never seen as big a Florida deer before nor since.

"What are we goin' to do with him, Billy?" Tarl asked me. "We can't tote him I don't believe."

"We'll go get Uncle Winton," I said. And there was goin' to be lots of times in the days to come when that turnt out to be the best prescription for a heap of things.

"Yeah, but we just can't leave this deer a-layin' here," Tarl said. "A bear might tote him off or hogs might find him or buzzards get on him. Me or you one has got to stay here whilst the other goes for Uncle Wint and his horse. You might get lost so I reckon I'll go."

Neither one of us didn't have no knife fittin' to dress out the buck and the shot had bled him out pretty good anyhow. Both me'n Tarl had helped Daddy butcher hogs often enough so we'd of knowed what to do and how to do it if'n we'd of had a good knife. Ours wouldn't hardly cut the stems of some green palmetto fans to lay over the deer to keep the flies off him. If there's one thing a hunter needs in the woods, it's a good knife.

Now, I never will forget the next three or four hours or however long it were. Three or four *years*, it seemed like. Don't forget I were only nine years old. Well, nearly ten, but I felt mighty little out there in them big woods even with the .44 which Tarl had left with me to guard the deer. I hadn't never fired it, of course, but I sure meant to if I seen anythin' comin'—panther, bear, boar hog or whatever. I do believe that island were the lonesomest place in the whole world. All kinds of thoughts kept goin' through my mind. What if Tarl got lost or snake-bit or somethin' or couldn't find his way back. Why, nobody wouldn't never find me. That were silly though, when I thought about it. That old .44 could be heered a long way and I had six in the magazine. I'd heered stories about fellers gettin' lost and never found because they wouldn't stay put and let folks find 'em, so I didn't figure on goin' nowhere. And I weren't about to leave Tarl's deer.

As the sun moved the light changed and things didn't look the same. A little old bush or stump or somethin' that I had been seein' all the time would get to lookin' like a varmint of some kind when next I looked that way. A gray light'd snag looked more like a big wildcat than a wildcat. I even sighted at it a time or two. Once a cat squirrel jumped onto a dead fan in the top of one of them cabbages and liken to have scared me right out of my britches. Later on a dern hoot owl let out one of them ungodly screeches like they'll do sometimes just before they hoot and I knowed for a second that I were about to be panther-caught. But in spite of bein' scared I were soakin' up the spell of the big Hammock—the sights and the sounds and the smell of the leaves—bay, cedar and pine straw.

It were a good three miles back to the River and by the time Uncle and Tarl got back and we could bring that deer in on his horse it were near 'bout dark. Ever'body come out in the yard to see the deer and old Tarl were some kind of proud. But he still hadn't got over his buck ague and would start shakin' whenever he'd start tellin' about it.

"Don't tease the boy," Daddy said. "When a feller don't get the shakes at a time like this'n he might as well lay down and die."

And I'll guarantee that's so. It's a long time ago since me'n Tarl and Blue dog done business on that swamp island but my neck prickles and my mouth still gets dry when I hear the hounds a-comin' on the trail of a big old buck.

Well, we pulled the peelin' on that deer down in the shed by the light of some pine knots and I'm here to tell you there just ain't never been no better-lookin' meat. Uncle explained that the ruttin' season hadn't started good yet so that old scaper hadn't run hisself down chasin' does. There was fat along his back a inch thick and them back strap steaks would melt in a feller's mouth.

"It's cool enough so he won't sour tonight, so we'll hang him in the smokehouse and carry him up to the ice plant tomorrow," Uncle said.

We eat the liver for supper that night, fried along with some of Uncle Winton's home-cured bacon and it even put a smile on Aunt Effie's face. Somebody had give Ma a big bunch of mustard greens and they was really somethin' fittin' too. Just before we set down at the table Uncle got out a jug and poured out some corn whiskey and him and Daddy drunk a toast to Tarley and Uncle Winton made him a poem, which Ma saved for him to pass along to his children if he ever had any. It said:

Tarley Driggers and my dog Blue
Done what they wasn't supposed to do.
But while they was at it they done it well
And finished it up, so what the hell!

Ma wanted him to change the last lines to, "While they was at it they done it right and all come home with their eyes alight."

"Froney Driggers," Daddy said. "That don't sound no more like your brother than I sound like Blue dog. So just shut up."

"Don't be a-tellin' my sister to shut up," Uncle said. "She's a fine Christian woman and she just don't like my language."

"And neither do I," Aunt Effie said, jumpin' into the argument. "But that don't mean you're ever goin' to change it. Now let's eat these here rations that the Lord and Tarley Driggers has put before us before everything gets cold."

Everybody said, "Amen," and we went to eatin'.

^{6}The Hammock—Talkin' Turkey

Thinkin' back to the days when we was stayin' with the Eppses and first gettin' acquainted with the River and the big Hammock and all, I realize they was some of the happiest days of my life—spite of Aunt Effie. Sometimes Daddy and Uncle Winton would take us boys along on campin' trips—plumb up to Spring Run and even Hickory Ford and Otter Creek. I'll tell you now that were some pretty piece of woods—great big old cypress trees along the sloughs and creeks and around the ponds, high islands of big pines and water oaks and magnolias and palmettos and gums and bays and cedars and hickories. A feller couldn't hardly see the sky and it sure was easy to get lost. Ever'body carried a huntin' horn, made from a cow horn, and many's the night I have laid in my blankets and heered some way-off horn a-wailin' and knowed that some poor sap-sucker had missed his trail and were callin' for help and bein' glad it weren't me.

I reckon the part of them huntin' trips I enjoyed the most were settin' around the campfire after supper and listenin' to Uncle Winton and the other hunters tell stories. Some of 'em I ain't forgot till yet.

Once the talk got around to mules and ever'body agreed

as to how ornery they was and how gassy they was. Uncle Winton told a story about a widow-woman who lived up on the shore—I forget where—Virginia or Carolina or somewheres. Anyhow, her husband had been a great fox hunter and after he died she had stayed on at the farm tryin' to look after the stock and all them dogs and all. Well, the mule got sick and were just standin' around all swoll up with its head hangin' near 'bout to the ground and it wouldn't eat nothin'. So she called the onliest doctor on the shore.

"Doctor Jim," she said, "this is Annie Cortland. Our mule is sick and won't eat nothin' but just stands around all swoll up."

The doctor told her to give it a pint of mineral oil but she said she didn't think she could get the mule's mouth open. The doctor told her that it weren't supposed to be taken by mouth but in the other end.

"How do I do that?" she asked.

"Use a funnel," the doctor said. "Pour the oil in the funnel."

Well, the poor old soul didn't have ary funnel so in desperation she taken her husband's huntin' horn down from the wall and went out to the barn. When she had the horn in place she reached up to the shelf for the mineral oil but she didn't have her glasses on and got a bottle of oil of turpentine. She poured it in the horn and when she did the mule made a new door in the side of the barn, knocked down two sections of rail fence and went off down the road blowin' that horn. All of the dogs thought there were a fox hunt under way and went a-tearin' after that mule. Every dog in hearin' joined in till there must of been forty in the pack.

The bridge tender at the Inland Waterway heered 'em comin' and thought it were a boat comin' through so he run out and opened the draw. Three dogs was able to stop but the mule and the rest of the dogs went right on into the water. The mule drowned but all the dogs made it ashore.

I remember somebody askin' Uncle Wint if he believed all that foolishness and he said, "I'll believe anything about a dad-burned mule. But you don't have to. I'll tell you somethin' else about a mule. If you ever give oil to one and just have to go somewheres, ride him don't drive him!"

Of course me'n Tarl was just shirttail boys then and

She poured it in the horn
and when she did—

naturally all them stories made a great impression on us. I'll probably remember more of 'em as I go along.

When we started huntin' in the mornin' they put me on a stand close to camp. I didn't have nothin' but my little old .22 single shot and I weren't suppose to shoot at nothin' but squirrels and not even them less'n they was up in trees.

"What'll I do if I see a deer or a turkey?" I wanted to know.

Uncle Wint had seen me hit the cow on a milk can at twenty steps so he said, "Well, sonny, if a old gobbler walks out close enough for you to see his eye, try him. And if a deer should walk up that close, wait till he turns his head and shoot him right in the burr of the ear and don't never think that little .22 won't kill him graveyard dead."

Uncle had whittled me out a cedar stick turkey yelper and told me how to use it. It were just a cedar stick, about as big as a ordinary lead pencil, run through a corncob and you helt it by the corncob and scratched the end of the stick on a piece of slate about as big around as a milk can—it could be either roundish or squarish. You cupped your left hand around the slate and helt the edge of it against your chest or, if you was kneelin' down, against your kneecap just above the joint. This was to give it a coarse sound like a old gobbler. If you helt it away from your body, you'd get a higher-pitched note like a young bird.

He said to always be sure to whittle off the end of that stick like you were a-sharpenin' a pencil. If it wore down smooth and round it would just skid on the slate and you'd have to chip off the end again. Uncle had both ends of the stick fixed just right so he could use either one and wouldn't even have to look down when he started yelpin'.

To keep the end of the stick from slippin' on the slate and makin' a false note, Uncle taken his pocket knife and scraped the slate till it got a little bit chalky. Man, he could imitate three or four different birds with that thing and cluck with it the most natural you ever heered.

"The main thing to remember about turkey huntin'," Uncle told me, "applies to life in general—which is don't talk too much. Get yourself hid in a good spot where you've seen fresh sign, but not so well that you can't see to shoot, and then send out a call now and then—but just now and then. If you get a answer be mighty particular about what you do because that old bird is standin' out there checkin' up and your second call is got to be just right. If he answers that'n, I generally shut up and let him look for me.

"There's all kinds of turkey calls and ever'body ought to use the one that is easiest for him. There's cedar boxes with a hinged top and there's cedar boxes you scratch with a piece of slate. Some fellers can call 'em up with a ordinary smokin' pipe and some fellers use the wing bone of a turkey. I even knowed of a feller who could cup his hands around the end of a soda straw and suck air through it. There's new-fangled calls with rubber diaphragms that are mighty good but the very best is the human throat—if a feller can hit the high notes."

My brother Tarl learnt to call 'em that way and he's the best I ever heered. Durin' the gobblin' season he could sound like a hen and a gobbler singin' a love duet and he'd flap his hat around in the leaves to where an old gobbler would near about run over him to crash the party.

Uncle went on to explain, "It's a heap better to be settin' backed up against a big tree or log or thick bushes than it is to be peepin' out around a tree trunk or somethin'. The main thing is to stay still and not move until you're ready to shoot. If you have to move to get a sight at him, move real slow and easy. Any kind of quick move will sure spook game of most any kind.

"I like to roost a bunch of turkeys," Uncle went on, "and one of these days I'm goin' to take you with me. We'll find us where they've been feedin' and scratchin' and we'll just sit quiet late in the evenin' till we hear 'em fly up. We'll get a pretty good idea of exactly where they's roostin' and we'll be right back there the next mornin' before day. Course a feller can sometimes outline 'em against the sky on a good bright moonlight night but that ain't legal no more."

When he said that I had to keep from laughin'. It weren't the law Uncle were skeered of, but runnin' up on a rattlesnake or a moccasin in the dark.

Uncle told me all this a long time ago but I ain't never forgot it. He said that like all wild critters, turkeys is interested in just three things—feedin', fightin' and you know what. So there really ain't too much difference between critters and Crackers, though us Crackers will sometimes sing, whistle or read a book. I reckon you could say a turkey likes music too, but only if you play the right tune at the right time—a old gobbler callin' to a hen, a hen callin' to a gobbler, a poult callin' to its mamma or a mamma callin' to her fryin'-size young-uns. The key is different but, like a heap of songs I hear today, the words is always the same—"Come here, baby! Come here baby! Come here baby!"

Uncle Wint always told us that in any kind of huntin', the first thing to do is find the feed. He said, "Critters spend most of their lives huntin' somethin' to eat. A old gobbler can't just go home and hang up his hat and set down to a table of good rations—his women folks is out scroungin' around for food too. And it takes up most of their time—dependin' on the season of the year, the weather, and the crop of nuts, bugs, berries or seeds. Down here we look for 'em 'mongst the oaks in the fall and winter and on the flats when the berries are ripe in the spring or out on the prairies or edge of the marsh, a-chasin' grasshoppers in the summer and they dearly love to get into a feller's chufa field or corn field or peanut patch if it ain't too far from cover."

Uncle went on to tell us that we shouldn't ever forget that when we go huntin' it's like visitin' somebody in his home. He lives there and he knows where ever'thing belongs to be. If he should come home and see a rockin' chair on the porch where a straight chair had been he'd say, "Oh-oh. Somebody's done been here." So if you're goin' to fix a log blind or somethin', fix it a long time before huntin' season and let the birds get used to its bein' there. Otherwise, make use of natural cover and don't change the looks or nothin' more'n you can help. They tell us a deer sees only black and white but a turkey sees color. Otherwise all them fancy feathers would be wasted. So wear dark clothes or camouflage clothes when you're turkey huntin' and always remember that a dern turkey is a suspicious critter. A deer looks at a man and sees a stump. A turkey looks at a stump and sees a man. If the wind is right and a feller don't move, he can set right out in the open in a bright red coat and a deer will feed right up to him. But not a turkey.

I never will forget the mornin' I called up and killed my first gobbler. Man! I were some kind of proud. That scoun'el had a beard a foot long and were just about all I could tote. Daddy put me on a stand near Dinah Pond that mornin' before it were hardly good day. Uncle Winton taken a couple of hounds and went north to get 'em started on a buck deer, if he could find a good track. He hadn't been gone twenty minutes till the sky began to get light and life in the Hammock began to stir around. Some wood ducks went a-screechin' over and a pair of them black mallards set their wings and whined into the pond. A squirrel were cuttin' the mast out of a green pine cone close by and way off down the slough a hoot owl hollered, "Who cooks, who cooks, who cooks for you all." When he did, a dern turkey gobbled! I mean right now.

It were early for the gobblin' season but Uncle told me later that a heap of times a gobbler will let go when he hears a owl, specially if he's just flew down from the roost. Well, I got out my cedar stick, scratched that slate with my knife till I had some chalk on it, cupped it against my brisket and yelped— just like Uncle had told me—four or five notes just about as fast as you'd count—one-two-three-four-five. Nothin' didn't happen so I waited about five minutes and yelped again. This time I got a answer so I put the yelper away, cocked my .22 and waited.

Directly, that old gobbler walked out into an open place up toward the end of the pond and I'm here to tell you that were some sight. He'd take a few steps and cluck and peep around this way and that. He were really doin' a piece of lookin' and I tried to remember to raise my little old rifle slow and easy. But between the cold and the excitement and the turkey cranin' his neck around, I just couldn't get a sight on that big old blue head with the red wattles. The sun had got up enough so that I even seen his eye glint! He kept on comin' and when he were about twenty steps away, I steadied my sights on that eye long enough to pull the trigger. Uncle Winton called it fine shootin'.

"Later on, Billy," he said, "when you get your own shotgun, you'll sometimes get a shot at a turkey flyin' overhead, like when some other hunter or a wildcat or somethin' has scared up a bunch. When you shoot at a flyin' turkey, lead him like you would a duck. He's so big you'll think you can't miss him, but he is ballin' the jack, so swing ahead of him. Like Lou Borden used to say, 'Shoot 'em in the head and the butt is bound to follow.' Some folks like BB's or even buckshot but I like fours or fives. I've even killed 'em with eights. I'd rather get a few fine shot into his head or neck than a buckshot into his body. I've knowed 'em to go on off a mile with two buckshot in the body. Anyhow, buckshot patterns out too sometimesy to suit me. I don't even like it for deer. I'm a rifle man for them skeesters.

"Another thing, Billy. If'n you get a turkey down with a busted wing, get to him fast. A winged turkey can really run. Shoot him again if you get a chance. It's better to pick lead out of some meat than to let a buzzard do it."

It's easy to get the buck ague over turkeys, specially when you see a old gobbler struttin' and you wonder whether he'll come on in range. I never will forget huntin' with Uncle Winton and a English officer when we got into a bunch of turkeys. The Englishman were carryin' a foreign-made double-barrel hammer gun somethin' like the one my daddy had. When them turkeys went a-bustin' out of there, some runnin' and some flyin', Uncle Wint killed two and I killed one but the Englishman didn't fire.

"What's the matter, Colonel?" Uncle asked him.

"Dammit!" the Colonel said. "I didn't have good cockage."

"Well now," Uncle said, "that's as good excuse as I ever heered in my life."

This same Colonel come back ten years later to hunt with us and this time he were carryin' another fancy, foreign-made shotgun he called a "over-and-under." He used it quail huntin' and he'd shoot twice at every bird that got up—once over and once under!

I've killed a few gobblers and talked with a heap of hunters since then—fellers who hunted turkeys all over—plumb to Arizona and Vermont. Conditions are different all right and the main feed is different but the nature of the bird is pretty much the same wherever you find him, from all I can hear. He ain't exactly what you'd call a trustin' soul.

⁷The New House

Ma always said, "Pride goes before a fall," and I reckon I bragged too much about my shootin' because one evenin', not long after I got that old big gobbler, I shot myself. It weren't really my fault but it sure taught me that what Daddy and Uncle Winton had told me about .22 rifles was true. They ain't playthings. It were on a Saturday and I had been let to go squirrel huntin'. All my family was workin' on the new house that day—even Tarl—and Daddy had got up on the roof to nail on some shingles—shakes we called 'em then. I set my .22 down on the front porch and leant it up agin a corner post. I should of unloaded it first but I didn't. Just forgot to.

Now, this were a little .22 single-shot bolt-action. The bolt had to be pulled back to cock it for firin' but of course it weren't cocked. Anyhow, there were a feller up on the roof helpin' Daddy and he jumped down from the porch rafters and when he hit the floor that little old rifle started fallin'—or maybe I should say slidin'. I had stood it up with the stock pretty close to the edge of the porch and when it slipped off it dropped down to where the bolt hit the floor and drove the firin' pin into the cartridge just as I grabbed the end of the barrel with my left hand. Off she went! That little old bullet went right on up through the roof and out through one of them cypress shakes just missin' Daddy. The trouble of it was that it went through my hand first, right at the wrist joint. So don't never think a .22 won't hurt you. If it hits you in the head, you're a gone goslin'.

Well, they carried me to a crusty old doctor down in Crystal and he put my hand on a splint board and said, "More'n likely there's bones busted in that wrist and you may wind up with a stiff joint. So how do you want your hand set—in a fist or straight out?"

"Curled just right to hold a gun," I told him.

"You crazy little fool," he said, "I've a good will not to treat you at all." But he rolled up some bandage and put it under my hand and curled the fingers over the end of the board like I wanted 'em.

Powder had got into the bullet hole and so they give me a shot in the back to prevent blood poison. That were a miserable time for me and I sure didn't get much sympathy from Aunt Effie. She drawed her lip down about three inches and said, "Serves the little skeester right. If he'd been workin' instead of off huntin' it wouldn't of happened."

"He weren't off huntin'," Uncle Wint said. "It happened right there at the house."

"Well, he were careless," Aunt Effie said. "Shouldn't of had a loaded gun around."

"That's where you're wrong," my daddy said. "A gun ain't no good unless it's loaded. It's the so-called unloaded guns that kill people. 'Oh, I didn't know it was loaded,' you'll hear somebody say after he's done killed somebody accidently. Well, I'll tell you now, any gun of mine is loaded—always loaded. When and if you need a gun, there ain't no time to mess around lookin' for shells and tryin' to load 'em. When I kill somebody, it won't be accidently. But I'll grant you the boy were wrong to leave his little rifle in a bad place . . . outside, around people."

Of course, Daddy didn't like to say too much to rouse up Aunt Effie while we was still havin' to live there with the Eppses, but I remembered all that he *did* say and it sure were the truth. When he done his final shootin', it weren't by accident.

I couldn't go huntin' for a spell with my hand all splinted

up, but I learnt a heap about the woods and varmints from just listenin' to Uncle Winton and I reckon the most important thing I learnt from him was to laugh. If he couldn't see a funny side to something he'd make one. He had his miseries—with his teeth, his women and sometimes his whiskey—but he could near about always laugh.

"Folks has got to laugh, sonny," he'd tell me. "If they don't they's either crazy or well-started." He couldn't hardly tell a funny story without it remindin' him of two or three more even funnier. I reckon some of that rubbed off on me because I just hardly can't keep from interruptin' my own self when I'm tryin' to tell about something. Like right now talkin' about Uncle Wint when I ought to be tellin' about the new house and all. If I was a coon dog where there was lots of coons, I sure wouldn't tree many.

North, our property run near about to the edge of the big Hammock and there were open glades where a man could find cabbage palms sixty feet tall and cut 'em for house logs. So that's what Daddy done. Most of 'em was almost straight as pine trees and some would make three cuts for a side wall, stood on end and capped over. If they's laid on their side, they'll rot but if the ends is protected from the weather they'll last from now on. When they's green, cabbage logs is some kind of heavy but we had got a old ox that could mortally drag 'em out of any place—high palmettos, mud or wherever.

I weren't able to tote much heavy stuff till my hand got well but I done what I could to help. All of us couldn't hardly wait till we could get moved in and away from Aunt Effie's sharp tongue. And to tell the truth I'd be mighty glad to get out of the sound and smell of Uncle's goats. He always had two or three favorites runnin' loose in the yard to keep the grass clipped off. The dern things has always been trouble to me ever since me'n Tarl was fire huntin' and shined the eyes of what we *thought* was a bunch of deer but weren't. I can't eat goat meat to this day. We killed five and crippled four more that had to be killed and Daddy made us skin and dress out every dern one of 'em.

Like everybody else in them days, Uncle let most of his stock run loose in the Hammock—hogs, cows and goats right out amongst the deer. So we had *some* excuse. But not enough. The ones we shot was his milk goats back in the pen—the dern mule we was ridin' had traveled in a circle without our knowin' it.

Later on, when we got our own stock we let 'em make their own livin' most of the time. If acorns were scarce, we'd put up a couple of hogs and fatten 'em on corn. In the open range, everybody had their own marks—ours were a crop and an under-bit in the right ear and two under-bits in the left.

When we had finally got the house all finished and moved in and started livin' there, Ma were the happiest I had ever saw her and gathered us all up every evenin' to read our Bible and thank the Lord for our many blessin's—for a good, gentle cow and a ox that could pull and all the fish and oysters and game we could want—deer, turkeys, ducks, squirrels—and acorn-fat hogs. There weren't a cloud in our sky that we could see then. This were the house where us boys was to grow up into manhood and where me and mine was to stay and raise our kids and have our own joys and griefs.

I'll never forget how glad Ma was to have her own room with Daddy off to theirselves. It were next to the kitchen at the east end and there were a big livin' room between it and the bedroom at the west end where me'n Tarl was. Most generally we'd eat in the kitchen but when company come we eat at the big table in the livin' room. Ma rigged a cowbell on a string to hang by the kitchen door so she could hear company, even if she were down the hall cleanin' up in our room. Me'n Tarl made our own beds and if we didn't we heered about it. And we had certain chores to do—Tarl's to tote in firewood and mine to tote the water. The river water were pretty and clean then but Ma boiled it anyhow for drinkin'.

I remember one time when we was huntin' with Uncle Winton and he dipped up a horn full of river water and drunk it and winked and said, "Boys, your mammy always has been right persnickety, even when she were a young girl. And if you know what's good for you, you'll do like she says." So when we was home we drunk boiled water but when we was huntin' we'd drink river water, creek water or pond water.

One of the first things Ma done were to have the church ladies' sewin' circle in for tea. We didn't have too much furniture then but there was seats for everybody. Me'n Tarl hung around for cake and cookies but Ma run us out of the kitchen so we didn't hear nothin' much interestin'—not at *that* meetin'.

But when the County Histerical Society met there later in the year some of the women folks bunched up in Ma's bedroom while us boys was settin' by the kitchen stove. Some of the cabbage logs in the wall had been a little crooked and didn't quite fit tight to each other. We hadn't got around to chinkin' and strippin' the cracks, so we could hear everything them ladies said. Some of it weren't fittin' for young boys.

There were one loud-talkin' lady none of us liked who told all about havin' to have her gall bladder out. She showed her scar but we didn't even peek. I remember thinkin' it must of been a big one to of took out all the gall that woman had. Another, Emily Baker, had just had a histerectumy and said she were glad to have that all over with . . . eleven kids was enough. She said Tim Baker weren't goin' to get his Baker's dozen . . . not out of her, anyhow.

Neither Ma nor Aunt Effie was in on all that talk. Aunt Effie had got mad about something and hadn't come to the meetin', and Ma were busy in the livin' room tellin' everybody the history of that dern cast-iron cockroach. Daddy and Uncle Winton had gone across River to look for some missin' cows. Seemed like somethin' always happened so that they couldn't get to these meetin's. Maybe they just didn't like tea.

Uncle Wint knowed near about everybody in Gulf Hammock from the Withlacoochee to Cedar Key and even down to Homosassa—fellers like Dad Easley and Frank Butler and Kelly Runnels and Tom Chaires and old man Hodges and young Randolph who got to be a senator later on. And everybody knowed Uncle because he sure did do a heap of prowlin' around. Of course he knowed all the great hunters and when they'd come to visit he'd bring 'em over to our house to get acquainted with Daddy. I wish I could remember all the mighty yarns I heered them fellers tell.

There was some outside hunters who wanted to do some fishin' too, so Uncle would bring 'em over and Daddy would carry 'em to the Gulf or, if he already had a party booked, he'd pass 'em along to the Yarnigan boys who lived down River and guided when they felt like it and was sober. There was three of them Yarnigans and they was all big old rough fellers that loved to play tricks on town dudes.

They'd punched three holes in the rim of a pie pan and brought three pieces of leader wire, all different lengths, through the holes to one swivel. When they was trollin' they'd wait till some feller had to go down into the cabin and then they'd tie this rig onto his line, throw it over and holler, "Strike!" Man, that pie pan would cut a flutter! It would go down deep and swim off to one side and then turn up flat and near 'bout snatch a feller's arms out of their sockets. Then it would swim the other way. They fooled me on it and it sure did feel like a big, heavy fish.

One day they had a feller aboard who were really punishin' the bottle. They was trollin' for kingfish about four miles off shore and he got so drunk he couldn't hardly stay in his fishin' chair. He did manage to catch one kingfish and then he went down into the cabin and crawled into a bunk. One of the boys got the kingfish out of the fish box, hooked it back on his line and hollered, "Strike!" The drunk crawled back up into the cockpit and the boys helt him to keep him from fallin' overboard while he reeled in the kingfish again. They done this to him six or seven times and when they got to Crystal River, he climbed up on the dock and told his wife, who'd come down to meet him, "Honey, just wait'll you see the string of fish I caught!"

Well, the boys brung out that poor wore-out kingfish and had their laugh, and that drunk wanted to whip everybody in sight—includin' the folks on the dock. He were a feller Daddy had passed along to 'em, so it weren't too funny to us. Daddy told 'em so right there on the dock and he didn't pull no punches. I thought for a while he might have to *throw* some punches but there were somethin' about the way Jim Driggers looked at folks that most always cooled 'em off in a hurry. It were that way with the Yarnigans. They'd been jokin' but he weren't.

When the bad thing happened and my dad got killed in the shoot-out over the closed gate at Gator Crawl, there come some rough days. But I have wrote that all out once* and there ain't no use dwellin' on it. Uncle Wint stepped in and helped raise us boys and Ma managed to keep things goin' with the help of the money the rich Yankee left us. I already told a heap of things we done and how Tarl got his vengeance against the feller who shot Daddy so it'd pleasure me to skip over it. Sometimes a feller just has to turn the page and never look back.

* *If Nothin' Don't Happen*

8 The Murderer Who Weren't

Sheriff Charlie Dean from over at Inverness in Citrus County use to come over bear huntin' with Uncle Winton and once in a while they'd go duck huntin' down in the marsh. They had took me along a time or two and I'm here to say that Sheriff Dean could mortally knock them high-flyin' pintails and widgeons out of the sky. When the huntin' season rolled around him and Uncle Wint would get together to make some plans and I happened to be down at Uncle's when this happened. I had carried one of Ma's special lemon pies down to the Eppses and I just set down in the kitchen and listened at them two cronies talk.

I don't reckon there were ary two better shots and better hunters in the whole dad-burned world. There's some fellers is good hunters but can't hit nothin' after they have found it, and other fellers who is fancy shots at county fairs and turkey shoots and such who don't know no more about findin' game than a blind hog knows about a eclipse. But when Uncle Wint and Sheriff Charlie Dean got together you had everything.

"How's the ducks goin' to be this year, Winton?" Sheriff Dean asked. "I mean out on the Gulf Marsh."

"Plenty," Uncle told him. "They's a heap of canvasbacks

and a jillion pintails and widgeons. And they's right smart greenheads and black mallards comin' in to the pot holes along the edge of the Hammock to get acorns. How is it on your side of the River?"

"That's what I want to talk to you about," the Sheriff said. "Do you know that string of cypress ponds about six miles south of here?"

"That's exactly what I want to talk to *you* about," Uncle said. "I mean them summer screamers is really comin' in there late in the evenin'. And there ain't nothin' better to eat or prettier to look at. The trouble of it is that it takes about four fellers to shoot them ponds or the birds will fly out of the first one and light down in the fourth one and then fly back to the first one if one lone hunter walks that mile to jump 'em up again."

That's when I put in my two cents worth and said it looked like the Sheriff of the county would know enough folks to find *forty* hunters for them ponds, let alone four.

The Sheriff laughed. "That's the trouble, son," he told me. "I know near about everybody and if I told forty about those ducks, they's four hundred would scream louder'n them screamer ducks."

"Well," Uncle Winton said, "four's the right number and we got four right here in the family."

"Who's that?" the Sheriff wanted to know.

"Me and my two nephews and you," Uncle said. "You can join the family temporariously."

So they planned they'd go the follerin' Tuesday and the Sheriff said he'd bring a little old duck boat in his truck and we could use it to pick up our ducks because there was holes out there deep enough to drown a man a hundred years old.

"If you don't want to bother to bring a boat," I told him, "me or Tarl will swim and get 'em. We don't mind."

"They ain't jokin'," Uncle Wint said. "They's a couple of tough kids and they dearly love to hunt."

"I know that," the Sheriff said, "but they ain't too tough for a big old gator to grab if they was to break through into his den. So when we get through shootin', the kids can take the boat and pole it to the dead ducks. It ought not to take us long to get all the birds we need, thick as they are."

I never will forget that day's shootin' because I sure were

proud of what I done. I knocked down seven of them summer ducks and picked up six. Four of 'em was drakes, the fellers with the green topknots and the pretty speckledy flank feathers with the black bars across 'em.

It were near about sundown when Sheriff Dean come drivin' up on the old sand road that run along the south side of that string of ponds.

"How many you got down?" he hollered to me where I were squatted down in the high grass.

"Six I can see. And maybe one more."

"The maybes ain't much good to eat," he said. "Jump in and we'll go pick up my birds and then come get these."

Well, that's what we done. As we was drivin' along the Sheriff asked me how many times I had shot and I told him I didn't have but fifteen shells to start with and I still had two.

"That's dern good shootin'," he said. "Anytime a feller puts one duck in the boat for every two shells he fires he's doin' extra good, considerin' he has to finish off some cripples. Ain't no use to let a hawk or a mink or a otter or a gator or a snappin' turtle eat your ducks—not with shells costin' near about five cents apiece."

When we got to the first pond where he had been shootin' I got into the little old duck boat and poled out and picked up his birds. There weren't no deecoys to pick up because we hadn't put out none—a feller didn't really need 'em for the kind of shootin' we was doin' because them ponds wasn't much over a gunshot wide. After I finished gettin' his ducks I poled on toward my pond. The water were low and I liken to have run hard aground two or three places in the shallow water connectin' 'em.

Sheriff Dean coursed me with the truck, polin' along about three or four miles an hour, which were about all I could do by myself. As soon as we got to the third pond, Tarley got into the boat with me and taken a paddle and we made short work of pickin' up his birds and movin' on toward the fourth pond and Uncle Winton. I don't mean to say Tarl hadn't got down his share of ducks but we could get to 'em so much easier when I didn't have to lose no headway while I laid down the pole and grabbed a duck.

The sun had set by the time we got to Uncle and we had to pick up his ducks in the light of the afterglow.

"Hurry up, boys," he hollered, "and let's get out of here. There's brassheads risin' out of this grass big enough to go to roost at night like birds. I slapped one on my neck a while ago that had more blood in it than a full dog tick."

"Your uncle don't fool around much with the truth, does he?" Sheriff Dean said, winkin' at me.

I reckon maybe Uncle Wint might of been a little crotchety because he didn't have but six ducks and one of them were a sawbill. When we got everything and everybody loaded and started for home it were black as the inside of a cow. As we was drivin' along, Uncle Wint said, "By the time them ducks got to me they was higher than the Georgia pines. You sky busters didn't let much come through unshot at. How'd the boys do?"

"They done all right," Sheriff Dean put in. "And that Billy can really handle a boat."

"He ought to could," Uncle said. "He were near about raised in one down on the Caloosahatchee."

"Why, of course," the Sheriff said, "Jim Driggers's kids would have to be at home in any kind of boat."

By this time we had got back to the old bridge across Coachwhip Creek where there were a fork in the road and the Sheriff said, "If y'all ain't in a rush I'll just swing off here and drive up to the Drewson place and take a look around. Major Drewson has been away and I promised him I'd check up on things now and again."

"Take your time, Charlie," Uncle said. "I ain't in no hurry to get back to Effie, and the boys' ma don't worry none about 'em when they's out with me."

This Major Drewson were a rich Yankee who had built him a great big old two-story house on a bend of the River. Near about everybody on the River knowed who Major Drewson *was* but didn't nobody really know Major Drewson. He were a shy sort of feller who kept to himself and spent a heap of time fishin' alone. His wife had died early in May and his son were off at some high-falutin' school up in New Jersey or somewheres. The boy were an onliest child and the Major would visit him up there and the son would come down here at Christmas and Thanksgiving and such. Folks said the Major were really wropped up in his son.

I had met up with the kid at the store two or three times

and he seemed friendly enough when I invited him to go a-fishin' with me. But he said he didn't have but a few days vacation and wanted to spend it fishin' with his daddy. He sure were proud of his daddy and told how he had done a special job for the army in the war and won a medal from the President, not to mention the D.A.R. I remember that at the time I were talkin' to the Major's son it reminded me of my own dad. I still missed him somethin' cruel.

Naturally, I got to thinkin' about all that as we come in sight of the Major's place. The moon were near about full and just showin' through the pines when we come to his fence corner. The house were about a full gunshot from the water and set in about a six-acre pasture and there was a nice carpet grass and 'muda grass lawn with a hog-wire fence around the whole place.

Sheriff Dean said, "He sure got him a nice set-up here but it's a wonder somebody ain't broke in when he's away. The feller who's supposed to stay here and look after the place is too sorry to trust with all the fine things in that house. He's drunk half the time and half-drunk the rest of the time and his gal friend is worse. She's supposed to come in and clean every Friday. I don't see how the Major puts up with 'em—probably they're all he can get to come plumb out here in the woods—no neighbors or nothin'."

Just about that time we seen a light downstairs in the house and a second afterward it went out. Sheriff Dean swung the truck around to go in the front gate but it was closed and a chain wropped around it. As the headlights swept across the yard we all seen a feller run out and head for the woods. He were carryin' a sack and I mean he were catchin' air.

"Git him, Tarley boy, git him," Uncle Wint hollered, just like he'd tell his catch dogs to catch a hog. Well, Tarl cleared that hog fence like a buck deer and tore out after the feller without even grabbin' a gun. I weren't far behind him but I grabbed my gun before I left.

There weren't no time to try to unwrop the chain on the gate so Sheriff Dean and Uncle Wint got over the fence and joined in the chase. They was both carryin' their shotguns, but Uncle Wint were also totin' some tallow around the belly like old fellers of forty most generally do so he were behind everybody when my brother tackled that burglar. And I mean ol' Tarl put a crusher on him. I felt almost sorry for the feller because he weren't a big man and he sure were the scaredest feller I ever seen before or since. He had dropped the sack and when he seen me and Uncle Wint and the Sheriff, all with shotguns, it didn't help him none. We didn't know it then, but he had a little old nickel-plated .32 owl-head pistol in his pocket and he might of shot Tarl. But my brother didn't scare easy and he hadn't hesitated a split second when he caught up with that feller.

"All right, Mister," Sheriff Dean said. "Stand up now and put your hands over your head and keep 'em there. Make a wrong move and you're dead. Turn him loose, Tarley, and stand clear."

There were somethin' in Sheriff Dean's voice that made a feller know he'd kill a man if killin' was called for and I reckon that burglar heered it plenty plain because he stood up and said, "I ain't about to move an eyelash."

"Search him, Winton," Sheriff Dean said, "and see if he's got a gun."

"Hold my shotgun, Tarley, while I check him," Uncle said.

Well, he did have, like I said and also a long, keen-bladed pocket knife, which Uncle Wint called a "Georgia pistol." All of this taken place in mighty poor light. We was a long ways from them truck headlights and the moon weren't high enough to help much.

"We're goin' back to the house where we can see just what's in that sack," the Sheriff said. "But first, has anybody got a piece of good strong fishin' line or somethin' to tie this feller so Tarley don't have to run him down again?"

"I don't aim to run him down again," Tarl said. "I aim to put the number fives to him." And there were the same tone in his voice that a feller could hear in Sheriff Dean's. I reckon the shoot-out and all when our daddy got killed had toughened my brother past his years.

"I got some trot-line cord," Uncle said. "Never go in the woods nowhere without it. Comes in handy for tyin' up a hog, a dog or a damn thief."

"Well, use it," Sheriff Dean said. "I got handcuffs down in the truck but I don't generally need 'em duck huntin'." Uncle could tie a bad boar hog's feet before you could hear the squeal

and it didn't take him long to get that burglar's hands tied
behind him.

As we started for the house Sheriff Dean said, "I want you
as a witness when we go into the house, Winton, but first I
want this feller dressed up with the real bracelets. I never seen
but one of your tied hogs come untied but it killed a dog and
put me up a tree. So, if you don't mind, go on down and bring
the truck up to the house—that is, if the gate chain ain't
padlocked." So that's what Uncle done. Then we all went into
the front hall and turnt on some lights and Sheriff Dean handcuffed the burglar and we got a good look at him. He needed a
shave but he didn't have nary beard or mustache and his hair
were black and straight as a Indian's. He looked to be about
fifty years old, best I could tell. He didn't have no kind of
identification on him but when they searched him they found
over four hundred dollars in cash money—four one-hundred-
dollar bills and some small bills.

"We'll give you a receipt for this when we lock you up,"
Sheriff Dean said, "and you can have it back when you get out
of jail—if you ever get out of jail—and can prove it weren't
stole. Now we'll just have a look around and see what all you
was up to in here. Then we'll check out what's in that sack."

I had brought the sack in from where the burglar had
dropped it when old Tarl had sacked him. We was all standin'
there in the hall right by a big wide door that opened into a sort
of combination livin' room and dinin' room and Sheriff Dean
flipped on the lights and we went in. On the left were a
swingin' door into the kitchen and then, first past that door, a
great big old sideboard. I mean that sideboard had been ramsacked and of course we figured all the silverware would be in
the burglar's sack, which I had set on the big dinin' room table.
But before we even started to look we seen a sight at the far
end of the room, the livin' room part, that I'll never forget but
wish I could.

Poor Major Drewson were layin' on the floor graveyard
dead. He had been shot in the left temple by a gun that
weren't no .22 and what was left of his head were somethin'
awful to look at. I almost had to leave and go outside for some
fresh air to keep from pukin'.

Alongside where the Major laid were his desk chair, turnt

over, and near by were another chair and little old table both
turnt over. The rug were scuffed up and everything looked like
there must of been a terrible fight before the Major was murdered. His desk hadn't been messed up much, though, a few
letters and books scattered around. The Sheriff checked on all
that later on but right then he said, "Looks like the Major
walked in and caught you red-handed and you shot him."

"I didn't shoot nobody. Check my gun—it ain't been fired,"
the burglar said.

So Sheriff Dean taken the little old owl-head out of his
pocket and smelt it and let us all smell it.

"It ain't been fired since it were oiled," Uncle said. "And it
wouldn't tear up a feller's head like that nohow. There's some
things here I don't understand all I know about. This ain't the
gun that done the job."

"Of course not," the Sheriff said. "So where's the murder
weapon?"

"Maybe the other guy took it," the burglar said. "I don't
know. I was just tryin' to get away myself. I hope he don't get
away with my car."

"Where's your car at?" the Sheriff asked him.

"Just outside the back gate. I left it there and was headed
back to it when you guys surprised me."

"Well, I'll tell you what we're goin' to do," Sheriff Dean
said. "This here big old mahogany sideboard looks like it
weighs a thousand pounds but it probably ain't over five
hundred. Anyhow, you just sit right over there with your back
to one of them legs and Mr. Epps and his nephews will raise
that sideboard and I'll just hitch you to that leg and there you'll
be." So that's what we done.

"Now then," Sheriff Dean said. "Winton you take Tarley
and the truck and drive out to the back gate and see if there's a
car there. I expect there is, though I don't believe there's anybody else involved in this business. But just in case there is,
have your guns ready." So that's what they done.

Whilst they was gone the Sheriff went over and looked at
the desk and we both read a letter that was layin' there.

"Don't touch nothin', Billy," the Sheriff said. "We got to
come back and bring the Coroner and take pictures and all. But
it won't hurt to read."

The letter were from the Major's son and the Sheriff read it out loud. Maybe he weren't too sure I could read. Anyhow he read it out and this is what it said:

Dear Dad:

Thanks for the check. I hope you are well and that your leg isn't hurting too much these days. I sure am looking forward to getting home for Thanksgiving and doing some fishing with you. Maybe we can catch old "Big Mouth" this time. I have told some of the kids that he has a mouth big enough to drop a football in!

Speaking of football I know you will be proud to learn that I have been picked as quarterback on the freshman team. I also hope to make the basketball team, though I am a little bit on the short side but maybe I can make up for it with speed and quick thinking, like you're always telling me. Maybe some day you can be as proud of me as I am of you.

Much love,
Chip

Whilst Sheriff Dean were readin' I thought I heered a funny noise and directly I looked over to where the burglar were handcuffed to the sideboard and he had his head bowed down and he was sobbin' right out loud. I hadn't never heered a man cryin' before and there were somethin' about it that made me feel terrible. About that time, though, Uncle Winton and Tarl come back. Uncle Wint were drivin' Sheriff Dean's truck and Tarl drivin' the burglar's car, a beat-up old Chevy.

"Didn't see no sign of another feller and don't believe there ever was one," Uncle Wint said. "But this gun business has got me bumfuzzled."

"You and me both," the Sheriff said. "And our burglar here taken a fit of cryin' when I read that letter over on the desk. I ain't surprised. I felt like it myself. Go ahead and read it, Winton, but don't touch nothin'. That kid is sure goin' to get a jolt over this. I liken to have choked up so that I couldn't read it."

Well, the burglar wouldn't say nothin' more but just set there and shook his head and groaned. Sheriff Dean taken a quick look into the sack and said there seemed to be a heap of silverware, jewelry and such in it but he were goin' to carry it on back to the jail and open it in the office in the presence of witnesses where it could all be listed and identified by the Major's son when he got there.

"I'll call him in the mornin'," Sheriff Dean said. "No use to tear the poor kid up tonight after he's most likely in bed and asleep. Wish I could be there to help him weather it. Now, let's take a look upstairs and around the house. Tarley, you stay here and be sure this feller don't run off with that sideboard. If anybody else shows up, challenge 'em and if they try to run or make a wrong move, holler."

"And put the fives to 'em," Tarl said.

"I reckon you know what fives will do at close range," Sheriff Dean said.

"I reckon I do," Tarl said, and he weren't smilin'.

There didn't nobody ask me to go upstairs, but then there didn't nobody tell me not to. So I went along. There was four rooms up there, two on each side of the hall. On one side were the Major's bedroom with a big old four-poster double bed that had sort of a silk tent on top, the fanciest dern bed I ever seen. In the closet was all kinds of fine suits and such and more shoes than the commissary store. A door opened into the next room, which were smaller and had a real nice smell to it. There were a big dresser and a little low dresser with a big mirror and some little bottles of perfume and powder boxes and all such as that. Some of the drawers was pulled plumb out and settin' on the floor and all of 'em was open and ramsacked and all kinds of woman things scattered around on the floor—stockin's and lace hankershiffs and shimmy shirts and such. The closet were full of dresses and coats and nighties and all kinds of shoes and fancy slippers. I mean Mrs. Drewson sure hadn't wanted for nothin'—clothes anyhow.

Across the hall was two bedrooms, one for company and one for the son who was off at school. The bathroom were at the end of the hall. There hadn't nothin' been messed with in the boy's room for some reason. All kinds of pennants and pictures and such was on the walls and standin' on the desk was a picture of the Major in his uniform with all his ribbons and medals on. And there were a mighty pretty silver vase a-settin' on the dresser. I read on it where Elsworth A. Drewson, Jr., had won it playin' tennis. It might not of been solid silver but it looked like it and if'n I'd been a burglar I'd of sure put it in my sack.

"Funny nothin's been disturbed in the kid's room," Uncle said as we went back downstairs.

The Sheriff nodded and said, "That's what I was thinkin'."

The last place we looked was in the kitchen and there didn't seem to be nothin' out of place there and the big wood range were cold.

Well, we went back in the livin' room and unhitched the burglar from the leg of the sideboard and he couldn't hardly stand up. He said he felt like both of his arms was dead and Uncle Wint said, "Both the Major's is dead as well as his legs and his butt and everything else, so shut up and be glad you ain't already been executed."

Then we went out to the cars and the Sheriff said to the burglar, "Get in the back. I'm goin' to padlock you to Winton Epps and he's a heap more active than that sideboard." Uncle smiled at the feller, just about as friendly as a ten-foot gator.

"Now, Billy," Sheriff Dean said, "you go get in with Tarley and we're goin' to your house and deliver you to your ma before she starts wonderin' what's happened to us sure enough. Park that Chevy up close to the house and don't let nobody mess with it or take nothin' out of it. Then tomorrow mornin' I want you boys to drive it back over here and answer any questions the Coroner might ask. Be here by nine or sooner. And before you go to bed drive down to your Aunt Effie's and tell her I have done deputized her husband and taken him to Inverness padlocked to a prisoner."

"That'll probably suit her just fine," Tarl said as they drove off. "But I sure don't relish wakin' her up to tell her."

Well, we sure didn't have no trouble gettin' excused from school next day. Ma went with us to see the teacher and asked him please not to tell nobody about what had happened or the whole settlement would be right out to the Drewson place before you could fix and just get in everybody's way.

When me'n Tarl got out to the Drewsons' there weren't

nobody there yet except a deputy who Sheriff Dean had sent out durin' the night to stand guard.

"The house is locked and I can't let you boys in yet," he said.

"We don't want in," I told him. "Now or no other time. I hope we don't never have to go in." I never will forget how I dreaded goin' back into that room.

Well, there was four or five cars come a-drivin' up directly—Sheriff Dean, Uncle Winton, the Chairman of the Board of County Commissioners, Doctor Herker, a newcomer, who were actin' as Coroner, another deputy with the prisoner, two or three newspaper fellers and a couple of fellers with cameras.

"Good mornin', boys," Sheriff Dean said to us as he got out of his car. "We'll call you when you're needed to testify."

After what seemed an hour, but probably weren't, the deputy called us. Them camera men were just finishin' up their picture takin' when me'n Tarl walked in. Man, I hated to go back into that room! Everything were just like we'd left it and we told the Coroner so. It seemed like he needed to find out, if he could, just how long the Major had been dead.

"We already know," Sheriff Dean said. "But Doctor Herker is also a duck hunter and he'd gone to his camp down on the marsh so we couldn't find him until this mornin'."

Uncle Winton were standin' with his back to the big rock fireplace listenin' and sort of teeterin' on his heels like he has a habit of doin' when he is warmin' his butt. Only there weren't no fire in the fireplace.

"I don't see why there's ary question about *when* the Major was murdered," he said. "I felt of his body when we first got here and it was still warm."

He went on to tell how there weren't no rigorous mortis and said he had dressed out too many hogs and goats and bears and buck deers not to know a heap about body heat and how long a critter had been dead.

"This was a man, not a critter," the Coroner said.

"A man's a critter," Uncle told him. "And sometimes a pretty dern sorry one." Then he scowled at everybody and turnt around facin' the fireplace. Directly I seen him starin' at somethin'. He put his face up real close to the chimney and kept lookin'. Then he put his big old hairy hands up and taken holt of a rock out on the shoulder of the chimney and I swear I seen it move.

"Look here, fellers," he said. "Just look here."

Everybody crowded around and then we seen what he were a-lookin' at. A string of little old ants was goin' into a hairline crack alongside of that rock and another string was comin' out and some of 'em was totin' somethin' in their bills.

Directly Sheriff Dean said, "Winton, them ants has found somethin' to eat back of that rock and I got a sneakin' idea that I know what it is. I've seen dark, rusty-lookin' flakes like that before and it ain't ashes."

"Dried blood," Uncle Wint said. "I found a big buck I had wounded one time by seein' a dern ant crawlin' down a stem of grass with a flake of it in his bill. I had done completely lost the trail of that deer and it would of gone off and died and been eat by the buzzards if it hadn't of been for that ant."

"Haul that rock out of there if it's loose, Epps," the Commissioner said. "And let's see what's behind it."

Well, the gun was in there—a great big old Colt six-shooter and the hammer were all the way down. There was still some dried blood on it.

"Be careful with it, Winton," Sheriff Dean said. "We might get some evidence off it."

"Maybe," Uncle said. "I'll blow these here ants off it . . . I reckon I got the strongest breath of anybody here."

"No doubt about it," the Commissioner said.

"That's the Major's gun* all right," Sheriff Dean said, "and I've seen him shoot it. He was a mighty fine shot—I seen him knock off a gator that had tried to catch one of his dogs. Bring in the prisoner."

Well, the deputy come in with the handcuffed burglar and he just taken one look at that hole in the chimney and the pistol layin' on the desk and plopped right down onto a chair and went to shakin' his head.

"All right now," Doctor Herker said. "Just tell us how you managed to sneak up on the Major yonder and kill him with his own gun. Just tell us the whole story right from the start. If

---

* The gun was a Frontier Model Colt .44–40. The hammer was all the way down on an empty shell, the only one that had been fired. The other five were two-hundred-grain, lead bullets which flatten and do terrible execution when striking bone.

you had an accomplice, who is he? You're goin' to get a long sentence and maybe life for armed robbery because you had that .32 in your pocket when you were caught with a sack of loot. So start talkin'. The more you level with us the better chance you got for a lighter sentence."

All the time the doctor were talkin' the burglar didn't look up. I could see that Uncle Wint were beginnin' to come to a boil and directly he said, "I learnt a good way to make a feller talk one time from the Indians. You heard Doctor Herker ask you a question. Answer him."

"We ain't Indians, Winton," the Sheriff said, "and I'm an officer of the law, so I'll handle this." Then he turnt to the burglar and said, "But you can have it easy or rough over in that jail so I advise you to tell us exactly how you killed this man."

Well, the burglar looked up for the first time and there were some fear in his eyes. "I didn't kill nobody," he said. "Please Mister," he said, "I got to talk private with you. You got to listen to me. You got to understand. I didn't kill that man as God is my witness."

"God was a witness all right," Sheriff Dean said, "and He's the best there is. But He's on the prosecution side. You are your only witness. But we'll hear your story. We'll go upstairs and set in that boy's room whose daddy you killed and you can have your say. But there's goin' to be two witnesses to everything you say. One is Winton Epps and the other is the Chairman of our Board of County Commissioners, a man whose word is Gospel in this county."

So they taken the burglar upstairs and me'n Tarl set around and listened at a lot of what Uncle Winton has a word for. Everybody had some kind of a theory and didn't mind offerin' it. All the time of course we was settin' there around that big old dinin' room table and my chair were the nearest one to the dead Major. Since we was little fellers Ma had talked about how a feller's mortal body weren't nothin' but a empty shell and his immortal soul had gone to be with the Lord or wherever it were goin' but all the same I got some kind of nervous and kept my head turnt away from lookin'. I sure hoped Uncle Wint and them would get through with their business soon.

After near about an hour they come downstairs and Sheriff Dean were carryin' what I thought at first were a dead black house cat. Then I seen that it were a wig and the burglar didn't have much more hair of his own than a week-old baby.

"All right, everybody," the Sheriff said. "We can all go back to town now. There ain't nothin' more to be done here."

"You must have gotten a confession," Doctor Herker said.

"I sure did," the Sheriff told him. "Right out of the wig!"

"Then the inquest is over," Doctor Herker said, "and we know who killed Major Drewson."

"We sure do," Sheriff Dean said. "I'll have a written confession as soon as I can get one typed up and signed. Now then, Winton, see if you can find that cleanin' woman and get her to come out and clean up after the undertaker leaves. I'll send him out soon as I can—most likely about three o'clock this evenin'."

"All right," Uncle said. "I'll send her out if she will go and ain't drunk."

We was all about to leave when the Commissioner hollered out, "Here's the pistol, Charlie. Don't forget the murder weapon."

"No indeed," Sheriff Dean said. "We sure mustn't forget the murder weapon."

The very next day after the murder, the burglar escaped from the Inverness jail sometime after noon. Uncle Wint had been called as a witness in a hog-stealin' case and let me go with him so we heered about it near about as soon as we got to court.

"The murderer slipped right out under the Sheriff's nose," somebody said, "and there's a rumor he stole a car and is long gone."

"Whose car did he steal?" Uncle wanted to know.

"Don't nobody know," the feller said. "There's another murder case and two rape cases comin' up and half of the county is here, parked all over town. But that ain't no excuse for lettin' a murderer get plumb away like Dean and his deputies is doin'."

"There's a hog-stealin' trial goin' on right now," Uncle said.

"Two of our county's three deputies is witnesses and so am I. Old Judge May is presidin' but don't let that stop you. Just go right on in and tell him what you want him to do and then listen at him tell you what *you* can do."

When a recess come, me'n Uncle Wint hurried across to the jail. The old Inverness jail were a big old two-story red brick buildin' across the square from the courthouse about as far as I can chunk a rock. Uncle Charlie Dean were settin' on the porch in a rockin' chair, drinkin' a cup of coffee, just about as unconcerned as a streaked-head turtle asleep on a log. There sure didn't nothin' faze that man.

"Howdy there, young sprout," he said to me. "Seems like I seen you somewhere before. Y'all come on in and have some coffee."

When we was all settin' drinkin' our coffee there come two or three fellers along the street and one of 'em said, "Sheriff, how come you ain't out combin' the roads for that escaped convict?"

"He ain't a convict until he's been tried and found guilty," the Sheriff told 'em.

"Well, he's a murderer and a car thief," a big rough-lookin' feller said, "and you ought to be a-lookin' for him."

"Whose car did he steal?"* Sheriff Dean asked.

"I don't know," the feller said.

"Neither do I," Sheriff Dean said, "and until I do, I don't know the license number, the color or even the make. And that ain't the kind of information I want to pass along to Marion, Sumter, or Levy County officers, not to mention my old sheriff buddy down in Hernando. After while, some feller will come in here and report his car has been stole and when he does I'll know what to look for and I'll go to lookin'—real hard. And I guarantee that the killer of Major Drewson won't get away."

"So will I," Uncle Wint put in.

After the fellers had left I asked Uncle Wint just what he had meant by that. "Maybe you'll know someday," were all he would say.

---

* The escapee had stolen a car from Scofield's garage and left it and stole another of which there was so far no trace.

"Let's go and set in the office," Sheriff Dean said, "before some more of them yayhoos come along askin' more stupid questions."

"They sure didn't seem very friendly to you, Uncle Charlie," I said.

"Son, when you have to arrest a man's brother for drunk and disorderly," the Sheriff said, "and forcibly take him to jail, you can be pretty sure his family ain't your best friends. Any law man who don't make some enemies just ain't doin' his job." Then we went into the office.

The Deans lived upstairs but the Sheriff had him a office downstairs where he kept his food accounts. He fed the prisoners on contract with the county, and I could smell some field peas cookin' in the big old kitchen just past the office door. I can still remember how good them peas smelt.

There were a desk and some straight chairs in the jail office and a little old safe settin' in the corner, where Sheriff Dean told Uncle Wint he kept his food accounts and private papers.

"I hope you got that confession locked up good," Uncle Wint said.

"You can bet on it," Sheriff Dean said.

"Can I see it?" I asked 'em.

"Not now and maybe never," Uncle said. "It all depends."

"Depends on what?" I wanted to know. But they wouldn't tell me nothin'.

"When did the feller escape?" Uncle asked.

"Right after the prisoners had their dinner—around one o'clock, I reckon. I had been over to the courthouse and was comin' back when the jailer ran out to meet me and said there were a prisoner missin' and he sure didn't see how come it . . . said he could almost swear every cell was locked. I told him not to worry—that that feller could probably pick the lock on the Pearly Gate, if he ever got there, so gettin' out of the Inverness jail was easy as takin' the ball away from a blind tumble bug."

Just about then there come a messenger from the courthouse sayin' old Judge May were just a-snortin' because Winton Z. Epps, a witness, had been called and couldn't be found, so we had to tear out for the courtroom. The case wound up with a hung jury. That hog thief just had too many cousins in the county.

I had to go back to school next day but Uncle Wint still had to go back to Inverness as a character witness, whatever that is, in one of them rape cases.

"He's a character all right," Ma said, "and I'm happy he's just a witness."

Anyhow, there was a lot of things happened that day. Chip Drewson and his daddy's lawyer had come in on the train and the lawyer had raised more hell than the gator did when the pond went dry. Uncle Wint said he looked like he were fixin' to have apple-plexy when he learnt the murderer had got away scot free and there weren't even a picture of him to show to nobody. Them photographers had been so busy takin' pictures of the body and all the turnt-over furniture that they hadn't took nary picture of the burglar. Uncle Wint said when the lawyer heered that he went to cussin' and usin' a lot of dirty words there in the hall of the courthouse. "Where's the law around here," he hollered.

"You're talkin' to it," the Sheriff said, "so cool off before I cool you off." After that the lawyer quieted considerable.

Chip identified all the jewelry and silverware and such and said there weren't nothin' missin' best he could tell. Sheriff Dean gave 'em the four hundred dollars and him and the lawyer left to take the Major's body up to be buried at where his folks come from—New York State somewhere. The lawyer come back in about a week to see about the place but Chip never did come back and I never seen him again.

Seven or eight years later—nineteen and twenty-two I think it were—Uncle Wint come by to show us a clippin' Aunt Rosa Belle had sent him from a Chicago newspaper. It said that Lieutenant Elsworth A. Drewson, Jr., of Levy County, Florida, had been killed when his trainin' plane crashed into Lake Michigan.

"So now," Uncle said, "there ain't no reason to hide nothin' no longer and the whole dern story can be told." So we learnt what the burglar told 'em that day upstairs at the Drewson place. Sheriff Dean turnt it over to the *Gazette* and they printed his whole confession just like he wrote it:

* * * * * * * * * *

THE CONFESSION

My name is Steven Raddy* and I used to go with a gal from up near Starke. When the room got too crowded I gave her up to some other guys but she had a lot of what it takes to call a feller back, so the other day after I'd been in Ocala on a short jail visit I drove over to Inglis to see her. There weren't but two bars over there and I found her in the second. She didn't work there but was a steady customer.

We had a few beers and she told me about this rich Yankee Major she worked for. She said he had built a big two-story house out on a bend of the River about eight miles from town and that it sure was a lonesome place—at least six miles from the nearest neighbor. She said the Major's wife had died in June, nearly five months ago, and that his only son was off at school up North and wouldn't be home till Christmas week. She said the Major had made her leave everything in the wife's dressin' room just like she had left it when they taken her to the hospital.

The Major sure was crazy about that woman, accordin' to Minnie† but she thought it were a cryin' shame somebody couldn't enjoy all them goodies. She said she had a good will to ask him for some of 'em when he got back from his trip and she went back to work.

"You're fixin' to get your butt fired," I told her. "Where did he go and when is he comin' back?"

---

* The name given by the escapee, according to Sheriff Dean, proved to be an alias just as expected.

† The woman referred to as Minnie either could not or would not give information as to correct name of escapee or where he could be found, and of course there was no picture to circulate.

By this time Minnie had had about seven beers and the information she gave me wasn't the clearest I ever heered, but I made out that the Major had gone to a specialist doctor in Atlanta for treatment of his leg. She said he might have to have surgery or radio treatment or both dependin' on what the doc said. Anyhow, he was due back on the evenin' train on the twenty-sixth.

I told Minnie I sure would like to see that place and I sure would like to sort of renew our friendship and that might be a good place to do it. She thought so, too, seein' as how her boy friend was down in Tampa and she was lonesome. We didn't go in the house but parked around back of the house near what she said was the back gate.

Of course I didn't tell her I was plannin' to go back and rob the place or I'm sure she'd of threatened to squeal without I promised to split with her. So I just said goodbye next day and told her I was headin' north—maybe plumb up to Chattanooga.

That evenin', the twenty-first, I drove back out to the Drewson place, arrivin' just like I planned—about first dark. I figured on finishin' my job and gettin' out of there by just creepin' along in the moonlight without no headlights. If I had met a car on the way out I would of just drove on and never stopped. But I didn't meet nobody so I parked out by the back gate again and walked to the house. While I was crossin' the yard I heard some gunshots way off to the west and figured some hunters was gettin' some good shootin'. Then I picked the back door lock and went in.

The first door on the left was the kitchen and the second opened into a long room with a great big rock chimney and fireplace at the far end. At the near end was the dinin' room and there was a swingin' door into the kitchen. There was a big dinin' room table and chairs and the biggest mahogany-lookin' sideboard I ever seen. I figured there'd really be some plunder in that thing. Right then, though, I went on down to the fireplace end and checked out a desk that set off sort of to one side, alongside a couch and a couple of easy chairs. The first thing I seen was a letter and I read it, since it was short and I weren't in no hurry. It was from the boy who was off at school like Minnie had said.

There weren't much in the desk so I went on upstairs after the jewelry, figurin' I'd get the heavy stuff out of that sideboard last. I turnt on some lights and pulled down the shades in the Drewsons' bedroom. The dead wife's dressin' room next to it was just like Minnie had said and I sure did make a good haul there. I didn't bother nothin' in the closet.

Back in the bedroom I found a little stuff in the Major's dresser, in the top drawer. There was some gold cufflinks, a couple of gold watches and a gold stickpin with a big ruby on it and a box with some loose change, just a few dollar bills—seven or eight bucks altogether. There wasn't nothin' of value to me on the desk but there was some pictures settin' on it and I couldn't help but think how valuable they must be to the Major. There was three of 'em in little silver frames—one of the boy in a football suit, another holdin' a big bass and a third with his mother when he was just a little booger. She sure was a looker and would make any man grieve. The frames looked like solid silver but I didn't mess with 'em.

Across the hall was two rooms, one for company and one the boy's room, where there was a lot of kid stuff—pennants, pictures and such—and a framed picture on the desk of the Major in his uniform with a lot of ribbons and medals. There was also what looked and felt like a solid silver vase but I didn't take that or nothin' else from the boy's room. The onliest bathroom were at the end of the hall and didn't have nothin' in it but a spider web and two dead roaches.

Then I turnt out the lights and went downstairs and found a whole drawerful of fine, solid silverware. I had just put it in my sack when a car drove up at the back. There wasn't time for me to do nothin' but just squat down behind the end of that sideboard and hold my breath. Whoever it was came right on in the back door, which I had left unlocked, and I took my pistol out of my pocket. I hadn't never shot a man but I just couldn't stand the thought of bein' locked up again. Jails just run me crazy.

The man who came in walked right past me, limpin' a little, and didn't even look towards the sideboard. He went to that chimney and taken out a loose rock and got a pistol from in behind it and come back and laid it on the desk and set down and wrote somethin'. Then he sort of shook his head and said, "God have mercy," and helt that big pistol to his head and shot himself dead.

I don't have words to tell what it's like to see a man just up and kill himself. It's twice as bad as seein' a feller kill another feller and it sure shook me up like I ain't never been shook before. When he had first got that pistol out of its hidin' place, I figured he must be the Major, come home ahead of time, and I thought maybe he had seen me somehow and would whirl around any second and go to shootin'. All the time he was writin' that note I just squatted there behind that sideboard tastin' my heart up in my throat.

When he fell over onto the floor I knowed it was time for me to haul buggy out of there but first there was somethin' I had to do. I had to see what he had wrote that might criminate me. So I went over and read that note and it sure hit me a lick. It was from the Major to his kid off at school and right then I decided to do what I done. I pushed the Major's chair over and I turnt over another chair and a little old side table and I scuffed up the rug so it would look like there'd been a fight. And I took that note and slid it up the back of my neck under my wig. That kid would never see that note if I could help it. And as long as I had it I had an alibi. But I sure didn't think I'd need to use it so soon.

Of course I had to do somethin' about that big old six-shooter. So I just carried it over and put it right back where it come from. Let somebody else figure how it got there, if anybody ever found it. When I was puttin' the gun back I seen a little money which I hereby confess to takin' since the law found it on me anyhow. After I put the rock back in place I got my sack and

was just about to leave when the truck-load of law
drove up. I know what I done sounds like a crazy
thing for me to do and hard for anybody to believe,
but my wife and onliest son had left me a long time
ago because she said she didn't want our boy ever to
learn that his daddy was a thief.

SIGNED: Steven Raddy

The editor of the *Gazette* was a kind-hearted man but he
insisted on seein' with his own eyes the Major's last letter to his
son, which Sheriff Dean had kept in his private safe.* Uncle
Winton knowed about it and the Sheriff let me see it but
nobody didn't think there were any need to print it in the
newspaper. This is what the letter said:

Dear Chip,

I hope you will forgive me. I have been having a lot
of pain lately and the Atlanta doctor's report was not
good, so I just couldn't face coming back to an empty
house without mother any longer. Remember all the
good days, son, and forgive me. I love you.

Dad

In talkin' to Ma about the Drewson case, Uncle Wint said
Steven Raddy wouldn't of even been mixed up in it at all if it
hadn't of been for a woman tollin' him back to the River. He
said it reminded him of the time old man Pete Brunson's
donkey got out and Sposey Jennings found him. Sposey were a
half-witted boy who lived out by the sawdust pile on the Ocala
road.

"How'd you manage to find that critter?" somebody asked
him.

"Well," Sposey said, "I just figured where I'd go if I was a
'scaped jackass and I went there and there he was."

"Only in the Raddy case," Uncle told Ma, "it were a Minnie
and not a jenny."

---

* The Major was indeed left-handed, as confirmed by the bullet
entering the skull at the left temple. He also wrote left-handed and the
suicide note was indeed genuine as confirmed by a comparison with
other letters written by him.

9 Billy Learns About Women & Is Saved by the Bell

Me'n my brother never hung around the schoolhouse long after that three o'clock bell rung—not durin' the fall and winter anyhow. All we wanted to do was hurry home, finish our chores and get in a little huntin' before it got dark. A feller could always pick up a mess of squirrels unless the wind were blowin' and when the wind did blow we'd get us some ducks. And over where Uncle Wint had some hogs in a chufa field there'd be a world of doves. I love to eat them scapers . . . I mean the doves, although I'd miss many a shot because I'd be busy eatin' them sweet little chufa roots. No wonder hogs like 'em.

Some of the bigger towns had football teams even back then and I remember Uncle Winton takin' us to Ocala to see 'em play Leesburg and even to Gainesville to see the Florida Gators. He were a sport and loved all kinds of athaletics. But our school at Gator Crawl were too small to get up much of a football team and even if it had we was too crazy about huntin' to fool with it—though I'll bet my brother would of been hard to stop.

But baseball were somethin' else. It come after the huntin' season so we got into it. I thought I'd be a pitcher but didn't nobody else think so. I just had two pitches. One were a ball and one were a strike and I never could control which it would be. So I decided I'd try for catcher.

Tarl, though, could do a heap of things with a baseball. He throwed a roundhouse outcurve, a sharp-breakin' inshoot, a drop, a out-drop and, once in a while, a knuckle ball. When he'd chunk that one I'd groan, because there didn't nobody know where it would go—him or me or the feller with the bat. Also, he'd chaw some slippery elm bark and use it for throwin' spitballs. That stuff is slipperier than six eels in a bucket of oil. He'd put just a little gob on top of the ball, under his two fingers and chunk it as hard as he could. Man! That crazy ball done more dipsy-doo-dads than a scared snipe. Half the time I couldn't catch it but most of the time a batter couldn't even touch it, so we done all right. We practiced a heap and later on won games against Crystal and Otter Creek and even one time against Inverness.

I do believe my brother had what it would of took to go into big league ball. Uncle Wint thought so too, and he had saw the best, includin' a feller he called "The Big Train," Walter Johnson. They got a lot of fancy names today for different pitches but there ain't but so many things a baseball will do and Tarl could make it do 'em. And he were *fast*. Today they call it *quick*. Anyhow, he had speed like Dazzy Vance and Dizzy Dean and Lefty Grove accordin' to Uncle, and he had knowed 'em all. He said that Tarl might even have made the New York Yankees and they was the acne of everything.

One evenin' me'n Tarl was playin' catch on the bank of the River near our house when Wilda Hunter come by and stopped to watch us. She were supposed to be my gal but I seen her cuttin' her eyes over at Tarl. That weren't nothin', though. All the gals did, him bein' such a big, good-lookin' scaper. Mostly he liked redheads and older ones at that. Wilda were only about my age and a honey blonde—orange blossom honey.

But I reckon every boy alive likes to have a gal look him over, so Tarl strutted his stuff. He'd wind up and chunk that ball as hard as he could, each pitch. I had learnt to center the ball in my big old mitt so that a hard-throwed ball would crack like a pistol shot. It helps to keep a batter from crowdin' too close over home plate. But I had also learnt that it were easier on my hand to soften the pitch and sort of give with it. Pitchers don't like that. They want to hear it pop. But I weren't about to help my brother show off to my gal. So I muffled down every pitch. Directly, old Tarl cut loose one of them roundhouse curves but he started it too high and I just were able to reach it at all. It hit the tip of my mitt and bounced off and took Wilda on the eyebrow, just over the left eye. Down she went and it liken to have knocked her plumb out.

I dropped my mitt and run over to her and so did Tarl. I were bendin' over tryin' to comfort her when she sat up and without sayin' a word, doubled up her little fist and popped me right in my left eye. Then she run over and grabbed the ball and chunked it just as far out in the River as she could—way out to where the middle current taken it. Then she went to cryin' and Tarl went to comfortin' her. If you don't think I were mad about then, powder won't burn. But before I could say nothin' she hollered out, "Billy Driggers, you're a old meanie— knockin' that silly ball onto me like that. You're just jealous. I never want to see you again." And she went to cryin' again and Tarl went to comfortin'. By this time she had a black eye and I did too.

"You'll see me if you keep on goin' to school," I told her, "but you sure ain't never goin' to see me up close again."

The trouble of it is that a feller can't be sure of what he'll do and won't do when it come to gals. I reckon that's because he ain't never sure of what they'll do or won't do. I helt out pretty well, though, until we had our school picnic over to that big blue spring near Dunnellon just before summer vacation. Them new, short little bathin' suits sure did make a difference. I don't know what I'd of done if they had been like the ones today.

It weren't long after the swimmin' party that I had my twelfth birthday and I taken a bad cold that settled in my bronichal tubes. Back in them days folks said you either had a "chest cold" or "the grip." Anyhow I were a sick somebody. Right at the first, when I started to feel bad I run a little fever and Ma made me get in the bed and stay there. About the second day Miss Pettijohn come to see me. That weren't her real name but it'll do. She were the fill-in teacher for the sixth grade. Our regular teacher had broke a leg runnin' after a naughty little third grade kid who had wrote somethin' dirty in the girls' outhouse.

But there weren't nothin' wrong with Miss Pettijohn's legs, I'll guarantee. They was long and slim and pretty all the way down or up whichever way you had a chance to look at 'em. How come her to be at our house was because Ma had asked her to look in on me while Tarl drove her over to Bronson to tend to some business. They was goin' to be gone all day Saturday and Miss Pettijohn said she'd be glad to take care of me. She meant that, too.

First of all she fixed me a cup of hot chicken soup. "Let me help you sit up, Bill," she said and reached over and put her arm under my shoulders. She were wearin' what I think they called a middy blouse and it hung down pretty loose in the front. I couldn't help but think of when Ma and Aunt Effie were laughin' about the little Ellison kid who'd said his first grade teacher was real pretty and when she bent over he seen both her lungs. Anyhow, Miss Pettijohn propped me up and not just with bed pillows.

Between the grip and the hot soup and the prop-up, my fever must have gone up at least five degrees and maybe more. Before I had quite finished the soup, Miss Pettijohn set the bowl over on the table and come and laid down by me and said, "Now let's just stretch out and relax, Bill." Nobody didn't call me Bill and it made me feel mighty big, I'll tell you. By this time my fever had moved up a couple of notches more. Miss Pettijohn flounced around gettin' herself comfortable and directly she flopped one of them pretty, smooth legs over acrost me and snuggled her cheek down against mine. I know her leg were smooth because I accidently touched it and I remembered Uncle Winton's sayin' somethin' were "smoother than a school ma'am's thigh." Right then I didn't see how that could be.

Now, I sure would like to be able to describe just what went on in my mind, let alone the rest of my body. To start with, I were scared. What of, exactly, I didn't know. Oh, I'd hugged and kissed Wilda and maybe two or three other little old country gals and I reckon I'd dreamed about havin' a woman. But when I come right up agin it I didn't know just what to do about it . . . or were scared to . . . or somethin'. All kinds of funny feelin's was goin' over me. I wanted to swaller but couldn't and my heart were thumpin' like a boat engine with the governor broke. My ears was ringin' and my eyes was burnin' and what my hands was doin' I didn't know. If that thermometer had been in my mouth the mercury would of boiled over—if I hadn't of already bit it half in two.

What would of happened next I'll never know because just then the cowbell went to clangin' and Aunt Effie hollered in the kitchen door, "Anybody home?" Then she come a-boilin' on in without waitin' for a answer and liken to have caught us layin' there in bed. As it was, Miss Pettijohn hardly had time to grab up the bowl and pretend to be feedin' me the rest of the soup.

"Well!" Aunt Effie said. "Well, I declare." And her lip were really drawed down. We wasn't foolin' her ary particle. She taken the bowl from Miss Pettijohn and said, "I didn't know you liked cold soup, Billy, or I wouldn't of bothered warmin' it when y'all was stayin' with us."

"This is Miss Grace Pettijohn," I said, and my voice sounded funny even to me. "She's our sixth grade back-up teacher."

"Yes, I've heered about Miss Pettijohn," Aunt Effie said, "and she's just as well to get her back up and out of here. Your Uncle Winton has gone to the woods so I'll just stay here and look after you till your folks get home, whenever that is."

Miss Pettijohn liken to have forgot to put on her shoes in her hurry to get out of there. All she left were the smell of her perfume on my pillow but my nose had got so stopped up I couldn't even notice that.

Aunt Effie must of really laid it on thick when Ma got home that night because I got a real talkin'-to next day.

"Son," Ma said, "that woman is old enough to be your mother. It's nice that she likes you and it was kind of her to come over but there shouldn't be anything between y'all but just a plutonic friendship."

"What is that?" I wanted to know.

"That's a friendship between a man and a woman where they are just friends and that's all—no sex at all; no huggin' and kissin' and such as that. Couldn't you and Miss Pettijohn have that kind of a friendship?"

"No way! No way!" I told her. "I'd rather this grip or whatever I've got would carry me off than ever get caught alone again with that lady. She makes me feel too funny." So there weren't no plutonic friendship.

When Uncle Wint come back from huntin' I asked him

"Well, I declare."

about it. "Did you ever have ary plutonic friendships?" I asked him.

"Three or four," he said. "But I always broke 'em up. There ain't nothin' more fun, Billy boy, than breakin' up a plutonic friendship." And he went to laughin' and slappin' his leg. Two weeks later I see him comin' out of Miss Pettijohn's house. He were smilin' so I reckon he had broke up another.

¹⁰Homosassa Springs

Dazzy Vance, the old ball player, had him a big old hotel down to Homosassa Springs and back in them days the bass fishin' were some kind of good in their river. Like Weeki Wachee and Crystal, the Homosassa River come right up out of the ground in a big spring of clear water. A heap of them old-time ball players use to come up fishin' and some of 'em stayed there to live—fellers like Bernie Neis, who purely loved his fishin'. Babe Ruth, Lefty Grove and other famous ones come there at different times when they'd be trainin' in Tampa or St. Pete or Sarasota. Old Dazz could—and did—tell some tall tales. I remember one time hearin' him tell some Yankees about the springs and the river.

"Fishin' is good and the scenery is beautiful and that big spring full of fish is a sight to see but we've got to have some good roads. I don't blame tourist folks for not comin'. I wouldn't travel plumb over here on that busted-up road from Inverness to see the Twelve Apostles swim the Homosassa River."

Later on when U.S. Highway 19 was built down the west coast, some fellers bought the springs and a lot of land around 'em and fixed a underwater gallery in the big spring where folks could go down and look the fish right in the face. There was lots of theories why all them salt water fish come up the river and collected in that big spring. Some folks said it were healin' chemicals in the water and others said it were because the water stayed seventy-two degrees summer and winter. This last kind of made sense because it seemed like more fish collected up in the springs when we had a cold spell.

There was mangrove snappers, jacks, redfish, sea trout, mullet, catfish and sheepshead, as well as fresh water fish such as brim and bass. And there was always a bunch of them big old lantern-jawed snooks. Some called 'em "soap-fish" and some called 'em "robalos." But whatever you called 'em, they was trouble on the end of a line. There was some down in them rock caverns that looked like they'd of weighed thirty pounds—just a-layin' there fannin' their fins. There weren't no fishin' permitted in the spring but now and again somebody would latch on to one of them bullies down river and have a fight on his hands—one of them "four-motor" snooks, as Mr. Ray Holland used to call 'em.

Me and Tarl used to go down there years before them Yankees bought the place and sit out on a little old rickety wooden dock and watch the fish. I still like to go there and look at 'em under water and now and again some tourist will ask me, "Why do all these salt water fish come up this river into this spring?" And I just tell 'em, "To see the people."

One thing I'll say about the folks who developed this place, they paid some mind to the beauty of the hammock and didn't cut no big old black gums or magnolias or big old pines. They made oyster shell trails all around the hammock, with bridges here and there, and went around the big trees so that even today the woods looks just like it did when we used to be in there turkey and deer huntin'. There's some fine old slash pines in there and I do believe one of 'em would cut near 'bout a thousand board feet. It must be over a hundred feet tall and I remember walkin' past it on the trail one day with a friend of mine who is in the lumber business.

"If a feller had about ten thousand acres of timber like that, he could sure retire," I said.

"Shucks," my friend told me, "if a feller had ten thousand acres of stuff like that, he could hire somebody to retire for him!"

One of the things I never could understand though about Homosassa Springs was the buildin' where they had their office. Accordin' to all reports, the Yankees, who had bought the place, had all the money in the world but instead of puttin' up a nice new brick buildin' they bought up a pile of beat-up old used brick from some tore-down courthouse or somethin' and on top of that they put a roof of cypress shakes. Hired a old Cracker to split 'em out and put 'em on just like the old days. It didn't make much sense to me.

But a feller can go there even today and walk around in the Florida woods just like it used to be—cedars and cabbages and red bays and sweet bays and hickories and magnolias and water hollies and big old black gums and I don't know how many other kinds of trees and bushes. I never go through there without thinkin' about how much I'd have give for one of them pretty trails when we was fightin' our way through the hammock fifty years ago, tryin' to catch up with a dern bear that wouldn't neither tree or bay up.

There were a small spring that made a little river that flowed into the main Homosassa River about a hundred yards or so downstream from where it come out of the big fish-bowl spring. The water averaged about four feet deep in that little river and were clear as gin. The bottom were rocky and they had fenced off a part of this stream for alligators, leavin' plenty of room for 'em to crawl out on the banks to sun and to dig dens down under and amongst the tree roots. It sure made a fine place for a feller to see gators in a natural-lookin' place and to watch how they can move under water. They had a couple of crocodiles in there with the gators and a feller could see the difference in the shape of their snouts and the way a crocodile's teeth showed on the outside of his lips. I knowed an old buck-tooth gal one time whose teeth done the same way but I ain't even sayin' what town she come from.

The trouble of it is that there's always some folks who are against everything and there was some of the local Crackers who didn't like the idea of the springs being fenced off and admission charged to somethin' they'd always been used to seein' for nothin'. Tarl said it reminded him of what had happened on our River and he never would go down to Homosassa after the Yankee folks bought it. I tried to tell him how pretty it was and how they hadn't done nothin' to spoil the woods but he wouldn't go nor wouldn't let me take Ma, even after the Yankees who had first bought it began givin' free passes to residents of the county. Of course that didn't last long after there got to be so many Yankee residents. No Yankee ain't goin' to miss ary chance to charge another Yankee.

Of course Uncle Winton had seen them fish plenty of times before from the old dock and I'll always remember what happened one day when we was down that way deer huntin'. We stopped at a little old cafe on the way to have some coffee because Uncle weren't feelin' the very best. The old gal at the counter must of been in a bad humor because when Uncle asked for his third cup, she slid it down the counter, sloppin' it over into the saucer and said, "You must like coffee, Mister."

"I do," Uncle said. "That's why I'm a-willin' to drink so much hot water to get some!"

When we started out of that place Uncle said, "Billy would you mind payin' for this? I didn't bring no money with me and come off in such a hurry I forgot to leave any at home."

"I believe that," the old gal said, slammin' the coffee pot back on the stove. "If'n you got a home!"

But what she didn't know was that Uncle Winton not only had a home but a whole lot of land and hogs and cows and timber and a woman that could be twice as ornery as she was.

One night some fellers raided the gator pen down at Homosassa and killed and skinned three or four right there alongside one of the trails. The story was that some fellers from Georgia had done it and that one of 'em were Speck Lukins.* There was several local gator hunters who hunted legal and illegal, but they had alibis. I think it were one of 'em who spread the story about Lukins. I know Tarl went down there and laid out a couple of nights with his rifle hopin' they'd come back. I couldn't talk to him and Ma couldn't talk to him. He just said, "I'd know that speckled s.o.b. on a dark night and it's pretty good moonlight right now."

He wanted me to go with him but Ma raised so much ruckus that I backed out. From what he told me about the mosquitoes, I was glad I did. He said they was lickin' off the

---

* One of the two men who shot Billy's father.

citronella faster'n he could put it on, and to make things worse, he stood in a nest of stingin' ants and they was plumb to his straddle before he knowed it and he had to come out of his pants.

After he got rid of them ants, he waited a while to let things quiet down and then slipped on toward the gator pool, makin' no more noise than a short-legged mouse wettin' on moss. That boy can sure travel the woods—day or night. He picked him a good place to sit, down in the leaves behind a big old sweet bay and the red bugs took over where the ants had left off. Yankees call 'em chiggers but to us Crackers they's just "red bugs"—tiny little old orangy-red bugs that a feller just can see with the naked eye. If you don't get him before he burrows in under the skin, he'll sure make you scratch.

When you first feel a place start to itch, take a good look and use a magnifying glass, if you have to. You'll see the scoun'el, just a tiny little orange-lookin' speck—and you can pick him off with the point of your pocket knife and wipe him off on a piece of white paper and see him good. There ain't but two ways that I know to get rid of 'em after they dig in and one's to hold a burnin' cigarette butt to the bite till it burns to where you can't stand it no more and the other's to dab pure ether on the place. That'll fix that bug. The trouble of it is that it's hard to get ether and when a feller's doctorin' himself with some-thin' like ether, he's got to be careful about fire, rememberin' how old Doc Joyner had set Uncle Winton afire with an electric needle that time he were takin' the mole off'n his hip and spilt the alcohol. Anyhow, Tarl laid out for two nights and nothin' didn't happen but bites. He had to wait for another time to get his vengeance.

That were a long time ago and the Yankees who had bought that big spring sold out to some other folks and they sold out to still some others. But there didn't nobody spoil the settin'. The big trees and the clear water and the fish and the birds is still there and I can walk them trails and dream of the old days when most of the country round and about were just like this—like God made it.

Speakin' of trees, the hardest wood I near about ever seen is one of them ukeliptus, specially after the tree dies. Man! It's purely impeccable, even to one of them big old lord gods— "pileated woodpeckers" the Yankees call 'em. There were one of them trees standin' at Pat's Elbow on the River about where the old Boyce place is at. It must of been ninety feet high before it died. The story is that Eddie Boyce clumb it and sawed off the top after the cold killed it back. It tried to sprout out and did, but two years after that there come another cold spell and that done it.

Anyhow, I were down there fishin' soon one mornin' and one of them lord gods lit on the flat top of that dead tree and went to hammerin' on it with all his might. I do believe you could of heered it a mile! He'd pound it and then raise up that big old red head and look around as if to say, "Let's hear you beat that!" Reminded me of a song that feller Len Stokes sung in the boat one day when he were over here fishin' with the feller from Leesburg. We was anchored near shore and I mean Stokes naturally made them woods ring with that song. It were somethin' about a water boy and I remember the words, "Ain't no hammer out on this mountain that rings like mine, boys, that rings like mine."

I never hear a peckerwood hammerin' on hard wood but what I think about that song and Len Stokes. I mean that old boy could purely sing. I told him so, too, but he just said, "You should have heard Paul Robeson sing it."

"If it were any better than that I couldn't of stood it," I said, "and I'll bet every coon and possum in this end of Gulf Hammock is in the top of the highest tree he can find right now."

The feller from Leesburg laughed and said, "Well, I heard Paul Robeson sing 'Water Boy' when I was having lunch with the Dutch Treat Club in New York, and he had a great voice and it's a great song and my friend Stokes here sure doesn't belittle it any."

"What are you talkin' about?" I said. "I don't believe nobody ever sung it as good—Paul Robinson, Jack Robinson, Red Robinson or even Robinson Caruso."

One mornin' while Stokes were still down here we collected up a bunch of hounds and put on a fox race for him. The feller from Leesburg brought over about ten and John Clardy come over from Ocala with six or eight. I taken three or four of ours and Uncle Kelly Runnels met us with two or three that he claimed was real wind-burners.

We went down toward Crystal and just after daylight we jumped a old dog fox in a little scrub near Red Level. He dodged around in that scrub for about half an hour and then come out and hit the open piney woods. I mean them hounds was mortally layin' it to him and about five of them fast, chop-mouth Walkers had a sight race on him and was near about grabbin' at him when they come by, not over fifty steps from where we was standin'. When they had got out of sight and the woods had quieted enough for a feller to speak, Stokes asked, "Do you reckon that fox was really doin' his best?"

Uncle Kelly Runnels looked at him like he'd lost his mind but I learnt right there that he weren't only a fine singer but also a great joker. I been knowin' him for forty years since then and ain't nothin' ever caused me to change my mind.

"Jokes That Backfired & the Double-Barrel Shotgun Wedding

One day I rode way up north along the edge of the Hammock lookin' for an old brindle cow and red calf that had turned up missin'. About noon I began to think about some lunch but when I looked in my saddle bags I found I hadn't packed it. I was hungry enough to eat a raw dog and I remembered there was a old colored feller called Bubber Clark camped in a deserted homesteader's shack about a quarter from there. The old feller was chippin' turpentine and I figured maybe he'd give me somethin' to eat because he'd knowed the Epps family for a long time.

I tied my horse under a big oak and walked on up past some guava bushes to the old house. But there weren't nobody there and I figured Bubber was still in the woods workin'. I looked at his campfire and hangin' over the ashes was a big iron pot with some hog chitlin's and rice already cooked up and nothin' ever smelt better. Just about then I heered Bubber comin' up the wagon road, hummin' a tune, and I jumped behind a bunch of guava bushes out of sight.

The old feller walked over to the back porch of the shack, laid down his ax, walked over to his fire and lifted the lid off his pot of chitlin's. I reckon it smelt good to him too because he rubbed his hands together and went back over to the porch and got his water bucket. It needed fillin' so he walked on down through the palmettos toward the old pump and when he did I jumped out, grabbed his pot and jumped back of the guava bushes again. I don't know what made me do it—just devilment I reckon.

Well, old Bubber got back, washed his hands, poured out a cup of water to drink, got his plate and fork and a old wood box to set on, and started for the fire. Then he slammed on the brakes like a bird dog comin' to a point and just stood there lookin' at the ashes where his pot had been hangin'.

Directly, he eased the box back onto the porch, laid the plate and fork on top of it, whirled around and grabbed his ax and started backin' up the road away from there, swingin' the ax back and to like he was fightin' off ha'nts. He backed about thirty steps, then throwed down the ax and I mean he caught air! He showed me the soles of his feet so often he looked like he was layin' down!

I ate some of the chitlin's and rice, hung his pot back over the coals and walked out to where I'd tied my horse. But that rascal had slipped the bridle and gone! I guess he'd got just as hungry as I had and knowed the corn was back at our camp. There weren't nothin' for me to do but walk and by the time I made it home my butt was draggin' out my tracks in the sand and it was black dark and Ma were just about two jumps ahead of a fit. My horse had come back and hadn't even lost my rifle out of the boot. When I told her what had happened, Ma said, "Served you right for playin' a prank on that old man."

"I didn't eat but part of his rations," I said. "There was plenty left."

"But he didn't know that and won't never know it!"

She were right because I found out the very next day that old Bubber Clark had gone in to Inverness to get Sheriff Charlie Dean. "Mister Charlie," he'd said, "I wonder if you'd take your pick-up truck and go out to my turpentine camp and get my beddin' and clothes and cookin' stuff. Somethin' got my supper with me lookin' right straight at it and I ain't never goin' near that place no more—daytime, nighttime or no other time!"

When Uncle Winton heered about this, he made me send the old feller more money than anybody has ever paid for a mess of hog chitlin's and rice. And I'll have to agree that it would be a right scary feelin' out in them big woods to have your supper disappear right out from under your eyes when you figured there weren't another livin' soul within five miles.

Sometimes, what's meant to be just a prank can turn into somethin' real bad and I remember one time when we were a-goin' on a deer hunt. There was a old Cracker boy from down near Tampa somewhere who'd already gone into the camp and taken his sister and brother-in-law along to help with the cookin'. We didn't know it right then but all three of them people really liked whiskey and they'd been workin' at it when we got there. Me and Tarl and Uncle Wint got into the camp about eleven o'clock at night. Uncle was horseback and me and Tarl rode the ox cart with old Buck. It were about a six-hour trip from our house back into the Hammock and the camp were just a old homesteader's shack hardly fit to sleep in. Uncle said the termites was just a-standin' around under it holdin' hands, which was all that kept the floor from fallin' in.

The woman and her husband had gone to bed but the feller from Tampa, Paul somethin' or other, was a-settin' on a box by the campfire, which was still burnin' bright enough to light up things pretty good. Uncle had just unsaddled his horse and leant his rifle up against a tree when this feller Paul spoke up and said, "Winton Epps, I hear you made a remark about my wife."

"Whoever said I did is a damn liar," Uncle Wint told him.

"My brother-in-law in yonder said so."

"Call him out here," Uncle said.

"I don't need him out here," Paul said. "I'll get my gun and . . ."

When he said that Uncle hit him right in the mouth and knocked him down. Then he picked up the feller's shotgun, pumped a shell into the barrel and throwed the gun down on the ground beside him.

"All right," said Uncle, "you wanted your gun. There it is. Pick it up. There's my rifle agin that tree. You're closeter to your gun than I am to mine. Reach for it . . . and when you do, I'll kill you! You ain't got ten seconds to live, you sorry bastard!"

Things was right tight for a second or two and I started to say somethin' to ease 'em off. "You boys keep out of this,"

Uncle said, "and stand back." Me and Tarl had our guns rolled
up in our beddin' in the ox cart so we couldn't really help none
no-how. But that feller Paul got a change of heart. He was
down on all fours and I don't believe two strong men could
have pulled his hand toward that shotgun. He started to cry
and he said, "I didn't mean nothin', Mr. Epps. I sure didn't
mean nothin'."

About that time, here come his brother-in-law out of the
shack with a big old long double-barrel with hammers like a
rabbit's ears and he said, "What's goin' on out here? What's
been a-happenin' to Paul?"

"Nothin' to what's goin' to happen," Uncle told him. "I don't
know who you are but I can tend to my own business."

"I asked what's a-goin' on and I want to know," the feller
said and cocked both barrels. When them hammers snapped
back seemed like you could hear 'em a hundred yards.

"Now if that's the way you feel about it," Uncle said, and he
picked up his thirty-thirty from where it stood and jacked a
shell into the barrel. They was a-standin' there and a-glarin' at
each other when out of the dark come a woman, barefooted as
a yard dog in that black hammock mud and her long black hair
a-hangin' down nearly to her waist. She just walked up behind
her husband and reached out and grabbed for the shotgun and
said, "Gimme that gun!"

The feller didn't say nothin'—just turnt around and hit her
a good solid lick right in the face. Down she went, but just for
a second. Then she raised up on her knees and began
screamin' bloody murder. There was a little trickle of blood
runnin' out of the side of her mouth. She reached up and
grabbed her hair with both hands and pulled it straight up as
high as she could reach and then turned it loose so that it all
fell down over her face. Then she'd do it again, all the time
keepin' up that moanin' and screechin'.

Well, I guess with the whiskey and excitement and all, the
feller Paul all of a sudden pitched a fit. He just fell over and his
eyes rolled up in his head and foamy hot water started runnin'
out his mouth and it took both his sister and brother-in-law to
hold him down. Both of 'em was so drunk they could hardly get
around but that got their minds on somethin' else. I'd heered of
fellers havin' fits but I hadn't never seen one and it sure were
kind of scary. Anyhow, the feller overed it and we unloaded

our ox cart, rolled out our bedrolls and got to sleep along about the time we should have been gettin' up.

We had expected a neighbor of Uncle Winton's to come in on the hunt and we didn't find out until the next day that he had already been there the night before. He was a great feller for pranks and when he heered about the big ruckus that almost turned into a shootin' scrape, he sure got tickled.

"When I got to that camp," he told us later, "everybody was mad at everybody else and plumb out of liquor. 'I've got a quart in my saddle bags,' I told 'em, 'and I'll make a deal with you. I'll leave it here, if you'll run Winton Epps and his two nephews out of this camp. He's a mean man and that biggest boy, Tarley, is awful bad about bullyin' women!' " So they agreed and he left them the bottle but what was just meant as a joke likened to have turned into a killin'!

Ma heered about the ruckus up at the deer camp and she sure got on Uncle Winton about it and never would believe that he had nothin' to do with it—even when me and Tarl told her just what happened. But she did go over to old man Jim Johnson's, the neighbor who had left the bottle, and give him a piece of her mind.

"I really gave that old reprobate a piece of my mind," she told Uncle.

"From the way he talks," Uncle said, "you gave him all of it! Ain't you ever goin' to learn that a feller has to have a little fun and a little drink will help him do it?" Ma just wouldn't answer him but turnt her back on him and went to singin'. This was one of the things that used to make Uncle Winton maddest—for Ma to sing what she called her "temperance" song at him. She'd just turn her back on him and go to singin'. I can hear her now.

> Ye drinks of men ye drinks of fear,
> Ye whiskies, brandies, lager beer,
> Begone, begone from here,
> Begone from here!

Then Uncle would sing her a song he'd made up in answer.

> There's lots of fun and lots of cheer
> In whiskey, brandy, lager beer,

So keep it near, so keep it near,
So keep it near!

Ma would get mad enough to bite a skunk—not only about the words but the way Uncle Winton sounded. He couldn't carry a tune at all and he'd sing out just as loud as he could, which made it all the worse, but then he'd give her a kiss, slap her behind and say, "Ain't nothin' the matter with you, Sis, but what a little drink would cure." Then he'd look at us boys and wink and get a wicked grin on his face like a old boar possum and Ma would take the broom to him.

Every now and again Uncle would get on a regular spree and stay liquored up for a week or more. Ma would get plumb out of patience with him and even old Doc Joyner got aggravated when Aunt Effie phoned him one day and said Uncle was drunk again and had took a big swig of kerosene from the wrong jug.

"What should I do for him?" she wanted to know.

"Stick a wick in him and light him!" Doc told her.

"Down his throat?" she asked.

"Any way," Doc said. "Just so it gets to the kerosene."

Aunt Effie slammed down the phone and said, "I'll declare that old doctor don't care what he says to nobody."

Uncle was layin' there near about dead but he spoke up and said, "Of course not, when he knows he's talkin' to nobody."

"I've a good will to let you die," she said, "if I knowed you'd go ahead and do it." But he didn't. There were many a jug yet to be sampled.

I were twelve in nineteen and fourteen when the Henry family come to live in the old Ellison place and that sure turnt out to be a big thing in my life. How me and my brother Tarl both fell in love with Lucy Henry, how we fought over her and what brought on the fight is a long story and I have done told it all once. Me'n "Loofy," as everybody called her, got married up just in time and Tarl did too. He married Morna McWirter, daughter of the man who had fenced off the River landin' and hired the guard who shot our dad. How all that happened is also somethin' I've done told once, a page that's done been turnt.

Like I said, both me'n Tarl got married up just in time. We had what you might call a double-barrel shotgun weddin' and afterward him and Morna built 'em a fine home but me'n Loofy stayed on with Ma at the house here on the River and added to it as our kids come along. Like all young folks we had our joys and our sorrows but we had learnt from our ma how to weather the storms by callin' on the name of the Lord and learnt how to laugh at reversity from Uncle Wint, so we made out all right.

12 · Troubles of a Family Man

I've got a heap of memories of them early days and I'll often come back to 'em—our huntin' trips with Uncle Winton and some of the funny things that happened to him and his huntin' buddy Sheriff Charlie Dean from Inverness over in Citrus County. We used to go over to Inverness to do our shoppin' now and then and after me and Loofy got married she'd often go over there with one or two of the kids.

We had seven kids—six boys and one gal. We named our oldest boy Jim after my dad. Winton, of course, was named for Uncle Winton and Kelly after Uncle Kelly Runnels, a great hunter from up River. We wanted to call the next one Tarley but old Tarl didn't like his name no better than Morna liked hers so we figgered "Charlie" was as close as we dared get and we all thought a heap of Sheriff Charlie Dean anyhow. We named the fifth boy David after a feller from Leesburg who used to come over here bear huntin' with Sheriff Dean. We named our youngest Burgoyne after one of Loofy's brothers, the one called "Goin'," who was killed in the First World War, but nobody ever called our kid nothin' but "Burr." We give all the boys the middle name Henry after Loofy's family.

We named our little gal Lucy Henrietta but she wound up

bein' called just "Etta." The boys started callin' her "Luce" but Ma put a quick stop to that . . . said she hoped no gal of ours would ever be loose or be called loose.

Tarl and Morna had just the one daughter named Lorna. Tarl had wanted to name her Morna after her mother but Morna just wouldn't have it . . . said she never had liked her name and wouldn't afflict it on nobody else.

"Well," Tarl told her, "we'll just call the kid Lorna and there ain't nothin' closeter to an 'M' than an 'L' and it seems to me like I've heered the name Lorna somewhere before and it sounds good to me!"

I remember way back when Loofy were in a family way with Jim, our first young-un. Her weak-minded brother, Gaynus Henry, had finally got better and gathered up enough sense to get married. Either that or he had got a little crazier. Anyhow he had married and were livin' up in Raleigh, North Carolina, where he wrote he were an executive with the city. When he come back to the River on a little vacation trip I asked him what he done on his job.

"Well," he said, "I ride around in a big truck with some other fellers and we take the iron lids off them holes in the street and put down a ladder. I take a bucket and a shovel and go down in that hole and fill the bucket. Then I pass it to the feller on the ladder and he passes it up to the feller on the street and he passes it to the feller on the truck and he empties it and passes it back to the feller in the street and he passes it to the feller on the ladder and he passes it back to me."

"That makes you an executive, eh?" I said.

"You're dern right," he told me. "I'm the bottom guy and I don't take no crap from nobody!"

Anyhow, all that dampness must have been too much for him because he taken the flu and there weren't nobody to look after him. His wife were long gone; must of just got tired of puttin' his clothes to soak.

"He's my brother and there ain't nobody to look after him but me," Loofy had said. "Mamma might could come when she gets better herself but she's in the bed right now with her arthuritis."

So I taken Loofy over to catch the train. We figured she might have to be gone a couple of weeks but her brother's flu went into pneumonia and then she taken the flu herself. Mrs.

Henry still weren't able to get about so Ma said, "I'm a-goin' up there to help that poor gal. We can't have her losin' the baby."

Well, thank God she didn't lose little Jimmy but what had looked like two weeks turnt into two months and the whole time I had everything to do by myself includin' the cookin' and dish washin' and I'm here to tell you now that a feller who has a good woman runnin' his house don't know how lucky he is till he tries to get along without her. Oh, I can cook all right— camp-style: flapjacks and bacon and eggs and all kinds of meat and fish but the main trouble were tryin' to figure out what to eat next meal. Ma would always ask right after breakfast, when I'd just eat a stack of pancakes and syrup along with some sausage and eggs, what I'd like for supper and I'd say, "Right now I don't feel like I want *nothin'* for supper. I'm full."

"But I've got to know," she'd say. "I'm a-goin' to the store."

Well, not many days passed after Ma left until I found out what she'd meant. So I tried to plan out what to buy and what to cook, but that's a dern job of itself. Anyhow, I learnt myself a heap of things that I hadn't knowed before—like how to cook young tender okra pods, baked yams and turnip greens and have 'em all come out even when the meat were done. I burnt up a heap of stuff and I chawed some half-cooked stuff, but I learnt.

My biggest trouble were cookin' too much beef stew or chicken purloo or whatever and havin' the ice box full of leftovers. On the other hand, I hated to throw away good food, so what I'd do would be to leave it in little old bowls or dishes in the ice box until it turned green or growed hair before I throwed it away. Then I didn't feel so bad about it!

I were sort of like the feller who were payin' a farmer five dollars a month to pasture his cow. But he didn't pay his bill for a long time—over a year.

"I just ain't got the money," he said.

"Well, you owe me ninety dollars," the farmer told him. "Why don't I just take the cow for the bill?"

"Seems like to me that cow should be worth more'n that," the feller said. "You go ahead and pasture her three months more and it's a deal."

A few times I made spaghetti and tried to copy Sheriff Dean's Spanish-style sauce, that he had learnt to make from the feller with the restaurant down in Ybor City. It turnt out pretty fair. The main thing is not to overcook that spaghetti and out at the camp he had showed me how to tell when it was done.

"Just chunk a piece up agin the wall," he said. "If it sticks it's done."

But my women folks didn't think much of that . . . no more'n I think of some of their doin's. Even today when I get to foolin' around the stove with cookin' I have to laugh when I think of some of the things women folks do, like when they open a jar of this here instant coffee. There's a paper seal under that there screw top and that's what keeps in that fresh flavor. Women know that, but nine out of ten of 'em will tear back just a part of that seal and leave just enough room to get a spoon in there. Every time I dip in a spoon to make a cup of coffee I hit that seal comin' out and knock about half of the coffee back into the jar or onto the table.

"Why do you do that?" I asked Tarl's wife, Morna, one evenin' when I were laid up with plumbago and she come over to cook me a supper and opened a fresh jar. "Loofy always does that and I just wonder why."

"For two reasons," Morna said. "First, it makes it easy to measure off a level teaspoon and second because it helps keep in the flavor."

"How?" I asked.

"That seal," she said. "That's what it's there for, stupid."

"Yes, but it's busted," I said. "It can't keep out the air no more."

"Well," she said, "it'll keep out *most* of it!"

Morna were a good cook and had brought over some fresh-shucked oysters so I didn't dispute her no more. After supper I hobbled over to the sink and said, "Now I'll wash the dishes. But I've got my own way of doin' it. You can help clear the table but don't stack the dishes."

"Why not?" she wanted to know, goin' right ahead and stackin' 'em.

"Because then you've got to wash both sides of 'em!" I said and I showed her. I just turnt on the hot water about halfway and helt the dish under while I taken the cloth and wiped it across a cake of soap layin' on the sink and then washed off the plate, rinsin' it at the same time.

"That's crazy," Morna said. "Why don't you draw your dish-
water in the dishpan or one side of the sink, shake in some
washing powder and wash 'em in a good Christian way? Then
drain 'em and rinse 'em with scalding water. Letting that
faucet run wastes an awful lot of hot water."

"I'll be derned if that's so," I told her. "I done checked that
out and by the time you fill up that sink with wash water and
again with rinse water you'll use up half again as much water
and time too. I'll be done through and havin' my pipe before
you're through rinsin'." But I couldn't convince her, and I never
have been able to convince Loofy neither.

But I were so glad to be shut of dish washin' myself by the
time Loofy and Ma come back from Raleigh that I were glad to
turn over the kitchen. I'll be derned though if I'll stack dirty
dishes even to this day. I'd rather make twice as many trips,
but I guess everybody has his own crankies.

I did learn a few tricks and combinations while I were
cookin' that I don't mind passin' along. A cousin brought me a
mess of bay scallops from Sarasota. Man! Them were the best I
ever eat. I had a few left over and I put 'em in a little dish and
set 'em in the ice box. Next mornin' I scrambled me some eggs
and just on the notion I throwed in them scallops and
warmed 'em up with them scrambled eggs. You ain't never eat
nothin' better.

I found that a green pepper cut up with some yeller crook-
necks takes about the same time to cook, makes a pretty color
combination and tastes real good. I decided while I were doin'
my own cookin' that women weren't just foolin' around when
they fixed up dishes to look pretty as well as taste good. If a
feller is off his feed a little, a tasty *lookin'* dish is just about as
important as a tasty *tastin'* dish.

One evenin' I made me one of my special scromelettes—
that's almost a omelette. I whip up a couple of eggs, pour in a
little milk and dump 'em in a pan greased with butter but not
too hot. I let that cook slow till some bubbles come through and
it's near about dry on top. Then I loosen it around the edges
with my pancake turner and flip it just like I flip flapjacks. I
ain't missed yet but I come close a couple of times! Then I cut
up a good ripe tomater and put that on top of my scromelette.
Once I had that with some fresh greens and that were as pretty
a plate as I ever seen—red, yeller and green on a yeller plate. I

almost hated to tear it up. I'd been feelin' puny but I went after that like a biddy after a worm.

Loofy had fell off some durin' all the sickness and worry and when I met her and Ma over at the Coast Line station at Dunnellon she didn't hardly look like the same gal. They come in on that early mornin' train—the Southland I believe it were—and Loofy said she hadn't slept a wink in that train bed—said she had chocked herself front and rear with pillers but even that didn't help much.

"I feel like I had been sent for and couldn't come and then got there and wouldn't do," she said.

"You'll do, honey," I told her. "Don't you worry. Everything is all right here. We got plenty of chickens and eggs and sixteen fat, slick shoats. I got a dozen ducks hangin' in the cold room at the ice plant and Tarl sent me over a side of fresh-smoked bacon and a few mullet. We'll put some meat back on your bones in a hurry." And we did. The trouble of it was that she and Ma went to fixin' all kinds of tasty rations for me so as to make up for the time I'd had to do my own cookin' and I mean I done some eatin'! Reminded me of the story old Doc Joyner used to tell about a country Cracker that come in to see him once who didn't know just what ailed him.

"I asked him where he felt bad," Doc said, "and he told me that he just felt logy and dopey and when he'd set up in the mornin' and reach down for his socks, everything would turn black and little spots would dance in front of his eyes. I told him it might be his diet and asked him what he eat in the course of a day.

" 'You mean when I'm home or when I'm in the woods hog huntin'?' he asked me.

" 'When you're at home,' " I told him. " 'Give me a idea.'

" 'Well,' he said, 'just ordinary food. For breakfast I like a pot of coffee, two or three slices of country-cured ham, some grits, a few fried eggs and four or five biscuits with syrup. Sometimes I'll eat a bowl of prunes, if I think I need 'em. At dinnertime I'll eat a couple of pork chops or a steak, some grits and turnip greens and maybe a couple of taters. Then I'll eat a pie and, of course, have a pot of coffee. I don't eat much for supper—maybe a chicken or three or four mullet and some cornbread and syrup. I don't drink no coffee at night but sometimes I'll have a pint or two of sweet milk or some clabber.'

" 'Drop your pants and bend over on that table,' I told him. He done so and I taken one look and said, 'The trouble of it is, you've only got one outlet!' "

Then old Doc Joyner would holler and laugh and say, "I've told that story to some other doctors and they all said it has sure helped 'em to diagnose a lot of patients."

Maybe that's what was wrong with the cowboy who got sick that time a bunch of us was camped in the flatwoods on the edge of the Hammock roundin' up a bunch of woods cows. He were a big, rough feller from up near Otter Creek and not the kind of feller to say nothin' unless he was sure enough a-hurtin'.

"Boys," he said, "I really got me a belly ache!"

It kept on a-hurtin' him until Uncle Winton decided that somethin' had to be done. He said, "This feller's goin' to die, boys, if we don't get him took care of somehow."

Everybody had been settin' around havin' a few snorts after a hard day's work and the cook was late gettin' supper, so just about the whole crew was feelin' no pain except that old boy from Otter Creek—and he was feelin' plenty.

Uncle Winton knowed a gal who lived a mile or so from where we was camped, and he saddled a horse and rode over there and borrowed a hot water bag. When he got back he said, "This dern thing ain't got exactly the right kind of nozzle but we'll try it." And he taken another drink to help his aim. Then he filled up the bag with hot soapy water, hung it up in a blackjack oak and a couple of the boys got the sick man and stripped him down. I don't know what he figgered they was goin' to do to him—maybe wash him down to cool his fever. I don't reckon he'd ever had a enema or even knowed what one was. Anyhow, when they had him tilted just to suit Uncle Winton, Uncle made a poke at him and he taken off through the woods, draggin' the two fellers with him and hollerin', "What do you think you're tryin' to do, Winton Epps, you drunk dang fool? Why you didn't miss stickin' that dern thing into me by over half a inch, you crazy dang fool!"

He never would let Uncle get near him again with that rig, which were too bad because the poor feller died the next evenin' and we might have saved him, if he hadn't been so touchy!

There were another old Cracker boy, from way back in the

Hammock, who were near about as ignorant or maybe more so. He had that same kind of trouble and told me, "I went plumb over to Ocala to the doctor and he said, 'What ails you, boy?' So I told him.

" 'Try these suppositories,' he told me. 'If the first one don't work, the second one should.' So I tried 'em. But nothin' happened so I went back to Ocala again.

" 'What now?' the old doctor said. 'Didn't they work?' I told him they hadn't and that they was the worst tastin' dern things I ever put in my mouth—just like chewin' beeswax dipped in assafetida. They hadn't done me no more good than if I'd stuck 'em you know where.

" 'That's what you was supposed to do with 'em, you dang fool,' the doctor said. 'They won't hurt, they're about the size of a stool.'

" 'You mean a spool, don't you Doctor?' I said.

"He'd been a-settin on a little old stool while he were talkin' to me and he liken to of fell off when I said that."

I remember a time when Uncle Wint were sure *he* had somethin' bad wrong and went down to what they called a "clink" down in Tampa. I always thought that were a jail but he said it were a place where they had a whole covey of doctors in one buildin'.

"I mean them scapers is all specialists and they sure knowed how to charge. It cost me three hundred dollars but they checked me from stem to stern."

"Great day in the mornin'!" I told him. "If it cost that much for that little bitty distance, what would they charge for a full length, up and down, head to foot, check-up on a big knocker like you?"

"That ain't what I meant," Uncle said. "I meant that they went over me with a fine-tooth comb."

"Well then," I told him, "the charge were reasonable. I'd charge that much to go over a hairy old booger like you with ary kind of comb."

"You ain't showin' much respect for your old Uncle," he said, laughin'. "Anyhow, them fellers cleared me and I come out of that hospital before you could say 'Red Robinson.' "

While he were in the hospital, Uncle Wint heered a story about a lawyer who was hired to sue a dentist up at Ocala. This dentist had been pullin' a feller's tooth and broke it off and busted his jaw at the same time. Naturally the feller took on somethin' scandalous and hired this lawyer.

"We'll have to have the tooth for evidence," the lawyer told him but the trouble of it was that he had done swallered the tooth. So they rushed him over to the hospital and X-rayed his belly but the tooth weren't there.

"It must have passed into the upper intestine," the stomach specialist said. "You'll have to see a upper intestine man."

So the feller went to the upper intestine man and got X-rayed again but *he* couldn't find the tooth.

"It's got by me," he said. "You'll have to see a lower intestine man."

So the feller went to the lower intestine specialist and he couldn't find it neither. "You'll have to see a proctologist," he told him.

A proctologist, they tell me, is a feller who takes the last look. If he can't find it it's done gone. Well this proctologist put the feller on his tiltin' table and taken one look and jumped back and said, "Good gosh man! You have a tooth in your rectum. You'll have to see a dentist!"

When I told this story to Loofy she couldn't help laughin' but she said it were not only vulgar but it were also impossible and she started askin' me questions like, "How long did all this take? Did the feller go to the lawyer first or the doctor first and how could he talk with a broken jaw?" All I could say was, "Loofy, honey—I don't know—I don't even know how long it takes for a acorn to go through a hog. It's just a story so don't worry about it."

13 Poems, Preachers & the Ticket to Heaven

One time the feller from Leesburg come over to go duck huntin' on what turnt out to be the coldest day of the winter. We come in before noon and was settin' in the kitchen with a pot of coffee tryin' to warm up when he asked me, "Any crazy folks in your family, Billy?"

"Two or three is all, countin' me," I told him. "Of course some folks used to think old Uncle Winton were on account of his writin' all them poems and puttin' 'em on markers on dogs' graves and such as that. I just figgered he was a lot smarter than most folks and done some deep thinkin'.

"There was two of Uncle Wint's dogs that had names near about the same—Brawler and Bawler. Brawler were a part bull and cur catch dog that would fight anything includin' a bear. Bawler were a black-and-tan hound with a big, bawlin' mouth you could hear a mile. He'd *run* a bear but if he ever *fought* a bear, I'll guarantee it were a pure accident. You might say he just misjudged distance. That's how come his epithet says:

> "*He met a bear and acted silly*
> *So now he's pushin' up a lily.*"

The feller from Leesburg laughed and said, "I remember his calling an epitaph an epithet."

"Well, what were good enough for Uncle is good enough for me," I said.

The feller from Leesburg laughed again and said, "Why not? I remember your Uncle talking about both dogs and I never could understand why he would give 'em names so much alike. How would they know which were being called?"

"They didn't," I told him. "But that didn't make no difference. Wouldn't neither one come when he were called nohow."

"What ever happened to Brawler?" the feller from Leesburg wanted to know. "Didn't he ever get an 'epithet' too?"

"Oh sure," I told him. "He even got a whole poem wrote about him:

"One time I had a dog named Brawler,
He met a hess and tried to crawl her.
She bit him through the mouth and nose
Until his mouth would hardly close.

"But he just took his punishment
And charged it off to funishment.
Then went right out and looked for more
And plumb forgot his mouth were sore."

"That dog must have been quite a stud," the feller from Leesburg said.

"He thought so," I said, "and a heap of dogs around here believed it. Some even showed it."

"Whatever caused his demise?" the feller from Leesburg asked.

"You know, it's funny you should use that word. Uncle knowed that word too and used it in a epithet about a feisty little old dog named Rip that would fight a bear to a fare-thee-well. And that's just what happened. So Uncle wrote:

"He tried a bear ten times his size
And that's what caused old Rip's demise."

The feller from Leesburg shaken his head and laughed and said, "Okay, Billy, okay. But what happened to Brawler? Didn't he rate a place in the dog graveyard?"

"Mighty right," I told him. "It's out there on a board with the rest of 'em.

> *"Old Brawler brawled just once too often*
> *So now he lays here in his coffin."*

"In his coffin?" the feller from Leesburg asked. "Did he really put his dogs in coffins?"

"Well, no," I said. "I reckon Uncle just couldn't think of a nice clean rhyme for dirt."

"He could have said, 'He got too *brave* and so he lies here in his *grave*,'" the feller from Leesburg said.

"I'll remember that," I told him, "if'n I ever start writin' epithets. And by the way, I found some more of them verses in a shoe box in an old trunk the other day—what the roaches and silverfish hadn't eat up—and I saved 'em for you, like you said to do. Here they are. Maybe they'll go in a book."

"Maybe they will," he said takin' 'em. "What are they about?"

"Near about everything Uncle liked," I told him, "baseball players, women, bear dogs, whiskey, politics, whatever."

The Leesburg feller leaned back in his chair and read one of 'em out loud:

> *"You'll often hear old-timers tell*
> *Of Rube Marquard and Rube Waddell,*
> *Of Grover Cleveland Alexander*
> *And Mays, a lefty underhander.*
>
> *"Three-finger Brown and Satchel Paige*
> *And others of that bygone age,*
> *Could chunk a ball so dadgum fast*
> *You'd hear it sizzle when it passed.*
>
> *"And Walter Johnson threw a ball*
> *A feller couldn't see at all.*
> *And Dizzy Dean and Dazzy Vance*
> *Could make a feller wet his pants.*
>
> *"But all them famous old-time buggers*
> *Had to face some mighty sluggers.*
> *When old Cy Williams took a swat*
> *You seen that baseball leave the lot!*

> "Sisler, Hornsby, Wagner, Waner,
> Ruth and Cobb and old Pie Traynor,
> Could clout that apple far away,
> I used to like to watch 'em play."

"Here's another one," I said. "Uncle must have wrote this'n earlier when he were workin' on a ranch down near Haines City one winter before he got married. Read this'n."

> "I've knowed a heap of pretty wenches
> And they was nearly all contentious.
> The only gentle ones I've seen
> Was very few and far between.
>
> "And one good-lookin' little filly,
> Who seemed so sweet and soft and frilly,
> Were really hard as anvil steel
> And bitter as persimmon peel.
>
> "She'd kick and stomp and scream and curse,
> You can't imagine nothin' worse.
> There ain't no cowboy from Kissimmee,
> Who'd hesitate if she said, 'Gimme.'
>
> "It's always take and never give,
> I just don't know how men can live,
> Unless they're lucky and can find
> A woman of the other kind.
>
> "My sister is a godly woman
> As fair and kind as any human,
> The Book says she's a priceless pearl
> I'm lookin' for that kind of girl."

"And he sure hadn't found her when he wrote this next one," I said, handing it to him. So he read:

> "I've knowed a heap of pretty women
> And half the time I've took a trimmin'.
> But what I've took the other half
> Would make a concrete monkey laugh."

About that time Loofy walked in to start dinner and said, "Man! If Aunt Effie'd ever seen that'n she'd of tore it up and him too!"

The feller from Leesburg laughed and said, "Human nature is human nature, Loofy, wherever you find it. If there was to come an earthquake over where I live strong enough to shake skeletons out of closets, a lot of folks would leave town. Don't be too hard in judgin' your Uncle Winton."

"Oh, I ain't judgin' him," she said. "He used to tell us that things ain't always what they seem. He'd say,

> " *The feller you might think a saint, ain't.*
> *The sweet young gal, you later learnt, weren't.'* "

"Sounds like him," the feller from Leesburg said, laughin' again.

"He'd tell us not to take nothin' for granted," I said. "He'd tell us,

> " *The dog they say will never bite, might.*
> *The mule that never kicks a man, can.'*

In other words, don't believe everything you hear. Ma used to quote near 'bout the same thing from her Bible . . . 'Prove all things, hold fast that which is good.' "

"Did you ever know Aunt Effie?" Loofy asked.

"Not very well," the feller from Leesburg said. "But I knew Winton Epps and I'm surprised that anything or anybody ever backed him off."

"He was a pistol ball all right," I told him. "But sometimes it got too much for even him so he'd go to the woods. But he always come back—I reckon on account of his sister, my mother. She was a wonderful woman and she sure had a tough job raisin' us boys after Dad got shot."

"Ma could near 'bout always find a way to do somethin' if she set her mind to it," Loofy said. "And she taught me a lot. She'd have been right proud of me over what happened when me and that preacher what's-his-name went to see poor old Mrs. Juddins."

"The name was Swindell," I told her, "spelled s-w-i-n-d-e-l-l, but you said it with the accent on the 'dell' to rhyme with hell."

"That's right," Loofy said. "Well, me and this Reverend Swindell went to visit old lady Juddins out on the Inglis Road. Mrs. Juddins was blind, or near 'bout it, and her place was some kind of a mess to hear the neighbor women talk. She hadn't never been much of a housekeeper or cook even before her husband died ten years before, and with her eyesight gone things had got even worse.

"When we went in, the place had a stale stink about it and there was dust all over everything includin' a pan of biscuits which was a-settin' on a piano in the hall. I remember thinkin' that I sure was glad that I didn't have to face eatin' them biscuits.

"I reckon I ought to explain why I was there in the first place which was because this preacher had come to our church to fill in for our regular preacher who had went on what folks call a pilgrimage to the Holy Land. So, the church ladies had asked me to introduce him around.

"Anyhow, Reverend Swindell was sort of a sissyfied feller but poor old lady Juddins didn't know how squeamish he was and went right to work fixin' a lunch. First of all, there was a big old cabbage leaf with veins as big as my finger and filled up with some kind of canned meat that had sort of a sour taste to it. Then I'll be derned if she didn't fetch in that pan of cold biscuits I had seen on the piano along with a piece of watermelon so old and dried out that the meat had drawed away from the seeds and the rind was sort of gall-bladderish yeller. Mrs. Juddins didn't eat nothin' herself but just sort of hovered around like a buzzard waitin' for a bogged-down cow to die. Of course the poor old soul couldn't hardly see nothin', much less how to fix a meal, but she sure had tried.

"Reverend Swindell taken his fork and lifted the stuff out of the cabbage leaf and pushed it around on his plate, pre-tendin' he was eatin' it. He'd just move it around in piles and then push it back together again.

"He didn't eat nary a bite, but I did. Two, I believe. But then I began liftin' it up to my mouth and spittin' it into my paper napkin. When my plate was near 'bout empty I pushed back my chair and told Brother Swindell that I thought we should have a word of prayer for Mrs. Juddins before we left. The Reverend went down on his knees so fast I thought he'd punched 'em right through that flimsy old floor! And he stayed down quite a spell too, prayin' for the old lady and her eyesight and for me and the children and their daddy. When he had finished, we stood up and he taken one look at his plate, which were clean as a whistle. His eyes sort of bugged out but he didn't say nothin'. When we had got far enough from the house so old lady Juddins couldn't hear us he said, 'All right, Sister Driggers. Where is it?'

" 'Where is what?' I asked him.

" 'You know good and well what I'm talkin' about,' he said. 'Where is it?'

" 'You better just pray it don't rain so that I have to open this umbrella,' I told him."

The feller from Leesburg got real tickled at that.

"Anyhow," Loofy went on, "our regular preacher come back and Preacher Swindell left to go somewhere up in Georgia—Tifton I believe it were. I disremember. I didn't miss him and I don't reckon many of our church folks did. I will say for him though that he sure laid it on the line and there wasn't no misunderstandin' of what he meant. I remember one Sunday mornin' after a hymn he told the congregation, 'The trouble of it is that y'all stand up and sing "Standin' on the Promises," but what most of you are really doin' is just *settin' on the premises.*'

"Another time he started off his sermon by sayin', 'First I'm goin' to tell you what I'm goin' to tell you. Then I'm goin' to tell you. Then I'm goin' to tell you what I told you!' "

"That ought to suit a Methodist," the man from Leesburg said.

"I wouldn't know about that," I told him. "I'm a Southern Baptist. What are you—a Baptist or a Methodist or what?"

"I'm a sinner," he said.

"I'll believe you," Loofy told him. "But what else? Maybe you're Episcopalian—I reckon that's how you say it."

"No," he said. "I'm Presbyterian."

"Some of the Eppses was them," Loofy said. "The Zeke Eppses in Georgia. They got in a feud with the Danielses about it."

"About what?" the feller from Leesburg asked.

"About predestination," Loofy said. "Believin' that what you do and when you'll die and where you'll go is already decided by God."

"Don't you believe that?" the feller from Leesburg asked.

"Do you?" Loofy asked.

"That's not exactly the way it is," the feller from Leesburg said. "I believe that what you'll do and be and where you'll go when you die are *known* to God but that you have a free choice."

"Ma always used to say, 'Whosoever will, let him take the water of life freely,'" Loofy said. "But that *whosoever* is hard to jibe with that *predestination*. What about the heathens who ain't never had a chance to know about none of this?"

"I'll tell you what I think about it," I told 'em. "I think our Creator is goin' to judge every man accordin' to his lights, like the Book says. If he's had lots of light and turns it off, that's his fault. If he's had little or no light, that's how God will see him. I was talkin' to one of them news photographers last week and he told me that if a picture didn't get quite enough light when it were snapped, it could be brought up in the printin' and helped a heap. God knows who the folks are who ain't had much light and maybe he can let 'em have a little more."

"Very well put," the feller from Leesburg said. "God is fair and just—we all believe that."

After he had left, I got to thinkin' over this whole thing, especially what that photographer feller had told me. And I thought of a boy whose daddy had been a fine, good, upright preacher who made his kid stand up and testify when he weren't but five years old. And yet the boy had turned out to be a nothin'—in fact a less than nothin'—and I just wondered if maybe sometimes givin' a kid too much light too soon would just plumb burn him out.

I don't mean to say exactly that bein' a preacher's son is a handicap to a feller but, on the other hand, it ain't no guarantee of goin' to heaven neither. There ain't nobody goin' to ride in on another feller's coattails—even a preacher's coattails, long as they are. Ever'body has to have his own ticket and that ticket ain't what church he belongs to or havin' a daddy for a preacher or a godly mother like me'n Tarl had. Havin' your ticket is havin' Jesus and that's all there is to it.

14 Babes in the Woods & Possum Trouble

Our first-borned, Jim, had been a big husky baby with a mighty appetite. Ma said he weren't nothin' but a appetite with some skin wropped around it. I mean he loved his rations and Loofy had to nurse him or fight him every hour, or so it seemed like. She'd had a cold that year when deer season rolled around but she decided to go along on our annual camp hunt, baby or no baby, cold or no cold.

"I'll take him to the woods and get on a stand with him," she said. "Start him off early."

"He won't be still. You won't see nothin'. He'll spook everything in half a mile," Tarl tried to tell her.

"He won't do no such of a thing," Loofy said. "He'll sleep all the time if he gets fed regular and that's one thing I can do out there in the Hammock without nobody watchin' me." Well, there weren't no changin' her mind. She loved to hunt as good as ary man of us so she got her way.

The first day she taken a stand near Dinah Pond, settin' on a great big old water oak log where it had blowed down in the herricane. Everything went just like she had planned. She had nursed little Jim right along with breakfast back at camp so he went to sleep quick as she set down on the log. It were a still mornin' and you could hear every sound in the woods. After about two hours, a big buck come slippin' along real easy right toward her. The trouble of it was that Jimmy boy had woke up and wanted some more of that milk and she were givin' it to him. The deer weren't over twenty steps away when she seen it and I just wish I had been settin' up in a tree watchin' what took place.

Accordin' to her own story of it, she just chunked little Jimmy down in the leaves but he didn't go easy. He had a good holt and good suction and he liken to have jerked a tit loose. It hurt and she hollered and that buck near about jumped plumb out of his skin. She grabbed up her gun and took a snap shot—and that's just what it were—a snap. She hadn't ever loaded her shotgun. She had a double-barrel but there weren't time to try to load both of 'em because that buck were really catchin' air. So she just fumbled around among the shells in her pocket, grabbed one and shoved it into the breech. But then the dern gun wouldn't close. It lacked about a half inch of closin' and she were tryin' to force it shut when she seen what the trouble was. She'd popped her Vicks inhaler into that gun. Of course by this time the deer were gone and the baby were hollerin' his guts out and there weren't no use in huntin' around there no more *that* day.

Little Jim growed up to be a big man   biggest of any of my boys—but he never were a good hunter and didn't care nothin' about it. I always will believe it were because of the rough treatment he got on his first trip. He's just lucky there weren't a rock under them leaves when his head hit the ground. Or maybe there was. There's got to be *somethin'* wrong when a feller don't like to hunt.

Of our other boys, Charlie liked to hunt but were always timid about gettin' lost; Kelly and David taken to the woods like ducks to the pond; but poor little Winton never had a chance to find out if he would be a hunter. I'll tell about Burgoyne later on. Etta didn't care nothin' for huntin', neither fishin'. She weren't a particle like her ma, because Loofy loved 'em both.

One time I taken Loofy and David along deer huntin' when he were only about seven years old. She'd done some deer huntin' before but always somethin' had happened to mess up her chances. I left her at a good crossin' where the lumber company had been cuttin' hard wood and the deer had been comin' in every night to eat them tops. I taken David on with me around the bend of the old road and we was just easin' along listenin' and lookin' when I heered Loofy squall.

"Billy," she hollered. "Billy come here."

I didn't know if she'd been bee-stung, snake-bit or bear-caught but I tore out, draggin' David by the hand. I don't reckon his feet touched the ground more'n about four times until we was back with Loofy. She were shakin' and cryin' and tryin' to talk but she couldn't and just went to pointin' back down the road. I looked where she was pointin' and there was fresh tracks of a deer with feet like a yearlin'. He had walked in our tracks where we had just walked in and had made a jump that sunk his hoofs six inches into that Hammock mud when he had started to leave. Loofy kept tryin' to tell us what happened but her mouth was so dry she couldn't talk.

"What ails Mamma, Daddy?" little David said and went to cryin' hisself. "What ails Mamma?"

"Mamma has the buck ague, Sonny," I told him.

"Daddy, I don't never want to have that," he said. "Not *never*."

By this time Loofy had got a hold of herself some and she blowed her nose and said, "But you will, son, just as sure as you keep on deer huntin'. And if the day ever comes when you don't get it that'll be a sad day for sure and you might as well stay home."

"But you're shakin' and cryin', Mamma," he said.

"I know it," she told him, "and I wouldn't take nothin' for it."

That evenin' after supper she told us all just what had happened. "I couldn't find ary log or stump to set on, so I found me a little low rock. There I sat, near about on the ground, with my legs folded up in front of me and my shotgun layin' acrost my lap. I'd been settin' there maybe thirty minutes—just long enough to start gettin' stiff and cramped up when some-thin' made me look around to my right and behind me. I didn't really hear nothin' I'm pretty sure, but I just knowed somethin' were there lookin' at me."

"And there were," piped up David.

"I mean," Loofy said. "A buck with the highest horns I ever seen and he were standin' there not twenty steps away; just standin' there lookin' with his head throwed up and his ears cocked forward and his nose a-workin' tryin' to puzzle out what he were seein'." She got so excited just tellin' about it that she had to jump up from the table and go to walkin' around the room.

"Then what happened, Mamma?" the kids asked all together. "Tell us. Tell us."

"Well, children," Loofy said, "the trouble of it is your ma is near 'bout as right-eyed and right-handed as ary body can be. If that buck had been to my left I'd of just raised my gun and fired and we'd be eatin' liver for supper 'stead of mullet. But there weren't no way I could turn myself around far enough to the right to aim without gettin' up. Did you ever try to get up from sittin' almost on the ground, holdin' a gun? There ain't no way. No way."

"I'll bet I can do it," Kelly said, grabbin' his BB gun.

"So can I," hollered Dave and Charlie. And they all tried.

"See what I mean?" Loofy laughed at 'em. "And when I moved, that deer mortally lit a shuck. He must of jumped thirty feet and ten feet high and that white flag looked a yard long."

"Hot diggety dog!" Kelly said. "I'd of laid the lead to him, been me."

"Aw hush," Jim said, "you wouldn't have done nothin'— just like Mamma done. Nothin'."

"Mamma pitched a fit," David said. "Daddy says it were buck ague and Daddy knows."

"You ain't jokin', son," I told him. "Daddy sure knows."

Ever'time I think about kids bein' out in the woods I remember a story some feller told about a little boy who lived with his daddy way back in the Hammock. His mother had died when he were just a baby and he hadn't been nowhere or seen nothin' but just his own place and his daddy. One time his daddy took him to town for the first time and he seen a woman walkin' down the street carryin' a baby.

"Look at that, Daddy. What is that?"

"That's a woman, son," his daddy told him. "A lady human like your mother was."

"Ain't she pretty," the boy said. "Do you reckon I could run acrost there and get a closeter look?"

"Sure," his old man said.

So the boy run up to the woman and said, "What's that you've got there?"

"A baby," she told him.

"What you doin' with it?"

"I'm nursin' it," she said.

"What do you mean?"

"I'm feedin' it," she told him.

"Do you feed it like that always?"

"No," she said. "After while I wean it."

"What do you mean?"

"I make it stop nursin' and I start givin' it regular food."

"It sure is pretty," the boy said. "Where did you get it?"

"I found it out in the woods," she told him.

"I sure wish I had one," he said. "I'm goin' to find me one."

When he got home he went out in the woods and started kickin' around in brush piles lookin' for a baby. The only thing he seen was a big old boar possum and he jumped on it and grabbed it by the back of the neck. It went to strugglin' and he decided the best thing he could do to gentle it would be to nurse it a little bit. So he unbuttoned his shirt and helt the possum up to his nipple. Well, that old possum latched on to him and he let out a squall and went to hoppin' around grittin' his teeth.

About that time a feller rode up on a horse and said, "What you doin' there, boy?"

"Nursin' my baby," the boy said with the tears poppin' out.

"He ain't turnt you loose yet has he?" the feller said.

"No, sir," the boy told him, "but if he ever does he's a weaned little s.o.b."

Loofy didn't like that story ten cents worth in commissary trade. "Just the thought of that old possum's sharp teeth latchin' on to that poor kid's bosom makes my skin crawl," she'd say. "It hurts me to think about it."

But she'd get real tickled at another possum story I had so I'd just as well tell it right here, even though it ain't got nothin' to do with babes in the woods. There were a drunk who were takin' a short cut home one night through a cemetery and fell into a fresh-dug grave. It had been rainin' and the sides of it

were so slick that he couldn't climb out. He hollered and
hollered and jumped and jumped but finally gave up and just
sat down in a corner to wait for mornin' and somebody to come
by and help him out.

After while a colored boy come along possum huntin' and
fell in the same grave. He made a few sashays but kept fallin'
and slippin' back. So the drunk feller spoke up out of the dark
and said, "Boy, you can't get out of here."

But he *did!*

I remember tellin' that story to Tarl when we was in the
car and he liken to have scared me to death. He just turnt the
steerin' wheel loose and went to laughin' and slappin' his leg
and hollerin', "I'll bet he did! I'll bet he did!"

Speakin' of graves, Uncle Winton fell into a grave once—a
special one. Accordin' to the story some of his buddies figured
they would scare him so bad he'd quit drinkin', so they dug a
pitfall about the size of a grave right in the path where he used
to take a short cut back home from the tavern through the
cemetery. They dressed one feller up with a sheet wropped
around him and a piller case over his head and all of 'em hid in
a pine sapplin' thicket.

Sure enough—Uncle fell into the hole and was layin' there
sprawled out when the feller in the sheet walked up and looked
down and said in a deep, shaky voice, "What are you doin' in
my grave?"

Uncle Wint just looked up and cussed and said, "What are
you doin' *out* of your grave?" He sure didn't scare easy.

Sheriff Charlie Dean were another feller who didn't scare
easy. Him and Uncle Wint was a pair. They hunted together a heap and seen eye to eye about a heap of things—
like Yankees, bird hunters and sorry dogs. I love to hear
Uncle Wint tellin' about some of their doin's—like the time
when the convicts escaped from the road camp and Sheriff
Dean caught 'em right in the middle of Inverness. Uncle
Wint had carried Loofy and little Kelly over to town to
get him some school shoes and they seen the whole shootin'
spree.

"Uncle Charlie ain't scared of *nothin'*, is he?" Kelly said on
the way home.

"Nothin' *I* ever seen," Uncle Wint told him.

But he did!

"I'm goin' to be a law man someday," little Kelly said, and he meant that thing.

If I could of looked ahead at that time I would of realized just how much he meant it and how proud I were goin' to be of him when the bad trouble came.

¹⁵ Little Winton

For a while we tried raisin' turkeys and I never will forget a sight I seen one mornin' in the field back of our cow pen. One of our turkey hens had hatched out six young-uns and they was about the size of pullets. The old hen were walkin' along on the edge of the field and really talkin'—"puttin'" we call it. She had her left wing stretched way out to one side, almost draggin' the ground, and the whole brood of young-uns was followin' along on the other side.

She were actin' so funny I started over there and then I seen the reason. A great big old diamondback were crawlin' along and that hen turkey were "herdin' him" you might say. When he'd try to turn in toward the field, she'd dust him with the tip of her wing and he'd strike at it—and of course hit nothin' but air or feathers. Why he wanted to come back into the field I don't know, but I'm glad he did, because it gave me time to get down there and separate him from his head with my hoe. I'd just worked out a row of mustard greens, so I had the best snake-killin' tool right with me.

One thing about rattlesnakes, if you ain't got a stick or a gun or a hoe right handy you can throw your hat or your coat down right close to him and there is a good chance he'll stay right there and watch it and rattle at it till you get back with some kind of weapon. I guess he figures it is somethin' that will jump on him if he tries to straighten out and crawl off, so he just stays there coiled and ready. I keep callin' this snake *him* but it were probably a she snake as they're usually the biggest—and this were a monster. That night at supper I told all the family to be careful—extra careful because it were gettin' cool and snakes would be movin' a-huntin' their dens.

One of our best deer dogs, old Belle, had whelped seven pups under the house and when them little fat scapers come out and began to wobble around the yard I seen we'd have to pen 'em to keep 'em out of trouble—or trouble off of them. I were buildin' a little old chicken wire pen but had to leave it and go over to the chufa patch where some hogs had rooted out. Little Winton had been "helpin'" me and after I left he stayed out there playin' around. Directly Loofy heard him cry out and she ran out into the yard. It were about a hundred steps from the house to where we was buildin' the puppy pen and when Loofy got to him Winton were just standin' and lookin' at his right hand. There was two little drops of blood oozin' up at the base of his thumb, almost on his wrist, and they was comin' from a couple of punctures about a half inch apart. Then Loofy seen the box of staples I had left settin' there. She picked one up and measured with it and it just fitted them two little holes.

"Did you fall into that box, sonny?" she asked him, but he just shook his head and sort of popped his lips and started to cry some more. So she picked him up and toted him into the house and washed off the hand and disinfected it with a little spirits of turpentine—and there ain't nothin' better.

But when I come back from the chufa patch in about a half an hour poor little old Winton were really in pain and his hand were swoll up so his fingers all was spread apart. His wrist and arm was startin' to swell pretty bad and he felt hot as a firecracker. I picked him up and walked him and said, "What happened, boy? Did that mean old staple stick you?" He just went to cryin' again and shook his head and made a funny move with his head, openin' his mouth and poppin' his lips.

"My God!" I said to Loofy. "Here, hold this boy!" And I tore out there to the puppy pen. Winton had dropped his little old blue sweater beside the staple box and I didn't have to look too hard to see what I were scared I'd see. There was a little diamondback, not over two feet long, cocked and ready, just layin' there beside that box. It were coiled and watchin' Winton's sweater, like they'll do when they think somethin' is goin' to jump on 'em. I did take time to kill it before I ran to the house. It didn't have but a button and one rattle so Loofy couldn't of heered it rattle if it had tried to.

"He's snake-bit!" I hollered to Loofy, who were rockin' him and puttin' some cold cloths on his head. "I'll get the car—you collect up the other kids and we'll leave 'em at Morna's on the way to the hospital."

My sister-in-law, Morna, had carried little Jim over to her house to spend the day with her young-un so there were only Charlie and Kelly at home with us. Loofy were seven months gone with David and already as big as a flour barrel. I just hoped this wouldn't cause her to miscarry.

There ain't no use in punishin' ourselves by tellin' about the trip to the Ocala hospital and all the rest of it. They done all they could and if they could have had an hour's jump on the poison they might have saved him. But the poison of a young snake is even stronger than a big one's—not as much, but stronger—and it had got right into one of them veins in his wrist. Poor little old feller, he done some sufferin' and he weren't even able to say "bye-bye" to us when the time come. He had learnt to say that . . . but not "snake."

There just ain't no way to describe what it does to a feller to watch one of his little ones die and not be able to do nothin' to keep him from goin', so I won't try. I'll just say I ain't never overed that and never will.

16 The Cranky Yankee

There used to be a rich Yankee feller named Vanherring come into Poor Boy's Restaurant to eat. He were one of them big business typhoons from the city and had built him a fine home on the River. I'd run into him now and again and we'd get to talkin'. He always sounded like he were tryin' to talk like a dern Britisher but couldn't quite make it. I'd often heered a real Englishman talk—old Mr. John Murray Davis who run the store and post office out at Lecanto.

I got so tickled one day at that store when Vanherring run into old man Digdon that I couldn't hardly keep from laughin' out loud. Old man Digdon were a real salty old feller from down near Pat's Elbow. He had a beard and looked to be about seventy. When he had a few snorts he were right friendly and he'd had a few. So when Mr. Vanherring walked up beside him at the counter he smiled and nodded at him.

"How do you do," Mr. Vanherring said in that uppity way.

"About oncet a week. How about you?" old man Digdon answered, quick as a wink. Mr. Vanherring didn't think it were funny, I reckon, because he sure didn't laugh or say nothin' more; just walked away. But Mr. Davis, the Englishman, said, "Ripping," and laughed right out loud.

Maybe Mr. Vanherring acted so cranky because he were an old bachelor and didn't have nobody to talk to. He didn't care much about sports but would just set in his back yard and read a paper called the *Wall Street Journal*. Once in a while he'd go bass fishin' down the River but there wasn't many guides liked to fool with him. Ever'thing had to be run accordin' to schedule—*his* schedule, of course, and he had one habit that liken to have run Spence Coggins crazy. Old Spence were one of our best guides.

"He's the beatin'est feller I ever seen," Spence told me, "No matter where we're at nor what we're doin' he's got to go to the bushes along about ten o'clock ever' mornin'—just as regular as the mill whistle. The other mornin' I pushed the boat through some awful heavy saw grass to get to a pocket of open water where I knowed there was some right big bass. I had hung and lost one there about a week before that would have pushed twenty pounds, I do believe. Just as I got the boat swung around and were startin' to tell him where to throw the plug he said, 'Sorry, Spence old boy, but I'm afraid you'll have to put me ashore.' I looked at my watch and sure enough it were ten minutes before ten.

" 'Mister,' I said, 'do you do this every day of your life?'

" 'Nearly always,' he said as cheery as could be, 'right about ten o'clock.'

" 'Great day in the mornin',' I told him. 'I do that about once a month and it near about kills me!' "

Of course old Spence were jokin' him and just said *month* instead of *week* to make it sound funny. Our Cousin Jeff Driggers had had trouble exactly the opposite of Spence Coggins. He had trouble keepin' from goin' until Doc sent him to a specialist in Fort Myers who operated on his spinster muscle. I never think about him but that it reminds me of a story Uncle Winton told about a city dude tryin' to buy a bear dog from his uncle up in North Carolina. Uncle Zack didn't have ary dog to sell him but he recommended a feller over the mountain and told the dude how to get there.

"I wouldn't know how to pick a good bear dog if I saw one," the dude said.

"Well," Uncle Zack told him, "just look at his rectum. The bigger it is, the better bear dog he is."

So the feller went on over the mountain to old man Platt's,

I think it was, and said he was lookin' for a bear dog—a real good one that would run and fight and tree a bear in their rodentdendren thickets. The old man showed him a great big red hound with the longest ears he ever seen, great big loose-hangin' lips and a voice you could hear a mile.

"He's young, but he's a dandy," the old man said. "Look at them ears—you could tie 'em on top of his head."

The dude walked around the dog a few times and shaken his head and said, "I'm afraid he won't do . . . a good bear dog, you know, has a big rectum and that dog sure doesn't have."

"Oh, that's all right," the old man told him. "Don't let that worry you. He's a all-around dog and a wrench goes with him. Right now we've got him tightened down on squirrels!"

I know we've done wandered a long way from Mr. Vanherring, the cranky Yankee, but I ain't forgot him. I just have to tell Uncle Winton's crazy old stories when they come to mind or I'll forget 'em. And this'n about the adjustable bear dog made even Mr. Vanherring laugh in spite of himself. Most generally he didn't even smile.

Loofy didn't like him, mainly I reckon because he didn't go to church and she'd heered him say he didn't think much of folks who did.

"Money's all that counts," he'd say. "I'm a self-made man and I don't owe a dime. I pay my bills the day I get 'em. Money's what counts, Mr. Driggers, and I've got it."

"Well," I told him, "if that's the way you believe, you'd sure better have some asbestos money for where you're headed!"

"Now that's ridiculous," Mr. Vanherring said. "When a man dies, he stops, and I don't take any stock in this talk about a life hereafter."

"Well, I do," I told him, "and I know where I'm goin'."

"That's what *you* think," Mr. Vanherring said, laughin'.

The last time we got in one of them hassles was about the end of March, when Mr. Vanherring were about to leave and go north for the summer. He had a place somewhere out on Long Island near New York City—near East Hampton. I believe he called the town "I'm Against It," or some such, and to hear him talk everybody out there had a roll of bills big enough to burn a wet mule. He were a fancy dresser and always wore a bright silk scarf around his neck—a "East Hampton bandage," I called it. Anyhow, Mr. Vanherring didn't get back until the

next January and we got to talkin' again one day at the restaurant.

"Do you still think you're going to an imaginary place
called heaven someday, Mr. Driggers?" he asked me.

"I sure do," I told him and I quoted some of Ma's verses
from the Bible to back me up. "Do you still think you're goin'
nowhere?"

"Exactly," he said.

"Well," I told him, "there's one thing for sure—we're both
one year closeter to knowin' who's right!"

Like always, he went back north in March but he didn't
show up the next January and in March a for sale sign went up
at his big house. I heered later that he had died just after
Christmas. So he knows now.

When a man dies, a feller get to thinkin' back to what he
might of said or done different to help him. It's a terrible thing
to think about a man goin' to hell. I know a heap of folks today
don't believe in hell-fire and say you get it all right here on
earth. But Jesus believed in hell-fire and said so over and over
again. And if we don't believe Him, we ain't got nothin'.

I remembered one of my last meetin's with Mr. Vanherring. I run into him at the fish house one day when Kelly were
with me. Mr. Vanherring started jokin' about heaven again.

"What about you, boy? Do you think you're going to
heaven?" he asked Kelly.

"Yes, sir," Kelly told him.

"Do you believe all your daddy tells you about it?"

"Yes, sir!"

"Do you believe the story about Jonah and the whale?"

"Yes, sir!"

"Do you think Jonah's in heaven?"

"I don't know," Kelly said. "I think so."

"Well, when you get there," Mr. Vanherring said, "you ask
him if that whale story is really true."

"All right, sir," Kelly told him. "But if he ain't there, *you'll*
have to ask him!"

After that we went home and I read the book of Jonah in
the Bible again and I'll be derned if I could tell just where
Jonah went after he died. He had set under a gourd vine and
pouted a heap but maybe God forgave him. One thing for sure,
I believe the whale story and I've told it to all my kids and all

my grand-kids. I tell 'em just like Ma used to tell it to me. She said that it was a straight-out miracle and that a feller just had to believe it. She told us that Jesus Himself said, "Even as Jonah *was* three days and nights in the belly of the whale so must the Son of Man be three days and three nights in the heart of the earth." If the Lord said Jonah *was* there, that's good enough for me! But I'll tell you one thing, if Jonah really spent three days and three nights inside that whale, he sure ought to be some kind of an expert on air pollution!

There must be a heap of fellers like Mr. Vanherring who claim they don't believe in heaven or hell or any life hereafter, but deep down inside they must be scared of somethin' or they wouldn't cuss like they do. I mean if a feller don't believe the Bible and its laws why don't he just go ahead and take the name of the Lord in vain instead of gropin' around for a substitute when he gets mad or scared or excited? You hear fellers say, "By gollies!" or "By Ned!" or "By jingo!" or "By gum!" or "By gosh!" or even "By damn!" Either their mammies taught 'em well or they're scared or both. Otherwise, they'd just go ahead and say, "By God!" or "By Jesus!" or "By Christ!"

One feller I knowed were a crank who didn't swear, smoke or drink whiskey, tea or coffee. If somethin' happened that called for strong language, this feller would say, "By George!" He might of been talkin' about George Washington or George Gobel. I wouldn't know. But that's all he'd ever say, no matter what. I remember takin' this feller deer huntin' in the Hammock one day and he were flanked off to my left about thirty yards. We was just slippin' along, still-huntin'—walkin' up-wind toward Dinah Pond—hopin' an old buck would get up in range. This was the feller's first deer hunt—I'll remember his name directly—and I was skeered he might be one of them hair-trigger skeesters that shoots at the shake of a bush. Well, I needn't of worried. Just as he went around the far side of a little red cedar thicket I heered him holler, "There goes a deer, by George! . . . Is it, by George? . . . Yes, by George! . . . Well, by George!" And he never fired!

"What happened?" I asked him after I got over to him.

"By George, I just froze up," Mr. Jenks said. That were his name—Horace Jenks, I remember now. He never swore or drank or fought. A right fine feller. He's been gone from here a long time though—got sent up for twenty years for rape.

17 Crazy Crackers

Our youngest boy, Burgoyne, were away from home a heap of
the time while our other kids was growin' up and learnin' to
hunt. We didn't talk about it too much but he had what the
doctors called dementia peacocks. This didn't mean he were
crazy about peacocks but just crazy, period. They said he
would probably over it when he got older and he did. But he'd
have spells when he sure acted like his nickname . . . *Burr*.
A burr keeps prickin' you until you get it plumb off of you so
that's what we done with Burgoyne—sent him off to what they
call a sanitarium whenever he taken one of them spells.

The trouble of it was that we couldn't never tell ahead of
time when he were goin' to go off on one. When he'd get one,
he'd be just like his Uncle Gaynus and want to fight about some
little old nothin'. And I'm here to tell you he were some kind of
a little banty rooster and it taken two grown men to handle
him. It's sure a good thing he outgrowed it because he wound
up near about as big a man as Kelly and just as strong or
stronger. I do believe he were most as strong as Mose Baldree
—and Mose were the strongest man I ever seen—white, black
or Indian.

Whenever Burr would start stayin' off to hisself and just

set starin' at nothin' it were time to watch him and even David were skeered of him. He never raised a finger toward his sister but Etta were skeered of him right on, specially when she were too little to understand his trouble. In between spells he'd be just fine and would laugh about some of the things he seen and heered at that sanitarium.

"There was a old boy from over near Inglis who was some kind of crazy when they first sent him up yonder," he told us. "They kept him four or five years and it seemed like he was gettin' better so they had him in to the head doctor's office to talk things over. A nurse told me about it.

" 'If we let you out,' the doctor said, 'what are you going to do when you get home?'

" 'I'm a-goin' to take a bath and get dressed in my own clothes.'

" 'That's fine,' said the doctor. 'Then what?'

" 'Then I'm goin' to make me a slingshot and come back up here and break every dern window in this place!'

" 'Maybe you'd better stay with us a while,' the doctor told him. So they kept him another six months before they called him in again.

" 'If we let you go home, Sidney,'—I believe the feller's name was Sidney—'what are you going to do?'

" 'I'm goin' to wash up and shave and get dressed up and make a payment on a car and start goin' around to see all my old friends.'

" 'That's fine,' they told him. 'Then what?'

" 'Then I'm comin' back up here and break every dern window in this place!'

" 'Well, maybe you'd better visit us a while longer,' they told him and took him back to his room.

"Next time they waited near 'bout a year and he seemed real good. So they brought him in again for questionin'.

" 'All right now, Sidney,' the doctor said, 'we're thinking of letting you go home. If we do, what'll you do?'

" 'I'll get me a shave and a haircut and a new suit and a car and a gal.'

" 'Yes indeed!' the doctor said. 'That's fine and then what'll you do?'

" 'Then I'll go out somewhere and park with that old gal.'

" 'Good!' the doctor told him. 'And then what?'

" 'Then I'll take off her dress and I'll take off her brassiere.'

" 'And then?'

" 'I'll make a slingshot with it and come back and break every dern window in this place!' "

"I don't believe he were quite ready," Loofy said.

"No," Burr laughed, "I don't reckon he was. And the trouble of it is, he never will be!"

When he were home and at hisself Burr told us about a heap of funny things that happened but when I went to see him up there two or three times I didn't see much to laugh at. Some of them folks was pitiful and some was so wild they was dangerous. I'd come back home and get the whole family together and thank the Lord we was all right and pray for Burr. One of them times he tried to kill himself that very same night but a nurse said somethin' told her to check on him one more time before goin' to bed.

Some folks will try to tell you that prayer don't count for nothin'. Don't tell me. I know better. I seen my ma's prayers answered too many times and even some of my own. She didn't do nothin', hardly, without prayin' about it and I might have saved myself a heap of trouble if I hadn't just waited until somethin' real critical come along before I discussed it with the Lord.

Raisin' kids and trainin' 'em to behave ain't too different from raisin' and trainin' bird dog puppies—or even hound puppies. If one barks and howls till you give him what he wants, he's got you. If he finds out it won't work, you've got him. It ain't no different with a kid that lays on the floor and kicks and hollers and has a tantrum. When he finds it don't work and might even get his little butt blistered, he'll quit. Of course there's a heap of difference in kids just like there is in pups. A sharp word will be enough with some but with others you've near about to knock 'em down. And once in a while you get one like David who never gives in or like poor little Burr who weren't to blame. A man needs a heap of understandin' to raise up a family and askin' the Lord to help ain't nothin' to be ashamed of.

There's some folks who ain't exactly crazy but just ain't got too good sense. Like an old feller named Jennings that Carl Ray used to tell about who had a few acres out on the Ocala road next to Pete Brunson's farm. Old man Jennings kept a few hogs but he didn't have no water on his land so Mr. Brunson told him he could water his stock in a little old pond alongside the road. Every day Jennings would load three or four hogs in a wheelbarrow and push 'em over to that pond, water 'em, and carry 'em back home in the wheelbarrow. Then he'd carry over another load. One day Mr. Brunson hollered out to him, "You're welcome to water but it looks like you'd save a heap of time if you'd dig a well on your own land."

"Oh, that's all right," Jennings hollered back. "Time ain't nothin' to a hog."

It's bad for anything to go crazy but it sure must be wonderful to get over it. I remember a feller from over near Mount Dora, I think it were, who got cured and come back home and lived a long time. He'd come over here to go grouper fishin' now and then and loved to play poker. One day they was a bunch havin' a game in the old fish house and this Mount Dora feller—Brackish, I believe his name were, or somethin' like that—made a statement and one of the Jernigan boys said, "You're crazy."

"I'll be derned if that's so," Brackish said. "I got a discharge paper in my pocket that says I *ain't*. I'll bet that's more than you've got—or anybody here's got. You're all crazy but *I* sure ain't." Then he'd haul out his wallet and show 'em the paper!

¹⁸The Hell Hole Bear

Mount Dora is over in Lake County and Mr. Brackish said that before he went crazy he used to go bear huntin' near there but when he got cured it cured him of bear huntin' too. In fact he said some folks claimed that bear huntin' caused his trouble in the first place . . . said he had got his tallow too hot one mornin' in a place called Hell Hole Bay. He told about a big bear that lived in Hell Hole Bay and said that it had to be big and bad to live in such a place, because no ordinary, little, half-handed bear could of traveled it. We had already heered about this bear from the Leesburg feller and it seemed like there weren't no dogs able to either tree him or roust him out of Hell Hole and so he just fattened on old man Milton Beck's hogs or Uncle Bos Royal's beehives. In between he had plenty of huckleberries and acorns and cabbage berries as well as cabbage buds. There was live oak hammocks and gallberry and blueberry flats and every dern thing a bear likes right there handy to Blackwater.

Blackwater Creek meanders through scrub and swamp and there is two hard roads crossin' it, both goin' to Deeland—one from Eustis and one from Altoona. The one from Eustis goes through Cassia, which is where old man Beck lived, right near the bridge. The one from Altoona goes through a little old town called Paisley, where Walt Disney used to come visitin' his aunt. This road has more curves than the Ozello River. It's somewheres about six miles between them two hard roads, on the average, but they come together at Crows Bluff near about at the big St. John River bridge a few miles west of Deeland.

The feller from Leesburg told us that this big bear ranged along Blackwater Creek all the way between them two roads and once in a while would take a sashay out across the lower one, State Road 44, and go south into Seminole Swamp and sometimes plumb to Double Bridges and the Fish Hole. There's a big scope of hilly oak scrub down there and a world of acorns in the fall.

It had been near about fifteen years since I had hunted that country. Me and Tarl had gone over there with Uncle Winton and old man Shorter and some other fellers and had camped in a old shack on Sulphur Island—a great place for bears. It weren't really a island, but Blackwater Creek circled it on one side and Sulphur Creek on the other. We had sighted a right sizeable bear on that hunt and it had went north across the hard road and Uncle Bos Royal had loped his horse on around toward Lake Norris and killed it near the little old log bridge over Blackwater . . . a great crossin' place for bears.

Once durin' the chase the bear had gone through the edge of Hell Hole Bay and I were tryin' to stay with them dogs. That's how come me to know what a hell hole it really were. Hell Hole Bay ain't a body of water like Red Bug Bay up where the gator caught the bear. That kind of a bay is a big wide place in a river, like Tarpon Bay up Big Shark River or Barfield Bay down near Marco Island. Hell Hole Bay is the name of the awfulest mess of saw palmetto and bamboo brier and bay trees I ever got into. The "Bay" part of the name is referrin' to bay trees and not to water. There's some water in it, all right, but it's just in swampy patches between the tussocks of ferns and briers and bay sprouts and saplin's.

I thought we had some bad places over on the coast, like the Devil's Pocket down on Chassahowitzka, but that Hell Hole Bay over on Blackwater Creek makes other swamps and bay-heads seem like county parks. It ought to be called Hell Hole *Bayhead* because that's really what it is—a hellacious big bayhead, runnin' for about two miles alongside the east side of Blackwater. It's about a mile from the creek out to the open flatwoods but I remembered that mile as the worst I ever seen. Uncle Bos though knowed every inch of that country, so he had just cut out and around for that crossin' place as fast as his old pony could run. That bear had weighed around three hundred and fifty and he had killed it with one shot. Now he were near about eighty and his eyes was bad so he wouldn't be goin' with us on this hunt.

When the feller from Leesburg had first told us about this bear he had said there were a old deserted homestead house on Bay Lake that we could camp in and he wanted us to come over there with our best dogs and take a whirl at that Hell Hole bear. Well, me'n Tarl had talked it over and decided we'd go. We figured we'd take old Bull, Jake, Belle, and Barrister and a new dog Tarl hadn't yet named so he just called it New or Newdog dependin' on whether he were out of breath when he called it. This Newdog were a big scaper and Tarl said, "The feller I got him from said he weren't scared of nothin' he'd ever met—boar hog, boar wildcat or boar coon."

"That don't mean nothin'," I told him, "until he meets old boar bear. Me'n you know that the scent of a bear is so overpowerin' to some dogs that they just have to go home and rest a while. You remember Charlie Dean's old Poor Boy that were so big and mean and what happened when he run onto his first bear? Why, that dog's tail hung down like a pump handle the rest of his life."

"Yeah," Tarl said. "I remember. But maybe old Newdog won't be like that. We'll just have to wait and see."

David heered us talkin' about the hunt and nothin' would do but that he'd have to go along. He promised to feed dogs, wash dishes, cut wood and tote up water from the lake. He was good with dogs and good in the woods and he promised to do like he was told so we let him go, though he weren't yet thirteen.

When we got to Leesburg we found our huntin' friend down with a extra bad spell of his arthuritis but he said for us to take some of his dogs and go ahead. Said old man Beck would show us the camp and go with us. So we taken a couple of his bear hounds and a big, brindled cur dog named Demon he had just bought.

"He's supposed to be a regular demon of a fighter," he told us. "Give him a try."

Well, him and old Bull tangled right off the bat. When we got them separated Demon tried Newdog and then old Bull got back into it. Each dog were grabbin' at whatever were handy and one time that were my left hand. We had a thirty-mile dog fight but finally got to Uncle Bos Royal's gate on the hill just west of Blackwater.

We drove on in to the house and found him home and he hoped us luck and said this devilish Hell Hole bear were the biggest and meanest bear he had ever knowed in his whole life and had been killin' hogs and tearin' up beehives around there for the last six years. One time it had come up to Steve Kirkland's house and killed a growed-up cow in the lot not more'n fifty steps from the house. The cow's bellerin' had woke old man Steve and he had run out in his shirttail and shot twice at it in the moonlight. He swore he had hit it but if he did the bear never paid it no mind—just run off toward Hell Hole. But at least it didn't get to eat no beef. Steve and his kinfolks done that.

The old homestead house where we was to camp on this hunt were on Bay Lake near where Bay Branch goes into it, about halfway between them two hard roads I spoke about and about two miles from Beck's home. Old man Beck went in to camp with us the first evenin' to show us the lay of the land and plan the hunt.

"The scrub acorns is ripe and if we can find where that devilish bear come out of Hell Hole and went up into the scrub we might could cut him off before he gets back into the Bay," he told us. "I don't know what you fellers has got in the way of dogs but up to now there ain't been no pack able to handle him once he's back in Hell Hole. He won't tree or hold up . . . just walks around in them vines and high palmettos slappin' dogs. And when he slaps one, it's a hurt dog. I got two or three old pups that'll help some but they ain't too eager when it comes to this particular bear."

"We got some with us that might just cut the mustard," Tarl said. "I got a new catch dog that the boys say ain't skeered of nothin' and my brother Billy brought old Bull along with our several hounds. Old Bull will take hold of a bear's butt if he gets a chance and if'n he does the bear will know it. Course he may get killed but he's fought right smart of bears and knows which end of a bear to go to. And we got three of the Leesburg feller's dogs includin' a new fightin' dog he calls Demon. Anyhow, we'll throw everything we got at this big mean bear of yours and see what happens."

"I'll be here at first day," Beck said. "I'll ride my horse so I can course them dogs wherever they go."

After he'd gone, David said, "I sure wish I had me a horse over here."

"Well, you ain't," I told him, "and just be thankful you're here at all. Just do like Mr. Beck tells you and stay where he puts you. We ain't huntin' in our own Hammock this time."

It rained some in the first part of the night but faired off and turned cold and there weren't none of us had enough cover. Our first real cold weather don't generally hit until late November or December and here it were only the end of October. By four o'clock I were shiverin' like a wet bird dog so I crawled out of my blankets and started a fire in the old fireplace. We was goin' to do our cookin' at our campfire out in the yard so had gathered up a few light'd knots and it weren't long until I had coffee. The feller who first brewed them beans hadn't been foolin' and I'm obliged to him every time I stick my nose into that steamin' flagrance.

We'd done had breakfast, the dishes washed and the dogs fed by the time the sky started to lighten. Way off to the east toward Lake Tracy I heered a flock of sandhill whoopers a-screechin' and I figured they must of been over a big saw-grass prairie that stretched way back into the scrub. Hell Hole Bay were to the north and west of our camp but Beck had said the big bear would now and then go over toward that prairie.

Some hunters don't feed their dogs nothin' before they go in the woods and I'll grant it ain't a good idea to fill 'em up. But Uncle Winton had always believed in puttin' a little somethin' in their bellies before a hard day's hunt so us boys had always done likewise. Loofy had baked up a couple of pans of corn bread and I give each dog a chunk, figurin' that if we jumped that Hell Hole bear they'd need it. We had chained 'em to blackjack oaks around the camp yard and they was all cold and hungry and rarin' to go. We figured we'd lead 'em all to start with so none of 'em would get after a deer or a bobcat or nothin'. One of the Leesburg dogs, a big red hound named

Stranger, weren't supposed to run nothin' but bears but we planned to lead him too, so that we'd have time to get our standers all in place before the action got started.

Old man Beck and Bill Beck come ridin' up next mornin' just as the sun were peepin', with four dogs a-follerin' the horses. Follerin' them come a big shiny Cadillac automobile, easin' along that old scrub road so the bushes wouldn't scratch it. There were a white frost everywhere and when Beck jumped down from his horse he liken to have cried when his feet hit the ground. "They're near 'bout froze," he said. "How did you fellers fare?"

"There sure weren't no roaches crawlin'," Tarl told him. "Let's get goin'. Come on David—let's yoke up them dogs."

Beck got me off to one side and said, "The feller in the car is Mr. Wells, one of the finest fellers I ever knowed. He's got a lot of money and he likes this country around here so we're hopin' he'll buy a few hundred acres and settle here. He's plumb crazy to get a shot at a bear so I'll put him on the best stand there is—right close to the little old bridge over Blackwater where it goes into Lake Norris. There's a place where a feller can see out through open swamp for a pretty good piece and Mr. Wells has a high-power rifle. If this bear decides to go north, the chances are he'll cross that old tram road within fifty steps of that bridge. A feller can hear him comin' for a long way, wallerin' along in the black mud along the creek and bustin' palmetto fans. If he goes north, there ain't hardly no way to miss him—even for a greenhorn."

David had slipped up behind me and had been takin' this all in. "Son," I told him, "you go where Mr. Beck says and stay where he puts you. That feller with the thirty-ought-six needs plenty of room around him."

"We'll all walk the scrub road from here," Beck said. "We'll put you fellers at the good crossin's and if this bear should turn back and get past everybody and go south, we'll just have to tear out back to camp, pile into our cars and drive over across Road 44 to Sulphur Creek and Sulphur Island and try to head him off at Double Bridges or the Fish Hole. We sure don't want to let him get into the main St. John River Swamp and Wekiva."

Well, we taken off on that old white-sand scrub road and a feller could see the tracks of everything that had walked it for the past several days—since the last rain. There had been some right heavy dew fallin' every night so some of the sign were hard to read, like tellin a coon track from a otter track where the webs on the otter's feet was washed out. But there had been possums and foxes and skunks and two different wildcats walked that old sand road in the last two or three nights, along with rabbits and gophers.

When I say *wildcats* I'm talkin' about what Yankees call *bobcats* and when I say *gophers* I'm talkin' about our land turtles—the ones that dig all them holes. Some Yankees will tell you that a gopher is what we call a salamander—the feller that looks like a big light-brown-colored mole and tunnels around underground and piles up them little mounds of dirt you see all over our part of Florida. They call him a *pocket gopher* on account of them pouches in his cheeks where he totes out dirt from his diggin' and piles it up. Other Yankees will tell you that gophers has got stripes on their backs and look like little old short-tailed squirrels. They say that a salamander is a sort of lizard. But I reckon a bear's a bear north or south and that's the track we was lookin' for in that old sand road.

We hadn't walked over half a mile from camp until we seen our first one. It were several days old and there weren't but three or four prints because the bear had gone straight across. Usually when any kind of a varmint comes to a road it will turn and travel the road a piece—sometimes a long way. Why, I don't know. But the big bear had gone straight across. Beck liken to have missed it because there was so many other tracks in the road. In fact, at first glance, it looked like where a couple of rabbits had hopped side by side.

"He was headed for them oak scrubs and hammocks over on Bay Branch," Beck said. "We'll see where he come back to Hell Hole if'n we watch sharp." And we did—about three hundred yards on down the road. But the tracks was near about blotted out by all the other varmint tracks. There must have been twenty coons walkin' that road and I seen where two good-sized deer had walked on the dew.

"It wouldn't take long to jump them scapers," Beck said, "and I know right where they is headed." But it were still October and the deer season weren't open yet.

To my way of thinkin' there ain't no better time than

October. The weather is gettin' cool, huntin' season is just
around the corner and the woods is sure pretty. Blackjack
leaves are startin' to turn red and so are the swamp maples.
Hickory nut and wild cherry leaves show yellow in the hammocks and creeper vines are bright red. Yankees tell me it ain't
a caution compared to the way their country goes to flamin' but
it looks pretty to me right on.

Where we was at the old sand road swung in close to the
swamp and I seen three cabbage trees with their tops mashed
down where a bear had climbed 'em and tore out the bud.
Turkeys will mash 'em down some too, settin' up there eatin'
the berries, but when a bear tears out the bud the tree will die.
These was so fresh the fans was still green.

Along about that time we found where that devilish big
bear had just come out of the bay and when he hit the road
had turned and follered it. We seen the fresh tracks on the dew
about the same time the dogs smelled 'em and Beck hollered,
"Hold them dogs back till we see which way he's headed."

Old Bull were standin' on his hind legs just chokin' to go
and the rest of the crew were just as rarin'. There was twelve
dogs and only four men a-holdin' but they managed to hold 'em
back till me'n Beck could go ahead and find where them tracks
turned off. They looked as big as dinner plates and where the
bear had walked a log when he turned east into the scrub he
had left the whole prints of his feet in wet sand. We was two or
three hundred yards away from the other fellers and them
crazy dogs, but even so Beck had to near about holler to make
me hear him. And his horse weren't too easy around that fresh
bear scent.

"I know right where he's headed," Beck said, "and I think
when the dogs get to crowdin' him he'll come back and cross
where I want to put Mr. Wells. But that dern bear don't always
do what a feller expects him to do. So he might could cut back
for Hell Hole most anywhere. Mr. Driggers, you go back and
tell your boy to stay right where he's at. It's a good crossin'
place. The road makes a bend directly just ahead of us and it's
only a short way to where I want to put Mr. Wells. Then Bill
will take you and your brother acrost the little Blackwater
Bridge and you fellers will take stands along the old road that
runs along close to the creek swamp. Just listen for the dogs
and try to head 'em if they come your way. I'll foller the dogs

on my horse. Now let's bring up them fire-eaters and start the ball!"

Naturally all hell broke loose when them dogs hit that hot scent. The trail were maybe three or four hours old but that is a fresh trail when it's made by a big old boar bear on dewy ground. The pack went a-boilin' off into the scrub—Jake, Barrister, the Leesburg hounds, old Belle and Beck's hounds all cryin' full blast and old Bull yippin' along with 'em. He didn't have much voice compared with them big-mouthed hounds from Leesburg but when he got there the bear would know it. Newdog and Demon took off with the rest.

We hurried on to the little bridge and Beck showed Mr. Wells where to stand and which way to watch. By this time the dogs was gettin' almost out of hearin' and Mr. Wells said, "They're goin' the other way."

"Sure they are," Beck told him. "That's where the bear has gone—up into them scrubs and hammocks where the acorns is at. He's a-settin' up there chompin' them acorns right now but he won't be for long. You just listen. Directly they'll jump him."

"What do you mean jump him?" Mr. Wells asked. "Do you mean jump *on* him?"

"No," Beck said. "I mean they'll start him runnin'. They'll interrupt his breakfast and he'll have to start runnin', walkin' or fightin'—whichever he decides to do. You'll be able to tell it from the sound just like if you turnt a faucet half on and then opened it all the way."

About that time it happened and even Mr. Wells knowed it. The sound of the chase had suddenly got louder and every dog were openin' every breath.

"They've done jumped," Beck said. "Watch sharp, Mr. Wells, and good luck." And he spurred his horse and taken off to the east. The rest of us moved on across the bridge and turned back up the creek swamp.

"I'll put you fellers on the crossin's," Bill Beck said. "Come on."

If there's anything more excitin' than the sound of a pack of hounds drivin' a bear, I don't know what it is and I sure don't want to hear it because I just couldn't stand it. Man, them boogers was tellin' the news as they hit the swamp where the ground were damp and the scent were steamin'. They hadn't quite caught up to the bear yet but were gettin' close and I expected every minute that Bull and Newdog and Demon would catch him. And they did! For a second or two there were a awful racket of snarls and yowls and yelps. Then the bear moved on. The hounds was a-bayin' him but there weren't nothin' stoppin' him—not even old Bull—and he kept goin' right on.

There weren't much use expectin' him to tree from what Beck had told us. No dogs had ever been able to put him up. It were a question of just stayin' with him until he run out over somebody's stand or somebody were able to get to him while he were backed up fightin' off dogs and gettin' his wind. From where I were at, the sound of the dogs would near about die out when they'd go over a scrub ridge. Then it would swell out strong when the bear turnt back our way acrost the ridge.

I didn't know just how far Tarl and Bill Beck had gone on past me but it weren't too far and I knowed they could hear the race good as I could. I called it a race without thinkin' because that's what we call it when hounds are runnin' a fox or a deer or a wildcat—a fox race or a cat race or what not. This were just a travelin' fight. Directly it topped a ridge and this time were comin' back—right down the swamp toward where Mr. Wells were a-waitin' with his rifle. I mean them dogs were makin' the woods ring and once I heered the bear beller when old Bull must of nipped him. It were enough to make a feller's hair stand up and I could just imagine Mr. Wells were a-shiverin' like a dog passin' peach seeds.

About that time a gun fired, but it weren't the crack of a thirty-ought-six. It were a shotgun and it come from pretty close to the bridge. In a few seconds the dogs hushed. Then there was a few barks and quiet again. I thought I knowed what had happened and I dreaded seein' old Beck. Here come Bill Beck a-gallopin' back on his horse and never even slowed when he passed me—just headed for the bridge. So I done likewise. When I got there, Mr. Wells was all alone and he asked, "What happened?"

"I don't know," I told him, but I felt like I were tellin' a lie. "Wait till Mr. Beck gets here. He'll know."

He knowed all right, and he were mad enough to bite a skunk when he rode up and got off his horse. "Your boy made a good shot, Mr. Driggers," he said. "But he didn't make it where he was supposed to. He left his stand and slipped on down this way and shot that bear ten seconds before it would have run right out to Mr. Wells here."

"Where is he?" I said. "I'll tell him about that."

"I done told him," Beck said. "I also told him to go on back to that camp and start packin' up. The sooner you Driggers fellers leave the better it'll suit me. I'm glad to have that bear dead but I sure am sorry my friend here didn't get his chance to shoot it like we planned."

Before I could answer, Mr. Wells said somethin' about the plans of mice and men goin' somewhere or 'nother. Then Tarl arrived and said, "Looks like David played hell again."

There wasn't nothin' I could say but apologize to Beck and Mr. Wells and say that we'd better go skin the bear and give the hide to Mr. Wells, if he wanted it. He were a good sport, that feller, and said that he would be proud to have the hide. It were a dandy and the bear must have gone four fifty or more. Mr. Wells said he couldn't blame the boy for gettin' over-anxious and leavin' his stand. But I could, and did, and told that young scoun'el it would be a long day before I'd carry him along on another hunt. What his Uncle Tarl told him I don't know but it sure weren't nothin' good.

Old Bull come out of the deal with only a sore shoulder but Newdog never raised his tail again and would bristle up and bark at every black stump he seen the rest of his life. Two of the Leesburg dogs was skint up pretty bad but would heal. They'd been right in the thick of it all the time. Old Belle and Barrister done real good and didn't get a scratch.

Demon were under the house when we got to camp. He must of run onto that bear and figured he'd made a bad mistake. Anyhow, the demon had done gone out of him. When we first got there he had come runnin' out waggin' his tail but I reckon we all smelt like bears carryin' that bloody hide and all so he went back under the house and we had a hard time coaxin' him out and loadin' him in the truck. He sure didn't try to start a fight goin' back—just set off to himself in a corner of the truck and had one hard chill after another. I started to tell Tarl maybe he could get up a trade with the Leesburg feller—Newdog for Demon—but he never was much for jokin' about a sorry dog when it happened to be his'n.

Beck had softened up some after we'd skint the bear and

said, "Tell our friend from Leesburg to come out when the deer season opens and we'll pull the peelin' off some venison. He keeps sayin' he's got arthuritis but I think it's just authoritis. He claims to be writin' a book."

19 The Big Cat
& Iambic Feet

There had been a bunch of turkeys usin' around the head of
Blind Creek and I had been keepin' an eye on 'em without
sayin' nothin' to nobody—not even my own boys. I specially
didn't want David to find 'em. That rascal would of sure busted
'em up before the season when they was hardly more'n half
growed. I planned on gettin' one for Thanksgivin' and I figured
my brother Tarley would want one too. We had always eat wild
turkey for Thanksgivin' and Christmas both. Old Tarl were the
best turkey hunter I ever seen and I done pretty fair.

There was half a dozen or so big old white oaks growin' on
a little high hammock about a quarter from where Blind Creek
breaks out into the open prairie and marsh. The acorns off
them white oaks is twice the size of live oak or water oak
acorns—even bigger'n blackjack acorns—and turkeys dearly
love 'em. It ain't no distance to the low prairies where there's
plenty of summertime food—cabbage berries on the cabbage
islands and plenty of huckleberries and grasshoppers on the
grassy prairies. So, every time I'd be in that part of the Hammock checkin' on hogs I'd ride over to Blind Creek and see
about my turkey flock. There was about fifteen or more birds in
it, best I could figure. I'd only laid eyes on 'em once but I could

tell pretty well by the tracks and scratchin' sign. And there was two or three hellacious old gobblers in the bunch.

Naturally I had to know that little piece of country pretty well, so when there were anythin' unusual it caught my eye. On this particular evenin' I'm talkin' about I seen somethin' I hadn't ever noticed before and I rode over toward it. As I got closeter I seen that it were a big pile of leaves and grass and pine straw and sticks five or six feet long and half as high. The ground around it had been raked pretty clean so that the old black hammock mud showed through and in that mud I seen somethin' that I hadn't seen in a long time—not since I had been down in the Big Cypress with Uncle Winton and Tarl years before.

The track I seen were a cat track, about the size of the bottom of a milk bottle so I knowed I were lookin' at a fresh panther track. I also knowed that bobcats don't often cover up what they kill and panthers do.

It were too late in the day to ride on home and get the dogs but I figured that varmint would be back that night to eat some more and I planned to be there soon in the mornin'. I knowed I shouldn't disturb that kill, but I were just too dang curious to leave before I found out what had been killed. I never got down off my horse but just rode off a little piece and cut me a long palmetto stem. Then I rode back to that heap of trash and poked around with the palmetto stem until I uncovered enough to see that it were a big black hog—most likely one of ours. It were nearly night when I got home and after supper I taken the car and drove up to Tarl's to tell him about the panther.

"I ain't told the boys," I said, "because I'm skeered they'll just get excited and make a lot of fuss and get in the way. I think just me'n you ought to slip out there with three or four dogs and take care of that gentleman."

"We'll just do that thing," Tarl said. "Your old Belle loves a bobcat, so she'll probably take to a panther quick as she smells him and I got two young dogs who like a bear even better'n a deer. So they may feel the same about a panther. Then, of course, there's old Bull. He'll run anythin' we put him after and won't go till we tell him."

"That'll be enough," I told him. "We can let old Bull travel but we'll have to take Belle and them two dogs of yours on our saddles. Old Belle would have a bobcat up and runnin' before

we got started good and them two fire-eaters of yours would
take to the first coon, possum, deer or hog they come to."

"We'll carry 'em on the horses," he said. "See you in the
mornin'."

It weren't no easy matter keepin' our plans from them boys
of mine when I got home. "Me'n your Uncle Tarl is goin' to try
out some dogs in the mornin'," I said.

"Can't we go?" they all said at once.

"It's a school day," I told 'em. "And besides a man has a
right to get off to himself with just his brother once in a
while—without a whole pack of young-uns underfoot."

Tarl were waitin' for me at the little bridge across the drain
where the road quits and the old hammock trail begins. I had
to laugh at him tryin' to handle Jake and Jane after I passed
'em up to him. It were their first horseback ride and they didn't
like it ten cents worth in commissary trade. But he had a
double swivel snap between their collars so they had to ride or
choke. Old Belle were quiet enough, bein' as it were an old
story with her. I just mounted my pony, patted my thigh and
she come a-sailin' right up into my lap and made herself as
comfortable as she could. I'd carried her this way many a mile
when I were goin' after a certain bobcat or bear in country
where there was a heap of deer.

Most any young dog would rather run a dern deer than
anything else. It just turned out, though, that this particular
dog taken a likin' to cat scent as she got older, and there
weren't no better strike dog on bobcats in the whole county—or
maybe the state. And when one took a tree, old Belle just set
up camp. She were a tree dog if ever there were one.

It taken us two hours to get out there to Blind Creek and
day were just breakin'. Ducks was beginnin' to move from the
marsh into the hammock ponds after acorns and two or three
of them big old blue cranes went sailin' over. Then all of a
sudden them dogs went crazy. We was maybe a hundred yards
away from that panther kill but they must have heard him or
winded him or somethin'. Anyhow, the scoun'el was layin' right
there eatin' on the hog!

"Throw down old Belle," hollered Tarl. "I can't handle
these crazy pups no longer."

Belle went to cryin' time her feet hit the ground and
headed as straight to that kill as a martin to his gourd. Old Bull

were right with her, yippin' away like a dern cur dog will do. Just the second I seen that they was after the panther I hollered "Turn 'em loose!" And Tarl chunked down Jake and Jane. They had big, bellerin' mouths and they was talkin' every breath as they tore out after Bull and Belle.

Now I've heard prettier hound music when there's been fifteen or twenty hounds drivin' a fox on a frosty mornin' but I ain't never heered nothin' that excited me more than them four bullies of ourn a-drivin' that big cat. There hadn't been no trailin' to it. The panther were right there and I do believe they must of got a sight race on him for a piece. What made him head straight west for the open prairie and cabbage islands I don't know, but that's what he done. Tarl had jumped down from his horse to look at the dead hog and see if it were one of ours but I spurred my buckskin after them dogs. I mean they were haulin' buggy!

I reckon the onliest animal in the world faster'n a big old Tom panther is one of them cheaters—them spotted cats from across the water that's half dog. But a panther is short-winded and can't keep up no great speed for very long, though this'n outrun them dogs for thirty minutes. I seen him once goin' from one little old cabbage island to another and he looked ten feet long the way he were stretched out with his tail near about straight up. I taken a snap shot at him with my .30–30, holdin' it out one-handed like a pistol. It liken to have jumped out of my hand and I never did see where the bullet struck. But it sure didn't hit the panther. The dogs got to crowdin' him about then and he run up a little old scrubby, leanin' water oak. There was plenty of cabbage palmettos taller than that, but I ain't never knowed of but one panther to tree in a palm tree and that'n just hadn't had nothin' else handy.

Old Bull were doin' his mortal best to climb that oak himself and a couple of times got up eight or ten feet before he fell out. Belle were just campin' under it tellin' the news. Jake and Jane could see the panther and I reckon that's all that kept them from goin' right off to look for somethin' else to run. They was sure full of vinegar but they seen that cat and smelt him and heered him growlin' and spittin' so they joined in the chorus.

The panther weren't thirty feet off the ground and he were a-windin' his tail, like all cats do when they're mad. Ever now and then he would flatten his ears down and spit and all the time he kept up a deep growlin'. He were a bad-lookin' thing, I'll tell you.

"Go ahead and shoot him, Billy," Tarl said when he rode up. "But don't cripple him or he'll kill a dog."

Right there was where I made a bad mistake. I should have stepped down off that buckskin but it were such a close, easy shot that I just raised my rifle and fired. The trouble of it was that just as I did, the dang horse moved and I hit the panther through the neck and not in the brain. Out he sailed and hit the ground runnin'.

Course old Bull took him almost the second jump and so did Tarley's young bitch, Jane. Bull had him by the cheek but the panther shook him loose and grabbed Jane and helt her with his forepaws while he bit her right down through the skull. Man, I hated that! And so did old Tarl. He come off his horse with his old .44–40 carbine ready and taken out through the grass after that cat and dog fight. By this time old Bull had done got his holt again and the panther rolled over on its back and brought its hind legs up under Bull to rip his guts out. Before he could do it, though, Tarl shot him through the heart. There weren't no way to shoot him in the brain without takin' Bull's brains too because they purely had locked heads.

"Damn it, Billy," Tarl hollered. "I told you to be careful!"

There weren't nothin' I could say, so I didn't try. Me'n my brother was too old to fight over a dead dog and of course old Tarl knowed I didn't go to do it. So I said I would tote poor Janie in for him on my buckskin, after we skinned out the panther, so he could bury her over in the field where Uncle Winton had had his dog cemetery.

It taken us a hour to skin that varmint, leavin' the skull and paws in the skin so old Oscar Swede, the taxidermist, could fix it up into a rug. It measured eight feet from its nose to the tip of its tail and we guessed it to weigh just about what I weigh and that's a hundred and sixty pounds. Tarley had to tote it on his horse because my buckskin got rollers in his nose quick as he smelt it. Dogs he didn't mind, but no panthers. This cat were just about the color of a deer at that time of year— sort of brownish, yellowish gray. It had black on the backs of its ears with a light-colored bar acrost each one and some black

He were a bad-lookin' thing, I'll tell you.

on its face where its whiskers was. It were much lighter-colored on the belly side—almost white.

On our way home, we stopped again to look at the hog the panther had killed. It were a young boar and didn't have no marks in its ears so it could have been anybody's. It had wicked, straight tushes about three inches long, yet that panther had taken that hog down and killed it without gettin' a scratch. And he hadn't took no long time or distance to do it, from the sign in the mud—maybe fifty steps from where he had made his first dash to where he ended up killin' and coverin' it up.

"How'd you like to have that feller pounce down on your back?" Tarl asked me. "I sure am glad we're takin' him out of the woods."

Since that day I've read a heap about panthers and talked to a lot of fellers who have hunted 'em all over this country and South America too. Seems like they don't hardly ever attack people and when they do it's what the book folks call "a rare exception." Well, I sure don't want to be that exception . . . neither rare nor well-done!

After we got home we stretched the panther's hide between some poles and salted it good and I taken poor little old Janie over to the field and buried her amongst all them other old long-gone pups. Next day I taken a hot wire and burnt what Uncle Winton used to call a "epithet" on a board which I put up on a cedar post to mark the place. All of Uncle Winton's markers was still up except one and I fixed it back with some nails. It were the one that he had put up over his old Bull that read—

> *There ain't no bear,*
> *Did ever dare—*
> *To show his butt,*
> *To this old mutt!*

The one I had wrote for Janie were just two lines and went—

> *Here lies a hound named Jane,*
> *A panther bit her through the brain.*

When Morna seen it she said it didn't scan right—whatever that meant.

"The first line doesn't have four iambic feet," said Morna, in her proper way of talkin'.

"Well, Janie had four ordinary feet and that'll do," I told her. "And I don't pretend to be no finished poet like my uncle were."

20 The Comin'-Out Party

When my brother Tarley's daughter Lorna turned sixteen they decided to put on a big comin'-out party. There hadn't been nothin' like that before in our little old town, but a bunch of Yankees had moved in over the last few years and some of 'em had more money than they knowed what to do with. There was maybe ten or fifteen pretty young heifers of the same age as Lorna and the comin'-out party were to "introduce 'em to society," whatever that meant. There weren't much society that I could see and everybody knowed everybody so there didn't need to be no introductions.

Well, old Tarl didn't go for the idea as much as his wife Morna, and he sure had a time findin' a party suit big enough to rent. This were what they called a "tuxedo" and made a feller look a little like one of the waiters at the Tampa Terrace. Tarl couldn't find nothin' big enough in Ocala and had to go plumb to Tampa. Even then he had to straight-out buy one. He were six four and two hundred and sixty pounds by then and there didn't nobody have a rental suit big enough. I think he had to shell out near about seventy-five dollars for that suit!

Everybody wanted me to go and of course Loofy wanted to go, so nothin' would do but for me to rent one of them monkey suits in Ocala. I had to lay down twenty dollars deposit on the dern thing and when I tried it on it looked like it had been to a lot of parties before. A feller could have shaved by the shine off the seat of them breeches and the knees was sprung so that it made a feller look like he were fixin' to jump. Old Bull growled at me when I put it on.

Of course both Tarl and me had to buy special shirts and stiff collars and I know now how a dad-burned turtle feels with his neck a-stickin' up out of a shell, although the collars was cut away enough to allow a feller's Adam's apple a little play. Uncle Winton thought the whole business was a lot of foolishness. We couldn't talk him into goin' and when he seen Tarl tryin' on his tuxedo and stiff collar he just shook his head and said somethin' about his big rough-tough nephew thinkin' he were Little Loyd Fondelroy or somebody. But I'll bet if Aunt Effie had still been alive she'd of made Uncle go anyhow.

Loofy got busy and made herself what she called a formal gown—three yards of cloth below the waist and not much above. The party were well-named a "comin'-out" party. I didn't see none come out but I were skeered several would. I hadn't seen nothin' like it since I was weaned.

All the daddies of all the daughters had chipped in and rented a lodge hall down at Crystal and hired a orchestra all the way from Jacksonville. Them fellers could mortally blow them saxophones and right when things was in full swing one of them big buxom Yankee gals come up to me and said, "Wouldn't you like to dance, Mr. Driggers?"

"Honey, I sure would," I told her. "If I had ever learnt how."

"Well, it's high time you did," she said and grabbed me.

Right about then the saxophone boys went to playin' one of them dreamy waltz tunes and that big buxom Yankee gal snuggled up to me and put her cheek against mine and I forgot all about Sherman's march. I reckon Loofy seen that the South were goin' under because she come up and said, "Billy, if you're goin' to make a fool of yourself on this dance floor, you ought to do it with your own little niece."

"Maybe I should," I told her. "The South will rise again some other time." So I found Lorna and said, "Your Uncle Billy has just done took his first dance lesson. Do you want to give him his second?" She did, so here we went—round and round and back and to. She were always a pretty little trick and the excitement had reddened her cheeks and her eyes was really sparklin'. And I will say she had on the prettiest dress in the whole she-bang.

Along about midnight, when the place were really jumpin', a dad-burn skunk come sailin' in the window. That skunk were fightin' mad and it let fly at the first feller it seen, which were one of them saxophone players. To tell the truth it liken to have lit right on top of him. He jumped up, hit at the skunk with his saxophone and missed and the skunk hit back and didn't miss. It weren't a very big skunk but it sure did pack a-plenty of musk and right about then is when the comin'-out party lived up to its name. Ever'body come out, not only the debutantes!

Naturally the kid brothers of these gals hadn't been invited to the party—just their special boy friends—"escorts" Morna called 'em—daddies and a few uncles, all dressed up in monkey suits too. Well, I reckon kid brothers has loved to devil their sisters and even gal cousins since time began, so what happened weren't no surprise. It were plenty surprisin' at the time, all right, but thinkin' about it later I might have knowed David Driggers would be up to some kind of devilment. He were about twelve years old and knowed how to drive but of course he didn't have no car of his own.

Humpy Todd's old man had bought him a beat-up jalopy to go to high school in and David knowed that Humpy were already red hot over losin' his gal to a visitin' Yankee boy. Humpy were about sixteen but kind of a runty kid. He had been goin' steady with Maybelle Morgan, who were one of them debutantes, and she had dumped him for the Yankee so he didn't have no friendly feelin' toward the party. David couldn't of picked a better partner for his meanness.

When them two kids had first started for Crystal they hadn't had no idea of just what they was a-goin' to do—just anything to disrupt the party I reckon—but they seen that skunk in their headlights about half a mile from the hall, so they stopped. It had went to prancin' around like skunks'll do, with its tail raised straight up, all ready to whirl around and fire that musk.

If you grab a skunk by the tail and lift him up real quick, he can't squirt on you. He has to press that tail forward on his back to do it. Of course you have to keep shakin' him down or he'll climb his tail and bite you. And I don't care how quick you are, he's pretty sure to get off a squirt or two when you first grab for him. That one had.

David didn't come home for two days and he still smelled of skunk. He'd tried to wash but everybody knows water will just tensify skunk musk. We washed him down with tomaters and I worked him over with a green bamboo though I didn't think it done much good. But it did make him tell me the details. He smelled like skunk right on and even his sister Etta told him, "You're just a plain-out little stinker." I heered that Mr. Todd taken the jalopy away from his boy for two weeks and made him walk four miles to school.

Anyhow, it had been some party and there was fourteen of them debutantes all told. Four of 'em was pretty, one were big and beautiful and three was pregnant, so they must have been introduced to society before! The other six didn't have nothin' special to extinguish 'em.

21 Sharks, Gators, Guns & Gravity

A feller can't spend as much time out on the salt water along the Florida coast as I have without learnin' somethin' about the critters that live there—sharks, manatees, porpoises and sometimes crocodiles. Ever'body seems to have a different idea about sharks. There's some that ain't supposed to be dangerous and some that is. There's nurse sharks, sand sharks, tiger sharks, hammerheads and them makos that'll jump like a tarpon when they're hooked on a line. And there's them big old pieded whale sharks that's so big you wouldn't believe it if I told you.

But the meanest of all and the one I'm scaredest of is a dern big hammerhead. Mister, that's a bad actor when he's stirred up. I'm tellin' you when a big old hammerhead, fifteen or twenty feet long, gets into a school of tarpon and decides to get one, it's a sight to see. Don't never think it has to be a hooked fish or a hurt fish neither. That shark will flat catch it! I mean! Oh, I reckon the tarpon could outswim him if it didn't panic, but it goes to jumpin' high and wild and about the third or fourth jump that big old hammerhead is there waitin' when it hits the water. There's a mighty swirl and some bloody foam and that is all.

My own scary go-'round was with a hammerhead we figured to be about a man's length less than our boat, which were a twenty-six-foot open guide boat. That big, vicious devil tried to take a six-foot tarpon away from us—tried to get it off the transom right while we was a-fightin' it off with a machine hammer and a polin' oar. If one of us had of fell overboard that shark would have took him like a bass takin' a bug. And there ain't nobody can tell me different. I can still see that shark's eye, in my dreams—big as a teacup out on the end of that hammer and with the most savage hate in it I ever seen in my life. Someday I'm goin' to tell that whole story in a book.

There's one thing about all sharks, though. They stay where the good Lord put 'em—in the water. If you stay away from the water you ain't in no danger from sharks—no kind of shark. This ain't true, though, of alligators. Them ugly scapers sometimes travel overland. There's always been a heap of argument about alligators—whether they done more good than harm and whether they was dangerous to humans or not. All I can do is tell about my own experience with gators.

To start with, any meat-eatin' critter that is twelve feet long and weighs six hundred pounds is dangerous. If you ever seen a big bull gator catch a dog or a hog, like I have, you'd hate to imagine a man in them jaws. When a big gator grabs somethin' he rolls over and over to drown and break up whatever it is that he has grabbed. It's a bad-lookin' sight.

I have caught a few gators out on land and when you get a rope around one he'll flip and roll the same dern way and you can feel how strong he is. And don't never think he can't move fast and turn quick. He'll bow his back till his tail is plumb around to his nose and when he flips that tail back he turns like greased lightnin'. And when he wants to run he'll raise himself up on all four legs till his belly is plumb clear of the ground and run. I don't mean walk, I mean *run*. It's only for a little piece because he can't go far that way, but he can travel faster'n you'd ever believe unless you was lookin' right at him yourself.

Back in the old days gators done a heap of good on the open range, diggin' dens where the water would collect durin' long dry spells and provide water holes for the deer and the cattle. Naturally frogs and snakes and turtles and mudfish and garfish would collect there and varmints would come after 'em.

So the gator was just providin' hisself with plenty to eat along with a place to live.

But when a country begins to settle up there ain't no place for big gators, specially when folks start feedin' 'em and they get tame and lose their natural fear of humans. I remember when I were a young feller goin' over swimmin' in Lake Charlie Apopka near Inverness. Some cousins had a grove over there and a dock built out into the lake. Me'n Tarl would dive into the lake and never give gators a thought. I remember one Sunday when there was two of the biggest you ever seen just floatin' out there in the lake with only their snouts and eyes and tops of their heads showin'. They wasn't a hundred yards out, but we didn't pay 'em no mind. And nobody else did neither. You never heered of any folks gettin' gator-caught—or hardly ever.

After gators got used to havin' people around it were a different story and there's been folks caught and killed and eat up by big gators. In some towns developers dig canals in from the big lakes and I knowed of a twelve-foot gator that were killed not fifty feet away from a feller's house—right where his dog and little boy would play on the canal bank. That gives me the cold chills. What if that gator had decided to travel over-land to the big lake right through their yard?

Gators used to be so plentiful that we'd shoot 'em just to try out a rifle. The hides didn't bring nothin' like they did later on, but even so there was some fellers who hunted 'em for a livin'. The way we hunted were with a lard-oil bull's-eye lantern on our head. This had a thick glass lens and we burnt a mixture of lard and kerosene. It didn't throw much light but would reflect a gator eye a long way. A flashlight will do the same thing but a big old gator that's been shot at—and maybe hit—a few times won't hold for a light that lights up the water and grass around him. On a dark night that bull's-eye lantern would pick up a gator eye a long way and it would glow like a red hot coal of fire. Moonlight nights naturally ain't much good for gator huntin'.

Before I get away from the subject of alligators I got to tell a story about a old feller who lived up on Red Bug Bay, near the mouth of Gun Barrel Creek, who had lost four good deer dogs to a big old gator. The deer would swim the bay and the dogs would start across and that old gator would get him one.

The old feller had a great story about what finally happened and he told me and Tarley one night when we stopped over there huntin' a lost dog of our own.

"One day my dogs got after a bear and it run for a while and then headed for the bay. Well, I taken a short cut to the bay and stood on a rock in the marsh where I could watch. The bear hit the water with a mighty splash and started swimmin'. About halfway acrost the bay a big wave rolled up and the bear went down. 'Oh, oh!' I said to myself. 'That gator's done caught hisself somethin' this time!' The dogs come to the edge of the bay and whined and cried and turned back but when I hollered to 'em they come around the shore and crawled out to me. They was standin' there shiverin' when there come a big commotion out in the water and that dang bear walked out on a oyster bar with that gator under his arm. He pulled up a couple of channel stakes off of that bar and he laid one acrost the gator's neck and stood on it while he taken the other one and beat that gator's brains out. And I never lost no more dogs in the bay!"

Always when a bunch of fellers set around a campfire there'll be some awful tales told about big gators and big bucks and big gobblers and huntin' dogs and guns—specially about guns. I remember one trip when the Sheriff told about his old frontier model Colt .45 six-shooter—the one with the bull's-head ivory grips—and he sure could use it. He said it were the hardest shootin' gun he ever owned and told about a shootin' he'd got into with a convict who killed a guard and escaped from the gang with the guard's shotgun and then forted up in a old homestead house on the edge of the Hammock. He'd buttoned a couple of Sears, Roebuck catalogs inside his shirt for armor—or maybe it were Sears on one side and Ward's on the other. Anyhow, when he raised the shotgun, the Sheriff killed him with that old .45 right through one of them catalogs.

Old man Otis said it sure were fine to have a hard-shootin' gun when you needed it and he told about a rifle he used to have that failed him. "That were the sorriest gun I ever owned," he said. "Just didn't have no directory." Which, he explained, was the way the bullet helt up against the force of gravity which kept a-pullin' it down toward the ground.

"The slower a bullet travels," he said, "the longer time it

takes to go somewhere and so gravity really gets a chance to work on it!"

Of course then everybody got in a big argument about whether to hold low or hold high when shootin' at a deer on the side of a hill above you or down in the swale below you. My teacher at school explained that real good to me one time and proved you had to take a fine sight and hold low both times—either up or down—because your gun was sighted to allow for gravity pullin' the bullet down. He said if you was to shoot straight up or straight down at a target, you'd shoot way over, because your gun was sighted to allow for the pull of gravity, and when a bullet was travelin' straight up from the earth, or straight down toward the earth, gravity couldn't affect its course; maybe its speed, but not its course.

I understood it, but I don't think them fellers did, and I never did convince old man Otis that he meant a bullet's "trajectory" and not "directory." He said he knowed dern well what he meant and he was ready to fight about it and I weren't, so I just gave up.

22 The Boxin' Lessons & Oucho Gaucho

One evenin' when Tarl were over to the house and the kids had went to a ball game he told me about how Kelly and Dave was gettin' along with their boxin'. My brother had fixed up a ring under some live oaks at his place and were teachin' seven or eight young sprouts how to handle their fists.

"Your boys are both quick as cats," he told me, "with David maybe a little faster'n Kelly– both on his feet and with his hands. That boy has a natural left jab that comes at your head like a snake a-strikin'. He pops me with it ever now and then and it ain't no love tap. The trouble of it is that when he gets a good jolt himself he gets mad. Just a few days ago him and Kelly was goin' at it pretty strong. David stuck that left into Kelly's face two or three times but Kelly just laughed and shaken his head and then crossed a right that would jar your kinfolks two generations back! Man, that boy is strong! I do believe he's even stronger than I was in my prime, much as I hate to admit it."

"What happened then?" I asked. "Did Dave go down?"

"Not quite," Tarl said. "But he liken to have. He wobbled around like a fresh-hatched whoopin' crane but directly his eyes cleared and he started tryin' to take off his gloves. 'To hell with this foolishness,' he said. 'If you want to fight, let's just take off these gloves and fight.'

" 'It's only for sport, Dave,' Kelly told him.

" 'Not for me it ain't,' David said. 'I ain't skeered of nobody—specially you, you big bastard—but there ain't no sense to this . . . hurtin' somebody just for fun.'

" 'Not if it happens to you,' Kelly told him. 'All your life you've been hurtin' things just for fun and you know it. Go ahead. Take off them gloves and I'll take off mine and whip you this time till you'll never forget it.'

" 'Simmer down, boys,' I told 'em. 'You young fellers come over here to learn how to box and I aim to teach you. I'll have no bare-knuckle business around here unless *I* do it.' "

I asked Tarl what they'd had to say to that but he didn't want to tell me. I could pretty well guess, though, what the answer were goin' to be and I was right.

"Kelly cooled off and stepped back but that dern young Dave just got that wild look in his eyes and said, 'I told you I wasn't skeered to fight nobody and that includes you, Uncle Tarley. And if I do, it won't be for fun.'

" 'No,' I told him. 'It sure won't. Get them gloves off.' I just did what I had to, Billy, and didn't mark him up none."

Well, it hadn't took long. Kelly hadn't seen it because Tarl had done sent him on home but Turkey-Neck Taylor's boy, Rudy, seen it and told me about it at the post office that evenin'. Rudy were Turkey-Neck's oldest boy, about seventeen and real big for his age—right at six feet and around a hundred and eighty. He had a name for bein' a bully at school and talkin' nasty to the gals.

"That were a sight to see, Mr. Driggers," Rudy told me. "David, he started that fancy footwork and popped Mr. Tarley a time or two with that left jab. Then Mr. Tarley caught him and that was it. I never seen nobody go unconscious before so fast he didn't even kick, but that's what happened. Nary a kick! After while Mr. Tarley throwed a bucket of water on him and told him to get his butt on home and not to come back."

All the time he were tellin' me about it, Rudy Taylor had sort of a pleased look on his face, so I asked him, "How about *you* and Dave? Can he whip *you*?"

Right away he got a ugly look on his face and said, "Me'n

him ain't never fought but twice—and then with them big old pillers on. Without 'em I might can whip him."

" 'Can' or 'could'?" I asked him. "You got any reason to fight?" He didn't answer me—just sulled like a possum and looked down at the ground, scufflin' his big, old stubby toes in the sand.

After he'd gone I went home and waited for David to come in to supper. There weren't ary mark on his face to show he'd been in a fight.

"Son," I asked him, "what's all this Rudy Taylor told me about your fightin' your Uncle Tarl bare fists?" Like I expected, Dave flared right up.

"So that damn Rudy has done talked already!" he said. "I sure got to teach that Cracker boy a lesson."

"What's wrong with Rudy Taylor?" I asked.

"Plenty," Dave said. And that's all he would say.

About a week later my brother Tarl come over to the house and I could see he were real worked up. "Billy," he said, "call Loofy and let's talk some. Ya'll won't hardly believe what I've got to tell." Well, about then she come in from the turnip patch so we set down on the porch and Tarl told us what had happened.

"I had just eat dinner," he said, "and were fixin' to grab me about a half hour's shut-eye before them kids begun showin' up for the boxin' lessons when I heard your boy David's voice out back of the barn. I had told him not to come back no more after what happened last week, so I couldn't hardly believe my ears. I pulled on my pants and hurried out there. It were David all right and he were jawin' with that big old Taylor boy.

" 'What goes on here?' I wanted to know. Dave spoke right up.

" 'I'm fixin' to teach this dirty-mouthed polecat a lesson,' he said. 'He can't even talk about my cousin like that, let alone try to lay hands on her like she says he done.'

" 'Who you talkin' about?' I asked David.

" 'Who you think?' he said. 'I ain't got but one cousin and that's your Lorna.'

"About then Rudy Taylor spoke up and said, 'I never hurt her . . . just felt of her a little bit and told her I'd like to get a piece of that. She ain't no angel, Mr. Driggers. She ain't got no wings.'

"'Shut your dirty mouth,' Dave told him, 'before I shut it for you!'

"'You and who else?' Rudy sneered at him. 'Just because her old man is here you think you can act big.'

"'I ought to stomp you into the ground,' I told him. 'But I'll just let my nephew handle it.' Then I set down on a sawhorse and said, 'Okay, Dave, he's all yours.'

"For a seventeen-year-old kid this Rudy Taylor has a real knockout punch. He's big and strong and if I could ever teach him his right hand could be used in defense as well as to slug with he might go a long way."

"Never mind about Rudy," I said. "Who whipped? Tell me about the fight."

"That's what I'm a-tryin' to do," Tarl said. "Like I told you, Rudy Taylor has a hell of a right but he ain't learned how to use it for defense and right away Dave went to stabbin' that left jab into his face and dancin' back. But Rudy outweighed him by twenty pounds and kept crowdin' in, sluggin' away with both hands so that some of them punches had to land. And they did. And they hurt."

"How bad?" Loofy asked. "And where is David now?"

"He's at my house—in bed. His nose is broke and one eye looks like a ripe huckleberry but Morna has a chunk of beef on it and Lorna is puttin' the ice to his nose, which has stopped bleedin'. He'll be all right."

"How about Rudy?" I asked. "Where's he? And who whipped?"

Tarl shook his head and said, "Billy, you're just as impatient as ever. Do you want to hear about this fight or not? If you do, quit interruptin' me!"

Well, the tellin' took a long time—what the newspaper fellers would call a round-by-round inscription. Old Tarl, naturally, bein' a fighter himself had to get into all the fine points of it.

"I was a little bit scared that maybe David might have what we call a glass jaw on account of how quick I knocked him out last week. But I had been mad and had hit him a real solid lick right on the button. It didn't take long to see there weren't nothin' to worry about on that score. Rudy nailed him a couple

of times with hard rights to the jaw and he didn't go down
. . . wobbled some but stayed on his feet. They both went to
the ground a couple of times and I seen that Rudy were tryin'
to bite and David were tryin' to gouge. That were the only time
I interfered.

"'Get up on your feet and fight like men,' I told 'em. 'You
ain't dogs.'"

"All right, Tarl," I said, beginnin' to get aggravated. "Who
whipped?"

Tarl grinned like a mule eatin' briars and said, "Well now,
Billy, judgin' from damage done and considerin' all punches
landed and what the judges call 'aggressiveness' I'd have
to say Rudy won. But judgin' from who were there at the wind-
up and who had quit and backed off and left, I got to tell you
that your boy David won. There just ain't nothin' that takes the
place of guts!"

"Well, he's got plenty of them," Loofy said. "And I'm glad to
hear of one time when he was fightin' on the right side. Ever
since that comin'-out party Lorna ain't been so shy of boys but
she sure ain't wild and ain't nobody ever said so before."

Tarl's account of that scrap reminded me of a story Uncle
Wint used to tell about two Irishmen who was about to tangle
and agreed to fight until one said "enough." They fought and
fought and fought and Pat whipped Mike and Mike knowed it
but kept on fightin'. After while Pat gave plumb out and said,
"Enough," and stepped back.

"Oh, be jabers," Mike said. "That's the word I been tryin' to
think of for half an hour!"

We taken Dave over to Doc Joyner's about his nose but old
Doc just laughed and said, "Let it alone and it'll heal itself. It
may be a little bit flatter like his fightin' uncle's but it's a Epps
nose and there'll be plenty left stickin' out." Doc didn't mind
what he said about anybody or to anybody. While we was in his
office some lady phoned in and said her young-un had
swallered two .45 caliber cartridges and what should she do.

"Give him a tablespoon of castor oil," Doc told her. "But
don't point him at nobody!"

Rudy Taylor never did show up for no more boxin' lessons.
Bein' whipped by a younger and smaller boy shamed him too
much. I've seen that happen lots of times with dogs . . . when
one dog whips another, the whipped dog don't never forget it.

He's meechin' and cowed down from then on whenever the other dog shows up. Of course there's exceptions to everything and I did know one old hound that never knowed when he were whipped and would fight the same dog forty times if it whipped him forty times!

Anyhow, it didn't make no difference in the boxin' classes and Kelly would of been top dog even if Rudy Taylor had of had guts enough to stay.

"That Kelly Driggers could go right to the heavyweight top if he wanted to," Tarl told me. "He's bigger and faster and smarter and nervier than ary boy in this county and maybe the state." And Tarl were right about that. Kelly could always hit like one of them Rocky fellers—Grazziano or Marciano or Battlin' Nelson.

Two or three times we all loaded up in Tarl's pick-up and went to Ocala to see some wrestlin'. Kelly had a idea he might like to try that. They was the first professional bouts he ever seen and the first one were between two foreign-lookin' fellers, one called Oucho Gaucho and the other the Bad Check, only they didn't spell it right on the posters. His real name, his full name, had near about all the letters of the alphabet in it.

Oucho Gaucho was a South American feller, real dark-skinned and with a heap of grease on his coal-black hair. His body were near about as hairy as Uncle Winton's had been. This feller's favorite hold were what they called a scissors hold in the newspaper write-ups. He'd get his legs around the other feller's belly or around his head and go to squeezin'. So now he kept workin' his legs forward toward the Check feller. The Check would reach down and snatch some hairs out of his thigh and old Oucho would beller and holler and stomp.

Directly, they both done a pinwheel in the air and went to the mat. The Bad Check had done got a toe hold on old Oucho and were flat puttin' the pressure to him. He bent that foot backward till Oucho's heel were pushed up agin his butt and he were poundin' the mat with his fists and rollin' his eyes and grittin' his teeth and hollerin' in Spanish. My own leg were achin' plumb to the hip just from watchin' all that pain.

About that time old Oucho looked acrost at his handler and nodded his head and kicked loose and before you could bat your eyes he had done jumped on the Check and stomped him unconscious—or at least till he pretended he was. The referee

patted the Gaucho's back and the match were over. A feller
come into the ring and announced that next week there would
be a return match and also a no-time-limit grudge match between somebody named the Vulgar Bulgar and a feller called
Fransaw Goatier who used a hold called the French Wrench.
Everybody hollered "boo" and we went on back to the River.

"It looked pretty fakey to me," Kelly told me next day. "I
think I'll stick to boxin'." And he did. Later on when he went
off to college to study law enforcement he wound up captain of
the boxin' team and State Heavyweight College Champion.

I reckon there's plenty of fakin' goin' on in both professional boxin' and wrestlin', specially when there's a heap of
money bein' bet. I never will forget a cartoon I seen one time in
Doc Joyner's office in a magazine named after one of our
Florida counties. That picture told the whole story. It showed a
couple of real rough-lookin' fellers locked in a clinch in the
ring with all the ringside crowd starin' up at 'em and one feller
was sayin' to the other, "Blow in my ear again and see what
happens!"

23 The Tollivers & David Does It

That winter there come a family of folks named Tolliver from North Carolina down to the old Riverside Lodge at Homosassa and David run into the old man while he were bird huntin'. When I say "bird" huntin' I'm talkin' about nothin' but bobwhite quail huntin'. Duck shootin' and dove shootin' is somethin' else. A bird hunter is a quail hunter in our lingo. Well, this Mr. Tolliver were a bird hunter from his heart. He had brought down four pointer dogs that was stem-winders and he hired both of the Barnes brothers to guide him. He rented a jeep, and him and his dogs combed that whole country. Money weren't no object with Mr. Tolliver as long as it were spent on bird huntin'.

Once when Jim Barnes were guidin' they hunted the country between Crystal River and Inglis. There's a heap of birds in that area but there's also a heap of lime-rock outcroppin' that'll tear up a dog's feet and the palmettos is so thick in places that a dog gets out of sight when he's fifty feet away. David were huntin' that country that same day and he had a slow-travelin' old meat dog that were just right for them thickets. He'd done killed his limit and most likely a few more when he met up with Mr. Tolliver and Jim and their jeep.

"Howdy, Dave," Jim had said. "This here's Mr. Thomas

Tolliver of Rocky Mount, North Carolina. And Mr. Tom this here's David Driggers, who's the only feller I ever seen that likes huntin' good as you do."

So that's how come my son David met up with the Tollivers. Old man Tolliver sure taken a shine to Dave and invited him down to hunt and bought his old meat dog Jumbo for three times what Dave had give for the old cuss. One evenin' the Tollivers had me'n Loofy down to the lodge for supper and we met the wife and daughter. Right away I seen why Dave had been cultivatin' them folks. I do believe that gal were the best-lookin' female I had laid eyes on since the day I first noticed Loofy Henry. But she were small, even smaller'n my sister-in-law Morna Driggers, Tarl's wife. And where Morna had jet-black hair this gal's hair were what they call auburn—rich, dark red-brown that really set off her creamy white skin and green eyes. I mean she were pretty—pretty as a fat little speckled pointer puppy, and their ain't *nothin'* prettier than that.

Her name were Ethel May and she were the apple of her daddy's eye. I could see David were gettin' real interested in her and it plumb skeered me. Most of the time when he took after a gal she either had to send him home or fight for her maidenhood.

The Tollivers stayed down at Riverside till the middle of March, long after the bird-huntin' season were over, because his Missus liked to fish. The old man would go but he weren't too crazy about it. The daughter went along because David had taught her how to cast and spent all his spare time down there goin' out with 'em. I could see by this time that he were gettin' serious about Ethel May and I hoped it would make a change in the boy. He'd knowed her for four months and she hadn't run him off. Best part of it were that her daddy hadn't run him off—which I were sure he'd of done if Dave had got out of line.

When the time come for 'em to go back to Carolina, Dave got real quiet and stayed off to himself even more'n usual. I seen him several times in his room writin' letters—somethin' he hadn't never done before that I knowed of.

"Wouldn't it be wonderful if that girl would inspire Dave to be a good boy?" Loofy said. "I'd give a pretty to see that happen."

Well, directly letters begun arrivin' from Rocky Mount and one day David come into the kitchen while Loofy were fixin' a mess of chitlin's and rice.

"Look what I got here," he said and showed us. I'll be dad-burned if the Tollivers hadn't wrote invitin' him to come up for a visit to their home. More'n that, they had sent him a round-trip ticket. Course I figured they had lots of money because a feller couldn't stay at Riverside for a nickel and a sweet potato, but I had the old man figured out as bein' right careful with his money about everything but bird dogs and anything that cute little daughter wanted.

We taken David over to Wildwood in the pick-up to catch the train for Rocky Mount, North Carolina, where Ethel May's people would meet him. They had sent him a ticket that included a bed in a sleepin' car and when he showed it to the feller in the waitin' room window he said, "That's in car S46. It'll be about ten cars north of the station."

Shucks! It were closer to a quarter mile! When the train come in that car went by the station twenty miles a hour and were halfway to Ocala when the train stopped. It were rainin' but there weren't nothin' to do but light out a-walkin'. We all got soakin' wet and David's new suitcase liken to have come plumb apart. At last we caught up with car S46 and a big, fat ginger-cake porter in a white coat taken a look at the ticket and said, "Lower eight," and grabbed David's suitcase and went up the steps and into the car.

"Foller him, son," I said, "and see where he puts it." So he did and after while he come back out but I said, "There ain't no place out here to get out of the rain so we're a-goin' back to the truck. I hope you have a good time and behave yourself. That little Ethel May is a sweet little old gal so treat her right." Loofy kissed him goodbye and about that time another train come in between us on a track alongside and we had to get out of the way.

It were at least five or six city blocks—like the ones in our towns anyhow—back to where the truck was at and it were a miserable trip. There weren't one shelter where passengers could wait and get out of the rain. Durin' the years I've took that train a dozen times, I reckon, to visit Charlie and other kinfolks and it seems to me that near about every time it has been rainin'. Once, when I had to go to Jacksonville I met some

of the high mucky-mucks of that railroad line and asked 'em
why they couldn't put up just one little old shelter for their
sleepin' car passengers who had to walk so far and maybe wait
a long time in the rain or the boilin' sun. They just laughed at
me and told me I could board one of the coaches right in front
of the station and walk on through the train to my sleepin'
Pullman car.

Huh! I tried that once, carryin' two heavy suitcases. Did
you ever try to make your way through twelve or fourteen
railroad cars, includin' a diner, filled with quarrelin' kids,
sleepin' old folks, pettin' newlyweds, popcorn, egg shells, half-
eat sandwiches, hat boxes and kids' toys . . . carryin' two
suitcases? No sir! No more! I'll drive or get me onto a airplane.

There was two trips when I rode them coaches. The seats
tip back and a feller can get fairly comfortable. They turn out
near about all the lights and if you draw a quiet seatmate, you
don't fare too bad. But I drawed a cranky old woman the first
time who either groaned or snored all night and the next time
a drunk who kept fallin' over onto me. So, no more! The only
bright spots on them trips was the pretty nurses who did try to
see that folks was comfortable. There was one . . . well,
maybe I better just skip that.

David were gone two weeks and, sure enough, it were
rainin' when we went to get him in Wildwood. This time I got
smart and drove my car way north of the station and parked.
Then we walked down through the worst sandspur patch I ever
seen, crossed over some tracks and got to where he were
waitin' in the rain. Ethel May's folks had give him a new
suitcase, though, made out of real cowhide that weren't
affected by the rain no more'n a gator would of been. But he
had got wet and started right in gripin' at his mother and me
like we was to blame. On the way home the rain stopped and
everybody dried out and he told us about his trip. The Tollivers
had drove him over to Asheville and then plumb over to Franklin and he had saw the big mountains and met up with some of
Uncle Winton's kinfolks.

He told us he had met some of them Plott fellers, the bear
hunters, and seen some of their famous dogs and, of course,
that had tickled him more'n anything else. He sure did fancy
the wild country. He told us he had talked to old Hal Zachary

at Franklin and a doctor named Angel who had a hospital and were a great trout fisherman and a bear hunter named Crockett whose great-grandaddy had been Davy Crockett.

"The bears up in them mountains live in regular jungles of rodentdendrens and it takes real fightin' dogs to roust 'em out and tree 'em," he told us. "And they got some wild boars up there a feller wouldn't hardly believe—tushes long as a new lead pencil."

We got home about dinnertime but the other kids had eat and gone over to Rainbow Springs swimmin'—all but Burr who had a sore toe. Him and David got to talkin' after dinner and went into Burr and him's room. They had left the door open and I couldn't help but hear the boys talkin'. David was tellin' Burr about his trip. "I was back in the club car havin' me a coke and there was this real good-lookin' filly sittin' at the other end of a little table. I'd seen her when I first went in and naturally I sat down by her."

"Naturally," Burr said, "knowin' you."

"She was drinkin' coke too and we got to talkin'. She'd been goin' to a college named Briar somethin'-or-other but had flunked out and was goin' back home to St. Pete. Seemed like she'd spent more time datin' and partyin' than she'd spent studyin'. We got pretty friendly—specially after the crowd thinned out in the club car and there weren't but just two or three folks at the other end. Along about midnight she said she'd better be goin' to her car so we left. This club car where we'd been sittin' was way back at the end of the train and we had to go through about five sleepin' cars to get to her car.

"Well, in the very first car, that crazy gal reached down and got a shoe from the floor under a bunk. It was stickin' out a little under them swingin' green curtains and she carried it down the aisle two or three bunks and swapped it for another shoe and then swapped that'n for another across the aisle. She done that all through four Pullman cars! When she'd come to the last bunk in a car, she'd take a shoe from there and carry it on through into the next car and start all over again!"

Burr said, "Man what a mess that would be!"

David laughed because that was the kind of trick he'd enjoy and then he said, "She didn't take nary shoe into her car though and when we come to her bunk she stopped and unbuttoned the curtains and we set down. I had held her hand a little in the club car and it had been cold but brother she wasn't cold. Not all over anyhow."

"What did you do?" Burr asked.

"What do you reckon I did? And I'll tell you now—if you ain't done it in one of them sleepin' cars, you ain't done it!"

I couldn't stand to hear no more and I walked right into the room. First, I told Burr to leave us alone and then I said to David, "Sit down and listen to me and don't open your dirty mouth. You ought to be nailed to a stump and pushed off backwards—cheatin' on a sweet little old gal like Ethel May. You're just like a dang chameleon. One minute you're one way and another the next. She thinks you're a warm-hearted, clean-cut young man of high principles when the truth is you're a lyin' young whelp with no principles most of the time . . . and I'm not forgettin' your standin' up for your cousin Lorna agin that Taylor boy. I'll give you credit for that. But even with me and your mother you only act nice when you want somethin' and when you don't get it, you change in one second to a surly, sneerin', impudent pup. You're just a dang chameleon, like I said before. Your color depends on the circumstances you're in!" He never forgot that talkin'-to.

Afterward I went out and found Burr and said, "Son, come on down to the River and let's set on the dock and talk some."

"Yes, sir," he said. He were always real respectful to his daddy and so were his brothers; all but David who'd just answer "uh-huh" or "yeah" or "okay."

We set down on the old board bench where me'n Uncle Winton and Ma had set so often when we had big talkin' to do and I said, "Now, Burr, I'm ashamed of David talkin' like he done in front of you—about that gal on the train and all. He didn't have no business speakin' about such as that."

"No, sir," Burr said, as serious as could be. "I just hope he didn't knock her up."

The trouble of it is that he did. And not only that but the dern fool had told the girl his name and where he lived.

24 The Outraged Father & Etta Learns About Boys

One day the gal and her father drove right into the yard without no warnin' whatever and I'm here to tell you that feller were some kind of on the prod. Over two months had passed and I had forgot all about David's train trip.

"Is this where a no-good young man named David Driggers lives?" he hollered out before he even got out of the car. I were layin' on Ma's old couch on the porch havin' a little after-dinner nap—or tryin' to would be more like it. There had been two dog fights in the yard and a couple of the boys had been playin' catch. Somethin' had disturbed the chickens and the hens was all a-cacklin' and the guineas hollerin' and now come this.

"Who are you?" I asked stickin' my head out of the door, "and what do you want of Dave Driggers? He's my son, but he ain't here right now."

"Where is he?" the feller asked, gettin' out of his Cadillac.

"Me'n you don't know," I told him. "He don't often tell nobody where he's goin' or when he'll be back. What's your business with him?"

"It's my daughter's business," he said, openin' the car door for her, and I had a chance to size 'em up. The gal were right pretty and stacked up like them underwear ads in the catalogs.

At least, I thought, Dave knows how to pick 'em. The father looked like a Yankee and talked like a Yankee and as it proved out *were* a Yankee.

All the guinea hens was goin' full blast as him and his gal come walkin' over to the house and he said, "I never heard such a racket in my life. Can't you make those birds be quiet?"

"Not me nor nobody else till they're a mind to," I told him. "They'll calm down directly and I hope you do," I said. "You look like a heart attack lookin' for a place to happen."

He had got red in the face and his collar were too tight anyhow. You could look at him though and tell he didn't buy his clothes at a commissary store. I'll bet that sharkskin suit cost him forty or fifty dollars, if not more, and he'd probably had it made to measure.

"Your son has gotten my daughter in trouble and I want to know what you and he are going to do about it!"

"He ain't here, like I told you," I said, "so I can't tell you what he will do. I can tell you right quick, though, what *I'll* do."

"And what is that?" he wanted to know.

"Just what's right," I told him. "Like I always try to do."

All this time we had been hollerin' at each other over the sound of them dad-blamed guineas and it must of woke Loofy from what she called her siesta. Anyhow, she come out and wanted to know what were a-goin' on.

"This feller claims our David got his daughter here in a family way and wants to know what we aim to do about it," I told her.

"Well!" she said. "Well! We ought to know about that kind of a weddin', oughtn't we Billy?"

"She means a shotgun weddin', Mister," I said. "Us Driggers men is inclined to be hasty. This here's my wife, Loofy Driggers, and she were two months gone when *we* was married."

"Pleased to meet you, Ma'am," the feller said but he didn't act pleased a dern bit. "My name is Edward J. Edwards and this is my daughter Edna."

For the first time the gal opened her mouth. "How do you do," she mumbled.

"Well, now," Mr. Edwards said, "what are we going to do about this situation?"

About this time old Blue come out from under the house

and when he did old Preacher took him. Them two dogs just naturally hated each other's guts. They'd team up on a bear and bite his butt till he had to climb but they'd fight each other to a fare-thee-well. They was both big, rangy, powerful hounds and the first thing they done was knock Mr. Edwards down and tear his breeches on the corner of the porch steps. Three or four more dogs come a-runnin' from under bushes here and yonder and joined in the fracas. All the time, the guineas was a-hollerin' bloody murder, Loofy was frammin' at the dogs with a broom and I were tryin' to separate them dogs before they ruint each other. It were right lively around there for a spell. Edna Edwards had run and jumped into their car and now she hollered out, "Daddy, let's go . . . let's get out of here. I'd rather have a bastard than be connected up with such people as these."

Mr. Edwards had crawled out from under the dog fight and he just ran to his car. "You'll hear from my lawyer," he hollered before he drove away.

But shucks, we never heered nothin' from nobody again and David told me later that the gal hadn't been no virgin nohow. I don't know how the Tollivers heered about the ruckus in our yard when the Edwardses was here, but they did and I mean that were the end of that. The letters quit comin' from Rocky Mount and when fall rolled around Mr. Tolliver and his folks didn't show up at old town (that's what we always called old Homosassa down on the River). I heered that they had gone to some place down near Punta Gorda where there was a heap of birds and good guides. Anyhow, there weren't no more free dinners and fishin' trips for David at Riverside.

"You done dropped your candy," I told him. "You put me in mind of a story Uncle Winton used to tell about two little colored boys back in the old days. They was real poor and neither one hadn't never had no money of his own. So when Christmas come their grandaddy give 'em each a dollar bill. This were back when a dollar would buy a Ingersoll watch and ninety cents would buy a pair of cotton drawers. They couldn't hardly wait to get to town. One had always wanted a watch so he bought hisself one and put it in his pocket. The other hadn't never had no drawers so he bought a pair and put 'em on.

"Not far from home they had to cross a foot-log over the

creek and it were their custom to do their doin's off of that log. So they stopped. Directly one said, 'That's funny, brother, I ain't done nothin' yet but I already gone *kerplunky!*'

" 'You know there's somethin' funny,' the other one said. 'I done somethin' all right but I ain't gone *kerplunky!* ' "

David didn't laugh or say nothin'—just sulled like a dern possum. "That's you," I told him. "You done gone *kerplunky* right in the middle of what'll probably be your best chance for a pretty wife and a good job and a father-in-law with more money than John saw Indians on the mountain."

"He ain't got no job I want," David said. "And there's plenty more good-lookin' gals."

Before I could answer him he got up and walked out of the room. I had a good will to follow him and give him one more good whippin'—as big as he was—but I knowed in my heart it wouldn't do no good. He were just a natural-born rebel.

When I get to thinkin' back on that whole go-round I can't help suspicionin' my own daughter of writin' to the Tollivers to tell 'em about David and the Edwards gal and the big ruckus in the yard. Etta had been in her room all the time and there weren't nobody else there but me'n Loofy and the dogs, chickens and guineas. Burr and Kelly had been playin' catch but they'd done gone off somewheres and David were already gone, like I told Mr. Edwards, God knows where. There weren't no near neighbors and if there had of been they couldn't have heard nothin' over them fightin' dogs and hollerin' guineas. So it had to be Etta.

For a long time I studied about askin' her flat out, but to tell the truth I were skeered she would lie and I didn't want to make her do that. She were always takin' up for David irregardless of whatever meanness he got into and I think she were just plain jealous of any gal she thought might take him away from home. In a way, you couldn't blame her because she were about the onliest livin' thing he seemed to give a real damn about—her and his cousin Lorna. I mean he'd whip ary boy that spoke nasty to them or around them and I never knowed him to be ugly to Etta about nothin'. Anyhow, both the Tolliver gal and the Edwards gal was now water over the dam and Etta seemed as happy as a little green toad frog in the rain.

One night I heered her cryin' in her room. Loofy had gone over to Morna and Tarl's to help nurse 'em. Everybody had the flu and their daughter Lorna liken to have died of it.

"What's the matter, honey?" I asked Etta when I got to her door. "Are you sick?"

"Come in, Daddy," she said. So I went in and set down on the edge of the bed. She had been to one of her first school dances with a boy named Rafe Henderson from over near Dunnellon. I didn't know the boy too well, but I knowed his folks a long time and they was good people. Etta were only fifteen and he had brought her home by eleven like he had promised. "It's about Rafe," she said.

"All right," I told her. "What about Rafe? Did he want to kiss you?"

She went to cryin' again. "He wanted to do more'n that," she said.

"Of course he did," I told her. "That's the nature of the critter. But you didn't let him and he respected your answer, didn't he?"

"Well . . . yes," she said.

"That's the difference between a man and a animal," I told her. "The difference between a gentleman and a s.o.b. Honey, you might as well get used to the idea that a young bucko like Rafe has got the same thing on his mind that most young fellers his age has got. He's made that way, and like your Bible tells you he's born a sinner. But if his folks have taught him right he'll have the fear of the Lord in his heart and he'll know the difference between right and wrong. I know *you* do."

"Oh yes, Daddy," she said. "Mother and I have talked about all this a lots. But I like Rafe Henderson real well and I just figured he'd be different somehow."

"Well, he ain't," I told her. "And don't hold it agin him too much. Just remember you're a Christian girl and that the Lord is always with you. If a feller don't respect that, he ain't the right feller and I'll make him hard to catch. But they'll all try, honey. If one don't, with a young gal as pretty and luscious as you are, there's most likely somethin' queer about him."

Etta shook her head. "I haven't met one like that yet," she said.

"Well, there is some," I told her. "The number of boys in Yulee High School ain't a very big slice of mankind. Now, I

reckon your mother has told you all you need to know about
your body and all that and you seen dogs and hogs and horses
and cattle and chickens and ducks and maybe even gators a-
breedin' so you know the way life goes on and I won't try to tell
you nothin' about that. It's the strongest urge there is and so
even if it should get the best of you sometime, don't you
hesitate to tell us about it. Me'n your mother know all about
temptation."

"And Jesus did, too," she said.

"He sure did," I told her. "And He said to that woman who
sinned, 'Neither do I condemn thee. Go and sin no more.' And
He also said for ary body without sin to chunk the first rock
and there didn't nobody chunk it."

"Daddy, promise me you won't say nothin' to Rafe," she
said sittin' up real straight. "If he ever gets too rambunctious
I'll tell Davy."

"All right, honey," I told her. "But he's a big old knocker
and Dave might not could whip him."

"Well, he'd sure try," she said. "And I'd a heap rather you'd
just stay out of it."

"Okay," I told her. "Only if you ever get in a family way by
ary boy, don't you fail to tell me and your mother first. Don't go
a-runnin' off somewhere or do nothin' foolish. Promise?"

"I promise," she said. And we talked a few minutes about
this and that and I kissed her goodnight and went on to bed.

I laid awake a long time thinkin' back to that night me'n
Loofy was in that pine grove while she were Tarl's gal and he
were in the army. It got so real that I come within a ace of
gettin' dressed and drivin' over to Tarl's right then and there
after her. A feelin' like that which lasts twenty years ain't
nothin' to laugh at or sneeze at or fool with. I had been seventeen years old that moonlight night on the pine straw and now
I was thirty-nine but my cravin' were just as strong. Or at least
I thought so. I know I weren't like old man Toskins who
married a real young gal when he were near about eighty and
claimed nothin' about him had failed but his memory. He said
that on his honeymoon they went to bed and after while his
bride said, "Old man, you have had it."

"And do you know," he told me, "I just couldn't remember
whether I had or not."

I hear a heap of stories about real old fellers who stay right in there pitchin' way up into their eighties and some of 'em ain't fittin' to be told and I try to forget 'em. But I did have to laugh when Doc Joyner said there were a old feller from up around Otter Creek who said that the second time he made love to his wife he'd always sweat pretty bad. The first time didn't bother him none.

"I can't imagine what would cause that," Doc Joyner told him. "Do you have ary explanation?"

"Well," the old feller said, "I got to thinkin' it might be the time of year. That second time is in July or August."

That story would of tickled my ma. She always said she couldn't understand why folks always wanted to get married in June anyhow. "Winter's the time, not June," she'd say. "It's natural for a couple of bodies to hug up close on a cold night. But in June a body don't want nothin' over it but a sheet—if that. And what about the poor doctors—specially Yankee doctors—havin' to get out and hitch up the buggy on them February nights?"

25 Trouble at Gator Den Tavern, Infomaniacs, Uncle Winton's Private Place & What to Do in the Red Alert

David had done got a name as a fighter, so when the trouble took place at the Gator Den Tavern folks was quick to say David Driggers were mixed up in it. He were there that night all right and had had a couple of beers. That were about all he ever taken, though, because he used to say enough folks were agin him already so that he didn't want to get into such shape that he didn't know exactly what he were doin' at all times and be ready for ary thing that happened.

Now, there were a family of people named Rainey who lived up near Otter Creek and was the quarrelsomest folks I near 'bout ever knowed. They wasn't no kin to old man Paul J. Rainey, the great bear hunter from up in Mississippi, who used to come huntin' with Uncle Winton. These here Raineys had a cousin livin' in Georgia named Doak Lee who would come down visitin' and who claimed to be descended from old Robert E. hisself. If he were, he had sure descended a long, long way. I can't imagine the General goin' into Gator Den Tavern, much less bein' throwed out of Gator Den.

On the night I'm talkin' about, this feller Lee picked a fight at the bar with one of the Reid boys and got his butt whipped. Lee's uncle, Horace Rainey, had to carry him home. Afterward

Horace come back and there was more jawin' and jabberin' until Horace jumped onto young Reid and liken to have beat him plumb to death. Horace Rainey were much of a man.

There had always been a heap of distention between the Raineys and the Reids and this ruckus just advanced the spark. Some said the original trouble come about because of a hog-stealin', others claimed it were all due to one of Jeremiah Reid's gals gettin' in a family way by Abney Rainey, Horace Rainey's youngest boy. The boy wouldn't marry the gal, even when her daddy threatened to kill him. He said he'd be derned if he were goin' to take credit for some other feller's work. All durin' this trouble I had sure kept my fingers crossed and my mouth shut because I wouldn't of bet a dime that David Driggers weren't at the bottom of it—which ain't exactly the way I meant to put it, but it will do. Anyhow, if he were the cause of the distention there didn't nobody know it.

Like I said, there had been bad feelin's between them families for a long time. One of Uncle Winton's poems made mention of that, come to think about it. I disremember the whole poem but one part of it went—

> *When Abney Rainey drawed a bead*
> *On old man Jeremiah Reid,*
> *A dad-burned rooster crowed and flapped*
> *And then his daddy's rifle snapped.*
>
> *And so I reckon you could say*
> *That it were not a Rainey day,*
> *Because old Jeremiah Reid*
> *Then fired and made young Abney bleed!*

After that shootin' the Reid gal left town and right soon afterward old man Horace Rainey shot and killed Jeremiah Reid. Young Abney Rainey were lame the rest of his life but there weren't no more shootin' far as I remember unless it's happened in the last few days.

Abney Rainey hadn't never amounted to much and after he got lamed he just wouldn't work. He'd give out and quit on ary job you'd give him. He didn't look puny but he sure acted puny. Most folks said he were just plain lazy. Then when he were about thirty he got married but instead of gettin' better after that he got worser.

"Couldn't his wife do somethin' with him?" Loofy asked me.

"Well, folks said she done it with him too much," I said. "She were another one of them infomaniacs, accordin' to the talk. Anyhow, Abney got sorrier and sorrier. A feller said he seen him sleepin' standin' up one time—just wouldn't make the effort to lay down."

"Whatever happened to him?" Loofy wanted to know.

"Well, he come home one evenin' and found another mule pawin' in the stall and he did get up enough energy to load his shotgun and shoot the feller. And he liken to have got two birds with one stone. Anyhow, he got five years for man-slaughter. Quick as they taken him away his wife moved in with a feller from Ocala and it weren't no time till *that* feller lost his job. Them infos sure is bad news."

I remember Uncle Winton tellin' about a cousin of his who married one. One day she told him to buy her a mouse trap when he went to the store. "Be sure it's one of them round ones with holes in it and not one of them little old sorry flat ones," she told him.

Well, Cousin Harry liken to have forgot all about the trap but remembered it at the last minute and the store didn't have nothin' but the flat ones with a wire spring that snapped. So he bought that and when his wife found it in the bag of groceries she just purely raised sand with him.

"I told you not to get that kind," she hollered. "All the neighbor women say they're no good, won't catch nothin'. I told you to get the other kind."

At last Cousin Harry got aggravated and said, "Of course it'll catch a mouse. If it wouldn't the store wouldn't sell it."

"It won't catch nary one," she said.

And then he said, "I'll tell you what I'll do. I'll set it and every time it fails to spring and catch a mouse I'll buy you a new dress. And every time it catches one, we'll have some fun."

"That's a deal," she told him.

Well, he set the trap over in the chimney corner and they blowed out the lamp and went to bed. Directly the little old trap went *snap!* Cousin Harry got up and sure enough there was a nice fat mouse in it.

"I just can't hardly believe it," his wife told him. "But I'll be good as my word." And she were.

In about ten minutes the little old trap went *snap* again and there were another mouse and another party. Cousin Harry were about to go to sleep when his wife punched him and said, "Harry, I heered that trap again."

"I'll be derned if you did," he told her. "I didn't set it!"

Uncle Winton had wrote a little short poem about him and his wife:

> *Cousin Harry Shallenback*
> *Married an infomaniac*
> *A year after Cousin Harry were married*
> *Were when poor Cousin Harry were buried.*

Whenever Uncle Winton had wrote somethin' that didn't make a good rhyme he would say he were just usin' his poetic license. I reckon he had one all right because he sure used it a-plenty, but I never did see it or find out where he had got it. I went in a bookstore in Tampa one time and asked how much one would cost and the feller just laughed at me.

I guess everybody has got 'em a special private place where he keeps real personal stuff that he don't want nobody to see. Of course he figures that someday before he dies he'll go through that stuff and burn most of it. After he dies, of course, he won't care who looks at it but until then he don't want nobody messin' around in that bureau or desk drawer or wherever he keeps it. The trouble of it is that he don't know when he's goin' to die—like Uncle gettin' killed by them wasps right in his own yard after all the fights and rough times he had had. But when we went through his things we never did find nothin' very private.

We did find a old shoe box with a few more of his poems, but I've already done told you about them. It weren't till nine years after he had died that I accidentally run up on his secret place and I ain't tellin' nobody where it is. I may want to use it sometime myself. There was two or three things in it that sure did surprise me—letters, mainly, from women folks who shouldn't have been writin' such to Uncle Winton. And there was two or three poems I hadn't never saw before and I don't reckon I ought to write 'em out. But one really tickled me, rhymin' a gal's name with a Georgia town. Yankees will say the gal's name don't rhyme with the town. They got a town by the

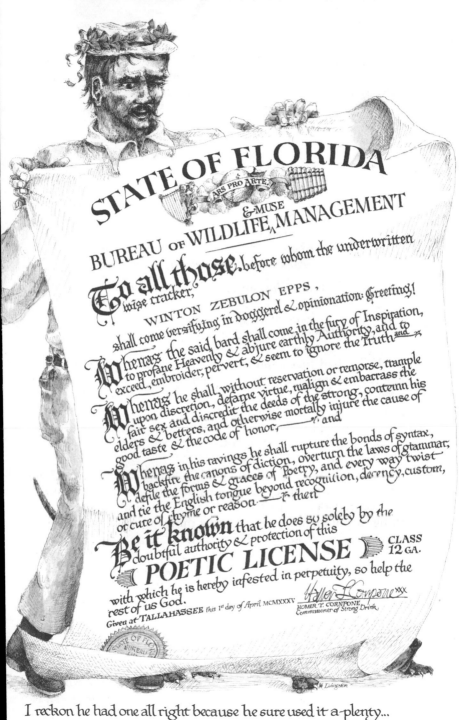

I reckon he had one all right because he sure used it a-plenty...

same name and can call it whatever they want. But Georgia folks call *their* town Al-*bá*-ny or Al-*bén*-ny. So the gal could be either Janie or Jenny. Anyhow, the poem went like this:

GEORGIA GAL

One time when I were in Albany,
I met a little gal named Janie,
And she were cuter than a bug
And, man! How she could kiss and hug.

She come from over south of Moultrie,
Her folks raised corn and hogs and poultry.
She called herself too sweet and charmin'
To waste her life on country farmin'.

And so she worked on country farmers
Like all the other two-bit charmers.
Instead of bringin' home the bacon
She packed and took it up to Macon.

Uncle had just happened to run into one of them women like King Solomon described in the Book of Proverbs—only he used words Uncle Winton didn't. But they was both warnin' against such women, whether they come from Moultrie or Beer Sheba, although, come to think about it, I reckon Uncle would of took the Beer and passed up the Sheba! But come to think about it again, maybe he wouldn't.

And speakin' of old King Solomon, I read in my Bible where he wrote there ain't no new thing under the sun. I believe that Book all right and I reckon there weren't no new thing to Solomon. But there's new things to me and I've been a lot of places—from Gulf Hammock to Memphis and back and to Atlanta and back twice. There's a heap of towns along the way and I pay attention to everything so I won't get lost comin' back but I ain't never seen a *Second* Federal Savings and Loan or a church with a board sayin' *Last* Baptist Church. Maybe there is such but I ain't seen 'em. And without meanin' to be sacreligious I'll bet old Solomon never did neither.

There sure weren't much new to my Uncle Winton but that old Grim Reaper slipped up on him too, like I said. And I reckon it's a good thing that don't none of us know when our time is comin' or what it'll be—bellyache, bee stings, snake bite, car wreck, coronation thrombos or whatever. Some folks got real churned up over the atomic bomb—and a heap of 'em still is. Well, I'll tell you how I feel about that. A sailor down at Key West told me they got a memorandum from Washington that told all office workers what to do in case of the red alert. "It told us to remove all metal objects from our pockets," he said, "push our chairs back about four feet from our desks, bend way forward and put our heads down between our knees and kiss our butts goodbye."

That makes as good sense as anything else I've heered, so I don't worry no more about atomic bombs than I do about some greenhorn hunter shootin' me for a deer. When you're dead you're dead and the important thing is to know what comes afterward and not be skeered of *that*. My ma weren't and I ain't and Loofy ain't. We done got our tickets to join Ma across the River. That ticket says, "Whosoever therefore shall confess Me before men, him will I confess also before My Father which is in heaven." When the Book says "whosoever" it's just a old-timey way of sayin' "anybody"—*all* folks, *ary* folks, and that includes me. So every time I tell this to men I'm just gettin' the Lord to stamp my ticket again. *Whosoever* even includes David Driggers if he'd believe it, but he never would pay much mind to nothin' connected with the Bible or church. He just seemed bound and determined to raise hell and put a chunk under it wherever he went. Keepin' out of the fracas at Gator Den were the exception.

26 The Dumb Feller, the Bitin' Bass & the Blind Man

For a while Early Byrd's daughter, Ima, were my boy Jim's gal and she'd drive her little old car over to see him. One day when she come over he weren't home. She visited with Loofy for a spell, waitin' for a hard shower to pass over. When she went out to her car I heered the starter grindin' away and after while she got out and come back to the house. I had started down to the barn and she hollered out, "Mr. Driggers, my car just won't run. I reckon you'll have to get it started so I can go home."

"All right, honey," I told her. "What seems to be the trouble—ignition or fuel?"

"What?" she said.

"Unless the pistons is froze in the block," I told her, "the trouble has got to be either no fire or no fuel. When a spark and gasoline get together there has to be a fire. When it's mixed with air in the carburetor there's got to be an explosion in the cylinder. Are you out of gas?"

"Nope," she said. "I got half a tank."

"Battery dead?"

"Nope. Not yet."

"Then it's near 'bout got to be plugs or distributor," I told her.

"Mr. Driggers, I don't know nothin' but to drive," she said and flounced back into the house.

Most women folks are like that—and the trouble of it is that a heap of men are too. One of my own kids, David, ain't got no more sense about mechanical things than a jay bird. He don't hardly know how to change a spark plug or a tire. But he can trail a buck deer out across the sand hills like a Indian or ride the meanest bull at a rodeo. On the other hand, our oldest boy, Jim, can take down and put together ary engine ever made but you couldn't get him within fifty feet of one of them Brahma bulls and he couldn't trail a deer if he wanted to— which he don't. Uncle Wint would have sure shook his head over him.

Old Uncle Wint would have been plumb helpless if he'd been faced with something like what's under the hood of one of these here modern automobiles. Back in the old days a feller could fix up his Lizzie with some balin' wire but today you can't hardly fix nothin'. If a little old plastic light switch don't work, you've got to buy half a dashboard panel to replace it.

I'll say this for old man Henry Ford, he made a killin' all right but he also made a automobile that gave folks their money's worth and would stand up under all kinds of treatment for a long time. They called 'em Tin Lizzies but they was built out of boiler-plate steel compared with what goes into these modern wonders that is put together out of metal just about as heavy gauge as a ordinary beer can. A feller could run into a cow with an old-time Ford and like as not have the damage hammered out at Luke's Garage without too much trouble. Today, if you hit anything bigger'n a house cat, you're "totaled." The trouble of it is that's the way the automobile people seem to want it.

Old man Henry Ford used to come down to visit Mr. Edison at Fort Myers and I remember seein' 'em both there comin' out of Mr. Edison's drive. We was in Fort Myers on our way to the Everglades huntin' and had drove out to look at the Edison home. That time they was drivin' a big shiny-black Lincoln and Mr. Edison were at the wheel.

Folks said that one year Mr. Ford brought Mr. Harvey Firestone and President Calvin Coolidge down to Fort Myers with him and they stopped to fill up with gas at old man Ed Brind's little old station at the bend of the Myakka. They was a-ridin' in Ford's Lincoln and old man Brind come out and looked 'em over and said, "I'll be dad-burned if that ain't the biggest, shiniest car I ever seen—near about as big as a Coast Line locomotive. I'll bet that's the finest car made in the whole dern world."

Accordin' to the story, Mr. Ford said, "Well, sir, I think you're right. I build this car in my factory in Michigan and know what goes into it. I believe it to be the finest car there is."

"Well, what do you know about that!" old man Brind said, walkin' around it and shakin' his head. "And them's the biggest wheels and tires I ever seen. Man! Just look at them tires! I'll bet they's the finest tires there is."

"I expect you're right," Mr. Firestone said. "I make those tires in my factory in Ohio."

Old man Brind walked around the car again and looked at all four wheels just a-shakin' his head. "And you make 'em?" he asked.

"That's right," Firestone said.

"And you make this car?" old man Brind said lookin' at Ford.

"That's right," Mr. Ford said.

Then old man Brind said, "The next thing you know that dumb feller in the back will be sayin' he's President of the United States!"

Now, I don't hardly believe this story and I'll tell you why. Folks who tell it say that old man Brind walked around the car several times a-lookin' at it and if he did, he had to be upwind from them fellers at least once. And if old man Brind walked upwind from anybody, whoever it was couldn't have just set there and said nothin'. So I just don't believe the story at all.

The feller from Leesburg used to tell some tall tales too but I never did catch him in a straight-out lie. One day when he were over on a huntin' trip I were a-tellin' him about Ima Byrd's car trouble that time and he said, "Now wait a minute, Billy. Don't tell me somebody's named Ima Byrd."

"I already done told you," I said. "That's her name. And she sure don't know nothin' but to drive."

"What ailed her car?" he asked.

"Distributor wires wet—that was all," I told him.

"Lucky," he said. "Usually when you go to help somebody you can count on ruined clothes, a mashed finger or a broken arm."

That sure is the truth. A heap of times when a feller tries to help somebody, trouble just keeps pilin' up. Look what happened to Frank Pemble and Bill Finlayson when they was fishin'. I never knowed either one of 'em but the feller from Leesburg did and he told me just what happened.

Bill and Frank was bass fishin' in Lake Griffin, a great big old lake near Leesburg which were one of the best bass lakes in Florida back in them days. Directly, Frank hooked a good fish—a four or five pounder—and Bill said, "Lead him around to me and I'll land him for you."

The fish was plumb wropped up in eel grass and Bill couldn't hardly see it or I don't reckon he'd ever have done what he done—and that was to ram his thumb into that fish's mouth and grab it by the lower lip.

Now, a bass ain't hardly got teeth enough to scratch you, let alone bite. And when you pick him up by the lower jaw you near about paralyze him and he can't do nothin'. But this weren't no bass! It were about a six-pound mudfish and it latched on to Bill's thumb and went to rollin' like a gator. In about three seconds it had done rimmed that thumb right to the bone and the blood was a-flyin'.

Well, they finally got the bleedin' stopped but it got to hurtin' Bill awful bad so Frank said he thought they should ought to get to a doctor pretty dern soon and they headed back for the fish camp where they had rented the boat. When they got to the camp the feller who ran it were gone but his wife taken one look at that thumb and said, "My, my, my, that's a bad-lookin' thumb."

It had started bleedin' again so she taken a old piller case and tore it up and made a bandage. Round and round she wropped it—round his wrist and up through his fingers and round his thumb and wrist again. Then she said, "I'd better disinfect that bite. Them mudfish bites'll poison a feller." So she poured about a teacupful of spirits of turpentine onto that bandage. When she did, old Bill went to cuttin' a caper. That turpentine was really a-burnin' him.

"Let's get to the doctor, Frank," he said and jumped into Frank's pick-up and stuck his pipe in his mouth. Just as Frank got in, Bill struck a match to light his pipe and *whoosh!* That bandage were a torch! Bill was a-tryin' to get the bandage off and Frank went to hollerin', "Get out! Get out before you burn up this car!"

So Bill jumped out, still tearin' at that flamin' bandage. Frank run after him and hit at it with his hat a couple of times tryin' to put out the fire but Bill would just jerk his thumb away. All the time he was a-tryin' to get that bandage loose but that old sister had really tied it on to stay. So Bill tore out for the dock and laid down and stuck his arm down for the water. But the trouble of it was that the lake were low that spring and he couldn't reach the water. So he just rolled on in—clothes, watch, wallet and all! That put out the fire but the thumb got infected after all from that old muddy water and he were lucky he didn't lose his arm. All from just tryin' to help a friend land a fish.

It's a feller's intentions that count, but sometimes what you might think are good intentions ain't good at all. Like the story about the feller with the seein'-eye dog—you know, one of them dogs that's trained to lead a blind man around. This feller started to cross the street with one of them dogs when a proud bitch went by. I ain't talkin' about a stuck-up, high-falutin' gal, but what us Crackers call a lady dog in season.

Anyhow, the blind man's dog sniffed and jerked loose and tore out after that lady dog, leavin' the poor feller right out in the middle of the city street in all that traffic. Two or three people ran out and stopped the cars and helped the blind feller to the sidewalk and by that time the dog come back. And right away the blind feller reached in his pocket and got a cookie and started to feed the dog.

"What you goin' to do?" somebody asked. "Reward the dern dog for runnin' off?"

"No," the blind feller told him. "I'm just tryin' to find which end his head is on so I can kick his butt!" So you see, things ain't always the way they look at first. That feller had *bad* intentions. But what I can't believe about the story is the dog comin' back so soon. The feller leadin' her must of got in a car and drove off. Once a dog takes out after a proud bitch, there ain't no use expectin' him back for quite a spell.

I remember Uncle Winton tellin' about a fox chase they had one mornin' down in the Weeki-Wachee scrubs. They had about twenty hounds and there was a feller from Brooksville had a little keen-mouthed black-and-tan bitch named Keenie, which everybody said were the fastest dog in the county. Anyhow, accordin' to Uncle Wint, Keenie was in season that mornin' and when the pack come out through an openin' where he could see 'em, he said she were leadin' the race with Bill Jernigan's Big Pup runnin' second, old Drum runnin' third and the fox runnin' a dern poor fourth!

I never did question Uncle Wint too close on that yarn but I do know that once when me and Tarl was on a panther hunt in the Big Cypress Swamp our strike dog, old Dolly, went in season and it sure broke up our hunt. All the other dogs wanted to do was just foller her around. But we never had no panther join the pack!

27 Tampa Fair, Boom Times & Bum Times

One time I taken the whole family down to the Tampa Fair to see the races and ride the Ferris wheel and all. It were durin' Gasparilla week and we seen the pirate ship go along the Hillsborough River. It's real pretty along that river where the college has them funny-lookin' buildin's with all them towers with the minuets on top of 'em. While we was in Tampa derned if I didn't run into Sheriff Charlie Dean from Inverness and old Jerry McLeod who had been up duck huntin' with us several times. He were Sheriff of Hillsborough County then and they'd just fixed up some right new jail cells in the court-house and showed me around.

"Billy," Jerry said, "just look in that cell. Ain't it modern and clean and nice?"

I walked in, just like a hog goin' into a trap—and that's just what I were! Old Charlie and Jerry slammed that door shut on me and then went strollin' 'off down the hall discussin' what they'd charge me with.

"I'd say we ought to charge him with first-degree hybotry," Charlie said.

"Right," Jerry said. "We ought to hold him for thirty days anyhow on that charge alone."

Well, them two crazy fellers left me in that cell for about fifteen minutes and it liken to have got to me, I'll tell you now. I never knowed I had cloisterphobia before but I found it out then. "What if there should be a fire or them two idiots was to have heart attacks and nobody knowed where I was?" I thought. And it were a scary feelin', I'm here to say! I felt just like that colored boy who asked me for a job and I were checkin' up on him.

"Have you ever been in jail?" I asked him.

"No, sir," he told me. "I ain't *never* been in jail . . . not even to see a friend!"

I know now why folks call it "servin' time." That fifteen minutes seemed like fifteen hours.

Speakin' of Tampa, my Uncle Winton used to go down there a lots and I remember his tellin' us boys about something that happened once when he were down there durin' Gasparilla, watchin' the pirate ship. It weren't far from the college that has all the towers with minuets on 'em There were a old feller near him a-smokin a big black cigar and the smoke kept blowin' back in another feller's face. At last this feller said, "How many of them stinkin' cigars do you smoke in a day, Mister?"

"I don't know if it's any of your business, but I smoke about six," the old-timer said.

"My, my," the feller said. "That's bad for your health. Not only that, but expensive. How much do they cost you?"

"Used to be a quarter. Now they're a dollar."

"My, my," the feller said. "How long have you been doin' that?"

"About forty years," the smoker said.

"Just think of that!" the second feller said. "Why, if you had saved and invested all that money, you might have been able to buy that tall buildin' over yonder toward the college."

"Do *you* smoke?" the old-timer asked.

"No."

"Do *you* own that tall buildin'?"

"No."

"Well, I do," the old-timer said, and he lit another cigar.

It turned out that he were Mr. Ed Bell, one of the richest fellers in Florida. To look at him you wouldn't have thought he had nothin'. He were wearin' a old beat-up, wide-brimmed, black hat and wrinkled-up denim pants, a plain blue shirt with the sleeves rolled up and high-top boots like a ordinary rancher or farmer. But folks said he once owned twenty miles of beach front and near about a hundred thousand acres of pasture. I reckon he must of sold durin' the boom.

Back in 1925 when we had the first Florida boom ever'- body went crazy. Land was sold and resold at prices a feller wouldn't believe even today when the price of land has again gone higher than the Georgia pines. Uncle Winton had always bought a little land as he were able to and he sold a chunk of it just at the right time. He never would say just what he got for that six hundred and forty acres except that it "brought more'n a high stack of otter hides." It didn't make him a rich man compared to some of them Brandybilts and such but he weren't hurtin' none and he left Aunt Jo pretty well fixed.

A heap of folks bought high and held on too long but the ones who sold at the right time made a killin'. I heered a story about a old boy who sold ten thousand acres of plain old palmetto scrub for two million dollars. His daddy had left him this land or he wouldn't of had nothin' because he weren't too bright.

All his friends said, "Fred, you'd better get you a manager to look after all that money or you'll sure lose it." So he got him a manager and the manager took him up to New York. They went to a couple of ball games but Fred didn't care about them. They went to some shows and even went to the opera but Fred didn't care nothin' for that. They went to the race track and old Fred pitched a fit over them runnin' horses. Boy, he liked 'em.

"Buy me some of them runnin' horses," he told his man- ager. So the manager did. And every horse began to win and the money rolled in.

Then they went up to Saratoga and he went crazy about them trottin' horses. "Buy me a bunch of them trottin' horses," he told his manager. And the manager did. And they all began to win and the money kept rollin' in.

So then they went down to Mexico and he seen some dog fights. "Man, I like them fightin' dogs," he said. "Buy me some of them." So the manager did. And every dog was whippin' the other dog and the money began rollin' in from that too.

Then they went up to Las Vegas and visited one of them

high-class sportin' houses. "How many girls you got here?"
Fred asked the madam.

"Thirty," she said.

"Trot 'em out here and let me look at 'em." So she did, and
they was all near about the prettiest things he'd ever seen.

"Buy me this place," he told his manager. So the manager
did. And the money began rollin' in from his sportin' women.
Likewise from his trottin' horses and his runnin' horses and his
fightin' dogs. By this time he was worth about five million
dollars and decided to go back home for a spell where one of
his old buddies said, "Fred, come on in and have a snort and
tell me about your trips."

"You know I never did drink," Fred told him.

"Well, you don't know what you're missin'," the friend said.
"With all the money you got, you ought to celebrate."

So he did. And he liked it and went on a big drunk and fired
his manager and put his runnin' horses to trottin' and his
trottin' horses to runnin' and his fightin' dogs to sportin' and his
sportin' women to fightin' and went broke in sixty days! This
story sure would have tickled Uncle Winton.

Even way back yonder when times was tough Uncle managed somehow to keep addin' a little land. He sure believed in
that real estate. "Everything else is just ' 'maginary estate,'"
he'd say.

The Epps place is down the River from us at a bend where
there were a high bluff lookin' out across the marsh toward the
Gulf. Panther Creek joins up with the main River just a short
ways past there. It sure is pretty property and I remember one
day when I were down there that a feller drove up in a big
shiny black Cadillac automobile and just set there in the yard
for a spell puffin' on a big fat cigar. Uncle Winton walked over
and asked him, "What can I do for you, Mister?"

"Pretty view you got," the feller said. "Wouldn't mind
ownin' it. Is it for sale?"

"Might be," Uncle told him.

"I'll give you two thousand dollars for the river-front land,"
the feller said. "You can keep the house."

"Well, now," Uncle said. "I'll tell you what I'll do. You come
back tomorrow with a wheelbarrow and I'll sell you two thousand dollars worth of it." Uncle weren't about to sell ary foot of
that land. He hung on to it rain or shine.

Of course us folks in the Hammock didn't have no such hard times durin' the depression as folks livin' over in the sand hills—places like Yalaha and Tavares and such. Why, Bert Hunter told me that near about everybody over there toted a bamboo moss-pullin' pole and a gopher-hook in their cars. He said if they hooked out a big gopher they'd trade it for groceries or a gallon of gas and take their change in little gophers. He said they knowed when things began to get better and was on the upgrade when a rabbit would run acrost the road and there'd be only three men after it!

The reason us folks in the Hammock never suffered so much hardship were on account of all the fish and oysters and swamp cabbage and squirrels, turkeys, ducks and deer we had to eat. A feller can't hardly make out on pine cones and black-jack acorns and gophers, which is about all they had over east of us. I reckon I'd better explain what a gopher is—at least what we call a gopher. It's a land turtle. Yankees call it a box tortoise and it digs holes about the size of a stovepipe. That's why them sand hill folks toted gopher-hooks. Bert said everybody were pretty honest, though, and if he pulled one out with a neighbor's brand on it he put it back!

We never did have enough Spanish moss in the Hammock to make it worthwhile to pull, so I can't tell you much about that. It don't grow too heavy in our part of the Hammock but over east there's patches of hammock with big old live oaks just loaded down with moss. Folks cut long bamboo poles and left some sprouts on the end so they could poke it up into a bunch of moss, twist it around and pull down a big gob near about every time. You'd see a whole family workin' under one tree, the grown folks pullin' and the kids gatherin' up and pilin'. Some people sold it green and some taken it home and hung it on wires to "cure." The outside would rot off and leave the wiry, black core which they used to make mattress stuffin' and auto seats in them days. Cured moss brought more than green, but I disremember what the prices were. I never did pull none—to sell, that is.

Back in them days we didn't have no welfare or unemployment payments or nothin' and it was "root, hog or die." Speakin' of welfare, I heered the other day about a woman who come into the office claimin' ten dependents and she had 'em with her.

"How old are they?" the government feller asked.

"Well, them two is three years old and them two is four years old and them two is five years old and them two is seven years old and them two is eight years old."

"Great day!" the government feller said. "Did you have twins every time?"

"No, sir," she told him. "Sometimes we didn't have nothin' at all."

28 Deputy Driggers

By the time Kelly were twenty-two years old he had growed to be six four and weighed around two forty. He taken after his Uncle Tarl but then his mother's folks had all been big old rugged knockers too. Everybody in the county knowed what a fine shot he had got to be—pistol, rifle or shotgun—so it weren't no surprise when Sheriff Tompkins asked him to go on as a deputy. And it sure enough weren't no surprise to me when he accepted.

I went up to Bronson with him when he were sworn in and remember Sheriff Tompkins sayin', "Now Driggers, you're a big, strong, young feller but I want to get one thing into your head right now. There's field hands in this county who are bigger men than you are and I don't want to hear of your scufflin' hand-to-hand with 'em. If you have trouble, use your gun. I don't want you killed."

I never forgot that but I reckon Kelly did because the third year he was deputy just such a happenstance come about. One of the loggin' crew cuttin' for the Cypress Company got in a ruckus one night at a juke over near Crystal River. He killed another black man with a knife and the Sheriff sent one of the other deputies to pick up Kelly and go after him. I just rode

along with 'em. This other deputy was an older feller named
Slim Jallup. He weren't a big man but he had a reputation as
bein' jumpy. Not exactly scary, but the kind of feller who gets
right keyed up when there's trouble. His voice goes up a couple
of notches and he'll grab for his gun and start shootin' at the
drop of a hat. I don't mean shootin' wild, because he's a good
shot, but shootin' quick . . . maybe too quick.

Deputy Jallup carried a .38 Smith and Wesson and, like I
said, were handy with it. They said that when he first got it he
went into Watt's Hardware and showed it to the feller who
clerked there—I disremember his name—and asked to check
and see if the same cartridges would do for it that worked in a
Colt .38 Special. The clerk got out a box of thirty-eights and
tried one in the cylinder of Slim's new Smith and Wesson—in
the first chamber to the right of the hammer. It fitted perfect.
Then he raised that pistol and aimed it at a picture on the wall
and said, "She sure is a sweet-pointin' piece of plunder." Then
he pulled the trigger on that double-action gun and *pow!* A .38
Special makes a heap of noise in a closed-in store and the
manager come a-boilin' out of his glassed-in office. He thought
a dynamite cap had gone off in the storeroom.

The trouble of it was that the cylinder of a Smith and
Wesson double-action revolver turns back to the left when you
pull the trigger and a Colt turns to the right. That clerk weren't
used to nothin' but a Colt pistol I reckon.

I don't mean to be confusin' when I talk about hand guns,
callin' 'em pistols one time and revolvers another time, so I'll
try to explain it. All revolvers are pistols but not all pistols are
revolvers. A revolver has got a revolvin' cylinder but some
pistols don't. They ain't got cylinders, but magazines, and the
action works by the force of the explodin' gases—firin' a bullet,
throwin' out the empty case, peelin' another one off the
magazine and settin' it ready to go in the barrel under the firin'
pin. It really should be called a "auto loader" but us Crackers
usually just call 'em automatics.

My brother Tarl learnt to use one of them .45 automatics
in the big war and taught Kelly to use it. Kelly liked it so good
that he ordered himself one of 'em. That's what he was carryin'
the night him and Slim went over to Crystal River to get that
logger.

If they had of took as long to find him as I have took tellin' about Slim and his gun, the feller would of done been across the Georgia line. But they didn't. They found him with a bottle of whiskey in one hand and a switchblade knife in the other—standin' everybody off and darin' 'em to try him. When Slim and Kelly got there, Slim drawed his gun and told the logger to drop the knife. He were a great big feller, over six feet, built like a bull and so black charcoal would of left a white mark on him. All he done when Slim spoke to him was to reach down and bust off the whiskey bottle about halfway down from the neck. He were holdin' it by the neck and what were left made a jaggedy, vicious-lookin' weapon.

"I ain't goin' to no jail house," he told us.

"Throw down the knife and the bottle and get into the back of this car," Slim said.

"I ain't gettin' into no po-leece car," the logger said.

"Well, now," Slim told him, "the ambulance can take you to the morgue or this car can take you to jail."

About this time Kelly spoke up. It seemed like he knowed the feller and called him by name. "Enos," he said, "didn't your daddy work for my Uncle Winton Epps one time?"

"That's right," the black man said. "And I know you and your daddy too and I don't want no trouble with you. You keep out of this. I done killed a man but I done it in self-defense. He had a razor and meant to cut my throat. You stand back and keep out of it."

"I can't do that, Enos," Kelly told him. "I'm an officer of the law. You have killed a man and you'll have to stand trial." All the time he had been talkin', Kelly had been sort of easin' up closer till he weren't more'n a couple of steps away.

It all happened so fast that it even surprised me—faster'n bats can do it and they do it flyin'. Kelly moved in and grabbed that feller's wrists and pushed him to the wall. With that Slim stepped in and fired two shots right under Kelly's raised right arm. The logger, Enos, sagged and slid to the ground and Kelly whirled around. I never seen him so mad.

"What'd you do that for?" he hollered at Slim.

"Because you were fixin' to get cut to pieces," Slim said, his voice real high-pitched.

"Man, what are you talkin' about?" Kelly hollered. "I had him. Couldn't you see that? I had him."

It all happened so fast that it even surprised me—

"You just thought you had him," Slim said. "If'n he'd got a hand loose he'd of cut your heart out."

"He wasn't about to get a hand loose," Kelly said. "I told you I had him. There wasn't no call to kill him."

I hadn't said nothin' till then but now I said, "Well boys, what's done is done. Let's take him to Bronson."

The Sheriff had gone to bed but we woke him and told him the story. Whether he were mad at bein' woke up or just takin' sides against Kelly I don't know but he sure gave him a fit.

"I told you not to get in no hand-to-hand scuffles with nobody," he told him. "You disobeyed my orders."

"Well, they're the last ones I'll disobey," Kelly said. "Here's your damn badge. It's lucky it ain't got a bullet hole in it. And me too!" With that he went a-stormin' out of the house. Slim Jallup followed us out into the yard and tried again to excuse the shootin'.

"Don't say nothin' more to me, Jallup, unless you're ready to do some more shootin'. Because I'll stomp you into the ground!" Kelly warned him.

Slim started to say somethin' but I interrupted him. "Better forget it, Mr. Jallup. Kelly's right worked up just now and I doubt if he'll even listen to his own daddy."

"What have *you* got to say, Dad?" Kelly asked, whirlin' toward me.

"Nothin' much, son," I told him, "exceptin' that I would of done just what you done and I don't blame you at all. If you said you had him, you had him, and there weren't no need for any shootin'."

Well, when the word got around that Kelly Driggers had quit his job and why, folks raised more hell than the gator did when the pond went dry. Most of the old-timers backed Slim Jallup, who claimed the logger was resistin' arrest with a deadly weapon and that he shot him just to protect his fellow officer. Other folks, includin' a lot of Yankees who had moved to Florida, raised a big stink about the poor black man bein' a victim of police brutality.

As for me, I didn't hardly know what to think . . . I had been there and seen it happen. I knew my own boy—that he was a big, powerful youngster but on the other hand he had holt of a dangerous feller who were much of a man himself and I had to remember that Kelly's left hand had had holt of

the logger's right wrist. And there's usually a heap of difference in the strength of right against left unless one of 'em is a
lefty. It might of been that Kelly couldn't of kept his holt and
that the logger would have got that knife into my boy any
second.

The Coroner's verdict was justifiable homicide, which I
reckon everybody expected but which sure didn't satisfy everybody. I believe that right then and there Kelly decided that he
was goin' to run for the office of high sheriff against Sheriff
Tompkins and beat him if it were the last thing he ever done.

The whole thing caused a heap of disagreement in our own
family. Etta was tickled to death to have her brother out of the
law business. "Sooner or later he'd be killed because he's big
and strong and not scared of anything or anybody," she said to
her mother.

"Oh, I don't know about that," Loofy said. "He's a pretty
level-headed youngster—as big and strong as his Uncle Tarl
but not near so hot-tempered. I think he was well suited to the
job and I hope he'll change his mind and go back to work."

Jim thought different. "He'll never do it. No way—no time.
Not as long as Sheriff Tompkins backs up that hair-triggered
deputy. Maybe Kel will run for the high sheriff's job himself. If
he does, I'll sure tear my shirt for him!"

David, as a feller could expect, started giggin' Kel soon as
he heered about it. "The big law man," he sneered. "He holds
'em while his partner shoots 'em."

"Son," I told him, "if you don't want to get bad hurt, you'd
better lay off your brother just now. He ain't in no mood to be
messed with."

But David kept on and kept on till Kelly jumped him. It
happened right out in the back yard one evenin' just before
supper time. David knowed from past experience he didn't
have no chance to stand up to Kelly bare fists so right away he
went to a knife. He got to make one slash with it before Kelly
had him down and was a-settin' on him holdin' his wrists.

"I had him," Kelly said, "just like I got you but there ain't
nobody goin' to shoot *you*. You're too sorry to shoot—a lyin',
thievin', tricky cur dog that don't belong to be called a
Driggers!" David kept strugglin', tryin' to hit his brother with
his left hand but it weren't no use.

Of course Loofy heered the commotion and come a-runnin'

out. "Billy Driggers," she said to me, "what do you mean just a-standin' there and lettin' your own sons fight in your own yard?"

"There ain't a better place for 'em to fight and David had it comin' to him," I told her.

Etta had run out and were a-beggin' Kelly to let David up.

"When he gives you that knife," Kelly said.

Well, I weren't surprised when he done just that. She could always do more with David than anybody and were always takin' his part against everybody. Now she reached down and picked up the knife where he'd dropped it and Kelly turned him loose and got up off him. There were a little red beginnin' to show on Kelly's shirt but the cut were shallow and had hardly drawed blood.

David didn't say nothin' to nobody—not even his sister—but just got up and walked off toward the settlement. He never looked back and we didn't hear nothin' from him or about him for near about two weeks. Then we learnt that he had enlisted in the army and got sent off to Camp Blanding. After a month or so he sent a card to his sister and said he had been transferred up to Fort Bragg in North Carolina.

"Well," I told Etta, "at least he's in a place with a name that fits him right to a T."

29 Kelly Meets a She Bear

Kelly met up with Ursula Staunton while he were deputy. He had to serve some papers on her daddy, Colonel Whitmore Staunton, who had bought the old Revels house and grove. I never could figure whether the Colonel were a Yankee or not. He come from Kentucky and sometimes he talked one way and some another; but he were a peppery little feller and spoke his mind. His daughter were sort of a block off the old chip, as Kelly found out. She were a big girl, near about six feet and her name meant "she bear," accordin' to Loofy, who looked it up quick as she heered it because it were a new name to all of us.

There weren't no doubt about *her* bein' a Yankee. She had went to one of the top ladies' colleges up North but I can't 'call the name to save my soul, though it's one of the commonest of all names. Anyhow, she had strong ideas about most everything and I just couldn't figure my boy Kelly with a ring in his nose. Of course, a feller could just look at this gal and see what Kelly seen, which were a great big, beautiful body with everything where it ought to be in just the right amount. I couldn't blame him and I remembered the way I had felt about his mother, Loofy Henry. She hadn't been no shy little flat-chested thing neither. I could of looked at this gal and done a little lustin' without half tryin', so I could understand how Kelly must of been messermerized—him bein' just twenty-five years old and all.

There had been some fireworks that first time they met, though. Some feller were tryin' to file a lien on the Revels property, claimin' he hadn't been paid for a roofin' job he had done for the Revelses before the sale. Old Colonel Staunton jumped all over Kelly about it and so did the gal. Kelly kept his temper, though, accordin' to what he told me and just said, "My job is only to serve the papers, sir. You can settle the matter in court."

Of course it never went to court and old lady Revels paid the feller what were owin' him. I don't know what excuse Kelly used for goin' back out there but he sure found one right soon and it weren't no time till he were datin' her pretty regular.

Like I said, Ursula had gone to one of them fancy women's colleges and it sure did hack her for Kelly to talk like a backwoods Cracker. "Kelly," she'd say, "you've been through high school and you've been to college yourself and you know better than to talk like a field hand."

"Oh now, honey," Kelly would say, "most of my dealin's are with country people and I don't want folks to think I'm tryin' to put on airs. I just naturally drift into talkin' with folks the way they talk."

Well, she tried to understand but there was some things she couldn't bear. One was like when Kelly was tellin' her about a shoot-out. He'd said that the robber had been "layin'" behind a car.

"You mean 'lying' behind the car," Ursula said.

"Sure," Kelly told her. "He'd been lyin' all the time—behind the car and everywhere else . . ."

"That's not what I mean and you know it!" Ursula snapped at him. "You people say, 'I'm tired and I think I'll lay down a while.' That's wrong. You *lay* down a book or you *lay* your weary bones down. You must have an object."

"Sure," Kelly said. "The object is to lay down."

"Kelly Driggers, you know perfectly well what I mean and you know perfectly well that I'm just trying to get you to use the English language correctly."

"I know it, honey, but the trouble of it is that *most* folks use it wrong and don't want to be told different. But if you've just got to correct 'em, I'll tell you a little story that you can use to explain it. An old feller and his wife were sittin' in the kitchen in their rockin' chairs and finally the old lady said, 'What's the matter, Elmer?' He heaved a big sigh and said, 'I just can't help thinkin' about our daughter Rose layin' in the cemetery.' 'I know it,' the old lady said, 'and I feel just as bad about it as you do. I could almost wish she were dead!' "

"Now, Kelly Driggers, that's a dirty story and you know perfectly well I'd never use it."

"Well then," Kelly said, "I reckon you'd just better leave it lay!"

Not long after that Kelly and Ursula was settin' on our porch steps peelin' and cuttin' up some sour oranges for Loofy to make up into marmalade. We had a tree growin' right up by the porch that Loofy had brought from the Henry place when we were first married. A lemon is sweet by comparison with one of them oranges and the air was heavy with the smell of 'em—strong but pleasant. Directly, old Drum come out from under the house and stretched and yawned before he trotted off across the yard.

"Whew!" said Ursula. "When you can smell a dog over these oranges you know he's rank. Kelly, you've just got to wash him."

Drum had killed a skunk a night or two before and when he passed by a feller could tell it.

"It'll just make it stronger to wet him," Kelly said.

"Well, do something!" Ursula said. "That dog really smells bad."

"No," Kelly told her. "He smells good. His odor may be unpleasant but he smells *good*—because he went right on huntin' and cold-trailed and jumped a fox the other night not thirty minutes after the skunk had plastered him. So you see he *smells* real good. I wish you would be more careful, honey, about the way you use the English language. The verb *smell* means to use your nose to pick up a scent or odor."

"You're right, but how do you know all that?" Ursula asked.

"Well," Kelly told her, "I read it in a book Uncle Winton had brought from North Carolina. It was his great-grandaddy's book and it was printed in England a long time ago. There was a whole chapter in it where this English lord was writin' to a friend to tell him how to get together a pack of foxhounds, train 'em and work 'em. He wrote that he was real particular about usin' the words 'smell' and 'scent' in their rightful meanin' and he told about a friend who spent most of his time in his stables and kennels so that he carried the odor of horses and dogs pretty strong. One night they were all at the opera, settin' in a box and one of the other fellers sniffed and said, 'Sir, you smell.'

"But the friend just smiled and said, 'I beg your pardon, sir. It is *you* who smell. *I* stink.' "

"Well, Drum stinks if that's the way you want it," Ursula said, laughin'.

"It ain't the way I want it," Kelly told her. "It's the way it is."

"All right, smarty," she said. "I give up. But I'd like to read that book."

"I'll see can I get it for you," Kelly said. "It must be in the house somewhere. Aunt Jo had it for a long time and promised it to Grandma Driggers. I reckon it's a right valuable piece of plunder by this time—if the roaches ain't eat it up."

"Haven't eaten," Ursula said.

Before Kelly could answer a dog fight started out by the road where old Drum had waylaid a passin' cur dog so I never did find out who won the word battle. But I said to myself, "That young lady better ease off pickin' on Kelly. He's a Driggers and don't none of us have the longest fuse in the world nor lead well with a ring in our nose!"

About a week later she come over to the house again and brought Loofy a mess of what she called artichokes—said a classmate from California had brought 'em to her and she wanted us to share 'em. There wasn't but three so it were a good thing everybody wasn't home. They looked like green pine cones and tasted to me sort of like a cross between a swamp cabbage and nothin'. After they were boiled they sort of opened out and a feller pulled a section loose, dipped it in hot butter and rasped off the meat with his front teeth. You could only eat down so far until you come to the part that give 'em their name—the chokers. That part weren't nothin' but little stickers like what's on a prickly pear and you throwed it away.

Far as I was concerned, you could have started throwin' before the cookin'. But I'll be John Browned if Kelly didn't say

he *liked* the dern things. That shows what bein' in love will do
for a feller! He even claimed they helped a feller's manhood.
He didn't need no help and it would of took more than eatin'
artichokes to of helped me.

After dinner Ursula asked about the old English book. We
had found it and Loofy brought it to the table. "Look at it all
you want," I told 'em, "but don't get no gravy or nothin' on it."

Well, you should have heered that gal Ursula carry on about
that book. The name of it were *Thoughts Upon Hunting* and it
were wrote by a feller named Teter Beckford. I hadn't read too
much in it myself because the people who printed it didn't
seem to know a "s" from a "f" for one thing. But she could read
right along in it.

" Seventeen hundred and eighty-four!" she said. "Isn't that
wonderful? Just think of it, Mr. Driggers, this little volume is
three times as old as you are!" And the way she said that
sounded like I was one of them redwood trees or somethin'.
"And look here," Ursula went on, "published by E. Easton,
Piccadilly."

"Like me," Kelly said.

"What do you mean?" she asked him.

"I pick a dilly too!" he said, kissin' the top of her head. That
were too much for me and I got up to leave the table but not
before Ursula said, "Now, Kelly, that's a poor pun and, in case
you don't know it, the very, very lowest form of humor."
She was still carryin' on the lecture when I left the room.
One of these days, I thought to myself, she's a-goin' to start
tellin' *me* how to talk. That day arrived a heap sooner than I
figured.

One evenin' after supper when we was just loungin' around
in the kitchen Ursula said, "Mr. Driggers, I notice that you
have a most original way of using the verb *to be*. One time
you'll say 'he were' and the next time 'he was.' Which do you
prefer?"

"Whichever is handiest and seems to fit best," I said. "It
were always a question with me ever since I was a little
skeester."

"There you go!" she said. "Right then you used the verb
erroneously."

"If by that you mean wrongly," I told her, "I reckon you're
right."

"That's exactly what I mean," she said. "The past tense of *to be* is *were* or *was* depending upon the preceding pronoun. For example, I *was;* you *were;* he, she or it *was;* we *were;* you *were;* they *were.*"

"I see," I said. "Everybody were."

"No-no-no," she said. "*Everybody* is really singular. It means every person so it would have to be everybody *was.*"

"Now, young lady," I told her, "if you want to give English lessons to my boy Kelly, you go right ahead. With all the plans he's got he'll need 'em. But my way of talkin' suits me fine and if you can't understand it, I'm sorry."

"Oh, I understand you perfectly, Mr. Driggers," she said.

"Good!" I said. And that were that.

30 The Wedding, the Honeymoon & Aunt Effie's Secret

Peccadillo Eppsii.

(Collard Pecadillo.)

But in spite of her fancy talk and Yankeefied ways, Ursula were a good woman and anybody could see she near about worshipped Kelly. And, of course, he were plumb foolish about her. So it didn't surprise nobody when they announced they was gettin' hitched. Colonel Staunton give 'em a right fine weddin' out at the old Revels place. He had got some grass growin' in the front yard and had tables and chairs set out there.

Loofy went over and helped with the party and there must of been near about a hundred folks there. The big house were fixed up real pretty and there was some big murials on the wall. The Colonel explained that his daughter had a natural bend for art and had studied it at college and had done some right good pictures. The murials showed the river and trees and some cows layin' around in the shade—real natural. But some of her pictures sure was hard to figure out. I remember one that looked like a fried egg havin' a runnin' fit. And there were several pictures of folks with three eyes and such as that. Her father said she were just followin' the style of Dolly somebody-or-other. There was one of a woman with two mouths and one eye down underneath her jawbone. When I seen that one I thought about what L. K. Hooper said one time when we was drivin' through his pasture.

"See that cow over yonder, Billy?" he said. "Well, that cow has five tits."

We drove up close and I'll be derned if she didn't. I'd never seen that before and said so.

"It happens now and then," L. K. said. "Even with people. I know a gal once that had three."

"Where was the third one at?" I asked him.

"Right between her shoulder blades," he said. "She weren't much to look at but she sure were fun to dance with!"

Well I'll bet there ain't no artist could of painted *her*—I thought to myself.

Kelly and Ursula went on a honeymoon trip to Daytona Beach for a week and when they come back they said it were wonderful over there.

"It's wonderful anywhere, son," I told him, "especially at the beach when you're twenty-five. But like your Uncle Winton says about sex, 'There ain't nothin' a feller can get further behind on and get caught up on quicker.' So, like your grandma used to say, 'Let your moderation be known to all men.'"

"It don't concern all men . . . just me," Kelly said. "And that ocean air is stimulatin'."

"I know it," I told him, "and I've a good will to try a second honeymoon over there myself but I'm scared I'd be like the old couple I heered about who went back thirty years later to try to relive their honeymoon. They went to bed and after a while the old lady said, 'Honey, thirty years ago you was so eager you bit my ear.' The old feller jumped right up out of bed and started for the bathroom. 'Where you goin'?' she asked. 'To get my teeth!' he told her." That tickled Kelly and he just started to tell me a good one when here come Loofy down the hall and he had to quit. She never would permit none of the kids to tell what she called "dirty" stories in front of her.

When they come back from their trip, Kelly and Ursula stayed on at the Colonel's. Mrs. Staunton had died four years before and he were glad for the company; and the Revels house were a big old place with a heap of room. It weren't far over to it from our house and the young folks spent near about as much time with us as they did at home.

One day when we was just lolly-gaggin' around on the porch watchin' the River go by Ursula said to me, "Father Driggers, I am thinking of buying one of those two-piece bathing suits that shows some bare skin between the upper and lower parts. Do you think people around here would look askance at me, if I should appear in such a garb?"

Now, to begin with I didn't like her callin' me "Father Driggers" like I were some kind of a priest. Most daughters-in-law around here would say, "Daddy Driggers" or "Daddy Billy" or maybe just "Big Daddy," if they had young-uns. The kids' own daddy would be "Daddy" and *his* daddy would be called "*Big* Daddy." But Ursula never would go along with our customs too much about nothin', though she were friendly enough and makin' Kelly a fine wife. So I tried to be patient with her.

"Honey," I said, "I've heered about 'castin' a spell' and 'flingin' a cravin'' but 'lookin' a skance' is a new one on me. Whatever in this world does that mean?"

"It means raise their eyebrows and be shocked or scandalized," she said.

"You can bet on it!" I told her. "If that's lookin' a skance, you can be sure we got a heap of skance lookers around this neighborhood."

I could just imagine what old Preacher Goodson would say. He were so strict with his own family that when he seen one of his girls cross her legs and show some calf, he'd take his cane and hook it around her ankle and uncross 'em. Of course this were a long time ago and I had to laugh when I thought about what some of them old-timers would say and do today. If Preacher Goodson had used his cane when all them real short dresses came in, he'd have revealed the whole world at once. And I wondered what my ma would have said, if she had lived to read the papers today. Why, they had a referendum over on the east coast somewheres on whether to let women keep on goin' bathin' with no tops at all! It were lucky they voted agin it or I'd of had to go plumb over there to see it before I'd of believed it.

I reckon everybody's got his own ideas about raisin' kids and what's too strict and what's not strict enough. Some folks is very strict about what they do or don't do on Sunday and I heered about a young preacher up in the city, just out of preacher college, who got a call to go preach at the big rich church across town from where he lived. He were poor, so he taken a street car. It stopped near about in front of the church and when he got off and walked up the sidewalk to the big stone front steps, all the elders was standin' around havin' their after-breakfast cigars and passin' around the latest gossip. They was kind of cool to him and he noticed they was absent from the service.

"What happened to all the elders?" he asked the janitor after church was over.

"Huh," the janitor said. "You don't think they'd stay and hear a feller preach who'd ride the street car on Sunday, do you?"

There's other folks who ain't strict about nothin' but matters of health. Anything else goes—just do whatever you take a notion to, so long as it don't endanger your health. Like Mrs. Ben Lasher who come home and found her daughter and my boy David makin' love in the front yard. They wasn't even engaged but still Mrs. Lasher just hollered out, "Mary Mae, are you crazy? Y'all git up off that damp ground and go in the house. Do you want to catch your death of cold? Don't you know your pores is all open?"

Another evenin' when Kelly and Ursula was over to the house I told 'em about a little poem I had wrote. Way back yonder, when Morna had got onto me about my dog poems, I had bought me a book and studied up on the subject. It showed all about accents and iambic feet and such as that. Some of it I couldn't understand but there weren't nobody I would ask because I didn't want nobody to know about what I were up to. But it were fun thinkin' up rhymes for words and I could see why Uncle Wint had wrote so many poems.

My spellin' ain't never been the very best and what bumfuzzles me most is the crazy way some words in our language is wrote. Sometimes there'll be one word that's spoke the same but has three different meanin's and is spelt three different ways. And sometimes it'll have three different meanin's and be spelt the same way for everything. So what about the poor foreign feller tryin' to learn how to *say* all our words irregardless of how they may be spelt.

Just doodlin' around one day I had wrote out this little poem that sort of shows what I'm a-talkin' about.

> *A tiny little nit on a tiny little gnat,*
> *There couldn't hardly be nothin' smaller than that,*
> *Unless it would be*
> *Somethin' so wee*
> *As a tiny little knot on the nit on the gnat!*

Of course I had to part company with the book when it come to some things—like rhymin' a word to another by the way it *looks* and not by the way it sounds. Old Delano used to rhyme *again* with *rain* but there ain't hardly nobody else does, includin' me. I say *again* to rhyme with *Ben* or *den* or *Len* or *men* and so on down the alphabet plumb to *wen* and *yen*. Ever now and then I get a sudden yen to write a rhyme, like this'n about clothes. I hauled it out of my pocket and passed it over to Ursula, wonderin' how she'd like it.

> *Silks and satins suit the Latins,*
> *Woolen and tweeds the Scotch,*
> *But cotton covers American men*
> *From head to toe to crotch.*

"Well," Ursula said when she had read it, "you've certainly been hiding your light under a bushel."

"A bushel of what?" I asked her.

"I'd just rather not say," she told me. "Since you have so often expressed your opinion of women who use coarse language. And while we're on the subject of clothes, what do you yourself prefer—as a representative Florida Cracker?"

"Cotton, naturally," I told her. "I like the feel of cotton. And then, too, I remember a story Senator Spessard Holland told me once on a huntin' trip about a member of Congress from Mississippi who visited one of them nudist camps and looked around and shook his head and said, 'Don't it just beat hell what some folks will do to keep from usin' our Southern cotton!'"

Ursula laughed and said, "Cotton's fine for summertime. But what about the cold weather when we get what you call a 'blue Norther' blowing in?"

"Then I want wool," I told her. "The feller at the store tried to sell me some new-fangled stuff that he said were just as warm as wool but I said, 'If that's true, why ain't it on a sheep?' "

While Ursula were over to the house I showed her some of Uncle Wint's poems and I remember she really took on about one of 'em that went:

> *I knowed a gal named Emma Drawdy.*
> *Oh lawdy, lawdy, lawdy, lawdy!*
> *I knowed a gal named Ethel Hubbell.*
> *Oh trouble, trouble, trouble, trouble!*

> *I knowed another gal named Lou*
> *And there ain't nothin' she don't do.*
> *I knowed one named Patricia Luffin*
> *But that old gal just won't do nothin'!*

> *And some are tall and some are short,*
> *They'll make a feller paw and snort.*
> *And some are fat and some are lean,*
> *And some are sweet and some are mean.*

> *The trouble of it is, I reckon,*
> *That when a woman starts to beckon,*
> *There ain't no way a man can tell*
> *Till after she has rung his bell.*

Ursula shook her head and said she had no idea that Uncle Wint had been such a Lothario, whoever he was—some Eytalian from the sound of it.

One day I heered Loofy and Ursula discussin' Uncle Winton and what they called his peccadillos. I never knowed him to have any of them things, but he used to tell about a real feisty little old wild hog they had out in Texas that they called a collard peckery—I reckon because it loved collards. And of course I knowed what a armadillo is. So I suppose a peccadillo is just a cross of some kind. I asked Ursula about this and she just laughed and said, "They turn out that way sometimes.

"When and where did your uncle ever encounter all those women?" she asked.

"Oh, he'd been to Chicago and Macon and Atlanta and a heap of places. Some of 'em encountered *him*. He told us that one of them gals up in Chicago tried to get smart with him. She said a feller should invite a gal up to his room to see his etchin's. He thought at first she had said 'itchin's' but she explained they was pictures. He told her he didn't have no etchin's with him and come off in such a hurry he forgot to leave any at home. 'What about all them pretty ones of Andrew Jackson I seen in your wallet?' she wanted to know.

" 'Bein' a Illinois Yankee,' he told her, 'I reckon you'd settle for old Abe. But I ain't in no spendin' mood and I've done checked out of my room anyhow.' "

"It's too bad poor Aunt Effie couldn't have written something to defend herself," Ursula said.

This were what I had been waitin' for so I told her to just relax and listen. Then I fished around in the bottom of that old shoe box and brought out a sheet of old yellow-lined paper.

"This here," I told her, "is a genuwine, hand-wrote poem by Aunt Effie herself. It's signed 'Euphemia Epps' and this is what it says,

> *"Winton Epps won't fix the steps,*
> *Nor either mend the fence,*
> *But still I stay and people say*
> *I just ain't got good sense.*
>
> *"His goats and hogs and huntin' dogs*
> *Is all he seems to care for,*
> *Or chasin' gals with drunken pals,*
> *I don't know what I'm here for.*
>
> *"He likes to spit, his teeth don't fit,*
> *There's always somethin' ails him.*
> *But he'll get well in spite of hell*
> *Unless his whiskey fails him.*
>
> *"He has more hair than ary bear*
> *And not all on his head.*
> *His nose is long, his breath is strong,*
> *But he is good in bed.*

"What good is that unless he's at
The proper place to do it.
So he should be at home with me
Or I will make him rue it."

"And did she make him rue it?" Ursula asked.

"Did you ever see her lip draw down?" I said. "But Uncle couldn't no more resist a pretty gal than a little boy can keep from pickin' his nose in church."

"Did Aunt Effie fool around any?" Ursula wanted to know. "Is that the way she made him rue it?"

"Knowin' my Uncle Winton—I doubt it," I told her. "That would of been right dangerous. I think she just picked and nagged at him, though I do remember there used to be a feed salesman that would come by now and then."

"Where in the world did you ever get that poem?" Ursula asked. "I just can't believe it."

"I'll never tell you," I said. "No more than that it come in the mail after she died. And I'll never tell nobody else." And I haven't to this day.

31 The Election of Sheriff Driggers

When Kelly announced for Sheriff there were a heap of procedures to go through over to the courthouse and considerable money to be spent for posters, handbills and cards and announcements in the *Tribune*, the *Chronicle* and the *Gazette*. We all had a pretty good idea of how folks was lined up but Kelly drove around and made a lot of speeches anyhow. And he were good and could make folks laugh.

I remember his tellin' about the time old Champ Clark come to Tampa and were listenin' to a young politician make a speech. This feller told how he had been Clerk of the Court and as Clerk of the Court he saved the people thousands of dollars and then he had been elected Sheriff. As Sheriff he had stopped most all the crime and then he had been elected to the House of Representatives and as a Member he had introduced many important bills and bragged on how he got 'em passed into laws. Now he were runnin' for the Senate and said if he was elected he would do some wonderful things. "And folks," he finished up, "I'm goin' higher!"

Somebody asked old Champ Clark what he thought about the speech and old Champ said, "Well, he told us what he's been and what he's done and what he's goin' to be and what he's goin' to do. And he says he's goin' higher. He's just like a dern monkey . . . the higher he goes the plainer he shows his backside!"

This story always drawed a big laugh but Kelly could be real serious too, when it come to serious and important things; like the night he were talkin' to a crowd over at the turpentine still. He noticed there was quite a few black people among 'em so he said, "And I want to tell somethin' to all you colored folks. If you vote for me for Sheriff and I am elected, it don't mean that next month all your problems will be gone. Your grandaddies and grammas was slaves for fifty years and you can't change all that in fifty days.

"But I can promise you one thing. When I'm elected you'll get fair treatment in the courthouse. You'll find me in my office ready to talk to you. And nobody—I mean *nobody* will mistreat you.

"And let me tell you another thing. Folks who break the law—black, white or Indian—will be brought into jail. My daddy and my uncle and me ain't never backed away from nobody or nothin' and y'all know it. And you know what happened to Enos Rhodes and how it happened and you know it weren't my doin'. I quit my job as deputy because of that and I'm askin' to become Sheriff so there won't be no more of that sort of thing. But it wouldn't of happened if Enos hadn't of defied the law. So don't defy the law.

"Now, I know some of you folks are bitter about slavery times and all that and some are tellin' the young folks to hate the white man because he carried your ancestors away into slavery. But don't forget that a heap of times one African tribe raided another tribe and captured slaves which they sold to the white traders. In some places over there Africans still got slaves of their own. So if old man Norton's folks hadn't of been sold to a white man in the U.S.A., Ben Norton wouldn't have wound up a free man makin' his own 'shine and livin' high on fat-back and collard greens right here in this county. He might be right back there cuttin' down thorn trees to make a fence to keep out the leopards and other varmints. Maybe someday slavery will be gone from over there like it is from over here and that'll be good."

When Kelly had mentioned old man Norton a few of the older folks had laughed and nodded their heads, so Kelly

stayed right on that subject. "And speakin' of old man Norton,"
he said, "I want to read you a little poem I found in a shoe box
up in the attic of my great Uncle Winton Epps. Some of you old
folks will remember Uncle Winton. He wrote this:

> *"A nip of old man Norton's likker*
> *Will make a feller sing and snicker.*
> *The next will make him snort and shout;*
> *The third will surely knock him out!"*

Everybody laughed then and two or three old-timers said,
"That's the truth" and "You ain't foolin'!" So Kelly went on.

"My uncle liked his liquor as most everybody knows but he
never did *sell* it. So don't think *you* can make liquor and sell it
because I'll bring you in and tear up your still. But I ain't goin'
to go pokin' around in your house to see if you got a jar of
somethin' workin' for your own enjoyment. You got nothin' to
fear from me. You won't have trouble unless you cause me
trouble. I'll be glad to have your vote."

I thought they received him right well and, as it turned out,
he got about sixty-seven percent of the black vote, which were
quite a victory when you remember that any feller holdin'
office is bound to have a pretty good machine workin' for him.
Of course, Sheriff Tompkins had been in office three four-year
terms and there was bound to be some black folks obligated to
him one way or another, as well as some who were just plain-
out skeered to vote against him. Anyhow, my boy Kelly out-
drawed him two to one.

There were a black preacher who had a little church north
of Crystal who helped swing a heap of his people for Kelly. His
name were Isaiah Hodgins but he called everybody "Brother"
so everybody got to callin' him "Brother" until that's all he was
knowed by. Well, Brother Hodgins come by one day and
offered kind of a swap for helpin'. He said he had a chance to
go to Tampa, to a big church, where he'd get about six times as
much salary and a fine place to live. All he had to do were go
down there and ring the bell with a real fine sermon—"sample
sermon" he called it.

Now Brother Hodgins were a stomped-down stem-winder
when it come to preachin' and he were a genuwine godly man
along with it, so everybody respected him. He told me'n Kelly

he needed fifty dollars to make the trip and we give it to him. That were a good chunk of money in them days. Anyhow he come back the followin' Monday and said he had give them his best and that the deacons was goin' to make a decision and let him hear somethin' real soon.

Well, two weeks went by and he didn't hear nothin'. He near about lived at the post office but still no letter from the big church. His wife, Mary, were up to our place helpin' Loofy can some guavas and he come by to drive her home.

"Heered from that board of deacons yet, Brother?" I asked him.

"No, sir," he said. "Not a word. Nearly three weeks and not a word."

Then Mary spoke up. "I tell him he's got to stop worryin', Mr. Driggers. The Book says, 'If God be for us, who can be against us?' "

"Niggers, that's who!" Brother Hodgins said.

And, as it turned out, they was and he didn't land the big church. To tell the truth I were sort of glad because he were a good man and a fine example to all the kids. We needed such in our neck of the woods. And he helped in the campaign, like he said he would.

Sheriff Tompkins made a heap of speeches and he were good at it as long as he stayed on county matters. But he got to spoutin' off on things he didn't know much about and Ursula said he were just a Charlotte Ann. But I had knowed him since he were a boy and I couldn't agree with her, no matter what else might be said about him.

Tompkins had a heap of kinfolks in the county and they was old-time Crackers who all knowed each other and most everybody else. On the other hand, us Driggerses was right well acquainted around too, so Kelly pulled near about half of the Cracker vote. Where he really done good were with the Yankee vote, which had got to be considerable. There was regular settlements of 'em scattered through the county—like Yankeetown, down the River, where old man Knott had settled way back in the early twenties. When he talked to them Kelly almost sounded like one himself and Ursula bein' along with him sure didn't hurt none. He talked about conservation and new roads and honest government and low taxes and he done his talkin' in his best college lingo. And, of course, he went strong on justice for the black man because he believed in it and he said the main reason he were now runnin' against Sheriff Tompkins was on account of the shootin' of Enos Rhodes by Slim Jallup. Them Yankees just naturally ate up that talk.

There come a feller named Peter to see us durin' Kelly's campaign who were writin' stories for the newspapers and collectin' antidotes for a book. He weren't Peter somebody but somebody Peter . . . I'll remember directly. Anyhow, we got to talkin' politics and this feller Peter . . . Emmett Peter, that were his name . . . sure did know a heap about Florida politics from a way back yonder and he told us one story that his grandaddy had told him about a real bitter campaign for governor in nineteen and twenty-four between Sydney J. Catts and John Martin.

Catts were a Baptist preacher and had already been governor from nineteen and sixteen to nineteen and twenty. Our laws didn't permit no governor to succeed himself so Reverend Catts had to wait four years to try again. Anyhow, accordin' to the story he had really been frammin' at the Roman Catholics and the danger of the country comin' under the damination of the Pope at Rome. He lit into Martin as a tool of the Catholic interests and kept a-pourin' it on until Martin finally got wore out with it and made a speech to a crowd one night in Orlando. Mr. Peter told us his grandaddy were right there and heered it. Mr. Martin said: "Folks, y'all know how my opponent has been carryin' on about the Catholics and the danger from Rome. But I want to point out to you that back there durin' Governor Catts's own administration the Pope died and our Governor, Sydney J. Catts, just sat back and let 'em appoint another one without even raisin' a finger!"

Some of our folks laughed but I didn't see nothin' funny about it. I doubt if old Spessard or Fuller or even Roy Collins would of stopped it either. Maybe old Fred Cone would of handled it. I don't know. I do know Claude Kirk wouldn't of done nothin' about it—he had enough trouble with *Senator* Pope from all I could hear.

When we first come to the River there hadn't been no Catholic folks at all but now there was quite a few and if a feller is goin' to stay in politics, he's got to respect everybody's opinions, even Yankees, if he wants their votes—black folks,

Jewish folks, Protestants and Catholics. And in our good old U.S.A. near about anybody can vote or run for public office and get elected regardless of race, color or greed.

There's still a few old Crackers, though, livin' way back in the Hammock who is suspicious of all newcomers and outsiders. I heered about a priest who come to the River lookin' for a piece of land some rich Philadelphia Yankee had give to his church. It were a sizeable chunk of Hammock along the outer edge near the Gulf Marsh and the priest hired a local Cracker to show it to him. They had to go the last two miles afoot through some real boggy places. Night caught 'em so they stopped by Uncle Joe Whisnant's place and, accordin' to the story, old Uncle Joe really give that priest a lookin'-over. Of course he hadn't never seed a feller in them black clothes, collar on backward and all. Well, Uncle Joe put the local feller in the bed with him and Aunt Teenie and give the spare bedroom to the priest. Next mornin' at breakfast the priest thanked Uncle Joe for his hospitality and said, "I specially appreciated that big picture of the Pope on the wall."

"Who?" Uncle Joe asked.

"Pope John," the priest said. "Pope John in his ceremonial robes."

"Well, dang that feed salesman," Uncle Joe said. "He told me that were Harry Truman in his Shriner's outfit!"

That may be just a yarn like Uncle Winton Epps used to spin but there's folks near about that ignorant of what's goin' on in the outside world. Anyhow, Kelly went after their votes, if they could hold a pen and sign their name, no matter how far back in the woods they lived.

The last few weeks of the campaign got right hot. My brother Tarley fought three of the Nash boys at the same time over near Inglis and got his ear near about chawed off and his lower plate busted half in two. One of the fellers had said he had a man workin' for him who had swore that he were at the juke the night that Jallup shot Enos Rhodes and that just before the shootin' Kelly had hollered, "Shoot him! Shoot him!" Old Tarl were about sixty at the time but he were still some kind of a man and when he got through with them fellers they looked like they'd been sortin' wildcats!

Naturally I done right smart campaignin' myself and did

have some real hot arguments. Most of the objections to Kelly was on account of his brother David and all the scrapes he'd been into. There weren't much we could say about that except that we was sorry. David had come back from the army because it seems like they was goin' to make a parachute jumper out of him but, when they got to checkin' him again, they decided his feet was too flat to the ground. "Fallen arches" they called it. Seemed like he would have to land in enemy territory and walk around totin' a heap of equipment—maybe for days at a time. Shucks! That boy could outwalk ary Cracker in Gulf Hammock. How come they missed his feet in the first go-'round I don't know. They said his eyes was okay; said he had 20–20 vision. I could of told 'em he had mighty good .30–30 vision too.

Anyhow, he had got a honorable discharge and I were glad of that. Tarl said he weren't surprised at nothin' the army or navy done—said they taken Cracker boys and like to of froze 'em to death on ships to someplace called Murmansk and Yankees from Minnesota got sent to sweat it out in Africa. Said it were just like Ma puttin' up guavas—all went into the same kettle—big ones and little ones, yellow centers and red centers and white centers, ripe ones and half-ripe ones. They all come out stewed guavas; said that were the way the navy done. Everything come out just gobs or guavas.

Course when you got a war to fight there ain't much time to spend on classifyin' folks. You got to have a heap of fellers ready to go and go right now wherever they might be needed the most. So I don't mean to be too critical of the army. But by this very line of reasonin' they was losin' a awful good fighter when they got cranky about David's feet. I often wonder how he would of turnt out if he had been able to cut loose all his meanness lawful-like. He'd of been a caution. I'm sure some of the church votes went against us on account of him but Loofy and me and the rest of the family was all known to be strong church folks too so we got our share of the Christians.

There was one big old red-necked Cracker from up somewhere near Morriston who were passin' out cards that read, "A vote for Driggers is a vote for niggers." I called him on it one day at the forks gas station. There was three or four cars stopped for gas and cold drinks and this feller were handin' them cards out to everybody. I taken one and read it and said, "What does that mean?"

"Just what it says," the feller answered, swellin' up. "You got any objections?"

"If you're referrin' to the shootin' of Enos Rhodes, I reckon I have," I told him. "There weren't no reason to kill that man. My son were just holdin' him for a fair trial, which he were entitled to and would of got if my son had been Sheriff."

"Well, you and your son can both go straight to hell," the feller said, "and all the niggers along with you. In the meantime I think I'll just whip your butt."

I didn't give him no time to change his mind but hit him just as hard a lick as I ever hit anybody—dead center on his nose and right cheekbone. My brother Tarl had taught me how to get all my body leverage into a short straight right and I hadn't forgot how. The feller had just started to move toward me and the punch broke his nose and cheekbone and put him out cold. It also broke my hand. But before I headed for the doctor I gathered up them cards—all of 'em—and put 'em in my car.

"Anybody want one?" I asked the little crowd standin' around. But nobody didn't speak up so I left and dropped 'em in the River when I got to the bridge.

In one of the precincts the votin' took place in Stonebrook's old grocery store up toward Otter Creek and me'n Kelly stopped by there the evenin' before election day. Just as we drove up and stopped the cold drink man come by.

"How many cases you want for tomorrow, Mr. Ed?" he hollered out.

"That all depends," Mr. Stonebrook said.

"Depends on what? You won't have over thirty or forty folks votin' here so it ought to be easy for you to figure out how many drinks you're goin' to need."

"Well," Mr. Stonebrook said, "the trouble of it is that I don't know what time the man with the money will get here. If he gets here early, two cases will do. If he don't get here till late and them fellers all has to stand around and wait, I reckon it'll take eight or ten cases."

Me'n Kelly didn't let on we'd heered nothin' but it sure

weren't *our* money man who was due there. I wondered how many other ballots was bein' bought.

While we was in the store I noticed there was a awful supply of salt on the shelves—box after box after box—and I said, "Mr. Stonebrook, you sure must sell a heap of salt."

"You know," he said, "that's a funny thing. I don't hardly sell no salt at all. But the feller who sells me salt sure sells a hell of a lot of salt!"

We left a few of Kelly's cards with Stonebrook but figured they was probably wasted, though there were always the chance that some folks would take the other feller's money and yet vote for Kelly.

The vote were goin' to be close, all right, and election evenin' I felt just like Doctor John Emmett's yardman when Doc took him for a ride in his little private airplane. When they come down, somebody asked the yardman how he liked flyin' and he said, "It's all right, I reckon, but I never did let my full weight down in that thing!" That's just how I were until the final count were in. I couldn't set still and must of walked twenty miles in one room.

We didn't have final returns until noon the next day but we squeaked through by forty-two votes. Kelly and Ursula come by that evenin' and we celebrated the victory by barbecuin' some ribs. Afterward I had a good talk with Kelly.

"I'm right proud of you, son," I told him. "But let me tell you that if you are plannin' to continue to work for the State, there's a few things you've got to understand. You'll hear politicians say, 'My purpose is to serve the people. I have no ax to grind.' Don't you believe it. Everybody's got a ax to grind or he wouldn't be after the job. If he's rich, he wants power and to have folks write 'Honorable' in front of his name—whether he is or not. If he's poor, he's lookin' for a chance to make money. Ain't nobody ever just purely wanted to serve the people but Jesus Himself or one of His followers.

"But don't misunderstand me. There ain't nothin' wrong with havin' a ax to grind or with grindin' it. Everything depends on what you're goin' to do with that ax when you get it sharp. If you're goin' to chop some wood for yourself or a good friend and it ain't off somebody else's land or will damage somethin' some way, there ain't no harm in it that I can see.

The trouble of it is that a lot of politicians are fixin' to chop off some other feller's legs—or his income or his good name or somethin'.

"When you hear a senator or a representative or a county commissioner say he ain't got no ax to grind, just discount it, son, about ninety-eight percent. All of 'em I ever knowed had good personal reasons for wantin' to get elected or they wouldn't of run in the first place. That ain't to say they was *crooked* reasons though. If a feller will go up to Tallahassee and watch that legislature operate a while, he'll see that it's pretty hard to put over a crooked, private-gain deal with all them other fellers watchin' like hawks. There ain't many really bad bills get passed into law.

"If you go into police work, you've got an ax to grind. You got to build yourself up as a man who ain't scary and can't be bluffed. You got to earn your money and you got to learn that there's more crooked deals offered to law officers than to most folks. So if you're goin' to be a officer of the law, be a stomped-down good one. Folks will know it and you'll get re-elected long as you do a job. Don't back up from nobody about nothin' when you're right and don't go along with nobody about nothin' when they're wrong."

32 The Ambush at Polly's Quarters & Slim Jallup Pays the Price

I reckon the closest call Kelly ever had were right soon after the election when he got ambushed in Polly's Quarters one evenin' just before sundown. There'd been some trouble in the Quarters and the law would make a sashay through there now and again just to let folks know they was around. This time Kelly were horseback, ridin' a golden buckskin mare that we'd raised from a colt from the same stock as Sheriff Charlie Dean's old Panther. When he come to where Cat Street turned off from Broadway a feller stepped out from behind a house and cut down on him with a 12-gauge shotgun loaded with buckshot.

Buckshot patterns out in a crazy way. Double-oughts are loaded nine to a shell—three layers of three—in a 12-gauge shell. Each shot is the size of a sugar-crowder pea. The pattern holds together pretty good in some guns but I ain't never seen a gun that would shoot anywhere near the same pattern, shot after shot. But at a distance of forty feet they bunch up pretty good and they're strong medicine.

Anyhow, two of 'em took Kelly in the left knee joint. The doctor said one hit his fibula and another went in by his tibia and busted his panatella. I didn't know what a cigar were doin' in his knee joint but Kelly said that it were *patella* and not *panatella* . . . that patella meant kneecap. Anyhow, all three names sounded to me like three Ybor City sportin' women. A Cubian doctor must of wrote the medical books.

Four of the other buckshots went into that poor mare—two into her lungs, one into her liver and one in her neck. She went down and died in five minutes. Naturally, Kelly went down with her but he managed to roll clear so she weren't a-layin' across his leg. Of course he couldn't stand up but he did manage to shoot two or three times with his .45 at the feller who'd shot him. But he must of missed because nobody couldn't find no blood.

At any rate, the feller got plumb away, even though they brought the bloodhounds and trailed him all the way over to U.S. 41. The dogs lost him on the pavement, so somebody must have picked him up. We didn't find out for a long time who the feller was or why he wanted to kill Kelly. When we did, we learnt why he had shot low and killed a horse 'stead of a man.

Kelly spent two weeks in the hospital and three more weeks with his knee still in a cast. It never did get plumb all right. At first it looked like it would sure put a crimp in Kelly's huntin' for that season. Up to then he had always been the one to do the drivin' on our deer hunts, either on horseback or on foot. I'd place the standers and he'd take the dogs and make the drive. Now he couldn't walk and neither step up on a horse.

"You'll just have to set on a stand like any other city dude," I told him. "You can enjoy the sounds of nature—cat squirrels cuttin' acorns, jay birds scoldin' at whatever catches their eye, jorees scratchin' in the leaves and maybe—just maybe—a old buck tryin' to slip through."

"Just bein' out there in the camp will be fine with me," he said. "And if ary old buck tries to slip by, we'll pull his peelin!"

And by grannies that's just what happened—a ten pointer come sneakin' along ahead of old Blue—a good twenty minutes ahead because Blue hadn't yet got in hearin'. Kelly were sittin' on a big water oak log where he could keep that leg halfway comfortable. The log were about eighty steps from the edge of Bee Tree Slough and the dern deer tried to ease through between Kelly and the Slough, keepin' to the high grass on the edge of the Slough.

"The scoun'el was almost walkin' on his knees," Kelly told us when we got there after the shootin'. "He had his horns laid back on his neck and he was really doin' a piece of slippin'."

This were a awful big deer but the back straps was tender as a yearlin' doe's. I never eat a better piece of venison than one of them steaks from that tenderloin.

Durin' the season Kelly got him another buck and two gobblers just settin' around in the woods. "See," I told him. "You remember my tellin' you that you'd see just as much or more game settin' still and lettin' it come to you than by frammin' around in the woods."

When duck season opened I taken Kelly to the marsh just once. We went in a little old duck boat he had bought from some Yankee hunter but we didn't do much good. We got four or five pintails and three or four widgeons and a couple of them old black mallards but Kelly couldn't get his knee comfortable in that little boat and he didn't dare step out into the marsh with that cast. So we come back in about noon and went fishin' that evenin'.

There had been a good cold spell and it had sure enough brought them redfish into the River. We caught twenty-six, I remember, some of 'em almost bull reds—twelve or fourteen pounders. Kelly loved to fish and I reckon he got that from his mother, though I always did like fishin' myself. My brother Tarl had never cared about fishin' much, specially after the year he spent at commercial fishin'. But me and my family all liked to catch fish and eat fish. When I looked at them big bullies layin' in the bottom of the skiff, I could almost taste that redfish chowder Loofy would make. The smaller ones—three or four pounders—would be some kind of good filleted off and broiled with butter. These fish have different names dependin' on where you're from. The Yankees call 'em channel bass. Down here we call 'em red drum or redfish. But whatever you call 'em, they're somethin' fittin'.

We done a lot of fishin' that fall and winter and it stayed good in the River most of the time because the weather was cold most of the time. We'd get our fish—trout, snappers, redfish and sheepshead—by trollin', castin' and bait fishin'.

Live shrimp were best bait for redfish and trout and fiddler crabs best for sheepshead.

David always liked to fish and were probably the best fisherman in the family but had always been so mean and ugly that nobody didn't want him along. Only his sister, Etta, would ever go with him and a heap of times she'd come back cryin' over the mean way he'd talk to her. Kelly wouldn't never go in the same boat with him and it got so that I didn't like to if I could help it.

He were probably the best deer hunter in the family but naturally didn't ever go with us no more and to tell the truth I was glad of it. He wouldn't pay no mind to game laws and I do believe he would shoot an old doe nursin' twin fawns on Mother's Day and laugh while he were cuttin' her throat.

All the time Kelly were laid up, his wife Ursula took care of the office and paid the deputies and fed the prisoners. The county allowed three dollars per day for each prisoner and even then there weren't much to spare. One day when me and Loofy was in the office, Ursula complained about the high prices of food and said it was just a precurser of things to come. Loofy asked me later what in the world was a precurser.

"Honey, I don't know," I told her. "Unless maybe it's a feller who can curse before you do when the boat hits a oyster bar."

About six months after the shootin' in Polly's Quarters, we found out who the man were who had done it. Seemed like he were the brother of the logger that Slim Jallup had killed while Kelly had been holdin' him. Most folks, includin' the black folks, knowed that the killin' had not been Kelly's doin's and that him and Jallup liken to have fought about it. I reckon the brother must of knowed this too and just tried to cripple Kelly.

Anyhow, he waited six months and then he come back and bushwhacked Jallup out where he had a little garden near the edge of town. Slim had got a job on the town police at Crystal River and were livin' up that way. He managed to get off two shots with his .38 Special and the second took the logger's brother in the groin and cut the big artery. By the time anybody got there Slim were dead and the black man near about it. Before he died he confessed to shootin' Kelly too and said he wished he hadn't of done it.

33 Tracks in the Sand & Punkchell Jack Is Late for the Duck Hunt

If a feller don't realize that the world is rapidly fillin' up with s.o.b.'s he ought to hang around a sheriff's office or a police station and just watch and listen to what goes on. Rape and murder and armed robbery, hog stealin', horse stealin', cattle stealin' and car stealin'. More car stealin' than anything else, I reckon.

Kelly learnt not to be surprised at nothin'. A report came in that a couple of fellers had stole a right new Buick car from Mr. Polk's yard. The car were standin' within twenty feet of the house between two rows of orange trees, and the grove had just been disked so the tracks could be seen in the sand plain as day. One set of tracks looked like the feller were wearin' sneakers. The other were hard heels. There weren't no other clues they could find.

Later in the day Kelly stopped in Hayter's Garage and were just passin' the time of day when Ed Hayter said he were shorthanded—his mechanic had failed to show up for work that mornin'. Said the feller were always on time so must be sick. Said he were stayin' at Mrs. Baker's boardin' house and there wasn't no phone there. Kelly said he were goin' that way and would stop by Baker's and see what ailed the feller. Ed

Hayter told Kelly the feller's name were Bruce Tister and he were a big, blond-headed feller about forty.

Old lady Baker told Kelly that the feller hadn't been home at all the night before and had left some stuff in the room—specially some shoes. "He said he were a shoe salesman when he first come to board," she told Kelly. "He were always gettin' samples but never would offer to let folks get any at a bargain."

Well, that were the answer. There were sixteen shoes in their boxes up in that feller's room but there weren't ary two that would make a pair. The samples was one shoe to a style—either left or right. Anyhow, Kelly knowed then that it were probably this feller alone who had stole the Buick and he knowed his name and description so he put out a flyer and some calls and in three days the Tampa police had the feller. He were wearin' mismatched shoes then, too.

Of course it were just a happenstance that Kelly stopped to get gas at Hayter's or he wouldn't of had no idea of where to start lookin' or for who. But a heap of times it's just such lucky breaks that'll catch a thief.

There was a feller named Jack D. Keene who had a cane-grindin' mill in on Gator Lake. There's some fine muck on the east side of that lake and Jack growed cane ten feet high. He made the best syrup there was to be had and were a good feller to deal with. Whatever he said he'd do he'd do and whenever he said he'd be somewhere's that's just when he were there, so folks got to callin' him Punkchell Jack. He loved to hunt and you could always count on him to meet you when he said he would—even if it meant bein' somewhere two hours before day.

There ain't nothin' worse than to have a duck hunt planned in a place that's hard to get to and where the daybreak flight is all there is and then to have to set and wait for some feller whose clock didn't go off or who forgot to wind it or set it or just plain forgot the hunt. It's worser when the skeeters is bad and you have to set around and slap 'em and watch the sky begin to get light and you're not even out to the marsh, much less on your stand with your deecoys all set out.

Well, old Punkchell Jack never failed to be on time so one mornin' when me'n him and Kelly was goin' to Brantley Marsh and he failed to show up we was worried. We had the boat all loaded and ready and was settin' on the dock listenin' to a couple of hoot owls discussin' the weather when Kelly said, "Dad, this ain't like Mr. Keene. Somethin's wrong. I've got a bad feelin' that somethin's wrong."

"Let's give him another fifteen minutes," I said. "With the wind like it is there'll be a big tide and the ducks should be flyin' all mornin'."

We waited fifteen minutes and there weren't no sign of Jack. "Well, what'll we do?" I asked Kelly. "Go without him or call it all off or what?"

"He's been so good about bringin' us all that fine syrup," Kelly said, "that I'd purely hate for him to get here and find us gone. Anyhow, I've got a real strong feelin' that there's somethin' wrong . . . bad wrong. I've never known him to be late before."

"Neither have I. Never before," I said. "Maybe we better drive up there and check on him. The ducks will keep."

It's about twelve miles up to Jack's from our place and part of it is over a road that even a gator would find hard to travel, so it taken us at least half an hour to get to Jack's place. His wife had died and he lived all alone because they hadn't never had no young-uns. Some of the time there were a sort of half-witted nephew who stayed with him and helped with the cane grindin' but this feller hadn't been around for two or three months. When we drove in the yard, Jack's two dogs come chargin' out from under the house barkin'. One of 'em was a mean black-and-tan, prick-eared rascal that some Yankee had give him. He called it a Doberman pincher but I called it a Doberman biter because the scoun'el had done bit me once before. So we didn't get out of the car—just hollered a couple of times. But there weren't no answer. Jack didn't have no car shed but just let his old Hudson set out in the weather in the yard. But it weren't there.

"What do you reckon now?" Kelly asked me. "He didn't start for the River or we'd have met him on the road."

I didn't know what to make of it and said so. "He ain't in the house or his car would be here. Maybe he got sick and headed for Crystal for a doctor or went to Ocala to the hospital."

"He'd have had to be awful sick not to get us word," Kelly said. "Let's go on down to Crystal and see if Doc Joyner knows anything about him."

So that's what we done. It were near about sun-up when we got to Joyner's house and old Doc were up and havin' coffee. Back in them days most doctors had their offices right at home and had plenty of time to see a feller. Today, if you get sick, you set around in a nickel-plated waitin' room with a lot of other folks and if you're goin' to die, you just have to wait your turn. Doc Joyner poured us each a cup of steamin'-hot boiled coffee and asked what he could do for us. We told him about our busted-up duck hunt but he said he hadn't seen or heered from Punchell Jack for a week.

"If it were his brother, now, Bat Keene," Doc said, "I'd say he were gone off on a big drunk. But Jack, no. He don't hardly ever take nothin'. So I'm afraid I can't help you fellers."

When we left Doc's and started back up toward Inglis we was near about to Red Level when we met up with Will Butler. He were horseback and had a couple of catch dogs with him, hog huntin', I reckon.

"Howdy, Billy," he said when we stopped. "And you, Kelly. What y'all doin' down in our county when you got all the game up north of the River?" He seen we was in our huntin' clothes.

"We got lots of ducks," I said, "and we was goin' after 'em this mornin' with old Punchell Jack Keene. But the rascal failed to show."

"That's a funny thing," Will said.

"What is?" I asked him.

"Why I seen his old green car yesterday evenin' just before dark but Jack weren't drivin' it and I thought that were a funny thing."

"Whereabouts did you see the car and who were a-drivin' it?" I wanted to know.

"Way in on the Ozello Road, near about to the marsh," Will said. "I don't know who the feller were—never seen him before."

Then Kelly spoke up. "Is there anybody livin' in that old homestead house on First Island?"

"I believe there is," Will said. "I think there's some folks there got a daughter who used to go with that old, sorry, half-witted nephew of Mr. Keene's. Come to think of it the car were right close to the First Island turn-off when I seen it."

"Are you sure that old Jack weren't in it?" I asked.

"He might of been on the floor but he sure weren't drivin' it.

I were sittin' on a stump, squirrel huntin' in that little live oak hammock there and the driver never seen me. But I seen him—good. And I didn't know him."

"Let's go, Kelly," I said. "There sure is somethin' funny goin' on. Be seein' you, Will. Stop in passin' if you're up our way."

The Ozello Road were just a dirt road and hardly wide enough for cars to pass so when we seen a car comin' and seen it were a green Hudson we speeded up till we come to a little oyster shell fill across a marshy place where two cars just couldn't pass at all. It were Jack Keene's car all right and when we stopped, a big, rough-lookin' feller climbed out and come a-walkin' toward us.

"What's the idea of blockin' the road, Mister?" he asked Kelly, who had also got out.

"We got some questions to ask," Kelly said. "My name is Kelly Driggers and I'm the Sheriff. This here's my dad, Billy Driggers."

"Yeah?" the feller said. "Let's see your papers—you ain't wearin' no badge."

"We were goin' duck shootin'," Kelly told him. "I never carry my papers when I go to the marsh and I ain't wearin' my badge for the same reason. Besides that, I'm on my vacation."

"Then by what authority are you stoppin' me?" the feller asked. Then's when I took over. I had just by force of habit taken my shotgun out of the duck boat. There ain't no gun of mine ever left layin' around by itself, so it were right beside me.

"By the authority of old lady Winchester and the six children," I said and pumped a shell into the barrel. "This first one is number five chilled and it'll knock a hole in your goozlum that a catfish could swim through so don't make a wrong move."

All the time we had been talkin' I had been bluffin' him out with a unloaded gun. I mean unloaded in the barrel, because I don't never carry a gun in the car with a shell in the barrel ready to go. I learnt my lesson about guns goin' off accidentally a long time ago.

"Now then, Mister," I told the feller, "where is Jack Keene and what are you doin' with his car?"

"I bought the car from him last night. He was at home out

in that god-forsaken place he lives and that's where I left him."

"No it ain't," I told him. "We was all goin' duck huntin' and he wouldn't of sold his car last night. So where is he?"

About that time I heered a kind of a thump and then I heered old Jack holler out—not very loud but loud enough. I'll be danged if that feller hadn't locked him in the trunk of his own car. I helt the shotgun on the feller while Kelly frisked him, took a pistol from his pocket then got the keys out of the switch and found the one for the trunk. Poor old Jack were in his underdrawers and were beat up pitiful. One eye were closed tight, some teeth had been busted out and his head were cut where he had been bangin' it on the lid of the trunk and he were shiverin' like a wet bird dog. We helped him out and I seen his eye gleam when he reckonized the big feller.

"Lend me your gun a minute, Billy," Jack said. "I want to kill me a snake."

I had half a notion to let him do it, but Kelly spoke up and said, "No, Mr. Keene. I'm a officer now and we got to do this all legal. So we'll just take this gentleman on up to Bronson. First though we'll go by your house and let you get on some pants. And you, stranger, you just crawl back there into that trunk and see how it fits you."

"Oh no," the big feller said. "Please, Mister, not in the trunk. I can't stand close places like that."

"You'll stand this one," I told him. "Get in before I kill you." So we made him get in and we pressed down the lid and locked it.

"Now then, Jack," I said, "I think you should let Kelly drive your car and I'll follow."

"Okay, Billy," he said. "I don't feel too peert, I'll have to admit."

So Kelly went around and climbed into the driver's seat. "You can tell me how all this happened on the way," he told Jack.

"Just don't hit them pot holes too fast," I hollered at 'em before they started. "You wouldn't want to jounce your passenger to where he couldn't talk some when he gets to Bronson. Maybe we just better leave him in the trunk and go on in ourselves in our car and tell the judge."

"Oh my God, no," the feller hollered. "What if y'all had a wreck or somethin' and didn't get back. What would I do?"

"The same thing Jack Keene would of done if you'd left him—probably die," I told him. "Think about that some."

Well, that feller were in about the worst nervous shape I ever seen a man in when we got to the jail. He were cryin' and shakin' and beggin'. Ursula said he must of had cloisterphobia when she heered about it—said some folks couldn't stand to be shut up in a close place like that. I remember Uncle Winton tellin' me about bein' scared to go down in one of them caves up in Tennessee when he were on a trip up yonder.

Anyhow, the big stranger were some kind of glad to get out of that trunk and he were ready to talk, I mean. It turned out that the gal who lived out on First Island were a cousin of his and she had told him about bein' out to Mr. Keene's place several times when she were datin' Jack's nephew. She said the nephew told her that Mr. Keene kept all his money in a shoe box under a loose plank in the kitchen. You had to move the wood box by the stove to raise the plank but he hadn't told her that. Said Mr. Keene never went to the bank except to change ones and fives to tens and twenties.

So when the big feller went out there and couldn't find the money he beat old Jack near about to death, even though Jack tried to tell him there weren't no money there. Then he taken him in the trunk of the car down to First Island to see if the gal couldn't tell him somewheres else to look. She weren't there so he were goin' to take old Jack back and try to beat it out of him one time more and then probably leave him to die. He'd hid his own car on a old sand road in a little piece of scrub about a quarter from Gator Lake.

"The trouble of it was that the feller wouldn't believe me," old Jack said later. "It weren't but just a month ago that I taken all that money in to the bank and told 'em I wanted it kept in a safe place. Didn't expect no intercourse from it—just wanted it kept in a safe place."

34 Sheriff Kelly Finds His Match

Generally speakin', though, things is right peaceable in our county compared with the old days, but along with the tourists headed for St. Pete, Tampa and Sarasota and all them towns on the way to Miami, there's bound to be some bad actors and I really got my dandruff up over what happened to son Jim not long after Kelly got to be Sheriff. Jim had saved right smart money from his mechanic's work and he opened his own little repair garage and gas station on U.S. 19 on the River near the bridge.

Ours is just a little old Cracker county—most of it covered by Gulf Hammock and what's in it. Fishin's always been pretty good—both fresh and salt water—and them who likes it can get a mess of ducks or quail or squirrels most any time or maybe a deer or turkey. Course we don't have fancy horse tracks or ocean beaches and we ain't got a Bok Tower but more and more Yankees keep findin' out that we got a lot of things in our favor—especially since U.S. Highway 19 was built down the west coast. So Jim got to figgerin' that the Yankees had to eat and drink somewhere along the way so he fixed 'em a place alongside the garage. I mean he fixed 'em a nice place, tablecloths and all. Not like Cracker Pete's whose idea of a seven-course dinner is a six-pack and a sausage.

Business got good with Jim. He give 'em Yankee cookin'—green beans without any pork, half-cooked beef with the blood runnin' out of it, green English peas 'stead of black-eyed, and store-boughten, wasp-nest light bread 'stead of good old corn bread or hot biscuits. For breakfast he give 'em grapefruit and wood shavin's and sawdust and all that kind of stuff along with bacon and eggs. And the bacon weren't the good old country-cured kind that a feller can taste but packaged and sliced so thin you could read a book through it and some of it smelt like last year's fish when it were cookin'. You could get grits if you asked for 'em but I swear I seen a Yankee put milk and sugar on 'em and it turnt my stomach.

A heap of Yankees want their eggs half raw, so trembly you can't hardly get 'em out of the pan before they bust and run. It never did seem quite decent to me to serve a egg without coatin' over that yeller eye with hot grease or else flippin' it over. But Jim give the Yankees what they wanted and directly had to build a bigger place and get him a full-time cook.

As business got better, Jim put up signs along the highway and spent money on other advertisin' tricks. He called his place "The Last Resort" which never made sense to me and I tried to get him to call it "The First Resort" but he just laughed at me. "Dad," he'd say, "you just don't understand." And I reckon I didn't.

I ain't knockin' the Yankees, but along with the nice ones that come through our county there's a heap of riffraff—gangsters and gamblers and bums. It's such fellers we have trouble with and some of 'em are pretty slick. They're used to foolin' big city cops so they figgered a country sheriff like Kelly weren't hardly no match for 'em.

Well, two such fellers decided to knock off Jim's place. They come in about ten o'clock that particular night, just as he was closin' up, and bought cigarettes, lookin' the place over. Then they pulled guns on Jim and the cook and told 'em to sit tight. Jim would have been all right if he hadn't been a full-blooded Driggers. All of us Driggerses'll fight. So Jim reached for his shotgun under the counter. One of them fellers parted his hair right down between the eyes with the butt of a pistol. Then they taken all the money in the cash box—about three hundred and eighty dollars—and went out.

Sis and Lou, Jim's two waitresses, was already outside, fixin' to go home in their own car and seen the two fellers run out and jump into a black coupe with a New York license. But they didn't get the number. They said it kept on north on 19 and was really ballin' the jack and they could hear it a long way.

It was just happenstance that Kelly got there about fifteen minutes afterward. If anybody had any doubts about my boy Kelly doin' his job or backin' off from trouble, they didn't have after what happened at Jim's place. This was his first tangle with some real dangerous characters after his election. There'd been a big ruckus over in the turpentine quarters and he was on his way up to the jail with a black man named Hog Dog who had got that name while he was a local prize fighter. There just ain't nothin' rougher, tougher nor braver than a hog dog— a dog that'll go right in and catch and hold a mean old wild boar. I'd seen Hog Dog fight several times and won a couple of pretty good bets on him myself. He was well named.

Kelly stopped at Jim's place for a cup of coffee before goin' on up to Bronson with his prisoner. "When I pulled up in front of Jim's," he told me later, "I said for Hog Dog to sit tight and I'd bring him out some coffee. Then I went in and there laid Jim on the floor. The gals had thrown some cold water on him and he was just comin' alive. The cook had a bottle of moonshine stashed away and was tryin' to give him a drink but his hands were shakin' so bad he was spillin' most of it.

"Jim began gettin' mad before he had good sense. At first he was light green and as he got madder he turned purple-pieded. As soon as he got walkin'-around sense and could talk to me he described the two fellers who had attacked him. One of 'em had had slick black hair and jet black eyes and looked kind o' like a possum in the face—close-set eyes and sharp nose. The other had been a big heavy-set feller about two ax-handles long with gray hair and a long gray mustache. Jim said he looked like he'd swallered a couple o' cat squirrels and left their tails hangin' out of his mouth. Sis and Lou, the two waitresses, backed up his descriptions of the two hold-up men. I was glad of that. Lots of times a good solid lick with the butt of a gun will addle a feller till he gets all mixed up—especially when he's mad too.

"The car had headed north, so I lit out. I told Jim to phone ahead to the police in Chiefland, Dunnellon, Gainesville and Ocala to be on the lookout for a black coupe with suspicious characters. But you know how that is. There's forty-'leven thousand black cars with New York licenses down here every winter and *everybody* looks suspicious if you get to lookin' at him hard enough.

"On the way, while I was drivin', I kept talkin' to Hog Dog. 'Hog Dog,' I said, 'you're a bad actor and you had no business cuttin' that gingercake boy like you done.'

" 'Swear I didn't cut him Mister Kelly,' said Hog Dog. 'I just stuck my knife in that nigger and walked aroun' him a little. Us was playin' a little game of poker an' that old boy had a marked deck.'

" 'Well,' I said, 'these two hold-up fellers I'm huntin' may be tough to handle if I find 'em, and I may need help. You do like you're told and I'll get old Judge Day to make it easy for you.'

" 'Yes, sir!' Hog Dog said. 'Yes *sir!*'

"About fifteen miles north, near where the Williston Road turns off, there's a juke joint that stays open pretty late and is run by a Greek named Nicky something-or-other. I slowed down to look it over. There were eight or ten cars parked and I thought I saw a black coupe with some fellers changin' a back tire. Just on chance, I rolled to a stop and cut off my lights. Before I could get out of my car, the two fellers had finished their job and was gettin' into the black coupe. Then they headed north again—this time toward Williston.

"I hadn't been able to check the license plate but I sure felt a stronger hunch than ever so I swung out and followed 'em, stayin' a long way behind. At last they pulled up to another beer joint, this one just outside of Williston near where U.S. 41 joins U.S. 27. I speeded up and pulled in behind 'em. If they were the two I wanted, they'd done switched licenses and now had a Florida tag on the coupe.

" 'Come on, Hog Dog,' I said. 'Maybe we'll have us a little fun here.'

" 'Yes, sir,' grunted Hog Dog. 'Mister Kelly, could I please have my knife back?' I gave him his knife and we got out.

"When I walked up to their car the two fellers were settin' there smokin'. One was a big stout feller all right, but bald as a grapefruit and without any sign of a mustache. The little black-headed feller had a black mustache.

" 'Good evenin', gentlemen,' I said, lookin' 'em over. 'Sure a pretty night.'

" 'Yeah,' said the little feller, gettin' out of the car real slow and easy. 'Guess we'll go in and have a beer.'

"When they were about halfway to the door I said, 'Hold it right there a minute.' The little feller started to reach inside his bosom.

" 'Mister,' I said, 'don't commit suicide. I'm the Sheriff of this county.' He stopped his hand and began talkin' to the other feller in some kind of foreign lingo.

"In spite of my tellin' 'em not to commit suicide, the little feller went for his gun. He was fast too, and his first shot took a button off my jumper. I shot him right under the brisket. That fixed his clock. The other feller opened fire on me and his second shot burnt me across the belly. I shot him twice in the short ribs and he hollered and went down. He was shootin' and missin' and I was shootin' and hittin'!

"Well, the big feller had fallen behind a car and was still shootin' at me. I tried to run to where I could see him to shoot him again and my bad knee buckled. Me and the big feller were layin' on the ground shootin' at each other when the door of the beer joint opened and one of the fattest fellers I ever seen in my life came a-runnin' out with two gals. His eyes were bugged out and he was really scared. Him and his two gals jumped into a car.

" 'Don't leave, Mister,' I hollered, but he didn't pay me no mind. I shot out one of his front tires as he started, and he went off down the road on the rim, knockin' fire out of the pavement. Then he turned over in the ditch. In the meantime, the feller who had been shootin' at me had quit, and I decided he had done died, so I got up and hobbled down the road to where the fat feller and his gals were. I thought they might be accomplices or something, but shucks, they were only tourists, as I found out later.

"I stuck my gun in the fat feller's ribs and ordered him and the gals back to the beer joint. He was the scaredest feller I ever saw. His old belly was just a-heavin' and his eyes were still bugged out like a blue crab's.

" 'Three men shot down right before my eyes!' he blowed. 'Three men killed! I'm goin' back to Chicago where everything's decent and law-abiding!'

"When we got back to the beer joint, the proprietor identified him and the gals as Yankee tourists. I told everybody I'd need 'em as witnesses and not to leave. Then I went to look for the hold-up man who had fallen behind the car. By gosh, he was gone!

" 'Hog Dog!' I hollered.

"By gosh, Hog Dog was gone too! My knee was hurtin' mighty bad so I sat down in the door of my car. Everybody in the beer joint was gathered around as well as other folks who had heard the shootin' and a couple of late cars which had stopped to see what was goin' on. Directly, here came the police from town and I recognized one of 'em when he walked up.

" 'What's the story, Sheriff?' he asked.

" 'Let me think a minute,' I said. 'In the meantime, scatter out and look for the man I shot.'

" 'He's a-layin' over there graveyard dead,' said the other officer.

" 'Not him!' I said. 'The other feller. The big feller. He was behind that car yonder but he must have crawled off somewhere.'

"About that time there was a blood-curdlin' squall from down the highway about a hundred yards. The two police ran off to see about it and directly they came back. They had the big feller, all right, and they had his gun—a .38 Special but it was empty. He'd never had a chance to reload before old Hog Dog had him. He wasn't as bad hurt as I had thought. One of my bullets had barely nicked him.

" 'Did he show fight?' I asked.

" 'How could he?' said the officer. 'There was a two-hundred-pound black man on top of him chokin' him to death.'

"I got so tickled I could hardly talk.

" 'That's my deputy,' I said. 'Bring him here.'

"Old Hog Dog was so scared he was plumb gray. The two policemen had him handcuffed.

" 'Tell 'em, Mister Kelly,' he groaned. 'Tell the white po-leece I was just helpin' you. I swear I never cut him, Mister

Kelly. Never even opened my knife—just a-holdin' him down so he won't 'scape.'

" 'Turn him loose, boys,' I said. 'He's actin' as my deputy.'

" 'Now, Sheriff,' said the Chief, who had arrived by this time, 'what's this all about?'

"I told him. I told him how these fellers had held up Jim's place, also the juke joint, and had resisted arrest. The Chief agreed they were my prisoners so I told Hog Dog to drive the black coupe to the jail and wait for me. Then I sat the dead feller in the back seat of my car and handcuffed the big feller to him.

" 'No funny business now,' I said, as we started back toward Nicky's, 'or you'll join your partner in hell.'

" 'You got nothin' on me,' he said. 'I ain't held up nobody. You can't prove nothin' on me.'

" 'We'll see about that,' I told him, thinkin' how tickled Nicky would be at the juke joint. That feller Nicky sure loves a nickel.

"Well, sir, when we got back to the juke joint things was a-goin' full blast.

" 'Hi, Sheriff,' said Nicky, as happy as a tree toad in a thunderstorm. 'Big night tonight. Kind of quiet earlier in the evenin' though.' I couldn't figure that.

" 'I got those two hold-up fellers,' I said.

" 'What hold-up?' shouted Nicky over the racket of the juke organ.

" 'The fellers who stuck up your place about two hours ago.'

" 'Nobody stuck up my place,' grinned Nicky, 'and they better not try.'

" 'Come out here a minute,' I said. 'I got a couple of fellers I want you to look at. One of 'em can't talk and the other won't.'

"Nicky took one look.

" 'Gosh a'mighty, Sheriff,' he said. 'One of 'em's dead.'

" 'That's right,' I told him, 'and I'm lucky I ain't the one. Ever see either of 'em before?'

" 'I wouldn't swear to it,' he said at last. 'But it seems like I remember their comin' in for a beer sometime before midnight. So many strangers come in and out I can't remember 'em all.'

"The big feller gave a sneerin' laugh.

" 'Sure we was in your place, you dumb cluck,' he said. 'Don't you remember my askin' you how far it was back to Tampa and you tellin' me? Tellin' me what good speed me and my partner had been makin?'

" 'That's right,' said Nicky, 'I do remember. You must've been steppin' on it.'

" 'We was,' says the big feller, 'until this hick cop gets tough and starts to kill everybody. Me and my partner thought *we* was bein' stuck up.'

"Nicky looked at me kind of funny and went on back into his joint. By this time I was doin' some thinkin' sure enough. Suppose Jim couldn't identify the fellers. Suppose I *had* got the wrong men. I remembered the big feller was supposed to have had gray hair and a mustache and now he was bald and clean-shaven, but wigs and mustaches are old stuff. I couldn't remember whether Jim had said the little feller had a mustache or not. There wasn't anything to do but wait and see what Jim and the waitresses would say tomorrow.

"When I got to the jail Hog Dog was there with the black coupe and after I'd locked the big feller in a cell and we had laid out the dead feller and called the undertaker I searched the car. It was plumb disappointin'. There was a pair of brass knucks, a couple of cheap suitcases with clothes, and that was all. No wigs and no mustaches and no New York tag. The dead feller had a couple hundred dollars in his wallet but the big feller didn't even have a wallet and nothin' in his coat pockets. There was nothin' more I could do that night, so I locked Hog Dog in a cell and went on home. It was two in the mornin' and I was give out. The crease along my belly had quit bleedin' but was gettin' sore so I cleaned it out with a little turpentine and slapped on a bandage.

"At first day I called Jim at his home and told him that I needed him and his two waitresses and the cook to come to the jail to identify the two fellers who had robbed his place and to be there as quick as he could. He started to tell me about some Yankee's car that had to be fixed but I told him to get his butt over to the jail and to do it right now—that I was fixin' to get in a jam.

"While I was waitin' I got plumb nervous. False arrest ain't any too good for an officer, and I'd done killed a man in the bargain. Of course the little feller had reached for a gun, but then the big feller could swear they thought they were bein' held up. I was certain I had the right men, but proof is the only thing that goes in a courtroom, and so far I didn't have any proof. Jim wasn't much help after he got to the jail and the girls was less. They hadn't brought the cook because it was his day off and they couldn't locate him at his home. We all walked over to the undertaker's.

" 'It ain't him,' said Lou, after viewin' the corpse.

" 'It might be him,' said Sis.

" 'I can't be sure,' said Jim. 'I remember the feller's eyes more'n anything else. They don't look the same.'

" 'Hardly,' I said. 'After a slug in the brisket anybody's eyes look different. What about the black mustache?'

" 'Yes,' said Lou.

" 'No,' said Sis. 'My boy friend wears one and I like 'em. The feller who held up the place didn't have nary sign of one.'

" 'Seems like he did, though,' said Jim.

"That gave me a thought. I reached over and jerked the little black mustache. It came off, slick as a whistle.

" 'All of you folks give me a pain,' I said. 'Your testimony ain't worth nothin'. Now come on back to the jail and see the other feller.' He was settin' on the edge of his bunk when we walked up and I asked him, 'Ever see any of these folks before?'

" 'Never in my life.'

" 'Ever see him?' I asked Jim and the gals.

"Jim looked at me like I was crazy. 'I told you the hold-up feller had gray hair and a big mustache. This feller ain't got neither.'

"I was gettin' sore by this time. 'Jim Driggers,' I told him, 'if you weren't my brother I'd beat you till you begged like a pet coon. The dead feller had a fake mustache. Why couldn't this feller have had one? And a wig too?'

" 'Put 'em on him and let me look at him,' said Jim.

"I felt like I was goin' to blow up. 'You find 'em and I'll put 'em on him,' I told Jim.

"The big feller in the cell just laughed. 'You're all screwy,' he said.

" 'What about it?' I asked Sis and Lou. 'Ever see this feller before?'

" 'Nope,' they said, right together.

" 'Go on home—all of you,' I told 'em, 'before I hurt somebody else. Now I want that cook. I'll get me a witness yet.'

"Several hours after they left, Ranse, my chief deputy, came into my office. He'd found some things and when he showed 'em to me I told him to bring the big feller in for some more questionin'.

" 'Now then,' I said, 'where were you on the night of the hold-up?'

" 'What night was that?' he sneered.

" 'Last night,' I said, 'about ten o'clock.'

" 'On the road between Tampa and Jacksonville,' he said.

" 'Did you stop at a restaurant called The Last Resort?'

" 'Never heard of it,' he said.

"I took a paper of safety matches out of my pocket, opened it, tore one out and tossed it on the table.

" 'I'm just a country sheriff,' I said. 'I believe anything anybody tells me. Did you go into The Last Resort and buy anything?'

" 'Never saw the place. The first stop we made was to get a beer at that guy Nicky's place.'

"I tossed another match on the table.

" 'Did you ever see the man and the two gals who were talkin' to me here at the jail today?'

" 'Never laid eyes on 'em.'

"I tossed another match onto the table.

" 'Do you remember sluggin' that man with the butt of your gun?'

" 'Nuts! Never saw the guy before.'

"I tossed another match onto the table.

" 'Where's the money?' I asked him.

" 'What money?'

" 'The money you stole from Jim Driggers's place—The Last Resort.'

" 'I never saw Driggers or his place and I never stole no money from nobody.'

"I tossed a fifth match onto the table.

" 'There's five matches,' I told him, 'and every one of 'em

says you're a liar. Because they all came out of this little folder with the pretty little cover that says "The Last Resort." And that little paper of matches came out of your car. The boys searched it good this mornin'. It had slipped down back of the front seat cushion like things'll do. Tell him what else you found, Ranse.'

" 'I found what I thought at first was a dead cat squirrel layin' in the grass but it just turned out to be a gray wig. When I got to lookin' real close, I found the critter's tails. Must have been a two-tailed squirrel,' Ranse said. 'We'll try 'em on you directly and see how they look. And here's a wallet with a lot of money and a driver's license for somebody named Califano from New York. That wouldn't be you—would it, Mister?'

" 'Where'd you find the wallet, Ranse?' I asked.

" 'Where do you reckon?' Ranse grinned. 'Old Hog Dog had it—said he found it in the grass alongside the road where somebody had been scufflin'. Said he just forgot to tell us about it last night. Said he didn't have no idea whose it was. I told him, "You knew dern well it wasn't yours, didn't you?" So he give it to me—money and all.' "

That wrapped up everything but the New York car tag. Nobody hadn't been able to find it nowhere. Kelly felt like it had to be around Nicky's juke joint somewhere because he was sure that's where they had done their switchin' to the Florida tag.

About dinnertime, while we was talkin' to one of the county commissioners about a cow-stealin' case that might involve David, the phone rang. It was a woman's voice.

"Sheriff Driggers?" she asked.

"That's me," Kelly answered.

"I'm Beulah Jones."

"Yes, Ma'am. What can I do for you?"

"I need help. I'm under arrest."

"On what charge?" Kelly asked. "And where are you?"

"I'm here in Daytona Beach—me and my boy friend. He wants to talk to you."

When the man came on the phone, Kelly thought he recognized the voice.

"Mister Kelly, this is Bill—Bill the cook—you know, the cook at Mister Jim's Last Resort."

"All right, Bill," Kelly told him. "What kind of trouble are you in—outside of runnin' off from your job and dodgin' your witness duty?"

"I ain't runnin' from no job, Mister Kelly," he said. "Today's my day off. It's my girl friend who is bein' held by the police."

"What did she do?" Kelly asked.

"Nothin'," he said. "The police was lookin' for a stole New York car—a black Buick—but she's drivin' her own little old white Ford. The trouble of it is that she's got a New York tag on it with some numbers they're lookin' for."

"Who is this girl friend and where is she from?" Kelly asked.

"She's Beulah Jones. You know, the cook at Nicky's juke joint. I swear us don't know nothin' about no stole black car."

"*I* do," Kelly told him. "Let me talk to the Police Chief over there. You come on home and I'll tell you all about it."

At the inquest all the witnesses told the same story that Kelly had told, but that weren't no surprise to me. Ever since he'd been a little skeester he'd told me the truth even if it meant gettin' his butt dusted off with a oleander switch. The killin' was ruled justifiable homicide and the big feller, Califano, was indicted and tried and put away for twenty years.

35 Caught in the Act

The county commissioner who had been missin' some cattle were a feller from Red Level who had a heap of cows scattered all through the Hammock from Spring Run to Otter Creek. They was just old mixed-up breeds, some red and some brindle, some black and some pieded—Angus and Hereford and Longhorn and even Brahma mixtures. They run wild and made their own livin' in the Hammock and flatwoods along the east edge. I don't reckon he knowed himself how many he had but he'd try to check on 'em now and again with his catch dogs and mark their ears, cut and dehorn the bull calves and of course butcher and sell the fat steers if there was any.

This same feller had several thousand acres down in Citrus County across the River and was already seein' what was bound to happen—that there would come a day when Florida would have a no-fence law and when that day come a feller could hope to raise some real good beef cattle. When I say a "no-fence" law I really mean exactly the opposite. Up to then, if you wanted to keep cows out of your orange grove or your garden you had to fence 'em *out*. Now you didn't. The feller who owned 'em had to fence 'em *in*. As long as we'd had open range—where everybody's cattle had just ran loose—it wouldn't do a feller no good to buy a fine big fat shorthorn bull for instance, and just turn him loose. Because that big old lazy rascal wouldn't have a chance against them scrawny wild range bulls—all neck and you know what. And I don't mean fightin'. I mean one of them range bulls would cover six cows while that prize bull was thinkin' it over.

But we had a governor about then named Fuller Warren and him and a lot of young fellers who called theirselves the Jaycees got together and passed a law requirin' cattle to be fenced. There had been a lot of folks crippled and killed when their cars had hit cattle on the highway and this new law took the cows off the road.

In the old days if you hit a cow and killed yourself and all your family, the owner of the cow could sue your heirs for damages. Now the owner of the cow would be liable—which is really like it ought to be. I must say though that a lot of old-time Cracker cowmen fought it—like old-timers will fight most any kind of change; especially if they think it is takin' away any of their rights. But this fence law sure did do a heap for the cattle business in Florida and improved the stock a hundred percent in just a few years.

This county commissioner I spoke about had already done fenced in his big ranch down south of the River and put in some prize Brahma bulls, "buffaloes" some folks called 'em. Man, them bulls was somethin' to see! But two had already been stole and Mr. Spicer were red hot. "Mr. Driggers," he said to me, "I ain't got no proof—yet—but the talk is that your son David is mixed up in this cattle stealin', both in our county and down in Citrus and Hernando. I hope it ain't so."

"So do I, Mr. Spicer," I told him. "But if he is, he'll pay for it. You've knowed me and my folks for thirty years and you know dern good and well we don't approve of no such carryin's on. If Dave is mixed up in this business, we'll find out."

I think Mr. Spicer believed me all right, but he grumbled somethin' about "no good young hellion" and walked on out of the courthouse.

It were about a week after that when the real bad thing happened. There were a big rancher down near Brooksville named Asa Parker who had a few head of cows in a pasture he had leased from the widow Latham up near Hickory Ford. I heered later that Mr. Parker had give them cows—about sixty head—to his only son, Herbert Parker, to raise and sell toward college. Mr. Parker's foreman, Yay Verily, was helpin' to learn young Herbert the cattle business and they went up to Hickory Ford on this particular Friday evenin' to check on a couple of new calves. Now, accordin' to Mr. Yay Verily, this is what happened. First, though, I've got to tell you about Mr. Verily.

Mr. Verily is well named. If there is one feller in this part of Florida whose word is took without ary question it is him. If Yay Verily said there was ninety-six bullfrogs in a pond, there was ninety-six. Not ninety-seven or ninety-eight, but ninety-six. I guess maybe he must of growed up feelin' the responsibility of his name. He were a slow-talkin' feller and you had the feelin' he were thinkin' things over before he spoke.

Well, him and young Parker drove down into the pasture and the first thing they run onto was my boy David and another feller kneelin' down about to take the paunch and guts out of a young brindle steer. They had a old beat-up pick-up truck settin' nearby. When Mr. Verily and young Parker come a-drivin' up David laid down his knife and picked up his rifle. He knowed he were caught in a bad act and expected trouble.

Naturally, when the Parker boy started to get out of his car he picked up his own rifle like any feller would do under them circumstances. Whether he ever raised it or started to raise it nobody will ever know because David opened fire with his .30–30 and he were plenty fast with it. The first shot killed the Parker boy right now and when he fell Mr. Verily pulled his pistol out of the door pocket. But before he could shoot or say a word, David blasted him too. The bullet went through his neck but it didn't get the spine or the jugular, just nicked the meat. Though the shock of it near about knocked him out, he did remember hearin' David cussin' his pardner for drivin' away without him.

Mr. Verily lost a lot of blood and were right addled when he come to but he were a tough old booger and managed to drive out of there. Of course he called the Sheriff's office quick as he could get to a phone and it weren't long until Kelly come a-rippin' up to the house to tell me.

"David has played hell this time," he said. "He was caught butcherin' a Parker steer and he shot and killed young Parker and likened to have killed Mr. Yay Verily who has gone to the hospital in Ocala. He can't hardly speak out of a whisper but he sure put the finger on David Driggers . . . and you know how folks are about Yay Verily. When he says somethin' folks take it as Gospel, like Uncle Winton's guaran-dam-tee. I'm on my way out to the scene of the shootin' right now and figured you'd want to go."

The buzzards was already down on the steer by the time we got there after followin' Mr. Verily's tire tracks down into the pasture. From the looks of things it must of happened like Mr. Verily told it. Him and the Parker boy had drove up almost to the carcass and then swung left to dodge a big old light'd log and a couple of blackjack saplin's. This had put 'em broadside to the carcass, so when the Parker boy had opened the door he would have been right in line and when he fell Dave could have seen Mr. Verily reach for his pistol.

Whoever had been with Dave in the old pick-up truck had left out of there spinnin' his wheels in the sand and had gone south to the fence where he'd cut the wire and got into a woods road. We followed the tracks a mile or two till they come to the old shell road and then we lost 'em.

The next day Doc Joyner from Crystal River was appointed coroner and him and six jurymen all went down to the pasture after first talkin' to Mr. Yay Verily in the hospital. Their verdict were that Herbert Parker had come to his death at the hands of one David Henry Driggers and a warrant were issued. The driver of the pick-up hadn't been recognized by Mr. Verily and couldn't be identified by nobody. He had drove off by himself at high speed, like I said, and a John Doe warrant were issued for him as an accomplice.

Loofy and Etta just wouldn't believe it, in spite of Mr. Verily's sworn statement and his reputation. "Why would David do a thing like that?" Loofy kept askin' me.

"Because he were caught red-handed in a man's fenced-in pasture butcherin' one of the man's cows," I said. "And he knowed he were in for bad trouble. So he killed a man and liken to have killed another. He's a outlaw and has been all his life—except when he wanted somethin' and were butterin' up somebody."

"I don't believe it and I hope they never catch him," Etta said. "And I'll bet they don't. He'll know where to hide. He knows that hammock and marsh from one end to the other like the back of his hand. They'll never find him out there."

"God help him," Loofy said.

"I don't know about that," I said. "God don't like thieves and murderers and our boy is both. And there's folks who'll be lookin' for him who know that country good as he does—one of 'em bein' his own brother."

"Oh my God!" Loofy said and went into the bedroom with Etta and shut the door and I could hear 'em prayin'. And it sure were time to pray.

I got down on my knees by the kitchen table and talked to God like I hadn't done since the night little Winton had been hangin' by a thread. "God," I said, "You made all us folks and You know what we're like inside and why we do what we do. Now, I can't tell You why my boy David is like he is. He growed up in the same nest, eat the same food, had the same teachin' and the same lovin' mother as the other boys, so it ain't what they call the evironment that's to blame. There's just somethin' in that boy like there were in Cain and Judas who we read about in Your Book. They're just bad. Maybe it's the devil got into 'em. You will know. And if You don't remember about the home teachin' our boy had, You can ask Ma who is up there with You. She can tell You that both me'n Loofy are solid believers in You and Your words."

I went on and reminded God that our boy's namesake, King David, done some awful bad things like gettin' a feller killed in the war so that he could have the feller's wife, but that God had forgave him and let him become a mighty man and write all them Psalms. So I asked Him to forgive our David and have mercy on him. Beyond that I didn't know what to ask because I didn't feel like I should ask God to help him get plumb away. I just asked for mercy in the name of Jesus, like Ma always taught us to pray about everything.

After while Loofy and Etta come out and dried their eyes and got supper and didn't nobody even mention our boy's name. But all the time I were eatin' I were picturin' him out somewhere there in the hammock or down in the marsh. I were glad he hadn't killed Mr. Verily and stole the car to add to his troubles. I hoped he had somethin' to eat and a shelter from the skeeters. To tell the truth, I reckon I were pullin' for him to get away. And, like his sister Etta said, he knowed that country out there like the back of his hand.

West from the widow Latham's pasture is nothin' but hammock and marsh plumb to the open Gulf. It's cut up with sloughs and creeks and there ain't but one or two families in the whole township. Mink Creek comes out of a little spring about thirty feet acrost and at least that deep. The water is clear as gin and a heap better to drink—to my way of thinkin', anyhow. It flows a good stream for three or four miles down through low hammock and open marsh until it runs into Grassy Creek. Salt water fish like redfish and trout and mangrove snappers go plumb up to the spring and, of course, there's bass, brim and shiners a-plenty.

There's islands scattered all along and some of 'em is really shell mounds where the Indians camped and eat oysters. If all them old-time Indians loved oysters as good as I do, it couldn't of took 'em as long to build a island as the history fellers try to tell us. A feller on the run could hide out amongst them islands and find plenty of game and fish to eat and good water to drink, specially along Mink Creek.

36 Blood Will Tell
—& Does

Mink Island ain't over ten acres big. It lays up near the head of Mink Creek, about two miles above where the creek joins up with Grassy Creek. From there it's about two miles on down to the Gulf and about three miles back up to where Grassy joins the main River. Nothin' lives on Mink Island but fiddler crabs, a few coons, sometimes a otter or two, some marsh hens and old man Elkins. A big gator used to crawl out on the west end of the island to sun itself but Elkins killed it after it caught and ate his dog. There ain't been a mink caught there in ten years, the time Elkins quit trappin'.

If you ever seen this old feller you wouldn't believe it. His head were bald as a grapefruit but he had a red beard that were turnin' gray on the edges and scraggly brindle mustaches. His eyes was set so far back in his head a Mexican buzzard couldn't pick 'em out and they was almost hid by the thickest eyebrows you ever seen. I'd knowed him for a long time but I couldn't tell you the color of his eyes to save my soul. He trimmed his own beard and it always looked like where a horse had been eatin' in the crab grass.

He must of been seventy-five but he were tough and wiry

and got around in the marsh just about as good as when he first started trappin'. How he managed to live after coon hides went down to nothin' I just couldn't figure. Some folks said he slipped down River at night in his skiff and brought in a load of liquor now and then from a boat layin' out in the channel. Some folks said he hid out a outlaw once in a while and he used to shoot plume birds back in the days when the feathers could be sold and smuggled out. He never had much use for civilization and didn't go to town hardly at all—would get the mullet fishermen to bring him his rations from the store up the River.

Nobody knowed just where he come from but it were somewhere out West and the story was that he had shot a couple of fellers and had changed his name. He come to Florida and built the shack on Mink Island about nineteen hundred and twenty. It weren't much of a house but it set well up on the shell mound above the storm tides.

Back in the old days me and my brother Tarl had a little old huntin' camp on another high little island across from Mink Island where we used to go to shoot ducks, and for a long time I used to take my boys down there. We'd shoot a mess of canvasbacks, catch us a redfish or two and have us a real stomped-down good time. David loved the place and spent more time there than the other boys, so naturally he got to know old man Elkins.

"That's a wicked old feller, son," I warned him one time. "I wouldn't hang around him too much if I was you."

"Yes, you would," David said. "If *you* was *me*. I like him. That old skeester knows a lot of tricks—about settin' traps and snares and such. He can make a water set for mink or otter that's the slickest you ever seen. And he knows that whole marsh and all the creeks and side creeks better'n you or me do—and I thought *we* knowed 'em." Nothin' I could say would change David's mind about Elkins bein' bad news. But then he hadn't never listened to me about nothin'.

So, when young Parker died in the pasture shootin' scrape and David had to hide out, I would of bet money on where he'd go. And, naturally, Kelly had the same hunch.

"I've got to bring him in, Dad," he said, "and maybe old man Elkins with him, if I find that he's been shelterin' a fugitive from the law. And that's what my brother is . . . a plain-out fugitive outlaw—wanted for cattle stealin' and murder."

And that's what it finally come down to—one of my sons goin' after the other with a gun—who also had a gun. It were all pretty dern bitter and sad to me and had hit Loofy so hard that she couldn't face goin' to the courthouse for the hearin'. So I think I'll let my son, the Sheriff, tell it like it happened. He's always told me the truth and I think he told the truth then. But . . . well, there's folks who heard two shots that night and Kelly's a deadly shot so . . . but here's his story that he told in the courtroom at Bronson—real formal like he learnt to talk in college. His mother would have been proud of him if she'd of been there. It's all on the record.

"My name is Kelly Henry Driggers and I am the Sheriff of this county. On the evening* of August fifth I went down River in my skiff, powered by a ten-horse Johnson outboard motor, to look for a fugitive named David Henry Driggers. Dave Driggers is my own brother, two years younger, and I had a warrant for his arrest on a charge of cattle theft and homicide in the shooting of Herbert Parker, son of the owner of the C-Slash Ranch down south of Brooksville.

"Because of my brother's frequent visits to one Jonas W. Elkins, commonly known as old man Elkins, I had reason to think that the fugitive might very likely be hiding out on Mink Island, or on one of the other small islands in that area of the Gulf Marsh. I therefore went ashore at Mink Island and found old man Elkins washing up his dinner dishes. I noticed that there were two cups and two plates and I asked him who his visitor had been. He swore that he hadn't had a visitor in over two weeks and that the dishes and cups were ones left over from his own breakfast. I then checked the rest of the house, which didn't take long, but saw no sign of my brother's having been there.

" 'Set and visit, Sheriff,' Elkins said. 'I'll be finished washin' up directly.'

"It was a hot day and I sat down in an old rocker near the window where there was a little breeze. Elkins was still in the kitchen at this time. I then noticed that a mosquito had been

---

* Sheriff Driggers used the word "evening" as it is used locally—to denote any time in the afternoon from twelve o'clock noon till dark.

mashed on the window pane and that it had been full of blood and recently killed because the blood had not turned dark brown but still showed deep red where the sunlight shone through it. I then took out my pocket knife and scraped off that mosquito and the dried blood into a cigarette paper and put it into a letter I had in my pocket. I had just tucked it back into my pocket when Elkins came in.

" 'How are things up River, Sheriff?' he asked me when he had sat down on an old couch. I told him about the shooting and finally asked him the direct question, 'Have you seen my brother, Dave Driggers?'

" 'Not for a month or more,' he said. 'He brought me some of the finest, fattest oysters I ever seen from over toward Gun Barrel Creek. He sure knows how to find them scapers.'

"That's all I could get out of the old man so I went back up River. Next morning I drove straight down to Tampa to the Police Crime Laboratory and within a very short time I found that my mosquito had filled up on blood type B which I knew was the same as my brother's and comparatively uncommon. On the way home, as I got close to Brooksville on U.S. 41, I remembered that there was a new hospital there and it seemed like I remembered old man Elkins having gone there when he had pneumonia last year so I stopped and checked. They had his record and his blood was type Ô.

"I got back home too late that evening to do what I had to do, but next day I hooked up my outboard on the skiff and took off for Mink Island again. This time I towed a little old duck sneak boat I had bought from a Maryland man. My father, Mr. Billy Driggers, wanted me to take him along, or at least a deputy, but I said, 'No. I have to do this job alone!'

"I waited till nearly sundown before running into Mink Creek and the sun was just dipping behind the marsh when I ran my skiff up onto the beach at Mink Island. Elkins came out of the shack right away and hurried down to the beach to ask me what brought me to his place again so soon. He seemed right nervous and didn't invite me to come up to the shack and get out of the mosquitoes. I asked him again if he had seen David and he repeated his statement that he hadn't seen my brother for over a month. The mosquitoes and sand flies were bad so I left pretty quick and ran back out to Grassy Creek. I had tied my sneak boat up under some myrtle bushes and I transferred to it after I had pushed the big skiff as far as it would go up under the myrtles and into the saw grass. I left the outboard running—I figured it could be heard a long way across the marsh.

"I knew that slipping up on my brother would be real chancy, because he has eyes and ears like an Indian, but I hoped my outboard trick would work. Never in all my gator hunting did I ever dip a paddle as carefully. I eased that little duck boat onto the shore without a sound. It was plumb dark but the moon was just coming up . . . about two nights past the full.

"Dave and Elkins were having a drink of 'shine at the kitchen table when I walked in. I had my pistol drawn and I told my brother he was under arrest. I could see behind his eyes that he was weighing his chances—that same wild, crazy look he always got when he was getting ready to make his move. He cut his eyes over toward his rifle, which was standing in the corner by an old couch and I said, 'Don't try it, Dave!'

"For a minute or two I thought he was going to try me anyhow and we stood there without speaking or moving. Elkins started to slide over in his chair and I said, 'If you move, Mr. Elkins, I'll kill you!' He didn't move.

"Finally my brother laughed and said, 'Well, I guess you win, Mr. Law Man.' I got out my handcuffs and he said, 'Don't try to put those things on me, Kelly, or I'll make you kill me!'

"I knew he would, too, so I said, 'All right. I reckon I have to trust you but don't make the wrong move. Stand up. And you, Elkins, don't get out of that chair. And don't go anywhere after I leave. I'll be back for you later.' Then I backed over to the corner, picked up Dave's rifle in my left hand and told him to walk down to the boat.

"This was the tricky time. And I knew it. So I stood firm on the land holding the .45 on him and ordered him to sit down and face forward. Then I eased the boat into the water, slipped the rifle under the back seat and got in.

"We were just coming into that long straight stretch of creek near the old Turner duck stand when it happened . . . as I might have known it would. I had my .45 on the seat between my legs and it didn't take more than one second to drop the paddle and grab it. Dave had slipped off his shoes and

"Dave and Elkins
were having a drink of 'shine..."

he just rolled over the side and into that dark water like an otter. The duck boat almost turned over when he went out because he gave himself a mighty push to start his dive but I managed to keep from going over. The moon was high enough so that when Dave's head came up about fifty feet away I saw the shine of it on his wet hair and on the ripples. I steadied myself and fired twice. I'm sure folks must have heard the shots. It wasn't over half a mile to the Barker place on Dove Island and not much more to Halfway Camp."

Kelly stopped talkin' right then and just set there in the courtroom with his head bowed. Everybody had listened to his story and Mrs. Barker and her daughter spoke up right together. "We heered it," they said.

Then the old lady said, "I thought at first it might be a gator hunter shootin' but then it were a bright moonlight night so I knowed that couldn't be it."

"I figured somebody had roosted some young turkeys before the season," Eunice said. "David Driggers, most likely."

"Them weren't no shotgun shots," Emmett Hawkins said. "I had my net set out in the mouth of Grassy and heered both shots plain. Them were pistol shots—heavy pistol shots."

Old Judge Day said, "All right. The Sheriff has so testified. They were from his old Colt .45 automatic and most everybody in this county knows that he can sure use it. So what we need to know now is *did they hit their target*? If they *did*, where is the body? If they *didn't*, where is the murderer? All we've got is his rifle."

There didn't nobody have the answer. Near about everybody in the settlement had gone down there next day when Kelly went after old man Elkins. He were there all right and Kelly brought him in. On the way back Kelly and three deputies searched both sides of Mink Creek and Grassy Creek for sign of a man havin' crawled out through the grass. There weren't no way a feller could go out through that marsh without leavin' a trail that any kid could foller. Of course there were gator trails here and there but a feller would be crazy as a outhouse rat to go a-wallerin' along in a gator trail at night. It gives me the cold chills to think about it even now. Gators don't often attack humans but I sure don't want to be the one who busts down into a den with a big old bull gator ten or twelve feet long.

And a heap of the marsh were saw grass marsh and that stuff'll cut a feller time he touches it. Furthermore, a feller always runs the chance of bumpin' into a dern cottonmouth. Rammin' around in the marsh at night ain't the smartest thing a feller can do—even if he's on the run. Anyhow, nobody found nothin'.

On the way home from the courthouse I rode with Kelly and sort of waited for him to say something. Most often a feller who is used to shootin' can tell when he is on target when he squeezes the trigger, but this shootin' had been done at night from a little old tippy duck boat that were already doin' a dipsy-doo. And don't think even a good shot can always hit a small target with a pistol—even in daylight on solid ground. That's just in the movies.

"What happened, son?" I asked him at last, when we was almost back to the River. "Did you really miss or did you pull to one side at the last second? You can tell your daddy. I'll never say nothin' to nobody."

Kelly give me a long, long look—till I was skeered he'd run off the road. "You were at the courthouse," he said at last. "You heard it all."

And that's all he ever said or ever would say.

Old man Elkins swore at his trial that David hadn't been hidin' out at Mink Island but had just got there and demanded a drink. And he just laughed at the mosquito evidence. "That skeeter could have bit somebody a mile away and blowed over here. If it were in my house, *I* killed it," he said. "You ain't goin' to convict a feller on a half drop of blood out of a dad-blamed dead skeeter are you?" And, as it turned out, that jury of country Crackers sure weren't either. But they was so down on my boy, David, that they gave old man Elkins six months just for drinkin' with him.

Weeks passed and we didn't hear nothin'. Currents run strong in them Gulf Coast creeks and rivers and a body would get carried out to sea, maybe, where sharks might cut it up. And if a man still lived in that marsh, he'd be bound to show some sign—he'd have to eat and he'd have to have fresh water. A hunter or trapper or commercial fisherman would see him or see his sign and report it, because there didn't nobody like David Driggers too much. But there weren't nothin' from nobody.

So then another of the family were gone. Folks'll tell you that the sharp edge will blunt after a while and nobody knows that better'n me. First it were Daddy, then Uncle Winton and then Ma and each time I didn't hardly see how I could spare 'em.

And when the snake killed little Winton both me'n Loofy felt like we wouldn't never over it. Nothin' ever come so close to makin' Loofy lose her faith in God as that did. I tried to help her by quotin' some of Ma's favorite verses but she didn't want to listen—just went into the bedroom and cried. And to tell the truth, I got a little bitter about it myself. There didn't seem no answer to why such a terrible thing could happen to a innocent little feller.

But this were different. David sure weren't no innocent little feller. I thought back on all the times I had maybe been too rough on him. Maybe he wouldn't of been so changeable. Maybe he were really skeered inside and just put on bein' mean and tough. Both his mother and sister would take up for him even when they knowed he were wrong but I had always whipped his butt when I thought he needed it—and that were right often. Well, now he were gone too and in a way I felt like a feller does when he's been totin' a big buck out of the Hammock on his back and somebody comes along with a horse and wagon. If David was dead, he was dead. And if not, at least he wouldn't be electrocuted—not until he was caught anyhow.

It were over five years later that the letter come from Pensacola. I had run up to the post office in my boat after fishin' a while and this letter were the onliest thing in our box—just a pencil-addressed envelope with one sheet of ordinary lined tablet paper inside. There weren't no writin' of no kind on the paper but folded inside were a little old wizzened-up dried-out leathery dead chameleon.

Man! That hit me right in my gizzard. The boy were alive! At first I were glad . . . until I got to studyin' what this would mean. Loofy would get all roused up again and I would have to report this to the law. Report what? I didn't have nothin'—no name, no address, no nothin' but a dead lizard. And there wouldn't nobody know the meanin' of that but me. I thought a long time. David would know, of course, that I would get the message but it were just like him to stick a knife in somethin' to see it squirm. He hadn't meant to do nothin' else. I reckon he hadn't anyhow because he hadn't give no name or address.

So I just shook that little old dried-up chameleon into the River. It started to float off and a mangrove snapper come up and grabbed it, chawed it once or twice and spit it out. "That's what *I* got to do," I said to myself, "spit him out once and for all." And I swung the boat into the current and headed for home.

I hope I done right in not tellin' Loofy and I hope I didn't do no wrong in not tellin' the law—though I really didn't have nothin' to tell. I do know that if he was ever caught and electrocuted, it would near about kill his mother She believed her Bible, though, and I had often heered her quote the verse, "Whoso sheddeth man's blood, by man shall his blood be shed." But a feller can believe in somethin' strict mighty easy until it applies to himself.

37 Summin' Up

The years have rolled by and we never heered nothin' more about David—at least I didn't. And if Loofy did, she never let on. In the meantime a heap of things have happened to us Driggerses—some good and some bad.

Jim always stayed a old bachelor. He made a heap of money out of his restaurant and garage and wound up drivin' around the country in a little old low-slung foreign-made sports car that didn't have much more clearance from the road than the butt of a goose. He got him a little old checked cap and went to all them road races—specially the one down at Sebring. But I will say, he kept sense enough not to try that racin' himself.

Charlie wound up workin' for his father-in-law in the tobacco business up in Carolina. He had four kids but two of 'em got took off in a flu epidemic. Then him and his wife agreed to disagree and he went with another tobacco company. When I seen him last he looked a little puny but said he were doin' right well and had his eye on a rich widow-woman from Winston-Salem.

Kelly served twelve years as Sheriff and then two years as State Representative. The Governor appointed him on the

Racin' Commission and after while he tried for the State Senate but didn't make it. Maybe he'll try again. He's a hard one to keep down.

Burgoyne moved to Sarasota and got in the real estate business with some feller down there who took him to the cleaners. He tried it again down around Naples and hit it lucky. He married a Bradenton girl who sure did stand by him through thick and thin—for a long time *real thin*. She give him four sons and every dern one of 'em was a healthy, husky little scaper. They done good in school and we're right proud of 'em.

Etta married a feller from Gainesville, a car salesman, who were doin' all right to start with. But he got on the bottle and wound up givin' her a bad time. It were lucky she didn't have no kids. When he beat her up one Sunday me and Kelly drove up there and I would of killed him if Kelly hadn't stopped me. We taken Etta home with us and that's where she is now and we're glad to have her.

Tarl's daughter, Lorna, waited till she were near about thirty to get married and then married a Yankee feller who had a heap of money and didn't do nothin' but study birds—a horny theologist I think they called him. Anyhow she got pregnant right off and had a boy baby. I mean old Tarl were tickled and had boxin' gloves on that kid before it were hardly out of its diapers. They went on and had six more—four of 'em gals, one an opera singer. Our kids' and their kids' doin's would make another book. The trouble of it is that I forget half of 'em and the rest I can't remember.

When I walked out to feed the stock this mornin' there was a light mist risin' off the River and a water turkey perched on the back of our dock bench. A covey of birds was scratchin' in a sandy spot by the cow pen and way back in the Hammock I heered a hoot owl still askin', "Who cooks, who cooks, who cooks for you-all?" Everything seemed near about like it used to be, right peaceful. "Serene," my daughter-in-law calls it.

But I knowed things was different away from here. The Israelites and the Arabs had done gone way back yonder into the Old Testament, the French and the Eyetalians was fightin' amongst theirselves, the Irish hadn't never stopped fightin', the Pandemoniums was raisin' sand again about who owned the Canal—them or us. Even some of our near neighbors had turned agin us and there just weren't no tellin' what the Russians was doin'.

Some folks will try to tell you that everything is gettin' better in this old world but I don't have to read my Bible to know that ain't so. The talk is gettin' nastier, the books is gettin' dirtier, the money's gettin' tighter, the morals is gettin' looser, the music gettin' noisier, the pictures gettin' sillier, the women gettin' harder and the men gettin' softer.

We had a big city preacher come to our church not long ago who preached about Jesus and the prophecies about His comin' back and how things would get worser and worser till then. After the service derned if some stranger didn't walk up and say to me, "I don't believe none of that second-comin' talk, do you? Jesus caused enough trouble in this world when He come the first time, let alone comin' back a second or even a third time like some try to tell us."

I don't know who the stranger were but I'm sorry for him because the trouble of it is he ain't got nothin' to hold to, nothin' to hope for and nowhere to go. But I have. And I don't know of no better way to end this here book than the way Jesus ends His.

A NOTE ABOUT THE AUTHOR

David M. Newell has lived fifty miles east of the Gulf Hammock in Leesburg, Florida, off and on for the past sixty-seven years—during which time he has been, variously, editor-in-chief of *Field & Stream*, roving editor of *Sports Afield*, and a special correspondent for *The New York Times*. Out of his knowledge and love of the woods and waters, he has written five books and dozens of articles and stories, and has contributed in numerous capacities (as actor, writer, narrator and producer) to the production of some thirteen films and numerous television programs.

A NOTE ON THE TYPE

The text of this book was set on the Linotype in a face called Primer, designed by Rudolph Ruzicka, who was earlier responsible for the design of Fairfield and Fairfield Medium—Linotype faces whose virtues have for some time now been accorded wide recognition.

The complete range of sizes of Primer was first made available in 1954, although the pilot size of 12-point was ready as early as 1951. The design of the face makes general reference to Linotype Century—long a serviceable type, totally lacking in manner or frills of any kind—but brilliantly corrects its characterless quality.

This book was composed by American Book-Stratford Press, Inc., Brattleboro, Vermont; printed by The Murray Printing Company, Forge Village, Massachusetts; and bound by American Book-Stratford Press, Inc., Saddle Brook, New Jersey.

Typography and binding based on a design by Earl Tidwell